Onkalot

Onkalot

Death Bringer Book I

Zodiac Universum

Adrianna Biełowiec

EPUB ISBN: 979-8-2015870-1-7
PAPERBACK ISBN: 979-8-9859170-9-3

***

WRITTEN BY ADRIANNA BIEŁOWIEC
PUBLISHED BY ROYAL HAWAIIAN PRESS
COVER ART BY TYRONE ROSHANTHA
TRANSLATED BY SZYMON NOWAK
PUBLISHING ASSISTANCE: DOROTA RESZKE

***

FOR MORE WORKS BY THIS AUTHOR, PLEASE VISIT:
WWW.ROYALHAWAIIANPRESS.COM

***

VERSION NUMBER 1.00

Table of Contents

The Ten Commandments
of the Kiritians

Worship whichever gods you want and as many as you want, you may not even worship any.

Take the god's name when you need it. Since the reason has arisen, you don't do it in vain.

You don't need to go to your temple unless you have a spiritual need. For the human heart is the only true seat of faith.

Love your mother and your father if they deserve it.

Above all, respect yourself and your neighbor's life and health. However, don't spare your enemies and all those who want to harm you.

Don't commit adultery.

Steal if you must.

Tell only the truth.

Don't covet your neighbor's wife. However, you can play the field with enemies from conquered planets.

Don't harm your neighbor in any way. If the situation requires it, oppress the subordinate peoples.

Prelude

Anna Sandstorm examined a small jade fighter figure for a moment, then extended her little hand to tap on the marble base. After a while, the statuette disappeared in the girl's embrace, as if it had been one of her tautori mascots - made of synthetics safe for the youngest - with which she loved to play.

"Leave it, or you will break it! It's not yours!" Julie Croft rumbled, trying to imitate the tone of her mother's voice.

Anne wrinkled her nose and pursed her lips. She looked angrily at her friend with intense green eyes, then, having squeaked dissatisfiedly, turned away, and obviously not even thinking about putting back the new toy.

"Come on!" Julie made the gesture of a slum child trying to steal jewelry from a wealthy passerby, but Sandstorm efficiently dodged.

"Nooooo!" She protested.

When into the guest room of Mr. Carlos Drunkenstein went his ten-year-old son Beliar, accompanied by two younger colleagues, he found Julie, puffed up, kneeling on a carpet and massaging her knee. Grumpy, Annie was sitting on a dresser by a window and was adjusting her sandal, which had shifted while giving her intrusive friend a kick. She pressed the fighter figure to her chest.

"Idiot!" Julie hissed. Annie showed her tongue in opposition.

"Wow ... You got hit again from the four-year-old!" Ari Croft chuckled at the sight of his roughed-up sister.

"That's not true!"

Jarret Nelson, the third boy, helped her up, although he was surprised that Julie didn't get up by herself. Nothing had happened, after all. He very often fought with his buddies and didn't roar on the floor when someone hit him with a slipper.

Beliar Drunkenstein assumed a frustrated face. He walked over to an armored window, taking up the entire front wall and overlooking his father's private airport. He surveyed a few of the visitors' flying machines in which they were to depart at dawn the next day with their host for some briefing, then approached Sandstorm sitting on the dresser and moving her legs vigorously. He smiled amiably. Though born in troubled times, when opposition adults had constantly struggled with the Kiritians occupying the Zodiac Universum, also known as the Immortals or the Infected, Beliar was cheerful and open-minded. He liked Annie very much. Although she was the youngest member of their gang of five, she showed tenacity and even a fiery temper. She always got her own way, even if it was to end with a reprimand of a nanny-android called Aga, or worse with a smack on the ass. She also never cried. She reared, thrashed, bit, lay down on the floor and hit it with her feet in anger, but didn't waste tears. She was the complete opposite of the exaggerating all and eternally aggrieved Julie Crybaby, the miss 'Wait on My Hand and Foot'.

Annie answered the boy with a smile, but embarrassing. Her cheeks crimsoned and she pressed her face into the puffed sleeve of her yellow dress.

"Will you give it back?" Drunkenstein held out his hand. Sandstorm hugged the jade beauty tighter and uttered a murmur of protest. The boy, undaunted, crouched down and smiled again. "Alright, take it for a while. But if you want this fighter forever, you must ask for my father's permission, but he will certainly give it to you. You know it's a prototype model?"

"What is a plototype?" Surprisingly, Annie gave him the figurine. Beliar stared at it like a modeler at a freshly glued work of art, rotating it at any angle.

"Prototype," he clearly repeated and accentuated the word, "is such a new thing that you test and see how it works. And if it works well, then more of these things start to be produced. Dad is a constructor of flying machines and supplier of new technologies for the rebels, and this fighter here is his project. It is to be designated XRS-14. In a few years our troops will commonly fly such machines."

"I aso wiy fly!"

The boy laughed.

"You're too little."

"But when I gyow up. I wam to be a pilot like my dad Kysan and Callos."

"Krystian and Carlos," corrected Beliar. Spending a lot of time with Anna, he decided to work on her pronunciation. He also tried not to talk naively to her. "Though your dad was born on the planet Calcaris in the Libra Universum, he has ancestors on Earth. It is the cradle of all the people who colonized the Zodiac Universum. You have the Polish-American origin from his side, Annie, and the Asian one from your mother Hanako's side. You know, I also want to be a Rebel pilot. My father claims that I have commanding qualities and that I'm destined to lead squadrons, maybe even an entire fleet. Anyway, in a few years, I will fuck up the Kiritians. Ohh ..." He covered his mouth with his hand and looked around, wanting to check if the android Aga wasn't walking around. Fortunately, apart from him and Annie, in the living room there were only Jarret, Ari and Julie, who had stopped sulking and now the three of them were fooling around on the couch, basting each other with pillows.

Sandstorm, however, was at an age when new words, she soaked up like a sponge.

"What does to fuck up mean, Beli?" She asked extremely seriously. And very correctly.

"Nothing. Forget it." Drunkenstein playfully brushed a strand of dark auburn hair off her face. The girl, giggling, retaliated by grabbing his blond bangs and lifting it up, ruffling it into a 'rooster' on his head.

"Hi, kids. What's up? Are you having fun?"

The five faces turned to Carlos Drunkenstein as he entered the living room accompanied by Krystian, Jarret's father and the Crofts' parents. Behind the group of rebel pilots, marched the graceful android Aga, dressed in a stylish, archaic, black and white maid outfit. On her head she had a bun supported by a red ribbon. She was carrying a tray with jelly-filled salad bowls.

Annie ran up to her dad and snuggled into the gray and silver pants of his uniform. Beliar took the opportunity to put the miniature fighter on the upper shelf of the cupboard so that the girl wasn't able to reach it later, unless she had already forgotten about it.

"What's going on, sweetie?" Krystian bent down and wiped the dirt off his daughter's cheek with his thumb. Then he knelt down and pushed her arm's length away, brushed the electrified hair off her eyes. He watched the child for a moment before he spoke again: "Listen to me carefully now. Daddy has to leave today, even though we were supposed to departure only in the morning, which is in so many hours." He stuck out his right index finger. "Our plans have changed a bit, but I will come back to you soon."

"I wam to see my mother."

The sound of those words made the forced smile fade from the pilot's face; a soft sigh escaped from his mouth. His partner Hanako, who had conceived Anna during a fleeting affair with him, had died over a terranic year earlier - but not at the hands of the Kiritian hegemons who had terrorized most of the inhabited globes of the Milky Way and Andromeda, but the members of the lycan sect nested on the planet H14. Its followers engrafted into themselves implants imitating wolf eyes, fangs and claws, or even used the genes of the predators they worshiped to resemble mythical werewolves. They didn't like the rebels who settled on the H14 and made of that quiet, forgotten planet their main base. But how do you tell about it a four-year-old who doesn't know the rules of the universe? Krystian used the oldest strategy in human history to deal with such cases: he lied, saying that his mother had left and would come back someday. 'She would come back at a time' when Anna would understand it without suffering psychological consequences. Or she would get pissed at him for deceiving her for so many years.

"I already told you mom is unavailable to us. While I'm away, your best bet is to stay in Mr. Carlos' residence." Despite his exhaustion and problems with the Kiritians, as well as a lot of other issues that plagued the opposition, Krystian tried to look cheerful, at least in the presence of his daughter. He smiled crookedly, a little disarmingly. "Look. He nodded towards Croft's siblings, who were also listening to their parents' instructions.

"Julie and Ari will also stay with Mr. Carlos. Jarret will be there too. And Beliar. Aga will take care of you as usual."

"Why can't I be home?" Annie scratched her nose. "On our panet?"

"Because it's not safe on Calcaris. Evil Kiritians may appear nearby. We agreed with the rest of the parents that you would stay in Beliar's house for a while."

"Onto the H14, Kitilians aso cam fly."

"Oh, I can see you remember the name of the planet well." The man patted Annie gently on the cheek, which made her a little cheered. "The H14 is safe. The Kiritians will not come onto it because there are a lot of opposition people here. And these evil invaders fear the good rebels." He always felt terrible when he lied like a rug to the little one. "Anyway, even if they appeared, Aga will throw them out of here." He supported his words with another fake smile.

"Cam, I fly with you?"

Krystian ostentatiously saddened.

"Unfortunately, not. We have a reunion at the mountainous North Pole where it is very cold. I explained to you once why we have to hold meetings elsewhere each time. And in places with electromagnetic interference, for example in specifically built mountains. "The day after tomorrow, that is, in so many days," he spread two fingers as if in a pre-colonial gesture of peace, "I will be back. In the meantime, Aga will take care of you. You like Aga, don't you?"

The girl nodded a few times.

Krystian took his daughter in his arms and hugged her tightly. Before putting her on the ground, he playfully ruffled the bangs above her tiny eyebrows.

"Take care, frog." He winked at her as he walked away. Annie watched as Dad put his hands on the shoulders of Julie and Ari's parents and spoke to them.

After saying goodbye to their children, the rebels went out into the corridor, where they unhooked their helmets from the magnetic buckles, then walked down the hall to the marble stairs leading to the first floor. There, more people joined the group. Soon the children watched through the window as a dozen flying machines come to life at the airport. Small, maneuverable machines, the smallest rebel units of a combat character, made a vertical take-off. They soared into the evening sky marked with orange and red by the setting star K'ajolom, made a V-formation, and moments later there was no trace of them. Though the Kiritians were unaware of the existence of opposition units on the H14, covered with jungles at the equator and mountains at the poles - at least that's what rebel intelligence claimed - all flying machines turned on masking fields that prevented both sensory and scanner identification. It wasn't the perfect defense against the Immortal with the best technology in the Zodiac Universum - the rebels had stolen it from them in the past, but now, in 2936, they had an old version - however, it did offer a sense of security. So the children couldn't follow the flight of the V-formation, which simply disappeared as if it had traveled thousands of kilometers in a second, having generated a subspace tunnel. This was the fastest form of transport between points in space that were far apart from each other. Unlike the rich Kiritians, it was, however, rarely used by rebels tightening their belts because of them. The subspace drive itself, professionally known as the Alcubierre engine, was created by Kiritian scientists from Dr. Maksimus Figam's team, who implemented and modified a project dating back hundreds of years, because from the end of the twentieth century, when the only planet inhabited by humans had been Earth. It was this invention that made it possible for the Immortals to rapidly conquer eighteen of the twenty-nine colonized planets that made up the Zodiac Universum; before that, the expansion of ordinary colonists from Earth had gone more slowly and bulkily.

"Please help yourselves." Aga cleared her throat significantly, then indicated dessert cups. "Croft, what have you got on your leg? Were you fighting again?"

Before Annie reached for the jelly, she watched as the scarcely bloomed bruise on Julie's knee disappeared mercilessly quickly after the android applied molecular glue. She felt remorse that she had kicked her friend so hard.

"Okay, kids, now I have to go away and clean up the rooms upstairs, and you have fun in the living room." The maid hid the medicine that was no longer needed into a portable first aid kit. "And no more fights, please."

"Can we walk around the house?" Beliar asked, bringing the spoon halfway to his mouth.

"Of course, just don't go to the administration wing or the briefing room. Mr. Drunkenstein doesn't want this. Anyway, you already know about it."

"Right. And can we play in the hangar?"

Aga frowned on the boy who assumed the face of an innocent.

"You can, but you are not to touch anything. And stay away from the control room," she added more sharply.

"So how are we supposed to play when we can't touch anything?" Beliar grinned with his dessert-stained teeth in a silly smile.

Aga put her fists on her hips.

"Beliar, don't be kidding. You are the oldest, so take care of your friends. I will visit you from time to time. Inform me via the intercom if you need anything."

The maid left the living room. She walked away down the hall, and the five sitting around the table remained motionless, listening intently and looking at each other meaningfully. When the sound of footsteps finally died away, the boys leapt towards the door and stuck their heads out into the hallway.

"Okay, she's gone," Jarret announced eagerly.

They rushed to the window to peek at the landing field, where more and more nightlight began to appear, though there was still some time to the K'ajolom setting. In the equatorial climate zone, where Carlos Drunkenstein's enclave was located, the late autumn period prevailed, but even the lowest winter temperatures here were rarely below five degrees Celsius. The few workers wandering about the landing field were dressed in airy nanotube work uniforms. In the evening, all the machines used during the day were brought back into the hangar. The next flights were also not expected, the last one in the daily schedule was the one that Carlos and the crew went on. Beliar found out about this by overhearing a conversation with the air traffic control tower. So, there should have been peace till morning. At least until Aga got them to go to bed, and that would happen only in a few hours.

"Are you sure, Beli, that no one is going to wander there?" Ari pointed at the tall building of the hangar with his chin.

"Probably not, after all, we often play there and no one picks on us."

"You forgot about the surveillance guys," Jarret muttered grimly. "And what are we going to do with the cellula?" He meant a fingernail-sized vision cell, also known as a mini-camera plate, which transmitted the vision to a capripod or other security receiver.

"This!" Julie proudly presented a sheet of synthetic paper with scribble and a caricature of Aga, drawn with colored pencils. At a time when the Kiritians were able to easily intercept messages flowing through the aether, paper got back in good graces, becoming the safest form of correspondence. However, the one used now was completely artificial mass, not made of wood as in the times before the colonization of space.

"It's so stupid," Ari snorted.

"You're stupid!"

"Alright, come on." Beliar started to leave. He paused in the middle of the room. "Just remember, you are not to tell anyone. Julie, won't you blurt out?"

"No," said the girl dryly.

"And you, Annie?" Sandstorm shook her head vigorously.

"Cool. Try to act naturally. Let the adults think we're going to play as usual. No nervous looking from side to side."

The children covered the same path as their parents fifteen minutes earlier. Being already on the edge of the landing pad, they headed towards the side entrance to the hangar. A technician leaving the hall smiled and greeted them with a captain's gesture, raising his hand to his temple. Anne waved to him cheerfully.

The kids, enchanted by the pilots' tales of fighting among the clouds and in outer space against the Kiritians, often played in the hangar between flying machines. They never did any damage, so they had been allowed to come here alone for some time. Beliar was responsible enough to look after two boys who were two years younger, seven-year-old Julie, as well as Annie. Besides, the spacious rectangular hangar was constantly monitored by cellula, the optical range of which also included the corners shaded by chests. And all thanks to the vision grid mode that allowed the cell mechanism to generate the observer an image behind each geometry inside the hall.

However, now it was different. The children had prepared a specific plan in advance, which they intended to implement soon. Therefore, it was difficult for them to act naturally.

Having made sure that they were alone in the hangar, Beliar climbed the technical ladder and fastened with wires in front of the Cellula lens, a piece of paper with Julie's scribble. The security guard working in the surveillance room immediately noticed the rather unusual flaw, smiled indulgently and shook his head, sure that, as usual, it was about the antics of the ingenious kids. Therefore, it didn't even cross his mind that they wanted to get precious moments of privacy, which could be disastrous.

Passing the silhouettes of fighters, transporters and small storm troopers, the group approached one of the four steel plates, where prototype objects, assembled according to the designs of Carlos Drunkenstein, stood covered with canvas sheets. Having gripped the corners of the fabric with both hands, slowly, as if solemnly,

Beliar began to slide the tarp down onto the ground polished by robots.

"Help me."

With Jarret and Ari, they jointly began to pull the stubborn material off the machine. Worried, Julie glanced nervously at the two technical entrances, despite Beliar's assurances that no one would care about their group.

They opened their mouths as before their eyes appeared a large, perfectly spherical white object.

"Wow!" Jarret whispered. Annie repeated the same.

"It's a six-man landing craft," said Beliar, proud of his father's accomplishments. "A technological novelty that the Kiritians don't know yet."

"What do you mean?" Julie asked, although she had no idea what the young Drunkenstein was talking about. However, she wanted to show that she was also interested in technology and was not a stupid, colorful doll, as her colleagues called her.

"That the Kiritians won't see it on scanners until they have gotten such an object, scanned it and entered the specifications into their systems. The shape and varnish are also important."

"That the White Ball is undetectable," said Croft at the same time.

"The White Ball?" Beliar blinked.

"That's what we'll call it." Ari began to walk around the transporter, running his hand over the smooth, Kevlar-like surface, except for the edges from which the cabin door slid out.

"I don't see any numbers. It needs to be named."

"The name of the White Ball is fine," Julie said. "Can we go now? Aga will kill us if she comes here. We'll have a one-year grounding. Hey, what are you doing?!"

The boys didn't pay attention to the protesting girl, who in addition ostentatiously stamped her foot. They looked at each other slyly and rushed immediately to the control room. Beliar activated the control panel and used it to open the door of the White Ball resembling a flower petal. It rose soundlessly until its lower edge pointed to the outlet bulkhead of the ceiling.

Moments later, the excited boys were simultaneously trying to get inside the machine.

"Me first!" Ari bellowed.

"No way!" Jarret cried, being pinched on the back by Beliar pressing forward.

"Calm down at last!" Julie grabbed her brother by the shirt, tried to hold him in place, but to no avail. He and Annie looked uncertainly into the blue-lit interior of the White Ball. The boys, happy, had already made themselves at home in three of the six radially arranged armchairs, smooth as the case of a transporter. They had even put on crude protective breast plates. A cylindrical control panel automatically slid out of a recess in the center of the floor.

"Come on in, it's fun," Jarret encouraged the girls. Despite Julie's disapproval, constant niggling and scaring with Aga, Annie went inside. She took a seat to the right of Beliar and smiled, biting her lower lip.

"You're supposed not to blurt out, understood?" Ari said. "Or you will get a slap on the wrist."

"I won't say!" Sandstorm gave him an oblique gaze, above which converged the tiny eyebrows tightly, and the forehead was cut by a frown. Croft almost laughed at the sight, because Annie reminded him of a pissed-off hamster.

Beliar slid the breast plate over her tiny body, almost as big as she was.

"Now you," he said to the other girl, still standing with a sulky face at the entrance. "Come on ... Everyone means everyone."

Julie finally let herself be persuaded and entered the machine. Drunkenstein closed the door with the illuminated control board; the hull of the transporter got sealed hermetically. The children quickly fell into a blissful mood, even Julie. They pretended to be flying from one planet to another.

At one point, in Ari's blue eyes appeared mischievous sparks.

"And the White Ball flies on its own like a patrol ship, or just drops from landing craft?" He asked Beliar.

"Flies, why?"

"Why don't we try it?!" Croft bellowed cheerfully.

"Hey, alright!" Jarret's face lit up like a young star.

"You know what. Why not?" Beliar smiled like a little devil.

"You are stupid!" Julie snapped. "We don't know how to fly! We'll kill ourselves! We'll get a spanking! I don't want it!"

"If we kill each other, we won't get it. Corpses aren't beaten." Jarret was going to punch his friend on the forehead, but he didn't reach out, being held by the breast plate. Anne giggled.

"I can fly," said Beliar seriously. "I flew with my father on patrols several times, he even allowed me to pilot. And the navigation system of the White Ball is not much different from those currently used in landing craft. Look, Julie," he extended his hand towards the control panel. "Everything looks complicated, but it's pure automation. You just enter the numerical bearings with a touch into this aquamarine field: planet number, sector, sector square, and destination point, and the transporter AI moves you safely there, unless you switch to manual control. And that's it. A cakewalk. I will also be able to come back, I know the location of my father's residence by heart."

"And what's the number of the H14?" Ari asked.

"Six." Beliar typed in the first number. He glanced at Annie and smiled brightly. "Do you want to go on a trip?"

"Sure!" The girl exclaimed enthusiastically.

"Parents will kill us," Julie muttered tearfully. She lowered her head so that the cascade of wavy blonde hair completely obscured her face.

"If you don't want to, you don't need to fly, cowardly creature." A malicious smile appeared on Ari's face. "Go play with teddy bears and blocks."

"I'm not a doll!" Julie's hair flew up furiously. Jarret was afraid of his friend, because for a moment she looked like pissed off Aga, who perfectly simulated human emotions.

"So, it's decided by the democratic majority." Beliar raised his fist, tapped it on his friends' hands. He entered four into the system. Apparently, it was a bearing of the tropical jungle densely covering the entire equator. The idea of a trip to an exotic forest where you could see fancy and colorful plants like in Carlos' conservatory seemed quite good. What to enter next - he had no idea. So, he let Ari and Jarret act, who chose five and eight. What was the difference where they would end up in the forest? Any area would be great.

"Where are we going, anyway?" Julie inquired.

"Fuck knows," Ari blurted out. Beliar pouted, transferred his meaningful gaze to Annie.

"I'll tell mom you curse!" Croft burst out.

"Hey, why are you picking on me, sister? Mother often says it when she doesn't know something, so it's probably okay."

"Alright, be quiet now." Beliar activated the take-off procedure with a punch of his fist.

Feeling the vibrations and hearing the rising hum of the engine waking up, Julie tensed all of her muscles. She gritted her teeth and gripped the breastplate so tightly with her hands that her wrists ached.

"We'll all die, we'll all die, we'll all die ..."

"They say you only live once, right?" Jarret said cheerfully.

"You must not fly away, without telling anyone ... Agaaaa! Mooooom!"

Annie was silent. Like the rest, she was moved by the first aviation impressions without the participation of adults. She felt a rush of adrenaline as regular vibrations began to pass through the machine. She also shared the enthusiasm of her colleagues who laughed louder and louder, whistled and mocked the panicked Julie. Sandstorm was absolutely not afraid, on the contrary - she was glad that they would have a fantastic adventure soon, even if it meant breaking all the safety rules that adults had put insistently in their heads.

Equipped with an anti-gravity engine, the White Ball began to rise aslope slowly and softly towards one of the ventilation tunnels, closed only in the event of threats or bad weather conditions. Such a small object didn't require the entire airlock to be opened.

The children fell silent. They stared at each other in fear, hearing the muffled, mesmerizing whine of the gongs that went off every time something left the hangar. They forgot about it completely. But no one tried to stop the White Ball, everything happened too quickly, and the young travelers easily found themselves outside.

Beliar, who had more or less grasped the operation of the control panel, managed to activate the thermal imaging area scanner. He and Ari watched as someone ran out of Drunkenstein's mansion as the machine was already high above the landing field. The cyan color of the mode indicated it must have been an android. Humans ranged in color from yellow to red, depending on body temperature, radiation, and emotional intensity.

"Aga!" The boys exclaimed simultaneously. Only one android worked in the small private rebel unit.

The thermal image of the surroundings changed immediately as the machine rushed ahead. There were chaotic readings as it rolled through the clouds like a thrown bowling ball - how to control rotation, Beliar had yet to grasp. Stains, bars and zigzags, meaningless for people not trained in interpreting aerial images, were displayed on the screen every now and then. Thermo vision indicated that there was no living soul within many miles.

"Right away someone will fly after us and bring us back to the base," Ari said. "I'm a little scared."

Drunkenstein replied by asking:

"Do you remember what my father used to say over and over about safety? The first rule that should be followed by any rebel in control of a ship or naval craft?"

"To take off only when we are sure that we will not be detected by enemy electronics?"

"This too. But that more important issue?"

"I don't know."

"He advised to always activate a protective screen around the hull. I just did it. We are invisible to human eyes, as well as to almost all types of scanners. The last point, of course, concerns the Kiritians. Co-evolutionarily, they are still one step ahead of us."

"Oh god ... How do you know so much and such strange words?" Julie asked sardonically, but she mentally admired Beliar's quick-wittedness. Sometimes she got angry when she completely didn't understand the erudition of her friends.

Drunkenstein smiled brightly.

"I'm interested in it. Anyway, I want to follow in my father's footsteps, so I have to study a lot."

Annie, as the daughter of the rebel, had repeatedly covered long distances in airships, and had also been in space a few times. But it was the first time in her short life that she dealt with such an extreme flight. The sensations she experienced made her hot. She began to feel that her stomach did weird things. Beads of sweat appeared on her forehead, not least due to the temperature of the perfectly air-conditioned cabin. The girl squinted and stuck out her drooling tongue. She saw that the faces of her friends were pale, and Jarret's was almost green. Each of them looked like after drinking Aga's energy drink 'full of health and vitamins'.

They quickly felt sick, just as quickly lost track in the windowless transporter of where was sky and where earth. Everything was spinning excruciatingly. The vehicle was rushing so fast, changing its speed, that it was difficult even to lift an arm or a leg. This was not how they had imagined it all!

Julie was the first to empty her stomach, starting a chain reaction. In less than a few minutes, the entire cabin, including the passengers, was covered with leftover food from the last few hours.

"Ugh. Jarret, goddamn it, you puked on me!" Beliar managed to brush off his filthy wrists. The smell was unbearable and the air purifier was working too slowly for his liking. He barely managed to keep from throwing up again.

The daring flight ended as soon as it had begun. The White Ball slowed down gradually, and when it reached zero speed, it began to descend gently onto the ground selected by the autopilot.

Beliar turned on the incomplete lighting in the cockpit, deliberately ignoring the airframe (that's what the hull or armor of any flying machine had been referred to for centuries - what an observer saw from outside). He didn't know where they landed and how they would be received here. If in some secret den of lycans, they could even pay for it with their lives when the wolf-people spotted the transporter glowing like one of the H14's two moons. The young Drunkenstein realized for the first time that his father's safety lectures, often too boring, were useful in practice.

The door rose, letting in stuffy air saturated with the intense scent of damp plants. The steps extended. Spider-like nanites removed organic waste, then took care of children's clothes, quickly restoring their freshness. Inside, the soothing scent of lavender began to spread, mingling with the flowing scent of the equatorial forest. The rubber and kevlar breastplates rose simultaneously.

The children, curious, approached the oval exit and began to inspect the surroundings uncertainly. For long moments, neither of them could say even a word. They stared at each other, endowing each other with surprised expressions, to fix their eyes again on the equatorial wonders.

It was a hot tropical night outside. The myriads of stars, two moons and the brown, rocky planet in the near area gave enough light for the eyes to catch the details of the immediate surroundings. A forest shaped by terraforming a few hundred years earlier, free from predators, was something unusual and fascinating for children. The intense, sweet scent of the flowers seemed overwhelming. Lizards of several species crawled over the large leaves. On their multicolored backs, swirled multi-shaped appendages with a fluorescent gleam. Above cycads and ferns that grew closest to the White Ball, hovered glow worms. One could hear the splash of water and the croaking of frogs nearby.

Chulimal, taken from humanoid jaguars and renamed H14, turned out to be a salvation for terraforming teams responsible for preparing celestial bodies for migrants coming from the cosmos, who wanted new life and space. In 2307, thousands of people settled in the first extraterrestrial colony on Mars, and since then the acceleration of general technology development had slowed down tremendously. Many things that facilitated existence had survived over the centuries in an unchanged form, since they worked well. In turn, the space industry moved forward, mainly regarding first interplanetary drives, then interstellar ones, the armaments industry and terraforming served by several companies, the largest of which belonged to the descendants of Elon Musk. The last process lasted from several dozen to several hundred years, depending on the conditions prevailing on moons or terrestrial planets, because only such objects were included in a framework of colonial examinations. They had to be similar to the Blue Planet, especially in terms of gravity, density and size, terraforming was cheaper then, and sometimes it turned out to be needed in a rudimentary form. After a thorough examination of the globe or the satellite, in the first stage of changes, a network of sky-high atmosphere synthesizers was spread, which in the complex processes of synthesis or treatment of elements changed the existing atmosphere or created a new one. Then the earth was transformed and enriched with elements suitable for farming, water tanks were created by chemical reactions or the water contained in the bowels of the planet was used if it was in a processable form. At the end, animals and plants from Earth, modificants or crosses, were brought in, according to the preferences and needs of the colonists. Hence the norm that the same species existed on the colonized planets, although they were not placed everywhere as in the case of sites used for testing weapons. Chulimal, however, turned out to be the exception. Terraforming groups saved many uinals, the official currency of the universes, introduced by the empire, because organisms similar to terrestrials developed here, and the transformation of the planet was practically a slight correction of the composition of the atmosphere. The change seemed small, but it nevertheless wiped out many of the native H14 species which, what shocked scientists and remained an unsolved mystery, shared genes with terrestrial organisms! Sixty percent of Onkalots' genes were human. However, biological niches were replaced by imported individuals that settled perfectly in the new conditions. Over time, indigenous and alien species interacted, and after several centuries, acquired the ability to interbreed. Centuries-long dependence, mainly competition and mutualism, led to the consolidation of new ecosystems on Chulimal, which in turn enriched the soil with valuable elements, and provided the air with oxygen in amounts good for people, so that the synthesizers of the atmosphere were turned off, dismantled and taken away by shuttles.

"Wow, its paradise" Jarret broke the silence.

"Well, paradise is the perfect word," commented Drunkenstein.

"It's beautiful!" Although Julie had been against the expedition, she was the first to leave the cabin and she climbed on a mossy boulder near a small pond.

"Julie, wait!" Beliar immediately found himself beside her. After a while, all the children tried to penetrate the thicket with their eyes, standing on the top of the rock.

"Is it safe here?" Jarret crouched down. He smiled as a bioluminescent fungus he tapped with his finger flashed red and began to exude a terrible smell from the coarse mycelium. "Wow, that's nice."

"Are we at the equator, Beli?" Ari was brushing off the flying spores with his hands.

Looking at the compact jungle and the dense treetops, Drunkenstein didn't reply immediately. He grabbed Anna's hand. With his other hand, he turned on the solar fluorescent lamp resembling a pillar of salt, he had taken from the transporter's storage compartment. He set the intensity of the glow so that they had an additional light source and at the same time remained invisible to the theoretical observer, far from their whereabouts.

"I think so."

"Then we are screwed when we get back to the base," Ari said, but in the voice of a person completely satisfied, as if he hadn't cared about the consequences of the forbidden trip.

"Why?" Beliar beamed. "Maybe there will be a slagging, but the White Ball has been tested."

"You're screwed!" Jarret pushed Ari off the slippery edge of the boulder. The surprised boy burst into the pond, screaming and waving his hands. To his relief, the water was warm. Creatures lying on the leaves and floating trunks jumped into the reservoir.

After less than a few breaths, Jarret landed in the water as well, being pulled by his leg by Ari. The other three jumped off the boulder and approached the edge of the reservoir.

"Are you normal?! There may be leeches here! And alligators! And piranhas!" Waving her fists, Julie invented more and more bizarre creatures that could inhabit this tiny pond. She stepped back to keep the drops and mud flying everywhere from landing on her new pants. The desire to protect the clothes from dirt, however, was unsuccessful, because Beliar, who stuck the base of the fluorescent lamp in the sand of a wind throw, pressed his hand against Julie's back so strongly that she flew into the water, screaming horribly.

Drunkenstein, still holding giggling Annie's hand, jumped into the pond with her, screaming loudly, "Wuhu!"

Alligators, piranhas and leeches - and more fantastic creatures - didn't attack the mischievous swimmers. Being held down by Nelson, Julie squealed and thrashed as if in the claws of a predator, when Ari, torn by spasms of laughter, tried to place a huge toad on her head. The girl finally broke free, ran out of the pond vigorously and rushed through the jungle, to avoid another encounter with the hideous, slimy amphibian. On the way, she brushed off with her arms large leaves and vines as thick as a human wrist.

The jog quickly turned into the run of an overjoyed child, having fun for the first time in its life without the presence of the guardians. After a few minutes, the frantic five were already rushing through the forest. They scared glowing insects, threw wind-pollinated seeds into the air, slid on their bottoms down slippery slopes, played tag between huge tree trunks.

Soon they reached a wet clearing bounded on one side by a jungle wall and on the other turning into a bald hill. Julie and Annie's attention was drawn to the congeries of small flowers with long stems scattered throughout the area. The boys began to play wrestling and jumping on the undulating carpet of the bog.

Out of breath, muddy Beliar, sure that the girls were busy making wreaths, which they had been doing a few moments earlier, paid little attention to Annie watching something from the top of the gentle hill. "She must have seen another interesting thing that she has not seen before," he thought, glancing at her briefly. He became interested in the mysterious object of observation only when Julie approached Annie and now both of them, standing motionless, were staring at something with excitement.

"What are you doing?" He walked over to them, brushing off the remnants of vines and threads of moss. Ari and Jarret also did themselves up and followed their friend.

Julie unnecessarily pointed at mysterious fires burning hundreds of meters away, in a tree-free forest enclave. They had strange colors, like friar's lanterns.

"You said no one was going to be here," Jarret directed his words to Drunkenstein.

"Well, because no one should be here." Beliar stared distrustfully at the fires. "Dad said that the H14 belongs mainly to rebels, the rest are apolitical civilians, i.e. farmers concentrated in warm zones, mainly growing corn and sugar cane, as well as residents of mining estates who extract minerals of volcanic origin in the mines. He argued that no one lived permanently on the equator, because nothing could be grown here or anything valuable in the ground could be found."

"Or maybe they are ... well ... some fractions?" Julie interjected. "Reclusions?"

"What reclusions, they say recluses," Ari corrected.

"I have no idea." Drunkenstein shrugged. He thought about something for a moment. "You know what? We can actually check it."

"Are you stupid?! What if there are monsters? Or lycans?!" The older girl shuddered at the very thought of the bestial wolf people, according to Aga, kidnapping naughty children. The adults too, because that is how Annie's mother had died - although no one had seen it.

"Devils don't exist, and there are no lycans in this region of the planet."

Julie didn't give up:

"Aga said that devils exist. Mom says that too!"

"Because your mom is stupid," Jarret mocked her, mimicking her nervous movements.

"You're stupid," Ari growled.

"Come on." Beliar decided to take matters into his own hands. He picked up a long pole from the ground and grasped it like a staff. "Who's in favor of checking these fires? This could be useful information for our parents. I'm for it." He hit the ground with the tip of the stick.

Jarret raised his hand first, glancing uncertainly at Ari. The friend did the same almost immediately. Anne also raised her arm, though she had no idea what it was about.

"We got four to one, so we're going." Drunkenstein gave his younger friend his hand. "Julie, grab Annie by the other hand. Everyone is to be silent from now on."

Croft obeyed, this time not opposing in any way.

They walked single file towards the valley, weaving between the trunks of trees and the tall vegetation of the underbrush. The closer they got to the fires creeping in the wind, the more slowly and cautiously they walked, carefully examining the surroundings. They saw nothing disturbing, no ground or flying vehicles. Also, no people.

They reached the vicinity of the light sources safely less than a quarter of an hour later. Drunkenstein turned off the fluorescent lamp he was holding with Annie, folded it at the push of a button and stuffed it into his pants pocket. It turned out that the wind-blown fire of an unnatural shade of turquoise and blue didn't come from the fires, but rose from porphyry bowls placed on stands. They edged a primitive stone road. Beliar had seen a similar one in Julie's holo-book about the ancient, techno lytic cultures of the Earth. This antiquity must have belonged to ancient times as well, for no one built such now, except in private gardens or amusement centers, but it was probably a remnant of exterminated Onkalots. The avenue ran towards a wide, jagged stairs that ended with a landing before the front facade of monstrous ruins. The children gathered in a tight group behind Beliar's back. Jarret swallowed loudly. Ari wanted to say something, inhaled, but only an incomprehensible rattle came out of his mouth. Julie gripped Annie's hand tighter. The girl, in turn, narrowed her eyes and stared curiously at the strange, decaying structure made of stone blocks, gradually absorbed by the jungle, at the square mouth of the portal leading to the dark, mysterious interior.

"What is this?" Julie couldn't take her eyes off the fascinating but terrible sight.

"Some old temple, I have no idea," Beliar replied in a whisper.

Having let go Anna's hand, Croft touched his shoulder.

"Maybe we shouldn't go in there ... We'd better go back ... Let's get out of here! Aren't you surprised there's a fire around? Someone has to live here."

Beliar turned to the girl.

"Relax, nothing is happening. We'll find out who's there and be right back. I promise. We need to know it."

"I'm not so sure." Ari ran a hand anxiously through his hair, clasped his fingers on the back of his neck.

Drunkenstein walked over to the nearest sand-gray stone stand, climbed onto a boulder slipped closer with his shoe. Instead of the branches and flammable fungi he hoped to see in the concave bowl, he found a beetle-sized black artificial fire generator. He stuck his finger uncertainly into the flame. It turned out to be a type of lighting that only gave light, but not heat. The boy suddenly realized one disturbing thing, looking at the remaining flames bubbling up in the rows on both sides of the road. Such a cold, colorful fire, came up with...

"The Kiritians," he whispered to himself.

Having turned off the flame, he put the generator in his pocket and jumped off the boulder. The group relaxed as it saw the fake smile on its leader's face. Drunkenstein pondered whether he would be right to tell them about his discovery. From an early age, he had been warned against the Kiritians and their cruelty, but, frankly, he was absolutely not afraid of them. He already knew life well enough to know that parents love to scare their disobedient children with alien invaders and monsters, and such stories are simply bogus. But now, standing in the middle of the dark jungle, hundreds of kilometers from Carlos' guarded base, facing the overwhelming structure erected by aliens' mitts, he began to feel irrational anxiety. Watching as the four charges walk around the stone courtyard and gaze with fascination at obsidian statues depicting large anthropomorphic, warlike cats, Beliar decided to keep his mouth shut. He would tell them, but later. Or maybe not. First, he should have learned more about the people who had left the fire (maybe they weren't villains or thieves, since they had lit up the courtyard in front of the ruins so brightly that you could see it from miles away?), even if, after returning to the base, instead of praise, he would get a decent spanking and a year-long ban on pleasures.

"Come on," he urged the others. Seeing that his friends were not moving from their place, he went to explore the objects of their interest. He walked around a pedestal with an amazing statue resembling a few meters high Onkalot, holding a shield in one clawed paw, and a javelin adorned with feathers in the other. The character was captured at the time of the aggressive attack.

"Are you afraid?" Drunkenstein turned to Annie. Sandstorm, staring at the portico yawning black, shook her head negatively.

"Don't worry, if something happens, I will protect you."

"Sure, you're only ten years old," replied Julie. "You're not even armed."

Beliar gripped the pole tighter. Croft gave him a wry look with a 'sure, you'll save us with the old stick' expression.

"This time my stupid sister is right." Ari stepped back as if he had seen something disturbing at the top of the stairs. "Let's get out of here better. This place gives me the chills."

Drunkenstein sighed nervously.

"Get hold of yourselves, people! Nothing will happen to us. We will quietly go inside, take a look and be right back. If there were any guards, drones, orbs, or other sensors, we would have been spotted long ago. We absolutely need to check what is happening. You understand? This is very important!"

Ari kicked a random rock and stuffed his hands into the pockets of his pants; Jarret nodded, but somehow reluctantly. Unwillingly, the group moved towards the entrance to the building.

They walked close to each other. They passed a dry and cracked pool, lined with roots. They crossed the square littered with broken columns and climbed the stone steps, sticking to their left side, because the other was badly shabby and overgrown with lichen. They stopped at the entrance to the dark corridor. Beliar lit again the unfolded fluorescent lamp, pushed aside the cobwebs dangling from the ceiling with his pole, and though he felt a sudden fear as he looked at the dark throat in front of him, he moved slowly. The rest followed single file the precariously walking guide.

The fear subsided, however, as the boy got used to his surroundings. The passage, built of perfectly even stone blocks, began to expand, and after a few minutes of walking it was wide and high enough for a tank to go through it. Rusty yokes jutted from the walls, without logs, but the corridor was illuminated by self-adhesive solar lamps. In the dim blue light, they could see the wall reliefs of the same humanoid cats whose stone images guarded the courtyard.

The corridor forked. They decided to go left. Soon before the group's eyes appeared four passages stretching in different directions. Beliar chose the widest of them, going through which, they soon reached an empty and not very large chamber. Behind the jagged door opening on the other side of the room, a further complex could be seen: the hall, and in it, stairs and passages lit with white. The boy concluded that they had entered some ancient sanctuary, forgotten by mankind.

The children standing in the center of the room froze as they heard voices coming from nearby. Panicked, they rushed forward and clung to the wall shaded by the pillars. Beliar turned off the fluorescent lamp. He put a finger to his lips as he looked at the rest.

The temple grew silent as a tomb.

The children waited. Each of them was afraid to move.

Breathing anxiously, Julie accidentally crushed the stone with her elbow, which fell and rolled a little with a thud. Ari closed his eyes, cursed in spirit his sister's stupidity.

"Are you there, Corporal Darkoris?" A powerful male voice thundered. The alien spoke Kiritian, the official language of most of the Zodiac Universum planets. It was derived from Anglo-American, once common on Earth, but many words were borrowed from the speech of the Onkalots. The newcomer, however, had a strange accent which made him difficult to understand. In addition, the sounds were muffled by the helmet mask, giving the words a synthetic radio sounding.

The nearest corridor got filled with the metallic clanking sound of several armored men.

"Shit, soldiers." Jarret turned abruptly and bumped into Ari, hitting him hard on the nose. Croft almost screamed in pain.

"Hurry up, we need to hide better." Beliar pushed the boys ahead and tugged Annie by the hand. Julie didn't need any encouragement to follow the escaping.

They burst into a small hall with columns and empty pedestals, where colored fires of small flames were burning in obsidian bowls. At the end loomed a door less passage. Two rows of short, winding stairs, fringing the pond branched off from the landing. The children, however, didn't manage to reach the steps: the clatter of soldiers' boots grew louder and louder.

Beliar, who had dropped his staff during the run, pushed Jarret into a darkened niche behind one of the platforms, threw himself at his friend like a wrestler and pressed him to the ground. Julie hugged Annie, Ari embraced them both and tried to flatten them as much as possible to the cold stone slab floor.

The children merged into one terrified mass of trembling muscles and worst thoughts.

Drunkenstein cautiously poked his head from behind the landing - and almost groaned in terror. He silently apologized to his parents for mocking their warnings.

Two powerfully built, armored ... Kiritians entered the chamber! Behind the right shoulders were the barrels of energizers protruding malevolently. Beliar swallowed. He companied this terrible weapon, capable of paralyzing the victim's nervous system for hours, making them look like a puppet with cut strings. From the perspective of the children, and almost melting into the ground, the Immortals were impressive, they looked like smaller versions of walking robots. Apart from the head, they were protected by a light, seemingly delicate, but extremely durable, and at the same time body-friendly bio metal. Possibly, androids passed by, flew through Drunkenstein's head, judged by the chalky like that of a corpse, faces above the communication masks. Or was it just a play of skimpy room lights? One of the men had blue eyes and black hair falling in pods towards his neck, the other looked like a stereotypical, crew-cut muscleman. Beliar had never seen a real Kiritian, only their likeness in the form of documentation and electronic notes, which were abundant in Carlos' base. From childhood, each rebel was instilled with information about the greatest criminals in human history.

Julie discreetly glanced at the center of the room, sticking her head out from behind the plinth, and turned pale like a wall. The Kiritians stopped right next to 'their' empty foundation. Ari, having noticed that his sister was moving her chest spasmodically, as before an asthma attack, or at least crying, covered her mouth with his trembling hand. Jarret looked at Annie and gestured to be quiet. The girl was the only one who looked at the imposing warriors without fear. She was too young to understand the seriousness of the situation.

"What's up?" A third soldier entered the room, also with snow-white complexion, freckled, with red strands of hair on the top of his head, locked in bio metal like his comrades. Beliar had heard that the Kiritians, no matter what their rank, were the same as far as their armor was concerned. By this visual equality they more than once referred to each other as an achij, which literally meant a warrior, but it was also common to call so a friend or companion; the word was taken from the onkalotian speech. Despite the lack of bars, thanks to the efficient electronic identification system, each soldier knew perfectly well who held what position among the militarized community. The goal of such a strategy was to confuse the enemy and the Oders in general - humans who didn't belong to the Kiritian people.

"You shouted, Corporal Victor Shane. Instead of yelling, you could call me."

"Was I supposed to give up on the sound of such a suggestive echo?" The dark-haired man called Viktor smiled fleetingly. "Now it's your turn, Darkoris. We are done with Shimizu for today." He nodded his chin towards the short-haired muscleman. "Nothing is happening, total boredom. Where did you lose Bradshaw?"

"He will come soon," Corporal Darkoris replied. Beliar, watching the men, hid as they moved slightly. He couldn't see them, but he thought the redhead smiled lasciviously, judging by the timbre of his voice. "Then have fun at the orgy."

"Thanks, but I won't use it. I have a wife. But you guys play the field with Bradshaw later." Viktor patted his interlocutor on the shoulder with a coarse gauntlet resembling a demon's paw.

"Corporal Shane, let's at least make fun of this new one," Shimizu said. "How is he called?"

"Private Tsar Seymour," Darkoris suggested.

"He's so drunk that we can prank him."

"But admit that his stuff is good." Darkoris grinned.

"Great, you and Bradshaw stopped being cats lately," Viktor recalled with amusement.

"Whatever. Do you think they will kiritianize him? It would be something to watch."

"New recruits are rarely infected," Shane said seriously. "They first have to get accustomed and train, too young age is also an obstacle. They'll probably inject him with a super virus no sooner than in two years. Alright, let's postpone the chats."

Both sentries from the ended shift climbed the steps and disappeared into the dark hall, while Darkoris went on patrol. He stopped and looked at the dropped staff. He shrugged. He bent down, picked up the item, and left.

"Let's run!" Jarret rushed from his hiding place as if he had been sitting on a hedgehog, as soon as the Immortals moved away. Beliar ran in a flash and immediately brought his friend back to his original place.

"Are you crazy?! Wait!" He said, finally allowing himself a deeper breath. "This Bradshaw or whatever he's called, might go this way any moment now. We have to wait."

"And if they find us? They will eat us, Beliar, you hear me, they will eat us!" This time Ari lost his temper. Drunkenstein couldn't stand it and hit his friend in the face.

"If you don't shut up, I'm gonna eat you myself! Think. Why would they look for us behind that landing if they don't even know we exist? Have you noticed that they don't use electronics to communicate or set any sensors outside? They also didn't have bio-opt visors or thermo-indictors with them, so they will not detect our bodies. They must feel safe here, do you understand? This patrol is also probably a routine and not a necessity. And they certainly didn't anticipate that we would visit the ruins."

"But why are they here in this part of the Milky Way?" Jarret asked. "The old folks say the Kiritians don't visit the Lion Universum."

"Apparently they are wrong," Beliar replied grimly. "The father thinks Immortal technology is light years ahead of ours, so it's no wonder they've been able to camouflage themselves so well. And on the rebel planet. We have to get out of here and let the parents know."

"Wait!" Julie yanked Ari by the katana. "Why did you say they would eat us?"

"You don't know?" Jarret was honestly surprised. "Kiritians are cannibals."

"Bullshit, don't scare her!" Beliar barked. "Don't listen to him, Julie."

"Isn't it like that, Beli?" Nelson looked his friend in the eye.

"It isn't. Only Forkis sometimes feeds on human flesh, but it's possible that it's just another silly gossip invented by scared people."

"Who is Forkis?" The questioning Julie's voice broke more and more. Ari slapped his forehead with his hand.

"First Galactic Dignitary, commander in chief and ruler of these usurpers." Beliar waved his hand in an undefined direction. "And shut up at last, or they will actually hear us."

Mysterious Bradshaw didn't appear for the next minutes. No one was passing through or near the chamber. Even the distant muffled conversation from the corridors died down, as if the Kiritians had left the temple complex. The children, however, were afraid to go back the way they had come here. Moving towards the winding stairs and the rest of the sanctuary was out of question. By a fortunate coincidence, Julie saw a hole covered with roots along the wall, with a dark corridor looming behind it. "Such a neglected passage is certainly unused," Beliar thought, and directed everyone there. He himself plunged into the darkness last, pushing Julie, who started waving her hands wildly as her hair was plastered with cobwebs and dried-up bits of plants.

They walked in complete darkness, touching the wall, now their only guide. Beliar didn't take a risk activating the fluorescent lamp. He kicked something openwork and rattling a couple of times. He guessed what it might have been, but didn't say it aloud. When the kicked something rolled on the floor with a rattle, Julie inhaled loudly and violently.

A dark, cool corridor with a low ceiling led them to a landing at the top of the spiral staircase that joined the two stories. The group entered a mezzanine without a balustrade - below which was a hall full of achijes. Beliar realized after a brief observation from his hiding place that it must have been a loose gathering: the Kiritians were laughing, shouting, talking, drinking, some were listening to an agitator as he spoke from a platform topped with a stone altar. At a colonnade on the edge of the chamber, where the light from torches and solar crystals was scarce, a few achijes kissed passionately women dressed in skimpy leather outfits, in imitation of those of Lycan warriors.

The boys grimaced, Julie on the contrary - she watched the love affairs with great curiosity. Annie wasn't interested in the Kiritians at all. Having crouched behind her friends, she started crushing clay pebbles.

"There are dozens of them ..." Ari whispered, fascinated and terrified at the same time. Beliar and Jarret yanked him sharply toward them as he unconsciously began to lean out of the shadow.

Drunkenstein intended to lead everyone out along the corridor which he believed extended to the exit of the temple. However, he pushed his friends towards the colossal blocks which were remnants of the long-broken wall, as a new group of Kiritians began to emerge from the perpendicular hall. The children lay down behind the rubble.

Beliar gritted his teeth and tapped his forehead in annoyance against the wall.

"Great, we're stuck here!" Everyone except Annie gave him a gloomy look. "Too bad, we have to wait out the briefing or whatever it is. Maybe we'll learn something useful, which we'll repeat later in the database."

"If we manage to survive," Jarret muttered glumly. His words remained without any comment.

***

Anne didn't try to melt into the ground like the rest, but, having settled herself on a boulder nearby between the remnants of a basalt monolith, she curled her legs up and hugged them. She wanted to pee, but she didn't tell anyone about it, seeing that her friends were watching the soldiers downstairs and talking in whispers. She decided to handle it herself.

Even though Beliar hadn't let her move away, she slipped off the seat and walked silently towards the stairs. She looked back, no one noticed she had gone this far. She shrugged and started climbing the steps.

Having reached the upper floor, she stopped in front of a corridor lit by blue lamps. This part of the temple looked completely different. The floor was covered with soft skins and shaggy furs. Bioluminescent insects hovered in the scented air, moving erratically like dust flecks in a draft. A lizard, attached to the wall with its paws, had spots on its back glowing in the spectrum of red. A cheerful smile appeared on the girl's face.

As soon as she took care of the need in a found clay amphora, she returned to the lizard to look at it closely. Upon seeing the great creature, the frightened animal fell off the wall, landed on the fur and began to run away in a flash, playfully flexing its torso sideways with each coordinated movement of its paws. It also ceased to be iridescent. Before the girl managed to grab the lizard by the tail, it hid in a crack in the wall. Sandstorm knelt down and peered into the crack, but then rose with a sour expression.

She realized that she had reached the further part of the floor. She noticed several rooms behind her back, protected by makeshift energy barriers of dark purple shades. She had seen alike at Drunkenstein's base, so she understood how they worked and what they were for, largely because of Beliar's fondness of explaining everything. The condensed, volatile particles of the shields formed structures dense enough to make seeing what happened on the other side impossible. However, some rooms didn't have such barriers and were covered with sheets of cloth.

All of the last category had no tenants. Except for one. The lodging was just around the corner of the corridor, slightly away from the rest of the rooms. Dancing light filtered through the narrow gap between the lintel and the synthetic fiber screen - the orange glow of artificial fire, something Anne discovered when she fell on all fours and peeked discreetly inside. Contrary to the previous chambers, where there were only bunks and barracks equipment, this one turned out to be richer furnished. A young woman in a white dishabille lay on the bed; holding her bent left leg, she looked relaxed and content. The girl crouching behind the threshold, smiled as she looked at her delicate face with bold red lips and the tangle of hair the color of the flickering fire. Naturally, she didn't know that the condition of the woman could be caused by drugs taken.

Sandstorm moved carefully to the screen to catch more details of the room, and saw that the woman wasn't alone. A tall Kiritian stood to the right of the bed. The most unusual man she had ever seen in her life. He wore incomplete, detailed, black-and-ink weapons with indigo elements. He didn't have a communication mask like the rest of the achijes, so you could see his handsome, slightly stern, shapely face devoid of any imperfections. The chest and abdomen were also exposed, while the arms and back were covered with bracers and other pieces of bio metal gear that Beliar would have certainly been able to name, indicating their purpose. On the powerfully muscled torso, were clearly outlined the ribs, and on the abdomen, what in his toy gladiators and mutants, Drunkenstein would have called the abs. Black hair flowing down the sides of his head contrasted with the pale face, as if the Kiritian had avoided the sun. This pallor, however, didn't scare the girl, on the contrary - in a way it attracted the eyes and scattered thoughts. The man sitting next to the woman looked just beautiful, like a top-class android. Or maybe it was an angel of war, about which Hanako's mother had once told her, which Annie remembered very vaguely? If he had had wings, he could have indeed been an angel of war. And while she had seen quite a few people, mostly rebels, passing through Carlos' base in her short life, none was as remarkable as the impressive two-meter Immortal. All of them, young and old, corporals and captains, she had once seen Commander Lacetti himself! - merchants, technicians of various kinds, scientists, inventors, a gardener who cared for the conservatory - none of them was the equal of this here, neither in height, nor stature, nor appearance.

"I'm really surprised that you decided to come here with us," the Kiritian said in a calm baritone. Anne took a risk and stood between the curtain and the doorframe so that she could see more. "It is as if a sheep were hanging out with wolves." A slight smirk appeared on his handsome face. The usurper rested his gloved hands on the sheets so that the girl was between his shoulders. "Aren't you scared?"

The woman rose on her elbows, chuckled, tilted her head back as the Kiritian tried to kiss her.

"No, you know the risk." said Forkis.

"You should. You should. Please Forkis..."

Anna blinked, felt the touch of thousands of moving legs of non-existent ants on her back. Wasn't that the name of the most important Kiritian commander? If so then ... it's ... amazing! She just had the strongest and scariest man in the universe in front of her! Except the Kiritian didn't look threatening at all. Beliar had lied to her. And I wonder what a cannibal means, which Sandstorm had sometimes heard in relation to the name Forkis. She concluded that it was probably some sort of achij military rank.

Embarrassed, she raised her hand to her eyes as the couple started kissing, and as they pressed each other so strangely and made terrible noises, she covered her face with her hands. Sometimes she just peered between her separated fingers, but each time she joined them quickly. She had registered that the man's face was weary. More than once, Julie had had such a face when Aga had told her to play with her many times the same day.

"I'm hungry," Forkis said when they finally stopped moving. "And very. You are so sweet. I would eat you; you know? Whole."

"Then do it." The woman stroked his chin with her hand.

Forkis hung his head, laughing as if insulting.

"But I'm not kidding. I was giving you a chance. I told you to let go and not give up on the modest but safe life. It was salvation."

"Eat me whole. I want this," the woman whispered in his face.

Annoyed, Anne raised her hand again to eye level, certain that these two would start kissing again. She would have also liked to cover her ears if she had had an extra pair of hands. In the end, she compromised and plugged her ears with her thumbs, and with the rest of her fingers, she covered her eyes, but she watched anyway.

"Whole. And fast or slow?" Forkis asked in a joking tone. Observant Sandstorm noticed a nuance in his expression. Seeming to be enjoying a moment earlier, he now looked a bit annoyed and disappointed, but he successfully covered up those emotions with a fake smile.

"Entire. And fast."

"As you wish." The Kiritian shrugged, then attacked the woman's neck in a flash. He bit into the trachea absolutely like a leopard, not giving the petite and much weaker victim even the slightest chance to defend herself.

Confused Anne's hands dropped as if the bones had turned into liquid. She opened her mouth in a silent scream, and with her eyes opened wide with terror, she watched the unimaginable monstrosities that began to unfold behind the synthetic screen. She stood paralyzed, unable to escape.

The usurper's mistress must have died within moments. The terrible mask of total surprise was fixed on the face as white as a canvas. Around the head lying on the pillow, began to gather blood, flowing profusely from the torn throat, soaking rapidly into the sheets.

Forkis gasped like a predator, tilted his head sharply, throwing into the air, scarlet drops and fragments of the body.

Blood.

There was so much blood everywhere ... So much blood! Little Sandstorm wanted to faint. No, she would have loved to die now! So that it was over, so that she didn't have to look at these horrors, off which she couldn't, however, take her fear-dazed eyes, as if her eyelids had been held up by some sadistic, invisible micro-bot.

Beliar had lied to her again: monsters existed. And one of them, very strong, deadly - and beautiful as an angel of war - was just a few meters away. In the human form.

The first bones from the torn flesh began to appear on the sheets.

"Run!" The voice rumbled in her brain. "But first, back off carefully!"

At one point, Forkis slowly turned his head towards the exit of the room, his wild gaze of the hazel eyes met the gaze of the girl scared to the extreme. Most of the Immortal's face was stained with blood that dripped on the sheets and bracers.

He smiled terrifyingly. He didn't seem surprised by the presence of the rebel child in the Kiritian nest.

Sandstorm lost track of time and reality. She wondered if she had mistaken wakefulness for a dream. Had she fallen asleep? Maybe she had passed out? Or maybe Forkis had torn her to pieces like that woman and now she was in heaven? What if she ended up in hell for escaping her friends and kicking Julie with the sandal earlier? What if there was neither heaven nor hell, as Jarret had often told her? What would happen to her then?

She remembered only scraps of reality, meaningless images with no rhyme or reason. Screams as if coming from another part of the planet. Beliar's panic scream. Julie's squeal. Ari's grumbling. Jarret's crying. Violently shaking her body. A sight of blue lights, someone's back, fast-moving legs, and a shifting floor. Muffled male voices, very distant. Close, distant again. Once more squeals, bellows, screams.

Someone dropped her on the stone slabs, picked her up again.

She was tugged painfully to the side, then she bounced again, seeing the back, legs, and ground endlessly.

The temple lights receded until they finally disappeared. The air temperature and the force of the wind changed. Or maybe there was no wind?

Branches and leaves struck her.

Julie was sobbing.

The earth shook, the area was filled with the howl of the jets of a spacecraft taking off, and a brightness so intense that it would have hurt the eyes even of a blind man.

The hiss of the propellers of the rushing support squadron pierced the air.

Beliar (I think) fell to the ground, groaned.

Anna also found herself on the ground. Her mind soon shut down.

***

She barely remembered the events of the trip to the ruins when later, after returning prematurely from the north, nervous rebels told her to remember it all. As if her memory had been reset like in the case of the toughest criminals as part of rehabilitation. Unfortunately, the macabre scenes left a lasting impression on her mind. As well as the image of the beautiful, cruel angel of war...

Chapter I
Descendants of war

The FX -94 Black Panther fighter set the fairing towards the Nephrid's equator and sped at full throttle towards the planet's exosphere. It performed the same maneuver as the seconds before, a white fighter, the XRS-14 Ghost chased by it. It would have seemed that both machines, having broken quickly through all layers of the atmosphere, would crash to the ground, but the professional pilots, who had been digging their job for years, at a critical moment brought them parallel to the surface of the planet.

The XRS-14 tried in vain to evade the pursuit. Even though it was a smaller and more maneuverable fighter, over the desert where the fighters were now, the advantage had the faster, though crude FX-94. So the white machine pilot could only feint and maneuver, which they were really good at. However, their opponent seemed to be superior to them in the skills.

Exactly, seemed.

"Not this time," whispered to themselves the pilot of the White, as they affectionately called their machine, in an emotionless voice.

A volley from the Black Panther plasma gun went over the sand; The XRS-14 made a sharp turn to the left. The pilot under fire entered the barrel figure, spinning around the fuselage axis, and with the chandelle, they tried to gain height. "As long as I play my intention flawlessly," they thought, "and make the classic loop, maybe I will be able to find myself on the opponent's tail." However, it was a vein hope: the FX-94 responded instantly to every maneuver, as if the minds of the pilots had been in tune.

The combatants reached low Rocky Mountains. The XRS-14 lowered the flight so much that it almost smashed the lake water with its oblique fins. Then it flew between the rocks, using natural tunnels and galleries as temporary hiding places.

The Black Panther rushed up and hovered in the air to scan the area above the peaks. Its hull geometry made it impossible to follow the target on the same track, unless the pilot's intention was to smash his fighter by breaking wings and fins against treacherous rocks. So they could only wait.

"You are, goddamn it," the pilot muttered with satisfaction as they tracked down the White, seeing it through the armored glass of the cabin at the same time. They dived towards it.

The clever opponent disappeared from the screens again, taking advantage of the rocks disrupting the electronics.

The FX-94 launched a small under swing rocket at the potential point of passage of the adversary. A powerful explosion shook the area. A third of the rock hit ceased to exist, boulders and debris flew in all directions.

The white machine emerged unscathed, flew skyward - and turned towards the enemy, flying at them frontally.

The Black Panther pilot accepted the challenge. They loved this type of psychic gameplay. Like their opponent.

The fighters were flying at each other at dizzying speeds. There were only two kilometers left to the frontal collision. One and a half. Eight hundred meters...

The pilots, high with adrenaline, screamed in their cabins, but none of them changed his flight path.

Fractions of a second before the impact, each of them turned to their right. The machines scratched each other with their fins, sparks flew.

The XRS-14 pilot glanced toward the setting sun, partially eclipsed by one of the four moons of Nephrida. They decided it was time to end this fun. After many breakneck maneuvers, they found themselves on the opponent's tail. The black fighter tried to elude.

The fighters reached the built-up zone, onlookers looked up at the skyward. Many smiled crookedly and shook their heads disapprovingly.

"Not this time, flower," the black machine pilot hissed desperately. Once the target was targeted automatically, they released an energy volley from both winged carbines. The opponent was hit several times, but not seriously. The White's fighter tried to elude again, but the FX-94 faithfully copied its every move.

The aviator didn't foresee only the immortal Pugachev cobra, combined with a sudden deceleration, i.e. lifting the fairing towards the sky.

The Ghost was left behind, the black overtook it.

The White's pilot tracked down the enemy in no time, accumulated energy and fired one large, overwhelming energy projectile.

The FX-94 got hit centrally, the partially deactivated machine started to freak out.

"The collapsed star, again?!" The man at the controls, according to the rules of the fight, should have landed at the point where he was hit, as a loser, but he decided to level the flight and he moved a bit above the ground to cool down. In the helmet communicator he heard Arcadius Croft's voice. The Splinter spoke in a joking tone:

"You lost, Beli. You hear me, you spilled, Mister Lieutenant. Stop fooling around and settle down."

"Alright," Beliar Drunkenstein sighed resignedly. But at heart he was pleased and proud of his opponent's progress.

The Black Panther turned gently in a wide arc so as to be able to fly ostentatiously over the opposition unit. Meanwhile, the XRS-14 Ghost decelerated to zero, changed the angle of the nozzles and settled on the landing pad of the spaceport.

Having moved back the tear-shaped cabin cover, the slim pilot slid onto the delta wing and jumped off. They were already standing on the ground, with their hands resting on their narrow waist when the airport servicing robots were heading for the XRS-14, intending to put steps under the pilot.

Satisfied as hell, Ari approached the winner with his arms wide open and greeted them in a friendly manner.

"The second lieutenant gave the lieutenant a hard time again," he said in greeting.

Anna Sandstorm smiled, removed her helmet, and handed it to one of the robots. Shaking her head, she tousled her beaten flat dark auburn hair, then tied it into a high ponytail. She raised her arms high in a gesture of victory. The members of the 78th Rebel Squadron, as well as a few pilots from other units, began to pour out onto the apron to congratulate the second lieutenant on another victory. Third in a row that month. Among the rebels as the space and planetary air force, there were rankings and names of formations as in the past in the land army, albeit in a truncated version. The opposition (as rebels were often named) took the nomenclature from the Kiritians, but in order not to resemble a hated enemy so much, the senior officers and admirals were taken from the former navy. Thus, the captain was followed by the rank of second lieutenant commander.

After landing, Beliar spent several minutes in the fighter before deciding to leave. He didn't have to squeeze through the crowd to reach Anna. The lower-ranking ones made a way for him. After all, he was the commander of 78th Squadron of the 99th the Rebel Fighter Regiment.

"Congratulations on your next victory." He and Anna shook hands in a manly fashion, and a moment later Drunkenstein pressed the girl and kissed her on the lips. She gladly replied with the same. The onlookers around them began to laugh, whistle and make cheerful comments.

"Thanks," Sandstorm replied, finally stepping away from Beliar.

Drunkenstein cleared his throat.

"Alright, ladies and gentlemen, party's over. And now everyone go to your task," he said to the pilots.

The company began to scatter. The Splinter (the nickname had begun to be used from the moment when Ari, as a freelancer unrelated to any regiment, had attacked a much stronger opponent with his flying machine, harassed them for a long time, was 'like a splinter in a butt', as his brave, even suicidal style of space combat was commented on at that time) said to his two friends from childhood:

"Are you out of mind?" He pointed to the white Sandstorm fighter. "To use live ammunition? So far you have done simulated sparring. With alleged energy bundles, which showed the level of damage on the calibrated meters. What were you thinking today?"

Lieutenant Drunkenstein, who had recently turned thirty, made a disarming face of a playful teenager. To heighten the impression of a distressed person, he even scratched his head.

"We wanted the fight to be realistic this time."

"Anyway, we had everything under control," added Anna seriously, taking up the game of her boyfriend. "We agreed that we wouldn't fire rockets or cannons at each other, only stun guns ..."

"We set them up in such a way," Beliar added, "so that ... the level of damage could be measured with the calibrated meters. Well, maybe not everything went according to plan." As he said this, he glanced at his fighter's airframe and its 'minor' flaws.

"You are insane. Completely insane!" Arcadius was angry. "You are setting a beautiful example for newbies." He pointed to the area around the landing field, where a lot of recruits had been stationed in makeshift barracks for several days. "And I sincerely congratulate you, second lieutenant. In the local month, you wasted seventeen underslung missiles, exhausted four power generators, and used forty plasma magazines. The taxpayers will beat us to death in the end. Resource replenishment is expensive, and we don't have such advanced self-renewal modules as the

Kiritians. If it goes on like this, we'll be forced to attack them with lances attached to the hulls."

"I just wanted to modestly note that for several decades the opposition has not fought any official battle with the Kiritians, not even a skirmish," said the girl.

"The devil never sleeps. Even if nothing changes over the next three hundred years, we should be prepared."

"You know what ..." Beliar began, but Ari, with a raised finger, ordered him to remain silent.

"Due to your aerial sparring, we will soon have to update the topographic map of the area. Why are you doing this anyway?" He asked sincerely.

"We're polishing our skills," the second lieutenant replied in a joking tone.

"Maybe instead of burning with mock jealousy, you'll just join us next time?" Beliar raised an eyebrow.

"No thanks, I'm not interested in threesomes." Ari chuckled.

The friends looked at each other seriously. First the Splinter's face muscles began to tremble. After a while he burst out in carefree laughter, infecting the others with it in no time.

"I love you my goddamn freaks!" He put his arms around Beliar and Anna, kissed them both on the cheeks.

"Alright, how much did you drink?" The second lieutenant asked.

"I'm not selfish and I don't drink alone," said Croft.

"If you like us so much, why don't you join the 78th Squadron? My people appreciate your aviation skills very much." Having heard the hum of activated cleaners, Beliar glanced at the recently arrived large delivery transporter. On the lowered unloading platform, walked two Onkalots with devices, representatives of a practically extinct species of humanoid jaguars. The anthropomorph in loose shorts, sensing the gaze on himself, lifted the jaguar's head and looked at Beliar with calm green eyes. Eyes no less intelligent than human. Drunkenstein hastily looked away for an undefined reason most comparable to a sense of shame.

"Something happened?" Ari looked at his friend searchingly.

"I just wanted to tell you that you are always welcome with us, so if you change your mind ..."

"You know me, I prefer to act as a freelancer. They say I'm a kind of antisocial, uncouth bastard who works best solo. But if needed, I can always serve as an extra pair of hands to help. Or I can enlist for a time during the crisis, but staying permanently is against my nature."

"And we will gladly accept such help." Anna smiled brightly. "We used to be a good team."

The first stars twinkled in the darkening sky as they left the spaceport.

"And seriously, mind your manners," Croft said, directing his companions towards the canteen, "because the subordinates might react differently when they see their commanders being such freewheelers."

"I have to practice," Sandstorm whispered more to herself. "They say that the Kiritian army is therefore so perfect, because achijes treat each other like a family. Their lives are guided only by the prohibitions and orders of the basic level, i.e., the Decalogue. It's so weird."

"What exactly?"

The girl fixed her eyes on a nearby robot loader, but she seemed not to see it.

"They're such motherfuckers, and they respect each other so well. Maybe this is the right method?" She looked at the Splinter.

"That it's worth being a motherfucker in life, as long as you meet some herd criteria?" Ari smirked.

"No, I meant the relations between achijes of different ranks."

Sensing that Anna was about to get thoughtful, which she had done too often, Beliar wanted to direct the discussion to mundane matters:

"You may be a great pilot," he said to her, "but you certainly won't absorb more Red Baron than your lieutenant!"

The Splinter made an eloquent arc with his eyes.

"And it begins again ..."

"You're drinking too much, Mr. Drunkenstein." Anna slapped her partner on his temple. "You weren't like that before."

"Ha! I knew you would wash out," replied Beliar.

"I would like to fly a little more tonight, until I have too many responsibilities. We will postpone the canteen, okay?"

"Complete freak," said the Splinter cheerfully.

"Anyway, I'm going to Julie for a girl's talk."

"I will be able to indulge in the pleasures," Beliar looked at the girl and smiled meaningfully, "only after the evening training."

"How many this time?" Sandstorm asked.

"About five groups. Only rookies." He waved his hand casually towards the tents in the barracks. "So, see you in the canteen in a few hours."

After saying goodbye, Anna returned to her fighter. She chased away the maintenance robots that had just finished refilling the fuel tanks, replenishing the supply of hybrid batteries and repairing the last minor damage. She climbed into the cabin and slid the cover closed. As she gazed thoughtfully at the semicircular instrument console, she didn't realize that the two companions were glancing at the White.

Concerned, Arcadius shook his head slightly.

"Maybe you spend too little time with her?" He turned to Beliar.

"I also considered it. But that's not it. We often deal with each other all day long."

"Maybe you just too rarely make ... you know." The Splinter prodded him in his shoulder. "Good sex is a cure for all ailments."

The girl had experienced a decent trauma twenty years earlier when she had met Forkis. She had lost her ability to speak for several years. Even the best specialists Krystian had brought hadn't helped her. Doctors with dozens of academic titles before their names had been helpless. The overrated neurological oddities, equipment worth hundreds of thousands of uinals, hadn't done much either." Beliar snorted. "Anyway, I don't need to tell you, you know the story yourself."

"Yeah ... I would probably have popped off in her place. I was scared with this degenerate from my childhood."

"On that unfortunate day, something happened with Annie that neither of us can understand. She fanatically hated Forkis, although, if you look closely at it, none of her loved ones died at the hands of the Kiritians."

"True. This is the rarest type of hatred, difficult to understand."

Beliar looked at the stars.

"She decided a long time ago that she would personally kill Forkis. Currently, it is her only goal in life, enhanced by the unhealthy passion. She counts on a space battle that has been impossible to arrange for decades. That's why she puts her through the hoops, wants to be better and better by taking advantage of the excess time." The lieutenant paused for a moment, wiped his forehead with the back of his glove. "It's stuffy today. Believe me, I did what I could. It is difficult to talk Annie out of this eccentric resolution."

"Nobody is judging you, man. It's her choice, we are adults after all. Everything will work out somehow."

Drunkenstein watched the White take off almost silently.

"Hopefully," he whispered grimly.

***

Flying at dizzy speeds was the only thing Anna really enjoyed. Seeing the fast-moving objects under the white fuselage of the White with a classic, ancient appearance (the shape and size of the airframe didn't matter in a vacuum, so the constructors didn't figure out too much and stuck to old projects that worked in the atmosphere, but also was used in space), she felt relaxed and calm. Then she felt free, uninhibited by anything, as if the worries, which lingered in her mind in a more and more heavy sediment, had had no access to her at such moments. They were left somewhere in the dust flecks behind the fighter's three rear blue hot drives. She could be herself. And she felt real freedom when below, she had clouds, a symbolic barrier separating her from the mundaneness.

Today, however, it was different. The grief endlessly lurking on the periphery of her consciousness, clung to her heart like an Onkalot cat to a tree with its claws, and refused to let go. The thoughts about the past and the present came to girl's mind, she was afraid to look to the future. Many friends from her earlier years had died, Anna particularly missed Jarret Nelson, about whose death had arisen many unknowns. The Kiritians were still the most powerful force in the Zodiac Universum. Beliar, falling into alcoholism, was not the same partner as he had used to be. They were supposed to be a pair, but mentally they moved away from each other like unipolar magnets. Even their intercourses didn't give the girl any pleasure. Not to mention, Anna had no idea what she was actually living for. Was the desire to kill Forkis really the point of her existence, or it was just an exaggerated goal that was practically impossible to achieve? And she stuck to him because she needed some kind of foothold, though that goal could have been quite different if she had only made more effort and done better? More than once she had heard that human life was senseless, unless it was given to it. She had set the goal for herself, but what kind of goal it was if she was going to throw a hoe at the sun? It was important, however, that she had something to analyze, that the goal existed at all, otherwise she would have fallen into madness like Drunkenstein slowly into drunkenness. Or maybe the cause of melancholy was the exorbitant bar of ambition, because of which she lost hope of a different form of existence and struggled with the blues every day? Maybe she should have thrown away the hoe and let the sun shine, at which it had been good for a long time after all?

She tried to chase away stubborn thoughts, which she did when she reached Mach five and kept increasing that speed as she flew over the desert. And as the first peaks of the low mountains appeared below, Sandstorm activated the XRS-14 AI.

"Good evening, Anna," said a synthesized youthful voice that filled the cabin.

"Hi, the White, give the same as always."

"As you wish," the fighter replied calmly as usual; a blissful smile bloomed on her face. The artificial intelligence of the most advanced machines focused on human interaction, especially fighters, could talk as if it were flesh and blood. Therefore, many pilots personified their machines and treated them like androids and even humans. Giving names wasn't uncommon, quotation marks weren't used with them unlike in the case of transporters, ships or shuttles deprived of AI. There were stories in the air, especially at bars on space stations, which once had been created a pilot AI so advanced that fighters using it, received military ranks, brawled with pilots, even revolted and refused to obey orders. Apparently, in the past, an entire squadron had escaped without the crew from some base, wanting to support a lone fighter calling for help from outer space. A similar story orbited a famous android mercenary Paul, the former security officer of the Terlendum III science facility on planet B9, the only working Liquid 5 model that was beyond control. However, Anna never encountered the phenomenon of any product of human intelligence causing her problems, especially the White. Nevertheless, the fighter already belonged to a generation with a more limited AI than in the previous series, and among other things, it was not able to operate independently of the pilot's will. There had to be something to it in the stories of rebel fighters and androids, then.

The XRS-14 flew up sharply, making a long barrel. It then proceeded to the chandelle, which he ended when the topmost cloud layer was hundreds of meters below its tail.

For some time, the White flew straight ahead. At twelve o'clock, one of the moons of Nephrida loomed, full and enchanting.

Instead of looking at the brightest and largest object in the area, Anna focused her attention on a small point - the triple yellow dwarf, where fourteen rocky planets orbited, and on one of them, traces of life had been discovered several hundred years earlier. Algae, as it turned out. It had undergone full terraforming, which hadn't killed the harmless native organisms, and had been named Calcaris. It was there that the girl had been born and spent the first years of her life. Both earth-like planets, although they belonged to other administrative zones called the Universes of Lion and Libra, were part of a sector free from Kiritian activity, often called rebel. Here were located, the largest bases of the opposition, and were stationed, the units, growing in strength.

The girl looked at the sparse cirrus as well as swirling clouds flowing much lower, which together formed a dense shroud covering the earth. Around the canopy, stretched out a space dome. Looking at it all was indeed calming, so that you didn't want to turn back down, where the monotonous reality of the weekday unfolded.

The XRS-14 entered a diving flight, crowning it with a spin. Moments later, the White was making its way through the cirrus, moving parallel to the planet's surface. Then it descended even lower to in the final, after leveling the flight, maneuver between the mountains. It made dangerous figures among monumental, fancifully shaped rocks. It flew through karst windows and open caves along the route Anna had perpetuated in the on-board memory a few flights earlier.

The girl allowed herself to be led along the canyon floor when a mid-range scanner detected three units approaching from the side of space. Since the distance was not significant for the technology of the XRS-14 Ghost, the on-board capripod, being the successor to the computer, immediately made their specification. Sandstorm blinked in amazement at the markings of the machines. Nephrida was being approached by fighter planes and a carrier from the 3rd Rebel Fighter Regiment, one of the priority regiments in the opposition forces, whose scope of activity covered the exo-planets of the Lion Universe, and sometimes even the life-threatening outskirts of the Scorpio, where the Kiritians had made their home.

Commander Aveo Lacetti himself and his entourage were moving towards the planet, so it must have been a priority case. They had few machines, because they moved in a safe sector, anyway the fewer machines there were, the lower the electronic noise and thermal trace.

"The White, go to meet them." After Anna's words, the fighter immediately set off towards space.

"Anna Sandstorm, second lieutenant of the 78th Rebel Squadron, 99th Rebel Fighter Regiment is reporting. To what do we owe your visit, Commander Aveo Lacetti?" The girl first gave her rank in accordance with the procedure, then asked the conventional question that must have been asked when someone from other cells approached the planet under the auspices of the military, regardless of the rank of the questioner and the questioned person. The task of surveillance belonged to the units currently patrolling the planet, which Anna, you might say, had been doing for the last quarter of an hour.

The narrow, dark face of a man in his forties appeared on the XRS-14 display.

"This is Commander Aveo Lacetti, the officer in charge of the 3rd Rebel Fighter Regiment," the chief officer introduced himself officially. "The purpose of the visit must temporarily remain secret. Please accompany us to your base."

"Yes, commander.

"The purpose of the visit is secret," the girl repeated in her mind. Obviously, such information wasn't disclosed to an ordinary second lieutenant who flew in orbit. She was hoping to find out quickly what it was about from someone of higher rank.

She positioned herself in a formation behind the commander's transporter and the two wing fighters so that the four machines formed a diamond, heading towards the base of the 78th Squadron.

Chapter II
The commander, the recruits and the goddamn pig

The unexpected visit of the commander caused considerable confusion at the base. Every officer who had nothing important to do at the moment summoned his subordinates so that they could line up on the landing field and pay their respects to the newcomer. However, before the visitors' machines penetrated the atmosphere of the Nephrid, Mr. Lacetti advised base commanders not to "do the mass scene outside" and to immediately call an officer's briefing, at which he wished to disclose the purpose of the visit. So, after the landing of the commander and his dozen or so men, honors were hastily exchanged with a few officers, then all went to the headquarters building.

Anna headed to an annex, where recruits were trained to inform Beliar about the briefing in an hour. She entered a darkened lecture hall where about thirty young people sat in a semicircle. They stared wearily at Drunkenstein, who was presenting what he was talking about with a holographic projection.

"Sit down." She waved at the rookies who wanted to stand up, seeing the officers' bars on her suit.

"According to the latest intelligence information, the number of the enemy is estimated at eight million achijes stationed in the Scorpio Universe," Beliar continued his lecture, noticing Anna sitting in the front row next to the novices who exchanged knowing smiles, one of them eloquently nudged his friend. "We have stayed out of each other's way for several decades," he said louder, drawing the attention of the audience back to himself. He motioned with his hand for Anna to wait a moment. "It is not really known why the Kiritians have not yet wiped us off the face of the planets, especially in a time when we were weakened from the decimation of our armies a century ago. As you probably know, after taking power on Earth in the twenty-sixth century, when they overthrew the global government and crushed its New Order Army, or NOA for short, they also dominated space and forcibly subjugated most of the planets colonized by the Oderses. According to Earth-derived Terran time, where the year is usually three hundred and sixty-five days, today we have 2956, but the Kiritian strength is still not weakened by the hybrid-totalitarian policies of Forkis, the First Galactic Dignitary who took many of the norms from the Onkalots. In the past, the opposition and the Immortals have had a lot of skirmishes, lost each time for our side, so for some time we have stopped mindlessly biting them and we are waiting for a good opportunity to finally take some thoughtful step forward. We also started to create our own inventions instead of using someone else's technology. But for a detailed history, irrelevant to our present case, I refer you, of course, to the database archives.

It is possible that their intelligence didn't actually establish where we are now. In my opinion, the truth is different: the Kiritians have left us alone because we don't pose any threat to them. This may be the second reason why we still exist. They are playing with us," the lieutenant folded his hands on his buttocks and started to walk around the room, "and either they wait for us to make the first move or," he paused for a moment, "they need us for something. Simply put, they keep us alive so as not to eliminate excessively the opposition soldiers from the Zodiac Universum, because they have a hidden purpose in it.

"So, cannon fodder?" One of the audiences asked as Beliar paused.

"That's possible." The lieutenant looked at the gathered. "Yes, I know, it sounds terrible, but it can be so."

"But who would endanger the Immortals?" Another person chuckled.

"Only aliens stronger than them, but such don't exist," said a boy from the second row in a joking tone. "The most powerful aliens we've found are polytheistic Onkalots. But they are practically animals that walk on two legs, can talk, and the pinnacle of their technical achievements are stone structures."

"Which doesn't mean that there are no stronger aliens in the universe," another recruit interrupted the conversation. "We still don't know much. We only examined a drop in the sea."

Smiling indulgently, Beliar let more comments flow. He moved towards Anna, who got up and also started walking towards him.

"Commander Aveo Lacetti is at base," she whispered at his ear.

Drunkenstein retracted his head like a startled turtle. The hall went silent. The recruits tried to hear anything.

"Really?" He looked Anna in the eye from under his eyebrows pulled together. "Why did he come here?"

"This is something important, there's a staff meeting. You must be there by 25.00," she instructed Drunkenstein, giving the meeting time in twenty-nine-hour Nephrid's daily system. "You have a message on the holo-display, but you probably muted it." It was about a small electronic assistant who was helpful in many areas of life, including sending orders. The Immortals used similar devices, but they were more advanced, and called PDAs.

"Yeah, right. Okay. Will you complete the training for me?"

"No problem."

"You have a list on the table. Two more items left, nothing but crap. I've already said almost everything."

"All right." Anna looked at the recruits.

For a moment the lieutenant's face was embellished by a malicious smile.

"And scare them a little."

The girl chuckled softly and shook her head.

Beliar introduced Second Lieutenant Sandstorm to the newcomers, then moved toward the automatically sliding door.

Anna put her hands on her hips, stood slightly astride and looked at the audience in front of her. They were tall men with soldierly, cropped hair, dressed in the uniforms of aviation cadets. She found the group without women, who were not uncommon in squadrons. Recruitment for the rebel space defense was carried out among capable seventeen-year-olds of both sexes. However, there were only a few youngsters in the room. Judging by their appearance, most of the recruits were already twenty years old, and a few were even older than Anna.

"Nice hair, Second Lieutenant. So long," said someone from the back row. A couple of recruits started cackling. Anna smiled slightly, expressionless. She had dealt with similar numbers hundreds of times. "Bad pickup," she thought, after all, she didn't have particularly long hair.

"Thank you. If you manage to survive in this nut house for the next few years, which I seem to be doing quite well, maybe you can grow one too," she replied.

The room burst out laughing, and the young man who had spoken, crimsoned slightly and began to scratch his neck, being prodded by his colleagues' hands.

"Alright, gentlemen. Enough of this sandbox. Where were you? History." Anna glanced at the sub points in Beliar's old stuff he had written probably a year earlier, judging from the crumpled pages, stiff with drinks spilled on them many times.

The recruits booed in protest.

"I know, it's boring, but you have to master the theory as well as your aerial and space combat skills."

"Why didn't they just give us entrasers?" Asked a dark-haired man from the third row. He meant a device which, when implanted in the brain, converted data contained in the carrier into electrical impulses. These, in turn, after modification by a micro-capripod, left relevant information in the memory centers. With the entraser, it was possible to master even the entire training material in a few minutes, as it took about this time for the brain to accept the information.

"Get up. Yes you." Anna pointed to the questioner. "Tell me, why is this happening? You don't know? I've thought so. Sit down. You get the first neg."

"We've just met, and you already give us dogs," it could be heard somewhere on the right. In this way, Anna obtained a candidate for the next grilling.

"Maybe you will know? Come on, up. Since you are sitting in the fifth row, you think you are invisible?"

"The implantation of an entraser can have side effects, and it is not always removed from the body," the recruit replied.

"Well, let it be. Sit down. You deserve a neutra plus." Sandstorm looked at the recruits seriously. "The fact is, this learning method is quite effective, and it allows you to master the material in no time." She began to move around the room like Beliar recently. "After use, an entraser should be automatically removed from the body along the excretory way, but this is not always the case. Sometimes it gets stuck in an area of the body where we wouldn't want it and has to be removed with bio-nanites. Permanently implanted versions are still in use. This is first. Second, the Kiritians can use them to overwhelm you, and sooner to fry your brains. Exactly with such a little shit. They could hack the entrasers and make us shoot at each other with equalizers. They go far beyond our capabilities and limitations." Anna stopped her gaze in the center of the room, got thoughtful. For a moment she said to herself, not to the recruits. "It's a bit as if they were protected by some incomprehensible force, because after all, the Kiritians are just like us. Have the same blood, the same bones, they have the same earthly origin. The only difference is that they are immortal. So why anyone can't beat them?" She cleared her throat, realizing she was making too many digressions. "Not everyone decides to take the entraser out if it turns out to be anchored in an inaccessible place. The more that it is not treated as a pathogen by the body. And thirdly: it is a human invention, and people, as you know, are imperfect and often screw up the job. That is why our little hero can't always give us all the coded information. So, instead of being lazy and fussy, you'd better set to learning with traditional methods, as our ancestors did for millennia. Amen, if there are believers here."

The recruits relaxed.

"Damn, nice woman," one of them said quietly.

Anna began to talk about how the Kiritians, created hundreds of years earlier by the agitator bizarrely called Xajb'a Kej, later named Forkis, had come to power. How they had begun to attack colonized planets and slaughter their populations. How they had massacred entire fleets with virtually no harm to their own side. How they had overthrown all paramilitary organizations and groups that had dared to challenge them. She also held forth for a long time on their flying machines, each of which had combat potential, from a cruise ship to a multi-kilometer astro-carrier, so ships and naval craft could take part in the battles. She said what she had heard once during training sessions, and since then the extent of knowledge about the Immortals - that is, the shred information itself, often passed on through word of mouth - had practically remained the same. For example, it had not yet been established how one man had managed to create the empire that stretched over the colonies of two galaxies, and why no one had opposed him. Why there were no conflicts among the Kiritians. No biological being, especially man, with own habits and needs, is able to live in constant peace with another. And finally: what had made their bodies immortal. For hundreds of years, no reliable answers had been found, only unconfirmed presumptions.

"I have a question," said the dark-haired man, who was the first to speak about the entraser. "Maybe a little ... well, I mean ... too bold."

"Go ahead," Sandstorm encouraged him, having finished her lecture on the weapons of the Kiritian infantry, the last training sub point.

"The second lieutenant is said to have seen him. Forkis, I mean. As one of the few people. There are ... some interesting rumors about it, but we'd rather hear the facts."

"And from a reliable source," another boy added seriously, nodding his head. "The guy doesn't seem to be dangerous. History knows many similar types. I bet he has a heavily armed retinue to protect his ass. What are they called, his protection? Lictors, right? Like those from ancient Rome."

"The information that he is immortal is also probably utter nonsense," another rebel joined the discussion. "They probably want to show the naïves from the Zodiac Universum that the guy doesn't pop off, so that we can live in constant fear of the Kiritians. The immortal ancient Persian kings and Egyptian pharaohs were also not supposed to die, and they liked to do it most with arrows and swords." He laughed at his own joke. "Hey, do you remember the guests who ate some sea algae on Mezzo, supposedly giving eternal life? For nothing in the universe, I would not like to have such a shit."

"Every Kiritian is said to be immortal," said another recruit. "You heard what was said during the lecture."

"The guy is not dangerous ..." Anna leaned with both hands on the headboard of a metal chair standing in the center of the room, on which there was a box of holographic cubes for presentation. Amused, she giggled discreetly, bent her head for a moment, and then raised it back. "There is nothing like repeating gossip heard from the grandfather of your friend's wife. In addition, such fairy tales are invented by people who have barely left their mommy's skirt or watch the universe through the armored windows of their headquarters, and are firmly convinced of their own omniscience. Haven't seen, don't tell nonsense. Better be silent and listen to those who have experienced the events the hard way. She turned to a random boy in the second row: "Yes, I was there, together with Lieutenant Beliar Drunkenstein, Julie Croft, who works as a waitress in our canteen, her brother Arcadius, a freelancer colloquially known as the Splinter, and the late Jarret Nelson."

"Was Jarret killed by the Kiritians?" the brave dark-haired man took the floor once again.

"No. Like Julie, he didn't intend to be an oppositionist. He chose the wrong path, and despite the fact that his friends tried to dissuade him from this lifestyle, he hit rock bottom. He became a gangster and, at the age of eighteen, was killed in one of the street shootings on Calvary."

"We are really sorry."

"Yeah, for a long time I also couldn't accept the fact that my friend was dead. However, I got used to the White Lady after joining the squadron. Although the first lesson, and perhaps the most important one, that life can end at any moment, I was given by Forkis twenty years ago." The girl took a short break to collect her thoughts, which quickly came in the deep silence in the audience. "After our parents left for a briefing, we sneaked out of

Drunkenstein's mansion in the prototype of a new transporter. We just wanted, as turds, to innocently try the White Ball. We were supposed to be right back. However, everything turned out differently. We got out of the machine and, fascinated by the jungle, we reached the Onkalot ruins of Ajb'atenaja, as the slaves working in our base call them."

"Ruins of the people-jaguars?" asked the rookie opposite Anna. She glanced at the patch on his sweatshirt: Tom Lewandowski.

"That's correct. Of those, our ancestors almost exterminated on H14. It turned out that Kiritians were stationed in Ajb'atenaja. So far, it has not been possible to determine what unit it was and for what purpose it stayed on the once rebel planet, but it was led by Forkis himself. I was a small child, but I perfectly remembered everything that happened then. A few terrible moments that haunt me to this day. I even remember a smell in that corridor and colored lights. I reached the private chambers of the usurper as I moved away for a moment from my friends watching the Kiritian's gathering. Forkis was having fun with a prostitute. I think he knew I was watching him from the corridor, maybe he had even known from the start that the bunch of kids had stepped into the ruins, but he didn't react." Sandstorm lowered her voice gradually, in line with the deepening silence. Nobody shuffled their chair, grunted, the treads didn't move across the floor. The corners of her mouth lifted slightly. The audience wanted a fairy tale with a strong punch line. Maybe she would manage to scare these newbies. When Forkis satisfied his desires, he took the girl's life, ripping her throat with his teeth. And then he began to devour the body, piece by piece."

"Connor's ass ... No way!" Tom referred to a scientist who reportedly had his buttocks broken off during an amateur trial with port technology. He spread his hands as if someone had poured coffee on his pants.

"Maybe it's enough?" the dark-haired man added. "I'm gonna puke. This guy is some kind of cannibalistic psychopath!"

Anna, however, remained ruthless and continued:

"The bland, sweet smell of human blood, the crunch of broken bones, the sound of tissues being torn - such things are never forgotten, especially when you saw the disgusting things, being four years old. Forkis started eating the guts out of the chest first, until there were only protruding red ribs left, then he began to gnaw at other parts of the body. Of course, he didn't stop there, as if his stomach had been a black hole."

"Now we know where this psycho gets so much strength from," said the boy sitting to Tom's right.

"And I watched it all the time," continued the second lieutenant. She closed her eyes for a moment, but quickly opened them as the scenes became too real under her lids. "Terrified, hypnotized, stiff and pale. Even slightly fascinated, but with what, I can't express it with words. Many sensations that I experienced then cannot be expressed at all, because there are no proper terms for them. Forkis looked at me at one point. I thought I was going to die. I even wanted to die. He had a lot of blood on him. I felt trapped as he stared at me with glowing eyes. He overwhelmed my mind, but my body also refused to obey. I was fully under his control. If he had ordered my heart to stop beating, it would certainly have happened. I saw the power behind those hazel eyes, completely incomprehensible and irresistible. I saw the being that couldn't be defeated. That will be followed by anyone who looks into those damn eyes. Forkis' disastrous charm has held me for many years and ... it hasn't faded very much so far. Looking at the problem in retrospect, approaching it maturely, I drew the obvious conclusions: this man cannot be annihilated. He's made of a clay similar to that of many historical usurpers who were eventually killed, but that clay is more perfect, harder, and unbreakable. Resistant to plasma, betrayal and intrigue. However, I decided not to surrender to this Nemesis. I don't know how my meeting with Forkis would have ended if Lieutenant Drunkenstein hadn't taken me out of Ajb'atenaja then. The Kiritians didn't pursue us. They probably hoped we would show them the way to the opposition base, or maybe they just didn't want to deal with such crap as chasing curious brats through the woods. When we returned to the residence by the transporter, of course, we got a christening from our babysitter Aga, and then from our parents, who with a bang left the briefing at the planet's pole as soon as they found out about their kids' wonderful idea. Moreover, we were interrogated by the rebel command and under the supervision of psychologists and doctors for a year. Carlos Drunkenstein forbade us to go anywhere without constant care. Beliar suffered the most for risking our lives, for first supposed lying, and then for telling the truth, showing his father a Kiritian fire micro generator that he had taken from the temple square of Ayb'atenaja as evidence of his alleged courage." Sandstorm took the item out of her pocket - a gift from the lieutenant. She lit it, generating a few centimeters long, cold flame and immediately extinguished it. The device was moved to the previous place. "They say, however, that every cloud has a silver lining. Perhaps thanks to us, were saved many rebel units, which immediately departed from H14 upon hearing shocking news, including the evacuation of the entire Drunkenstein's base. The planet is almost completely deserted. Today there are only the bravest families who work mainly in agriculture, and processing volcanic rocks. Honest, poor people who don't care for interplanetary conflicts. In turn, the opposition moved to the other end of the Lion Universe, where the squadrons known to you in their present form began to be formed." She pushed the chair to the desk with the projector. "That's it, ladies and gentlemen, when it comes to the history of the Liberation and Immortal Armies." She smirked. "I wish you all a good night and pleasant dreams."

***

"What did you tell them?" Beliar asked with mild amusement two hours later, meeting Anna in a projection room where she was watching movies to pass the time, and waiting for him. "The guys are subdued, as if the world was to end tomorrow. At least the little ones. Before their mouths never shut up."

"The truth and that's it. I got a bad feeling about this, since they bring us so fearful young ladies. Say, how was the briefing?"

Drunkenstein sat on a hydro-couch next to the chair the girl had taken.

"We fly out the day after tomorrow at dusk, or at dawn in two days. This is still to be agreed. Everybody. The entire squadron. They told us to get a good night's sleep tonight, so everyone departing got a leave pass."

"What are you talking about?!" Anna stood up abruptly, opening her eyes wide.

"Sit down." Beliar seemed deeply concerned. He looked at his partner with a stony expression on his face. "We will launch an attack on the Kiritians, the first in several decades. One of Commander Lacetti's intelligence squadrons, which tried to spy on the enemy on the border of the Scorpio Universe, informed him of Kiritian units that will be leaving Eos Endymion in fourteen Terran days. Lacetti's poor boys paid their lives to get this information, but fortunately it was dispatched and seized by the competent authorities."

"This information is confirmed? What is this planet?"

"Yes, confirmed. The Kiritians of Eos Endymion had been under surveillance for two years, but unfortunately, they spotted the intelligence units and smashed them to pieces. Fortunately, the message regarding enemy activity had been sent earlier. As for the planet, it is a rocky little thing on the periphery of the Scorpio Universe, with gravity twenty-three percent lesser than that of the Earth. There are no cities or strategic objects there, just a sort of harbor for the achij troops waiting for permission to go into the Universum. Anyway, I sent you a detailed report on the holo-display, study it meticulously by noon tomorrow." Beliar pulled his own electronic assistant out of his pocket for a moment to make sure the recipient had received the message.

"Information may have been intercepted, and the Kiritian's plans changed."

"It may have, but the probability is as minimal as being hit by a meteorite on Nephrid. The defeated intelligence took all precautionary measures, and used our latest technology to send this information into the air."

"You mean that technology smuggled out of Calvary?"

"Exactly. The Kiritians probably thought they had destroyed a bunch of spies who were just about to split on them." Drunkenstein sighed. "At least I would like to believe it ..."

"Hey, are you okay?" Anna waved her hand gently in front of his eyes, which clouded with a haze peculiar to people lost in thought. The man emerged and looked at the interlocutor with scared eyes. "What's wrong?"

"Nothing." The lieutenant looked away, ran a hand over his face, and rubbed his forehead with his fingers. "I'm a bit tired."

"You looked like you saw a ghost."

"I'm fine, okay?!" He growled. "Ehhh ... forgive me." Surprised, Anna observed his bewildered face for a moment. She shrugged. "Everyone has the right to privacy," she thought, "and certain limits must not be exceeded, even if they are created by the closest and trustworthy people." Anyway, Beli would probably confide in her when he cooled down a little.

"Okay, nothing happened. Better tell me who this Kiritian group is. Why are they so important that our commanders make us travel almost one-seventh of the Milky Way?"

Beliar pursed his lips. He stared at her discerningly, as if he had been considering the right choice of words, before he confessed:

"Forkis is supposed to fly in this squadron. We can't waste such an opportunity to eliminate the bastard."

Anna sighed softly, her heart skipped a beat, for the second time during this conversation, and she opened her eyes wide. She looked at the lieutenant as if he had had a deadly poisonous spider in his hair that must have been removed carefully so that it didn't bite out of fear.

Drunkenstein noticed that the girl's green irises flashed in an instant with a wild desire to act. It only took one sentence to say about her greatest enemy. She hadn't looked so animated in a long time, as if she had fully woken up from a long lethargy. Beliar didn't know if he should have been happy or worried about it.

She stood close to him.

"Are you sure?"

"Commander Lacetti would rather not bother us with rumors." Beliar grabbed Anna's forearms and forced her with a slight tug to crouch in front of him. "Tonight, unfortunately, is off, I have some work to catch up on. But you get a good night's sleep. We have two weeks of travel ahead of us. Okay? Promise me that you will skip the evening party with Julie and rest. You've been too tense lately."

He hugged Anna for long breaths, played with her soft hair, kissed her lips and neck. Finally, he got up, left the room, and walked down the hall toward the headquarters building.

***

Anna, however, wasn't going to rest that night. Not only because she wasn't willing to sleep and she despised all sleeping pills. First of all, she was too excited and worried about the revelations. She was aware that the flight to the Kiritians could end catastrophically for many opposition pilots, and that even no one may survive. As a soldier, she wasn't scared by the specter of death. Donning for the first time a silver-gray uniform with the image of a maokan, a Nephridan bird that was a symbol of the sky and aviation, she accepted all the dangers that her fate would surely pose on the chosen professional plane. The job was risky, but at least she felt that she was alive, that she was fighting on the right side, although she still needed a lot to be happy. She couldn't imagine herself in a different profession, such as an eccentric scientist who could stay in claustrophobic laboratories deep underground for years, or a sickly clerk who differed from an android only in that they sometimes had some biological need. Office, home, office, home, office, home, office, home ... No, it wasn't for her.

From the projection room she went to her two-room apartment in the officers' building. She read the report from Beliar on her holo-display. Then she took a shower, dried her body and dressed in an airy, amaranth sweatshirt with a wide cut for the head and pants with loose legs, to this she added chic low-heeled shoes. She winced as she looked in the mirror at first at the ponytail, then at the hair tied too high, finally let her hair down and left the room.

Being in front of the building, she walked towards the canteen connected with recently added cafe and drawing room. At the disco counter, she met Julie Croft, a very attractive blonde whose beauty and shapes were additionally emphasized by a tight red dress. The Splinter's sister just finished work; she was talking to some nice-looking woman. Sandstorm made a wide circle with her eyes, she couldn't not smile, because Julie was surrounded, as usual, by a group of admirers, from local soldiers to non-local civilians. Croft never aspired to be a pilot unlike the rest of the inseparable childhood gang. For her, an exalted coquette trying to keep class, this type of job was on a par with splashing in the mud. Although sooner in an extremely dangerous, liquid lead sprinkled with blood. She preferred to live a calmer life, to be the center of attention. And to have around, men admiring her.

"This is Marlena, my friend from the town of Ramondoor," Julie introduced to Anna a brown-haired, well-padded girl with whom she was just chatting. Unlike Croft, she looked modest and didn't have even a milligram of makeup on her face. The girls shook hands. "She is the owner of a pastry shop."

"Why is it so crowded here today?" Marlene looked around at the colorful lights-dotted, semi-dark disco hall. In fact, Anna noticed that all the tables were occupied mostly by rebels, with too many people sitting at every second. Additional chairs and benches had to be brought from the barracks, and quite a lot of it.

"See how many newbies we have." Julie was finishing correcting the already strong makeup in front of a pocket mirror. "Don't tell me you didn't see them on the way from Ramondoor to the base? Do you know what a mess we had today? In addition, two cleaning robots discharged and the employees had to take over their duties."

"We depart the day after tomorrow on a quite important mission. Everyone wants to get crazy," Anna announced.

"Really? Where do you go?"

"To someone we don't like," Sandstorm replied grimly. "Admittedly, to the squad small like my ex's cock, but well ... This enemy is powerful. Don't tell me, Julie, that nobody talked about the flight in all this mess." She waved toward the drawing room."

"That sounds bad. I hope everything goes your way," Marlena said honestly to Anna.

"Thanks. I also wish us this."

"I still don't know what it is about," muttered Julie.

"And you are not to know it, because you're not a soldier," Sandstorm replied.

Marlena snapped her fingers.

"You know what, girls? Let's go to the town. Recently, a couple of new facilities were opened there, where we will have peace. We are unlikely to have any fun here, unless we organize a dance competition on a square centimeter of the floor."

"Great idea, I'm in favor of the change of place," said Croft. "It'll be good to see some new faces."

"Are you bored of the old stuff from our base?" Anna jabbed her in her arm with a finger. "A couple of thousand healthy, strong guys? Man, you're good."

"Hey, come on!" Julie was indignant.

The three of them burst out laughing. It was rumored that Croft used her potential in other ways than by carrying out trays of food and drinks. Some of her friends knew, however, that there was an extremely fine line between such rumors and facts.

Anna liked Julie, they had known each other since childhood, but she was sometimes irritated by the temptation of her older friend, her unfailing ability to charm and seduce almost every guy in the base. She wanted to believe that Beliar had a good head on his shoulders and was faithful to his beloved who pleased him. "Wait, what kind of thinking is it, anyway?" She scolded herself in spirit. Why would have Beliar been interested in Julie, if he had always preferred her, his little Annie, who got angry in moments of sadness, but never cried?

"Then I invite to Ramondoor, let's go on my skulak," Marlena suggested.

They headed towards a visitor parking lot. Julie was accosted by two tipsy recruits on the way who began to pay compliments. Anna chased them away, and when the youngsters were gone, she loudly let out the air she had sucked into her lungs and shook her head eloquently.

They got single file onto the skulak, an anti-gravity vehicle that resembled a four-seater version of a motorcycle without wheels. After Marlene activated the two motors, it rose a meter and moved smoothly forward. Sitting at the control board, she avoided the recruits' barracks in a wide arc and steered the machine towards the wastelands, taking a shortcut. The town of Ramondoor was about a hundred kilometers from the base, so the journey passed in no time. Fearing about her hairstyle, Julie protested when her amused friends refused to pull out a shield over the hood, but after reaching the town they all cackled, looking at their tousled hair.

"Are you from a settler family?" Anna asked Marlena as they walked along the kermesite road towards the buildings, having left the skulak in the parking lot under the care of robots.

She had rarely visited Ramondoor, preferring the more remote, larger poleis to the west of the zone. Now she was rediscovering the charms of the town. She was studying the numerous spherical houses that looked like gigantic puffballs of cream color. Every of them had a garden hugging the curtilage, where exotic plants grew more often than vegetables and fruit trees. Various species of animals splashed in the ponds. Behind the residential area there was a market, where were sold goods imported from all over the Lion Universe and even from neighboring sectors. However, only a few stands, mainly alcohol ones, traded at such a late hour. Further there were company buildings, production halls, a hospital, and local office and entertainment venues. The city of Ramondoor had been established recently as a support area for the airbase, and was slightly remote from it due to the rich underground water resources discovered after rebels expanded in the vicinity. It developed dynamically, providing the opposition with necessary everyday goods and military equipment. In return, it received protection against corsairs and other bandits from outer space, as well as less frequently attacking thugs from the Nephrida itself.

"Mhm," Marlena replied. "I like life here, it is very quiet, business is booming. I don't need anything else for today."

"Better tell Annie about your hobby," Julie suggested.

"I'm not sure if it's a good idea." Marlena looked a bit embarrassed. "She seems a hard realist to me. People react differently to it."

"Come on. Don't hesitate," Anna encouraged, seeing Marlena shyly scratching her nose. Croft relieved her, joyfully announcing:

"She is a traditionalist fairy!" She had rarely used such difficult words.

"Oh, quite an interesting profession, especially in our time. Do you have many clients?"

"You'd be surprised how many," replied the fairy. "They come for herbs. They want me to read the cards, pieces of wood or a glass ball. Sometimes they ask for trivial life advice as if I were a psychologist. These types of professions are immortal. Even if people don't believe it, they at least have a kind of mystic-like entertainment.

"You must make a lot of money from it."

"And here you are wrong. Yeah, yeah, I know perfectly well what you mean." Marlena laughed. "I don't take money for telling the future. Nevertheless, I will not be angry if someone voluntarily gives me a few uinals or brings a nice gift as a thank you, when it turns out that everything I had anticipated, really happened."

"Maybe you will tell us something?" Julie suggested eagerly. "Annie, come on!" She added, seeing the hint of skepticism on the rebel's face. "You're leaving the day after tomorrow, so you should use your pass and have fun on many fronts!"

"All right, so be it," Sandstorm muttered. "Actually, why not? When I was fourteen, my buddies and I conjured up ghosts, and since then, I haven't had anything to do with the supernatural."

"The supernatural, come on," Marlena chuckled.

"And? Did you conjure up something?" Croft asked. Sandstorm shook her head.

"Not a thing, but the fun was great. You know, the effect is not important, but the path itself leading to it. The grown-ups yelled at us that such things brainwashed, even if they were fictional." She smiled.

They reached a confectionery. Marlena put her hand on a dermato-glyph scanner built into the wall. After a while, a steel door sliding upwards was open. Inside the room there was a wonderful smell of fresh bread and pastries, which looked as delicious as they smelled, lying on shelves and under the glass of an arched counter. Everything was done according to patented family recipes, as Marlena explained on the way to a basement, where her private, mystical universum was located.

"Sit here for a moment, I will call you when I prepare everything." She pointed to chairs in an old Indian style waiting room. Only a plasma ball didn't match the rest of the decor, nevertheless it added to the charm of the atmospheric place.

Julie and Anna looked at each other and collapsed into giggles. After a quarter of an hour, dressed up Marlena walked over to the threshold. With loose hair, wooden beads, large crescent-shaped earrings, numerous bracelets, in a dark blue dress embroidered with ancient ornaments, she looked like a book enchantress.

"It's so that I feel more into the atmosphere." She winked at Anna, intrigued by her bizarre clothes.

"Go first." Sandstorm gave Julie a little push.

The waitress brushed the bottom of her clothes off the iridescent brocade stuck on the chair and disappeared behind a wooden door that in the thirtieth century might have been found a museum relic. "Marlena took care of all the details," Anna thought as she walked around the waiting room and looked at the peculiarities of the times when the stirrings of famous ancient civilizations began to form.

Satisfied like a child, Croft returned twenty minutes later.

"How was the fortune telling?" Sandstorm asked casually as she perched on the edge of the table.

"Oh, I can't tell you, because if I will, it won't come true. You also don't tell anyone what Marlena will tell you. This is exactly what the whole thing is about!"

Skeptical about astrology, but eager to learn something new and enjoy the evening, Anna walked to the door. It creaked in protest, intentionally unpreserved, as she pressed her fingers against it.

Inside the room it was dim. Several candles dripping with wax burned in stands. The greatest flame flickered in the center of a wooden table where Marlena sat with a bundle of cards in her hands. The entire wall was covered with the depiction of the Aztec calendar created with colorful paints. From the joists hung straps carrying dummy bones of small animals, pierced precious stones, and feathers, dried fruits of various trees and bags of aromatic herbs. In a slight draft, waved a half-meter-long dusty cobweb. The center was guarded by a huge Indian totem made of wood and fur, covered with patterned scarves and dream catchers of various sizes.

"Shuffle." Marlene handed Anna the stack of cards as she sat down. Sandstorm complied with a mischievous smirk. The fully focused fairy shuffled the cards one more time, took out ten and spread them out on the table in a Celtic cross composition. She explained the meanings of the cards one by one. She started with the aura surrounding Sandstorm, to the forces acting on her, the goal she pursued, the causes of her current situation, the emotions tormenting the young lieutenant. Even though she described everything in general terms, Anna felt a little surprised. For what she heard, fit her person perfectly. However, she quickly came to a logical conclusion that prevailed over the more and more intensively working right hemisphere of the brain, responsible for emotions and belief in supernatural things - probably Julie had talked about it with Marlena.

"In four hours, you will experience a great shock. Huge. Something that will make you see your own life through a whole new prism. It will be painful for you," the fairy prophesied, putting aside another deciphered card.

"It's pretty gnarly. But rather, it won't happen," Anna spread her hands helplessly, "because what could happen to me tonight? Will a gold meteor fall on my head? We will swig a little, then I'll come back to my dwelling and pad down. At most I will not like the vodka or it will spill on my pants. And that's it for the anticipated impressions."

"I only anticipate the future with ..." The fairy froze like a deactivated android as she reached the card showing the future.

"What's there?" Leaning her entwined arms on the tabletop, Sandstorm bent to peer at the rectangle of paper held in the frozen hand.

Marlene got up. From the card she held in both hands, she shifted her gaze to the rebel, then back to the card.

"Amazing," she whispered. She tossed the deck on the table, mixed it with her hands with the swiftness of a street hustler playing mugs, then ordered Anna to draw three cards. "I can't believe it." She sank heavily into the chair. She made a gesture as if she had been going to wipe her forehead with the back of her hand, but she withdrew it. "Twice the same, identical, so it can't be a coincidence."

"But what is it about?" Sandstorm blinked. She stifled a yawn with difficulty.

"According to the cards, you will make a great change, the greatest man can do: you will change the face of the universe. You will lead to great death or great peace."

"Excuse me?!" Anna almost burst out laughing. "Holy cow ..." The fairy placed the cards in front of her. The first one showed a skeleton, the middle one depicted what looked like a lightning bolt crushing a block of stone, and on the third one there was an image of a departing pigeon with a green branch held in its paws.

"Well, at least I won't die of boredom in the future." Sandstorm smiled, shrugged, and left the room, completely unconcerned with the prediction.

***

In the premises where Marlena led them there was a pleasant atmosphere, intensified by lively electronic music, the play of lights in the spectrum of green and blue, and the smells of incense emanating from the perforated walls. Over a hundred people had fun here, dancing on a floor around a fenced water reservoir, laughing at the counter and tables, playing games of chance or cheering under a huge holographic monitor for a Nephrida football team that was playing a match against an opponent from another planet.

The women immediately acclimatized to the friendly environment, where the sounds filled the spirit with positive emotions, and robots the size of dwarfs flew between customers, ensuring that order was always kept and everyone had a good time. Anna recognized two people from the base. She said hello, raising her drink glass, as did the plainclothes pilots who had come here with their girlfriends.

After some fun on the dance floor, out of breath, the girls took their place at the counter. Marlena almost immediately engaged in discussion with a fellow bartender; Julie, stabbing a lemon in her glass with a straw, was leaning besides, sometimes adding something to the conversation and often giggling; Anna was looking at the party people.

At one point she stiffened. She held her breath. She made sure that it wasn't a play of lights distorting the features of the face. That she, being a bit dazed with alcohol, mistook the person twenty paces away for someone very similar.

She wasn't wrong.

The light wasn't at fault either.

Neither alcohol.

Among the playful people there was plainclothes Beliar. He danced with a black-haired woman who might have been Anna's age. When another piece of music sounded in the room, slower than the previous one, they both started embracing each other more and more passionately, and ended up with a very long, sensual kiss as well as probably affectionate words that couldn't be heard due to the noise in the room.

"How many, you said, Marlena? Four, damn it, hours?" The rebel snapped.

"Excuse me?" The fairy glanced at her, as did the bartender and Julie.

Clenching her teeth, Sandstorm, whose heart must have pounded faster and harder than the beats that caused the dance floor to vibrate, covered the distance to Beliar, striding.

"Annie?" Drunkenstein seemed as surprised as she had just been a moment earlier, seeing his girlfriend's face more saddened than enraged not far from his own. Perhaps already ex-girlfriends. His black-haired partner was also confused. She looked repeatedly at the man and at the stranger who had disrupted their dance. "What ... What's going ...?"

"You have a lot of work to do tonight, right?" The second lieutenant slapped the lieutenant's face, effectively extinguishing unspoken words. "I'm not enough for you bastard?!"

"Uuuuuuh, you got fucked up dude!" A party animal, grinning besides, commented, seeing the whole incident.

The friends at the bar didn't interfere, waiting for Sandstorm to deal with the awkward situation on her own.

"Maybe I will say," Anna still didn't let Beliar get a word in edgewise and she didn't care that more and more people were starting to look at them, "for you all that you will probably come up with: forgive me, honey, it's not what you think, let me explain it, I have nothing to do with this woman ..."

She lost her temper. Not wanting Drunkenstein to see germs of tears or a shaking lower jaw, she turned abruptly and headed for the exit.

Pushing her way through the thicket of the dancing people, she stopped for a moment and looked back. The tiny glimmer of hope went out immediately. Beliar ran after his new black-haired beauty, who also left the dance floor.

Seeing the surroundings as through a dense fog, Sandstorm, instead of going out, found herself in another part of the huge disco - the zone of games of chance, where the music wasn't so loud.

"Hello, Ms. Officer," said someone nearby.

It was only after a long moment, in which she stared at the speaker with an unconscious eyesight of a junkie, that she recognized the recruit from the lecture hall. I think his name was Tom Lawendowski. Or Lewandowski. He was also in civilian clothes. So he had a pass. "Is he going to the Kiritians with us?" She wondered. The commanders sent such newbies into space? And to attack the Immortals? Was it so bad - which no one below the rank of captain knew, of course - that they needed recruits, not wanting to lose professionally trained people? Poor kids. Or maybe nothing happened, and the recruits accidentally got days off at the same time as the members of the selected squadron?

"What a messed-up life." She leaned her forearms on the counter. She tried to limit the glances towards the already drunk neighbor, not knowing the condition of her face, which must have looked terrible.

"Please don't be angry about what I'll say now," Tom began timidly, "or about what I saw, but ... it was just a coincidence. I was on my way back from the bathroom. I won't tell anyone. Actually, what the hell." Frustrated, he slammed his open palm down on the table top. "Damn, I've always been bad at choosing words. Let's have a drink, officer! It always helps! There is nothing to be embarrassed about. We are civilians here right now, so we're equal."

He pushed a mug of foamy beer with a hint of vodka under Anna's nose, which she accepted without thinking.

"Thank you for your beautiful succor, Tom Lawendowski!" She screamed almost in his ear as the music was turned up.

"Lewandowski!" He corrected, smiling. "You're welcome!" He raised his glass in a gesture of toast.

After half emptying the vessel, she did feel better. The drink trickled down the esophagus in a scorching stream, stirring up a pleasant sensation in the stomach. The fire spread rapidly to the blood vessels, stimulating the entire body. She thanked the young one once more, with a smile and a nod, Tom replied with the same.

Sandstorm made an effort and took a few more sips. Screw Beliar. Screw the Kiritians. Glory to strangers. Glory to the drinks of the gods. The cursed predictions do come true.

Chapter III
To meet the enemy

It was not the end of adventures for Anna that night. Less than half an hour after she returned to the apartment in the officers' building, driven to the gate of the unit by Marlena, Beliar began knocking on the door. He talked classic male nonsense on stilts appropriate to the situation he had caused in the restaurant. Anna mispronounced a curse, grabbed her head and rested her forehead on the table where she had been sitting idle since her return. Aside from the fact that Drunkenstein had ridiculed himself and her in Ramondoor, now he decided to repeat it in front of the entire officers' building.

Unexpectedly, she thought of the Kiritians and the rigor in their army. The opposition closely watched Forkis' troops and transferred some customs to its own units. It considered their methods to be perfect, because from the beginning of the nation's existence they had not suffered a single defeat. Not even one. An exemplary norm among the Kiritians were looser, even friendly relations between achijes of different levels. For them it worked, but for the rebels it ended in a mess instead of an increase in the efficiency of the army. It was also a fatal mistake to allow relationships between men and women with different military ranks. Maybe it was time to quell their ego and recognize the Kiritians as better in every way? Again, it boiled down to the unknown how one man managed to create and maintain such a colossus.

Mumbling, Beliar hammered on the door; Anna was unknowingly stroking the tabletop with her fingers, making a circular motion with them. "Yes," she thought, "this was the fault of the imperfect opposition parroting the perfect opponent. Definitely!" Rebels of all ranks shouldn't have gotten friendly with each other, at least not show it off in public. Why, Connor's ass, were those damn Infected like some demigods?! Without any blemishes, scratches and scores. They always got what they wanted. Was it because Forkis, whose origins are unknown, trained them to be extraordinary soldiers, built from scratch the greatest army in human history, while the opposition descended from an oppressed underground that managed to merge in the name of an idea, for revenge or for an ordinary fun-filled brawl? What was the military success most about? A self-assurance? Personality cult? Fanaticism? Technology? Biological features? A corrected genetic code?

Anna couldn't define exactly who the modern rebels were. She remembered best the version passed on to her by her parents that they were the good ones who rose up to fight the bad ones. Most accurately, it could be summed up that they were an intermediate stage between amateurs operating in the military arena and the regular army. A stage that stood still when it comes to the way warfare was conducted, and evolved only in terms of technology (to put it another way: it stole these technologies more than devised them). Real professional armies were smashed by Forkis as he grew in strength. The historic date was September 11, 2517, when, as a result of the coup in London, the cradle of power and finance, the parliament was overthrown, at the same time bringing about the collapse of the earth's global government.

Sandstorm began tapping a finger against her mouth unconsciously. She was thinking about Forkis himself. That mysterious emperor, the First Galactic Dignitary, who had turned her life inside out so much. He had an impact on its subsequent stages.

She shuddered at the harder tapping on the metal. Beliar kept hammering on the door and babbling something futilely, mostly apologizing eagerly and explaining himself miserably.

She remembered Julie's lecture on the way back from Ramondoor: that a guy was such a material devoid of morality and conscience that should have been used, and then thrown away, and you should have looked for another, because they deserved nothing more. Anna didn't agree with the waitress, they had a different view of reality. Julie had never been in a relationship, and even though she constantly changed men like one change shoe, they clung to her like insects to a beautiful, fragrant, always fresh flower. She had a lot of partners, so a lot of experience - Sandstorm only four, including Beliar. Rebels, relationships with whom, didn't work out. She seriously began to consider whether it was the correct formula for her private life, albeit immoral according to her criteria: fleeting affairs, meeting needs, and lack of obligations. As was the old saying from pre-colonial times: "Scour your nest, but more often away." And what if Beliar, despite his assurances of fidelity to the one beloved woman, also had shared this selfish view, and for a long time? Anna leaned back in her chair, letting her loose hair hang freely behind the backrest. Did something in her life have to constantly go haywire?

"The universe is crap."

Beliar, who had always been her best friend, almost older brother, had left to train as a cadet when she had been twelve. A few years later she met a great boy who turned out to be cheating on her left and right with other 'Annas' unfamiliar with life. The second relationship, also perfect at the beginning, didn't work out. The partner was a female boxer, and since Sandstorm also had the ability to punch without finesse, feeling threatened, one time they both nearly killed each other. The third guy, a taciturn, noble sergeant from another squadron, also cheated on her, and with Julie Croft, who had no idea her new partner was in a relationship with Anna (or at least that's what she claimed). The appearance of Beliar at the base two years ago was for the young second lieutenant like a return to the old, childhood joy, as if the angel of happiness himself had descended from the heavens.

An angel who turned out to be fallen, using halo and white wings to disguise his true nature.

Sandstorm closed her eyes. As usual, she turned her sorrows into repressed anger, which she hoped to release some day in one mighty blow. That's why she needed Forkis. One day she would take it out on him for contaminating her childhood with endless trauma.

She heard one of the officers leave the apartment and exchange a few words with Beliar. He had to escort him to his room, for there was a blissful silence in the corridor. Anna breathed a sigh of relief. Drunkenstein would probably take a tablet to neutralize and break down alcohol in his blood, which would allow him to sober up in a few minutes. It was a common and completely harmless method to quickly return to full functionality. Beliar had gotten heavily stewed several times in the past year. He had done stupid things due to it, but hadn't been relegated. Despite his weakness for alcohol, he was a great commander and a talented pilot.

Anna couldn't sleep for a long time. She lay on the bed, staring at the ceiling with glassy eyes. She changed her position nervously every few minutes, but each time she felt uncomfortable. Annoyed more that sleep wasn't coming than because of Beliar's cheating, she finally took a hated tranquilizer.

It helped immediately.

She dreamed about Forkis, or more precisely, his few days old carcass lying in some wilderness, half eaten by animals.

***

The next day was not a good time to contemplate the evening's unpleasantness, as the base boiled like a hive with the first rays of the star warming the Nephrida. Reconnaissance and combat machines belonging to the 98th and 114th Fighter Regiments settled on the landing field, so wherever Sandstorm looked, small and medium fighters, storm troopers and chasers proudly presented their various silhouettes. The arrivals also landed on the smoothed-out periphery outside the unit territory. The additional hectares hadn't been used so far, as in the twenty years of the base's existence there had never been such a stir as today.

The squares, hangars and landing sites were swarming with people and robots. The equipment was checked, fuel and ammunition replenished so that each machine reached its maximum combat weight. The transporters went in all directions, directed to new tasks as soon as the previous ones had been dealt with.

Anna looked at it all through the ajar door, standing by the White inside the hangar. Despite the fact that the maintenance and technical robots had already gotten the inspection of the fighter over, she decided to check everything herself. And then again. Taking care of anything helped her not to think about Beliar. She was even more furious with him than a day earlier, because she learned from the White's AI, who used to activate in the cockpit when people were nearby, that the lieutenant had cheated on her with Julie. And that while playing with her near Anna's machine. After cooling down, she was going to take Beliar aside and tell him that their relationship was over. She wanted to close the topic before departure, but realized that it could undermine the morale of not only both of them during a difficult mission, but also random witnesses of the argument in the junior officer corps. So, she decided to leave the matter at the present stage. This monkey Julie, pretending to be a good, compassionate friend, she would also give on. At least for now.

Beliar came to see her an hour later, while she was sitting in the cabin of the fighter, once again studying a previous day's report, almost knowing it by heart.

"I know what you're thinking," the lieutenant began with a theatrical sigh. Standing next to the White, he looked sadly up; Anna thought she was going to vomit in a moment. "That girl means nothing to me. I admit, I had a couple of drinks, she wasn't sober either, and so we started a dance with a little ... bonus at the end. And that's it. I love only you."

"With a little bonus? You have the nerve to joke so ineptly about it?!" She boiled again, as if inside her there had been a phenomenon that might once have been the origin of her name. "When you had fun with Julie, you were also wiped out?" She growled, not taking her eyes off the holonot screen. She had intended not to speak to Beliar all day, but the emotions prevailed. "Surprised? The White's AI told me. And you know what?" She said nonchalantly, turning her face to him. She liked the consternation on his face, it was fun to look at it from above. "Better take care of your own matters, because you probably have a lot of them on your mind. And save yourself any further embarrassing deliberations, Lieutenant."

Beliar stood motionless for a moment, staring confusedly at Anna. He didn't answer anything. Well - if they were to speak to each other officially, so be it. It was no longer up to him to dictate the terms of their further relationship. He hoped, however, that there would come a time for sincere conversation and repentance in the near future. Perhaps. Unless the Kiritians would solve their existential problems sooner, eventually and forever.

Beliar moved away. Anna fixed her absent-minded eyes on the nozzles of the fighter standing in front of the White and sat for a good few minutes without thinking about anything specific. She was brought back to reality by a decent metallic bang next to the loader, from which someone accidentally dropped a box filled with hundreds of kilos of equipment. The operator smiled apologetically at the other employees.

She scanned the lines of the report once again. There was a mention of some mini-capsule around Forkis' neck that the First Dignitary reportedly wore always. He didn't allow anyone to touch it, which was pointed out by the opposition intelligence during the long-term observation of the Kiritians' commander. Anna vaguely remembered the incident from the fateful day she had met him. Before murdering his mistress, he had slapped her hands as she had grasped the metal capsule mentioned in the report. So, the object must have meant a lot to him. It is possible that it was the source of the emperor's strength, as was assumed several times in the reports of Commander Lacetti's spy batteries. Even hostile to the Kiritians, private intelligence agencies on several planets came to similar conclusions. There had to be something to it. But what? Was Forkis carrying a peculiar drug? Was it a kind of first aid kit? Rather, the radical atheist was not a superstitious person, believing in the power of talismans like Marlene's clients.

Preparations for the departure lasted until the middle of the night. No one was allowed to leave the base. Anna's squadron was enriched with machines of a few young men who were stationed under tents in makeshift barracks. Among the recruited was Tom Lewandowski, landing at the designated spot.

"Are they coming with us?" She asked Beliar, commander of the 78th Squadron, passing by. She spoke the words matter-of-factly, as if she had been directing them to Lieutenant 'Some', seen for the first time, who took command thanks to the assignment.

The officer also replied distantly, looking at the new squadron recruits:

"They haven't taken part in any hostilities other than simulated ones yet, but they fly very well. They can be useful to us. The Splinter is also flying with us, but accompanying the 98th Regiment as a freelancer." Among the rebels there was a smooth air formation called an accompanying squadron, to which usually belonged patriots who didn't want to join the army. It included freelancers like Arcadius Croft. They were disciplined, well-trained, and although they didn't obey the opposition leadership's orders, they synchronized with their squadrons and acted as support where they were needed. They operated as escadrilles, groups of several people, and even singly, changing places frequently and joining permanent squadrons. Anna nodded.

She was looking forward to the upcoming skirmish, which would be the perfect opportunity to vent her emotions and lace into the enemy. Although agnostic, she silently prayed that whoever responsible for creating reality would lead the rebels to confront the Kiritians.

***

The machines took off at dawn. The thick clouds that lingered through the night gave way before the first drives thundered, as if nature hadn't wanted to disturb the solemn mood of the moment. The polished hulls reflected the red rays of the sun and three of the four Nephridian moons. There was no one who was not impressed by the collective start, the first one in the history of the base. The onlookers shouted, waved their hands, wished a good hunt.

"This is what the beginning of any military expedition should look like," Sandstorm thought. This is how the hunt for Forkis should have begun: daringly, in good mood, with ecstasy and enthusiasm flowing from the hearts. To pass the time, she started to review the space map with the help of the White's AI. Thanks to the synchronization of the helmet sensor with the console display, it was possible to mentally select a specific object and view it along with the adjacent area with a large radius. However, the map was not displayed in real mode, at least when it comes to objects from sectors controlled by the enemy or criminals. For example, destroyed asteroids from one belt became visible on the grid even years after their liquidation. The Milky Way and Andromeda were still huge for Oders technology, and many changes were learned after a long time, usually when someone accidentally made a discovery. The Kiritians were probably better at it.

The 78th Squadron of the 99th Rebel Fighter Regiment together with the recruits' fighters consisted of a total of forty-five machines divided into three escadrilles. The frontal one was led by Lieutenant Drunkenstein; Anna took command of the left-wing escadrille. Six squadrons of the 98th Fighter Regiment, two of the 114th Regiment and a squadron accompanying freelancers also rose from the airstrip.

The rebels, flying in neat, synchronized V-formations, broke through all layers of the atmosphere and headed towards the exoplanet Mezzo, orbiting a few light years away. There, one hundred and sixty machines of the 3rd Rebel Fighter Regiment led by Commander Lacetti, who was in charge of the entire expedition at the same time, were to join the armada. Joining forces took place after a dozen or so Terrenic flight hours, one of which was sixty Earth minutes.

New types of machines that didn't have specifications in the Kiritian registry - at least according to opposition intelligence - long before approaching the border of the Lion Universe activated stealth masking. Also, the invisibility allowing pilots to 'see' their neighbors only with scanners aimed at the coded parameters. The micro-heads on the outside of the hulls generated an anti-g field around each aircraft: the armada was about to develop a dizzying speed, at which the pilot, exposed to horrendous loads, wouldn't have survived more than a few seconds. Due to the high energy costs, it was not planned to make subspace jumps allowing to cover billions of kilometers in a few minutes through a generated intercosmic tunnel. The flight was to be standard, from A to B, which each of the pilots could analyze thanks to the simulation provided by the command. Only the Kiritians had enough energy-saving technology to afford to jump with Alcubierre drives between universes.

Thanks to the trip, Anna stopped worrying, and even was good-humored. The rest shared a similar mood. Every now and then the joyful voices of pilots were heard on the common channel, exchanging reports or trivial comments.

The armada made its first stop a few days later, at asteroid stations right on the border with the Lion Universe, in a relatively safe sector. Fuel and energy were replenished, and minor faults caused by the meteor shower fixed.

Another stretch of space, called the Libra Universe, was poorly colonized; all inhabited globes, like Calcaris, bordered on the Lion. The mass of the rocky planets was uninhabitable. Gas giants dominated. The enormous amount of asteroids, frequently falling out of their orbits, made life impossible. The region was mainly used as a travel route between the more populated areas of space. The Libra was also one of the unattractive mining sectors: the same raw materials could be extracted in other universes, with lower transport costs.

The armada pilots were divided into three groups. When one was asleep and their machines were controlled by AI, the others were flying actively, ready to wake up resting companions in case of problems.

The Capricorn Universe, the last stretch of the route before reaching the target Scorpio, turned out to be an area as dangerous as the Kiritian's zone. On a few colonized planets and moons, and floating free space stations, had settled representatives of all underclass.

From gangsters, anarchists and psychopaths to deserters, corsairs and savages who worshiped pagan gods. It was the perfect place to hire hitmen, mercenaries - even entire platoons - or spies for a variety of purposes, such as driving illegal refugees off the planet. Intelligence services operating in secret and fear of the Immortals, not wanting to risk trips to Scorpio, sometimes hired people here and paid their intifadas dearly. Incidents with the Kiritians almost always ended in the mercenaries' death or their escape, but hundreds of thousands of uinals were able to blunt the survival instincts of most thugs. Needless to say, the privilege of hiring thugs was reserved for the richest. The Kiritians cared little about the pathological hinterland that flourished in their sector, though they could easily wipe them out of the Milky Way in a matter of weeks. They often visited Capricorn themselves and hired informants who worked for them in universes where, at the sight of the Immortals, the autochtones were able to leave the star system (Forkis, over the centuries of rule, learned that better benefits could be obtained from planets not affected by perturbation, therefore, after gaining absolute power, he changed his policy from dictatorial to stabilizing one. He ordered taxes to be collected, he regularly controlled the planets with achijes, limited their technological development, but generally allowed the population to live as they please, as long as they didn't harm the Kiritians).

The rebel armada had to be on guard at all times. Communication silence was ordered with the exception of priorities. Sleep was forbidden. Aveo Lacetti chose a route with the fewest ships, scanning space for millions of kilometers. He wasn't afraid of detecting the fleet invisible to the eyes and foreign scanners (the rebels had better technology than the criminals from Capricorn), but in the event of collision courses, hundreds of machines would have had to be directed the other way.

They reached the frontiers of the Scorpio Universe without any incident. Lacetti's plan was simple, albeit risky, but the opposition's leadership agreed with it because it could prove effective. It assumed a complete kill of the Kiritian unit on the outskirts of Scorpio and volleying itself into space before the enemy squadrons stationed in the depths of the sector reacted. Then the rebels would be too far away to be tracked. Therefore, the attack should have been ruthless and quick. Maybe it would even be possible to cast an energy net blocking targets before the fire took place, then the enemy would not send a request for support. If this was successful, Lacetti would lose few machines, and the Immortals, even with their intelligence, would have a hard time finding the aggressor. Capricorn, who was indifferent to the rebels' fate, would most likely be retaliated. To the pilots, the plan seemed suspiciously simple. But wasn't it easy to attack a powerful enemy who had long ceased to protect his back and foreground, convinced that he had baited the entire Zodiac Universum?

"It could actually work," Anna thought, feeling excitement building up with each light minute traveled. Unfortunately, there were also doubts. What if Forkis wasn't there, they were trapped, or it turned out that Lacetti was many board days late? What if it went well at first, and then they were chased and smashed into space dust? The flight might have turned out to be a kamikaze attack, a one-way ticket, but no one spoke these uncomfortable thoughts aloud, though everyone was tormented by similar ones.

They crossed the boundary of the Scorpio Universe.

The communication silence became total. Everyone knew their task and the details of the role that would soon be assigned to them.

Together with the silence there was consternation that seemed to wrap the fleet in a cocoon of baryonic matter.

Armada slowed to one-eighth the speed at which it had traveled in the Capricorn Universe. And it kept reducing it, as it was approaching the asteroid belt.

Sandstorm began to look around through the thick canopy of the cabin. The Kiritians' territory turned out to be a miracle of nature. Or of the Creator, or many of them, according to the will of believers. The view definitely let you relax before the storm. The space was dotted with myriads of stars arranged into constellations alien to the inhabitants of the Lion Universe. On the port side - as was commonly and traditionally called the left side of a vessel - you could see a breathtaking nebula, the name of which Anna didn't know, and she wasn't willing to look for it on the map or ask the White for the bearing. Perhaps it belonged to the Large Magellanic Cloud to which they were quite close on a cosmic scale. The outer planets of the nearest planetary system could be seen with the naked eye. The globe from the shore seemed to be the size of a soccer ball, the farthest - a bright pinpoint, and how easy it was to mistake it for a star. Among these globes, orbited Eos Endymion with its unpopulated moon U1. The Kiritians hadn't installed any detectors there, so Lacetti ordered a stop on them and the preparation of an ambush.

They didn't notice the activity of the Immortals, as if they had fled into a sector as empty as the Libra Universe. However, these were appearances. The very heart of Scorpio - the planet

Morascrik, with its extraordinary capital city with the bizarre Onkalotian name of K'otz'ibaja, was teeming with life.

U1 resembled the Earth's natural satellite from the solar system, except that the moon they landed on was younger and more volcanically and tectonically active. Geological factors, as well as the bombardment of the surface by asteroids from the nearby belt (Eos Endymion wasn't affected by it, as the Kiritians had deployed cannons in its orbit, breaking up dangerous objects, long before it reached the Roche boundary), caused that U1 wasn't developed. Therefore, the idea of an ambush in such an unusual place had a chance of success.

Secured by stealth fields, additionally protected by a high mountain range, the machines were ready for departure at any moment. Aveo sent a squadron on reconnaissance to monitor space from the other hemisphere. The pilots could finally unkink decently after the long, wearisome flight. However, they had to leave their cabins in suits, as on the moon deprived of a friendly atmosphere there was a shortage of oxygen. A day passed and nothing happened. Then another one. The rebels became more and more impatient. To pass the time and calm the nerves, some of them started gambling. Although the fuel should have been enough for the battle and the return to the Lion Universe, some placed solar panels on the machines to accumulate in photon batteries, which were a backup source of power, as much as possible star energy dispersed in space.

Anna discussed stupid things with the Splinter and the alien squadron rebels, even with Beliar, to keep her mind occupied. However, this didn't ease the tension she had felt since crossing the Scorpio border. She felt like a child waiting for surgery as it approaches a medic.

The enemies were spotted fifty-four Terrenic hours later. Their activity was reported by the reconnaissance squadron, which returned through a mountain labyrinth to a makeshift camp at the foot of an extinct volcano.

"The situation doesn't look good," said Lieutenant Cirix to the commander and squadron leaders gathered around. The conversation was listened to by pilots waiting for orders. "We counted about two hundred units, all personnel combat carriers."

"That's good, isn't it?" A rebel whispered behind Anna's back to his neighbor, who turned out to be Tom Lewandowski. They all looked alike in the prescribed suits, so she glanced at the badge.

"It sucks, not is good," Tom replied. "How are we going to track down the regiment commander, if at all a regiment can be called a group of transporters, since they are all the same?" Kiritians and their stupid tactics, as if they were constantly afraid of someone ... Regardless of the ranks, they can use the same machines in a whole regiment, and without markings. It was in training, man." He slapped the man on the helmet with his glove.

"It doesn't matter. We'll smash them anyway," replied Lewandowski's brother, trying to be joking.

"That's right. We'll bump these bastards off!" Someone else said cheerfully. People around them came to life, started quipping and making bets.

"Is Forkis going with them? Have you established it?" Lacetti asked the scouts.

"We don't know, sir," replied Cirix.

"Never mind. We are prepared." The commander looked at Tom and his brother. He smiled. "We're gonna smash them."

Beliar nodded to him.

"Anyone want to say something? Add? Suggest?" Lacetti looked at the crowd. "Great, screw truisms. So here we go, good people!"

The rebels cheered as they walked eagerly towards their machines.

Within minutes, the last vehicle was above the surface of the moon with its camouflage and anti-g active.

The initially created armada column formed a battle array, i.e. three groups flying at a certain distance from each other: two flanking and a central strike led by the commander. The rebels moved along the belt asteroid path, which provided them with additional physical and anti-scanner protection.

Anna was in the squadron of the right group; Tom and the Splinter were flying nearby. Beliar was out of range of the White's muted scanner (they were supposed to tighten the formations in the moment of the attack), but she knew he was somewhere in space on the port side.

It was estimated that, at the current speed, the confrontation should have occured within a Terrenic hour.

Although the enemy was still beyond the reach of the scanners, the opposition knew what machines they would face. The target seemed easy, especially since the carriers left Eos Endymion without any shields, even their hull lighting was on.

"Where could Xajb'a Kej be, sir? Despite being ordered to limit messages to priority ones, Sandstorm dared to accost the commander on the shared channel so that everyone got an answer.

Lacetti smiled indulgently. Lieutenant Sandstorm's 'Forkis disease' was widely known among people associated with her squadron. The girl had the opinion of such a great pilot that she could actually shoot Forkis down if she had known which machine, he was flying in. He gladly gave a factual answer:

"We haven't been able to figure it out, Lieutenant Sandstorm. Forkis is probably in the center. So, make sure that no one gets separated from the enemy's column in the moment of the attack. No Kiritian can survive this attack. And now I really ask everyone for silence."

Intuition told Anna that Forkis, a symbol of many failures in her life, as well as of all the evil plaguing humanity, was flying in this column. It was enough to track him down and kill him, though it wouldn't be easy. Otherwise, he would have died a long time ago in one of the countless assassination attempts. Like all Kiritians, he was beyond the reach of disease, old age, and death from their consequences, but he could be annihilated like any living thing. Only you had to get close to him first.

"You will die by my hand," she hissed, clenching her fist. Almost immediately she laughed at these so infantile words. She thought over the course of the battle in which she would achieve exactly what she wanted. It wasn't uncommon for her to fantasize about Forkis: she imagined how she would kill him. Whether with the help of the White's cannons, or with conventional weapons in direct combat, if fate gave her a chance to meet him on the surface of a planet. She wanted nothing more than to see his blood and bones, and his belly slashed open. She wanted to do to him what he had done with the bodies of the killed women. She regretted that the moment of eliminating the target would be short. It seemed that the White would do all the work, and at best she would be able to admire the explosion of the Forkis transporter.

"To all units: full combat readiness," said the commander of the squadron to which she was subordinate. In her ears, the words sounded like the most delightful music.

So, fate chose the clash to take place in space.

Chapter IV
Vivere militare est

Despite the utmost caution on the part of the rebel fleet, the Kiritians realized that they were being attacked a few minutes before the enemy V-formations embedded in their column. They dispersed immediately like an attacked school of fish - and set off to counterattack.

This confused the rebels, who expected the smaller and less armed enemy to simply flee.

But not the Kiritians.

What was commonly said about them, however, turned out to be true: The Immortals wouldn't have chickened out, even if the opponent had had a hundred-to-one advantage, and they had been aware that none of their achijes would survive the battle.

The skirmish was inevitable, both parties were flying on a collision course.

"Take the stealth covers off, we're just losing energy," Commander Lacetti ordered on the general channel. "The element of surprise went to hell."

Within a quarter of a Terrenic minute all the machines in the Lion Universe were visible in space.

The Kiritians and rebels reached combat speed. However, they had to maneuver because asteroids swarmed around. Admittedly, they were sometimes tens of thousands of kilometers apart, but it lost significance at breakneck speeds.

"We chose a nice battlefield," Beliar said to Anna. The latter didn't catch from the voice timbre distorted by the communicator whether the lieutenant was pleased or rather worried. She came to the conclusion that most likely the first. After all, they had both practiced breakneck maneuvers for years, choosing the most dangerous rocky and mountainous areas of the Nephrid, where it was not difficult to crash the fighters. The only downside was that they trained mostly in the atmosphere. In space, too, but there were no asteroid belts in the sector where Nephrida orbited. Now they would check that the time spent on the simulated combat hadn't been wasted.

"They are smarty-pants ..." Sandstorm heard the lieutenant's voice again, this time on the private channel.

"What's going on?"

"The Kiritians decoded us and just instructed the commanders on the channel that we shouldn't resist and let them escort us to Eos Endymion, or they will smash us. And stuff like that, procedural blah blah blah. Frigging beggars."

Anna blinked.

"They literally said so? That they would smash us?"

"No." Beliar laughed. "I'm telling you so."

Sandstorm couldn't not to smile.

"I understand Commander Lacetti gave an answer that they didn't like."

"The answer may have not pleased them, but they probably like the prospect of being able to attack us."

"So, he told these guys to go screw themselves," she guessed.

"More or less."

"Did the commander talk to Forkis?" Asking that question, Anna felt her heart beat faster.

"No. Only with Kiret Biffter. This is his lictor, sidekick, right-hand man, and Second Galactic Dignitary."

"Nice collection of titles."

"Looks like we have the whole flower of the adjutant centuria in front of us."

"Just wonderful," she whispered to herself.

"What are you saying? I couldn't hear you, as there is too much noise in the air."

"If Biffter is there, there must be also Forkis," Sandstorm spoke softly, trying to focus.

"Sorry for everything, Annie," Beliar spoke again, timidly. "No matter what you think of me, I've had to tell you that again."

"Let it go. See better what is happening in front of us."

"Will you forgive me?" The lieutenant asked seriously. He stared indifferently at the advancing enemy machines.

"I don't know. Do we have to talk about it now?"

"One of us may not survive the skirmish," he growled. "The fallen star, we both can die!"

"Are you serious?" Sandstorm laughed nervously. They got a signal from a flagship machine. At the order of the commander, rebel units went to the 'shoal'. A coordinated attack in a trident formation made no sense since the enemy column had dispersed on its own.

There were only a few kilometers left before the head-on fight.

"Screw it all," Anna said, more to herself than to Beliar, who was embarrassed at the ambiguous words. The girl was glad that she no longer had to fly in that damn V-formation and wait in the sweat of her brow for orders, but to attack as she saw fit. The 'shoal' meant that, despite a group attack, each pilot fired on a target ship without an order. They had to have a perfect sense of the moment and be able to quickly asses their own situation. It was necessary to cover both oneself and the neighbor. To be a little brain attuned to the big one of all the attackers. Therefore, only the best aces were recruited for the squadrons that operated in this way.

"We'll see if you guys are so good!" Anna's voice was more like an angry she-wolf's roar than a human's. Beliar was relieved. But she meant the others, not their relationship.

Sandstorm fired the first shot in this battle from a White's tamari cannon. It was a new type of energy weapon capable of piercing through metal. In a moment, they were to find out whether it was able to deal with the armor of the Immortal ships.

Resembling giant daphnias, the two Kiritian combat carriers bounced off each other violently. The beam of energy flew harmlessly into space, where it was quickly absorbed by the endless blackness.

Kinetic, energetic and rocket volleys spilled densely out of both fighting sides. The fleets mixed up. There were individual duels and chases, in which often took part several machines.

The ears of the opposition pilots were bombarded by the messages of the subordinates to the commanders and vice versa.

The Kiritians, on the other hand, rarely communicated, treating the whole incident as something slightly more serious than good entertainment.

On Anna's starboard, one of the rebels was hit by a guided rocket in the very center of the lower abdomen, began to sail away into space, driven by the force of inertia, and crashed against the edge of an asteroid. Sandstorm looked around in the cockpit, as she couldn't see if the misfortune catapulted in the rescue cyst or crashed with the machine.

The second lieutenant sighed nervously. Her hands were sweating in the gloves. She spoke to her friends - including Beliar - to see what the situation was. Fortunately, none of them got hit.

"The White, put out your front guns," she said to her fighter, whose AI was actively supporting her in combat. She began to intently watch the environment flashing with battle fire. She was desperately trying to figure out which machine Forkis was on. Logically, she was looking for the most covered one.

Opposite her, an enemy combat transporter unexpectedly appeared. Protruding beneath the fuselage were blades of dhurnstal, the hardest alloy used exclusively by the Kiritians. The girl corrected the motion vector by turning to starboard, thus avoiding damage to the airframe. Meeting the lances meant the blade plunging into the composite with the ease of a knife sliding into the human body. All shields of the opposition machines were electronic in nature, they protected against energy and electronically controlled weapons, but not purely physical ones. History had documented cases where small Kiritian units penetrated even the thick shields of space shuttles, causing compression shock.

The rebel rose relative to the enemy and made a long flip over the wing to turn around and find herself on the other's tail. However, she lost sight of the machine she was pursuing. All the transporters around were the same and seemed to fight with the same ferocity as the Kiritian, who had nearly damaged the White a moment earlier.

There was, however, an exception.

"I have!" Anna flinched as Splinter roared excitedly on the general channel. "I think I have Forkis! I marked the target with the laser, I send the bearings to everyone."

Sandstorm looked at the image that had appeared on one of the screens. With a red triangle was targeted the transporter distant from the combatants. It didn't take part in the battle, was protected by several machines. Selected fighters were already flying towards it. Anna also wanted to join the attackers, having received the order to fire from the squadron commander, but at the same moment a Kiritian transporter and a rebel stormtrooper brutally collided in front of the White's fairing. There was an explosion. The swirling, hot scrap metal crashed into the XRS-14 cabin cover, but didn't damage the armored glass several dozen centimeters thick. However, the entire hull shook anyway.

"Anka, are you alive?" It was worried Beliar.

"Nothing ... It's nothing." She exhaled only after a moment. "Nothing happened. Fly with me."

She found Drunkenstein and followed him through the flickering hell. They were both headed towards the Kiritian ship, which was fiercely - and successfully - being defended by the guards.

Anna didn't take her eyes off the target machine; she furrowed her eyebrows suspiciously. The object was slightly different from the other transporters: it was more streamlined, flat and smaller. The cockpit seemed too cramped for a pilot, unless a dwarf was at the controls or the vehicle was controlled by an AI.

Unexpectedly, security ceased to offer fierce resistance and escaped in all directions. The lone ship began to flee, pursued by the entire squadron of the opposition.

"Beliar, something's wrong," Anna said hesitantly. "Forkis would never hide behind the backs of his achijes." The enlightenment came immediately, when she remembered that her father Krystian had once told about this tactic. "Connor's ass! Call them all off!"

"What's going on?" The lieutenant asked confusedly.

"It's a trap!" Anna wasted no time explaining, and without further ado and fear of breaking the rules, switched to the general channel and communicated:

"Don't chase the fleeing unit. There's an inhibition bomb on board. Hold your fire."

People who knew Anna reacted immediately, accepting the judgment of the recommended second lieutenant, and stopped firing. Others preferred to wait for confirmation from their commanders. Some of the pilots began to change the direction of flight, some still kept the designated course.

Sandstorm was right, detonation came seconds later. It was as if all the water from a great lake had been ported into space, and spattered radially, sweeping away the machines closest to the epicenter, like polystyrene ships launched by a child into the waves. The White, located tens of kilometers from the source of the explosion, was also shaken. It took a few moments for the rebel to regain control of it.

"Well done, Second Lieutenant Sandstorm," Commander Lacetti said to her. "Congratulations on your good judgment."

Anna noticed with regret that many of the opposition's machines maneuvering closest to the explosion had become paralyzed and drifted as if they had lost all engines and propulsion systems. However, she couldn't continue to evaluate the losses as she was attacked by a rocket.

"The White, the rear plasma rifles. Bring down that crap." The rocket speeding towards the XRS-14 was difficult to shoot down. It responded to plasma beams and changed direction very quickly, as if it hadn't been moving in the vacuum. Anna tried to bring it down by hand, assuming that the missile's guidance systems knew the program of the White's AI and therefore had no problem predicting its moves, but the alternative method also failed.

Sandstorm shut down the assistance system completely and switched to manual control. She was going to get rid of the intrusive rocket in the oldest possible way of air defense: outmaneuver it and then crash it into an asteroid or an unlucky enemy combat transporter. This method also failed, for the Kiritian missile faithfully copied the moves of the white fighter at the same time as Anna tilted the stick.

As she began to be pissed off as much as worried, the missile was shot down by one of the rebels.

"Thanks, Tom." She recognized the shooter thanks to the markings on the speeder airframe, who immediately began to move away to find another target.

Anna made a quick reconnaissance. She noticed that Beliar was unable to deal with a certain Kiritian who was constantly on his tail. She immediately moved to support him. Three other fighters from the accompanying squadron also came to help the lieutenant.

And they were all annihilated in less than a minute.

The girl was speechless. The small Kiritian air carriers were known for their maneuverability, and the pilots who were flying them - for their perfect aviation skills. However, this one here seemed to trump everything she had seen so far in training and in practice. And she was diligent in her duties, she had watched hundreds of recordings of skirmishes with the Kiritians, she had analyzed some of them many times.

Lieutenant Drunkenstein was hit by an incapacitating beam from a cannon that looked like a plasmoreactor core. He almost completely lost control of the machine as it began to fly away from the battle zone into space.

"Beliar!" Sandstorm received no reply. The lieutenant was alive, however, because he managed to set his fighter so that he could touch with its underbelly a several-kilometer-long asteroid drifting nearby. The rebel hoped that Beliar only lost his communication system, but on the FX-94 might as well have been activated an autopilot that was trying to land safely on the huge, coarse rock.

Anna, however, wasn't able to check what really happened, as when she scarcely moved to help Drunkenstein, she herself was attacked by some achij.

It took her a good few Terrenic minutes to get rid of the intruder, who turned out to be a good pilot. Nevertheless, she didn't destroy the target, because it cleverly avoided her missiles, but only damaged it, which however, was enough for the intruder to retreat and disappear among the swarm of fighters.

She didn't manage to take a deep breath, as she was attacked by another combat transporter - the same one that had defeated Beliar. She recognized the machine at once, because it was the only machine that moved in an amazing, specific way. Every maneuver was perfect, error-free. She wreaked havoc among the rebels, racing through the skirmish area like a god of war.

"He's tough guy, isn't he? Maybe we will face each other?" The second lieutenant directed the White towards the transporter and immediately proceeded to a concentrated, concussion salvo from both front tamari cannons. At the same time, she tried to estimate where the opponent would be the next moment.

The Kiritian turned back with a wingover maneuver. He was flying towards Anna now, having opened fire as well. Orange energy shells were hitting the XRS-14's canopy intensely and steadily, until Anna, clenching her teeth, was forced to make a sharp left turn. The relentless pilot would most likely have crashed into her, had she not been the first to yield. As a result, she lost the mental duel. She was furious with herself.

"What a bastard!" She shouted in her mind. For a moment she lost sight of the Kiritian who disappeared also from the scanner. The fighter's warning system reported that the outer layers of the cabin were slightly damaged. There were indeed tiny, cobweb-like cracks where the concentrated fire had previously hit.

The intruder didn't let it go, he appeared on the tail of the XRS-14 at a distance of two kilometers. And immediately began firing.

Anna managed to avoid the missiles - though not always - but the pursuer himself followed the White persistently and didn't let her outmaneuver him, as if he had been reading the second lieutenant's mind and reacting infallibly to her moves.

After the Terranic quarter of an hour, both machines receded from the skirmish zone; The fighters, without words, decided to settle the duel on the sidelines. The Kiritian pursued Anna as she navigated among asteroids. The woman was furious, the intruder had a counter-maneuver ready for her every catch, even for those that had fooled pilots as good as Beliar and Splitter. In addition, he played with her as if he had known her possibilities perfectly well.

"Goddamn you ..." she growled through clenched teeth. "I'll take you down anyway."

To her boundless amazement, the Kiritian replied in an electronically distorted, thin voice. Getting trounced by some young private was the last thing she needed then.

"A bet, miss?" On the White's screen appeared a silhouette of the pilot clad in a helmet and black and ink armor with indigo elements.

"About what?"

"Nothing," she retorted thoughtlessly.

"You will have a hard time realize such a bet if I win." The Kiritian laughed cheekily and didn't speak again. The chase seemed endless. Sweat poured down Anna's face and back. As soon as she managed to hold the target in the line of fire and release the missile, the Kiritian immediately escaped from her. She wasted more than half of the rockets on him, of which only one managed to crease the hull of the escaping machine harmlessly.

She lost track of time. She stopped looking at the watch synchronized with the armada, because it didn't matter now whether they had fought for Terrenic quarter of an hour or a day.

Worse, communication with the rebels was severed because of the distance.

The girl completely indulged in emotions. She allowed herself to be driven by anger and lost herself in her hatred of the Kiritian people. In a state of agitation, she threw herself at the transporter. Even if she had to ram it and lose her mind at the same time, she would do it, the collapsed star! This damned game had been going on too long.

The asteroid belt had been long gone from their scanners. They did feints, combat turns, spins, chandelles, loops, Immelmann turns, and spirals because they didn't have to worry about any physical or gravity obstacle. Anything that didn't mean flying in a straight line could turn out to be beneficial.

Anna was being pursued almost all the time. She had received a diagnostic report that the White's hull was sixty-seven percent damaged. Her nose was bleeding, her ears were wheezing terribly. She felt as if she had been about to vomit her own guts, as the anti-g shield was failing more and more. She thought that she would suffocate right away.

To her satisfaction, the Kiritian was also hit.

Doing a feint, a little thoughtlessly, she fired her penultimate rocket.

It hit him. Finally!

The damaged machine of the enemy, being gutted by a spherical flame in the area of the nozzles, started to ... flee. It was heading towards some unknown, nearby gray-blue planet, which Sandstorm, plunged in amok, hadn't noticed before. Most likely, the pilot intended to extinguish the fire in the atmosphere.

"Your hull is battered! You'll burn in the thermosphere!" She called on the same frequency on which the intruder had previously accosted her. It sounded neither like a warning nor ironic. She didn't care about the pilot's fate and she was sick and tired of this idiotic fight that almost led to the destruction of the White.

The escaping man continued the kamikaze flight. Anna wondered if he had ignored her deliberately. Or was unconscious, was a corpse, or perhaps he was descending, being pulled by the gravity of the planet, having completely lost control of the vehicle. Or maybe, with tainted honor, beaten up by the rebel girl, he actually wanted to commit suicide. Whatever the cause, he rushed straight towards the illuminated hemisphere, accelerating steadily.

Following her target, curious and sure that she had defeated the enemy, she realized too late what it was about. She screamed in anger as the pilot unexpectedly entwined the white fighter with an energy net that blocked all its circuits.

The opponent's mocking laughter resounded in the White's cabin. Now both machines, one damaged and the other blocked, were falling towards the planet. They entered the upper atmosphere.

The XRS-14's AI also didn't work. The girl got roused from the battle rage and began to panic. She was fully aware that she would die soon, dashing on the surface of the globe if she didn't think something up quickly.

"The White, go off, Connor's ass," she tried to control the fighter by manual override.

As she passed through the thermosphere, she thought she was going to be burned alive. The skin stung as if dampened with acid and set on fire. Tears were pouring out of her swollen, aching eyes.

She didn't know how she had managed to activate emergency systems cooling the cabin, or maybe they went off themselves, but the jets of icy gray coolant that spouted from several sides at once, saved her life. Everything for a short while. Too short for a human to be able to control the failure and get out of it unscathed.

The earth, spinning on its axis, was approaching at breakneck speed. From hypoxia, Anna began to have hallucinations.

She noticed a distant explosion over sandy hills. Her enemy had just died - and she would share his fate in a few seconds.

"Get out of here, Anna Sandstorm. Save yourself." The White's AI somehow managed to break free from the blockade's operation. The synthetically sounding voice crackled like in a faulty android. Despite the progressive deactivation of subsequent systems, the fighter tried to save its pilot's life. Anna knew that the deteriorating White had crossed the Kiritian barrage only to, in the last surge of energy, give her a chance to be saved. She felt sorry. "Dear old machine," she thought as she placed her sore hand on the instrument panel.

Around the second lieutenant and her chair, closed with a bang a rescue cyst whose flaps slid out of the floor. The duralumin-lithium-composite ball, used to catapult the pilot in space, enabled them to survive even many decades in a state of anabiosis and hibernation. It worked worse in the atmosphere of the planet, serving the living contents a carousel with huge loads.

Further events unfolded at nanosecond speed. The second lieutenant felt a strong jerk up, then felt sick as the catapulted cyst began to descend. The whole system was jerked again as the anti-gravity drive went off. Her body was shaken vigorously; she hissed in pain. She vomited, then her eyes moved into her skull.

She even rejoiced to be drifting away into blissful ignorance of death. At least she would stop to feel that excruciating, crippling pain and pressure in her chest that made her realize in the last flash of herself that she would die from suffocation, perhaps from her own vomit.

Chapter V
A smile of fate

Q'ualel sat on the dilapidated wall, enjoying the terraformed air his body had long gotten used to. He pressed his chin against the top of his paw resting on the knee brought to his chest, and stared at the ruins of the pyramid he remembered from the time when he had come here as a kitten. A few hundred Terrenic years earlier, proud and tall, it challenged the K'ajoloms in its heyday. The once beautiful structure turned into piles of boulders, stone blocks, sloping walls and cracked stairs.

It was not the destructive passage of time that had caused it - humanoid jaguar's pyramids could survive millennia - but the attack of the colonists who had annihilated the Onkalotian nation and its civilization simply because they had wanted new living spaces and the planet's prizes. They hadn't cared about the creatures that had looked like two-legged jaguars. For the militarily and commercially aggressive settlers of the solar system, it hadn't mattered that the autochtones had been as rational as humans, also long-lived - the oldest members of the elders had been over a thousand years old at the time of the attack on Chulimal in the Terrenic year 2509. The Onkalots had been classified as zero point two on the Kardashov scale and it had ended there. Animals, savages, slobs. Unfortunately, the people of Jun Kame called One Death had made a great contribution here. The cruel cannibals had spoiled the opinion of all tribes.

Q'ualel moved a leather sheath with an obsidian dagger attached to his belt so that it didn't get in the way of his moving tail. He got up and brushed ants off his mottled fur. The small, persistent arthropods weren't a local Chulimal species. People had consciously brought various animals and plants with them, but sometimes something had come by a shuttle without their knowledge.

In addition to the belt with the dagger which was a gift from the farmer John Schindler, with whom he had lived for seven years, Q'ualel wore a necklace made of the teeth of a local predator (he had killed it in defense of Schindler's daughter) and a long loincloth. He liked to be dressed like his ancestors; cat's fur was ideal for the subtropical Chulimal zone. He hated uncomfortable human body-covering clothes, though he sometimes wore them when the situation called for it. Once, due to racism, he had had to hide his tail in his uniform and wear a one-way mirror-type helmet to cover his muzzle. However, the denizens to the space stations where Schindler had taken him to help with the crops trade, had gotten to know the identity and nature of Q'ualel and had liked him. People had started to treat him like a human being, they had stopped paying attention to him. Subjective observation had killed rumors of the aggressive and brutal big cat. Q'ualel - like most of his nation's tribes in the past - had proven to be a calm, intelligent, life-and-nature-respecting creature, affectionate to his friends and family. But also, once as a priest-warrior, dangerous to all who had wanted to destroy these sacred values. The incidents when he had killed his enemies, acting in defense of the Schindlers or his own, had occurred several times at the trading stations and near a lonely farm beside a jungle. Q'ualel had once stabbed radicals who wanted to get rid of him. Another time, he had gotten a robber who had been going to rob John's field and rape his daughter. He had also beaten-up corsairs from a small corvette when they had settled on the planet due to a breakdown and wanted to 'visit' the Schindlers. Killing in self-defense hadn't been punished, especially when witnesses and monitoring had been involved, which had luckily happened in the fights of the humanoid jaguar. Nevertheless, such incidents had been exceptions. Rarely did anyone land on H14 because of the Kiritians, even though they had been seen last twenty years earlier near the Onkalotian ruins of Ajb'atenaja. The planet was inhabited by ordinary families. They lived alone or in small clusters, as in the case of the Schindlers, taking advantage of the alienation and notoriety of the Chulimal, to live in peace, dealing with agriculture and mining crafts, and selling the goods they obtained at trading stations, numerous in the Lion Universe.

"Aggroteh!" Q'ualel turned, hearing the name given to him by the humans. The Onkalotian one was difficult for them to pronounce with the right accent. "There you are. I was looking for you."

The golden-haired Eredal, the twenty-year-old daughter of Schindler, trotted towards him, panting. Aggro smiled slightly, baring his fangs, and came to meet her. He grabbed the girl's waist and spun her. More than once he thought how lucky he was that he had come across the Schindler family, who, apart from taking him in, treated him like their friend and son. He was reminded each time of the grace of fate by Eredal's cheerful smile and her radiant face.

Like his old friend from Chiq'aq city known as the Place of Fire, where they both had grown up, he could consider himself the chosen one. Since the massacre, Aggro hadn't encountered any other Onkalots. He thought that maybe they had all been killed or they were hiding well somewhere on the planet. The humanoid jaguars were closely associated with nature. They believed in the myth that their ancestors had explored the secrets of the cosmos and Chulimal itself, thanks to which they had learned to control and use the forces that governed nature. Other spokes of powerful beings called Nimja, the Great Family, or the Ancient Onkalots who had given their descendants a particle of divinity. Each Onkalot at birth had been endowed with a psionic gift that had manifested itself earlier or later. Q'ualel had become a psychometrician, he was able to recreate in his mind events and even the appearance of people by touching objects belonging or related to them. As with ancient human civilizations, many of the skills that the ancient Onkalots had once used, had been lost over the course of the millennia. Q'ualel and his friend loved to explore these mysteries of the past - and that's what saved their lives. Shortly before the colonist attack, they accidentally launched a Nimja porter in the archaic temple of Toniatuha and moved to the planet Aj. They wandered through cold, alien ecosystems while their Chulimal people were either exterminated or taken captive. When they managed to return, they found on their home planet strange two-legged creatures devoid of fur and tails, building their own cities on the Onkalotian ruins. The trauma experienced then devastated Q'ualel. All he wanted was to hide in some inaccessible place and cut himself off from the universe. His friend reacted differently - he swore a vendetta.

Then their paths parted. Aggroteh's companion vanished without a trace.

Soon after, deprived of his will to live, Q'ualel was captured by slave hunters from Calvary. He was sold at an interplanetary market. For four hundred years he served various masters. Sometimes he was treated like a hard-working scum, other times he was taken secretly to the beds of his jaded female owners, who got bored of playing with representatives of their own kind.

More than fifty years ago, a certain change had taken place in tormented Q'ualel - he had decided to end his damned vegetation. Even though he believed in Toniatuh and thought it was his most important god who had reminded him of his inheritance and made him act, he supposed that he had won with apathy thanks to his friend. For he had found out by accident that he had been safe and sound. However, the things he had done were beyond Aggroteh's reasoning.

So Q'ualel escaped from the last owner in a stolen transporter and flew to Chulimal. Returning to his birthplace, he wanted to mentally renew himself. Unfortunately, he was disappointed again, because all the Onkalotian buildings, symbols of his carefree childhood and adolescence, had been turned into ruin. Everything he knew had died. He hid the transporter in a cave and holed up in the wild for decades, living almost like an animal. As a socially highly developed creature, he began to be bothered by loneliness. He was drawn to human settlements, conversations and reasonably decent civilization. He spent more and more days near villages and settlements. Once he dared to get closer to the Schindlers who lived near the ruins of one of the Onkalotian cities. The calm, peaceful family eagerly welcomed the exotic guest, especially little Eredal liked him. Q'ualel decided to stay with the Schindlers. He helped them to cultivate profitable bulbous onions that grew well in the wet subtropical soil, and to exterminate fanatical lycans and predators present in this part of the jungle. The assumption during terraforming was to create a planet free from larger carnivores, but these appeared anyway, bought at interplanetary bazaars and then released into the forests by the bored buyers.

Q'ualel witnessed how Eredal turned from a mischievous girl, always covered with mud, into a beautiful young woman. In addition, she had a crush on him, which her parents didn't oppose. He also liked Eredal with her pure heart and an eternally childlike gaze. He was still young by Onkalotian standards, a healthy and capable fighter who contemplated a long-term relationship with someone. However, he was afraid to stay with Eredal not only because of the huge genetic gap and short life of Oderses, but above all because of the unjustified aversion of many people to Onkalots. He suspected it was due to jealousy, especially when it comes to psionic abilities, and that it was human nature to hate anything that represented a higher level than their own.

"No," he thought firmly, jokingly putting the girl down. It was better for her to get to know a man of her own kind. Anton from the Rafens would have been a good catch, although Aggro didn't like him. This farming family lived closest to the Schindlers.

Eredal kissed his cheek, ignoring the long cat mustache she had gotten used to long ago.

"Can you help us with the onions?" She asked.

"The harvest is today? I completely forgot. Sorry, I don't have a farmer's soul."

"It doesn't matter. Let's go." The girl looked over Q'ualel's shoulder at the Onkalotian ruins, her smile crawled off her face. "I understand why you come here so often." She slipped her narrow, delicate hand into his strong, clawed paw with human fingers. "You miss that life."

"Sometimes a little. Sometimes very much."

She hugged him, and Q'ualel wrapped his arms around her, though he had done it reluctantly lately. He wished she wouldn't get too used to him. He didn't dare to tell her, though, and he hated to see bitterness on Eredal's flawless face. However, it had to be clarified eventually.

"So, are we racing to the field?" He asked.

Eredal smirked like an imp, jumped away from the humanoid jaguar and rushed to the jungle across the open area. Q'ualel huffed in amusement, pressed himself to the ground like a real hunting jaguar, and began a slow countdown by wiggling his tail sideways. It was one of their favorite games - sprints, in which Aggro gave the girl a bit of an advantage.

"Seven, eight... ten!" He moved. He easily caught up with her in the jungle. The girl was running on the ground, squealing and giggling, while Aggro efficiently jumped over trunks, windthrows and branches.

They reached the mud field at the same time. The girl almost bumped into her younger brother, Darius, throwing with a pitchfork from one place to other thick layers of compost, under which, in warm, humid, and at the right pressure, were ripening bulbous onions. Q'ualel caught up with Eredal and fell over, pretending that it was a big cat attack, then they both began pelting each other with weeds from the mound. Darius put his fists on his hips and shook his head disapprovingly - then laughing, joined the fun.

A quarter of an hour later, the three of them were already working hard, picking watermelon-sized onions from the ground and carrying them onto trailers, the contents of which, ready for sale, would land in the hold of a farm transporter the next day.

This time Q'ualel had no intention of going into orbit with the host. Before the whole family sat down at home a few hours later to eat a supper prepared as usual by Mrs. Schindler, he quietly accosted John and asked him for a longer conversation in private.

After the meal, as the K'ajolom slowly began to set, giving way to two moons in a navy-orange sky, the two met in a boulder field near the jungle, where they sat by family fires or burned weeds.

"So, I'm listening." The full-bodied host put a straw in his mouth. "What's bothering you, my friend?"

"Do you remember our last visit to space, a month ago?"

"Perfectly. We made a lot of money." The man bared his teeth in a slight smile.

"Back then, I spent a lot of time talking to merchants and pilots, generally people who traveled and knew a lot about what was going on in universes. I found out everything I wanted about my friend."

The farmer raised an eyebrow.

"The one with whom you survived the massacre four and a half centuries ago?"

"Yes."

"Why do you never mention his name? He has a name after all."

"Yes, he does. However, I would prefer not to disclose it. And not because of a lack of trust in specific people," the Onkalot looked kindly at John, "but ... because of some complications that could arise afterwards. Huge ones." He sighed, lowering his head, then raised it and looked into his blue eyes. "There are matters that we should settle only among ourselves. My friend - if I can still call him that - lived only for revenge on the colonists ... that is, the entire human race. He fed on this hatred. Of course, I didn't take his talk seriously, sure he would burn out over time, just as a heavy criminal stop escaping from a red security prison after years of trying. However, I found out, to my great surprise and disappointment, that he had achieved his goal, and with interest, as you say at the stations. He messed up terribly. And I have to clean it up."

"Onkalot?" John scratched his three-day mustache and ran his hand down his beard that had been growing for a year. "Nobody mentioned any humanoid jaguar interfering with people's affairs. Are you sure? Maybe the guys you spoke to talked flummery drunkenly or joked?"

"I'm sure. I know this Onkalot too well. He acts from the shadows." Aggro's eyes narrowed menacingly. "I can even guess how. He is so well disguised that the chances of him being detected are zero. However, if he doesn't stop doing what he does, it will lead to real perturbations in all planetary arenas. There will be too much death. He can't live long without it. That's why I decided that I had to do something about it. Fly to him and try to argue with him, long and intricately, if need be."

"Alright, buddy." John pressed his thumbs behind his belt and let his hands hang freely, "let's finish this froth. Tell me right away it's about Eredal." He smiled at the sight of a surprised expression on his muzzle. "You want to leave because you are afraid that you will ruin her life. But I'm telling you, directly, honestly and openly," he took the straw out of his mouth and began tapping it on Onkalot's chest to the rhythm of the spoken words, "that I have absolutely nothing against this platonic relationship. Neither of the family or our neighbors living far from us in this wilderness do. And when someone teases you at the stations, punch him in the face! Well, although hitting in the face isn't a good idea, since you've worked towards your reputation for so long. But we'll come up with something."

"No no!" Q'ualel waved his paw negatively. "I'm not making it up. Eredal is a completely separate topic. I just don't want to tell her about it. I'd rather leave without saying goodbye." He ran his fingers over his ears. "I may be acting like a coward, but I wouldn't like to change my mind because of her, and Eredal will certainly try to dissuade me from this trip. Then it will be harder for me to focus on the things I plan to do."

"Aggro." John put his hands on his shoulders. "You're like a son to me. And I try to be a good father and I don't want to spoil the prospects of my children. As long as they are wise and prudent. If that is your decision, I can't forbid you anything. No matter what drives you." His expression got rigid. "Unless the decision is not wise and prudent. But knowing you, I don't have to worry about anything, right? Come here."

The squat farmer hugged the much taller humanoid jaguar and patted his back with his hand. Aggro stood as rigid as a pole for a moment, then hugged him back.

"Go then. Do what you have to do and I will let you go without interfering with your affairs. I only have one request," he pushed Aggro an elbow away, "come back to us when it's all over."

The Onkalot smiled artificially.

"I'll be back."

"Let your god Tonatiuh be with you."

Aggro smiled inwardly as well. In fact, it had all started with this god.

The memories of the last days came back when some time later, carrying a bag with necessary things on his back, he ran through the jungle.

Aggro was an extremely religious henotheist. He worshiped the most Tonatiuha, the god of stars and warriors, according to the beliefs of the Onkalots, wandering around the universes. He wasn't sure if it was, he who had brought him back to the temple with the porter, or he had reached there by accident, wandering around the jungle. He felt, however, that it was rather His will that had brought him there. God demanded something from him. Q'ualel remembered clearly the temple inside the mountain from several centuries ago: reliefs with the jade faces of warriors and the muzzles of animal gods, a sculpture depicting a sacred tree of the cosmos, and the other Tonatiuh, a serpent fountain filled with underground water, a trough with a magic flame, a stone altar and a porter platform behind it. Then Q'ualel had stoked up the sacred fire while his friend had studied the mathematical signs of the ancient Nimja and the seals of the device. Aggro remembered best the sunlight, which had brought the temple to life at noon, thanks to the clever construction of the tunnels and appropriately inclined prisms of precious stones. Tonatiuh's strength was greatest at this time of day, perhaps through his intercession they had managed to activate the ancient mechanism that flared up with supernova power.

But all that had been long over.

Now, if he didn't know what to look for, Q'ualel would have found the hill that concealed the cave-temple ordinary and without secrets. The ground had collapsed enough that the entrance corridor had turned into a little dangerous tunnel through which you could only crawl, preferably holding your breath. The reliefs seemed to represent the menacing faces of the skulls, not the expressive muzzles and faces. The tree of the cosmos had collapsed. The basin resembled a grave hole. The well casing of the fountain had cracked. The altar had collapsed. The porter had been down for a long time. The temple had been shrouded in darkness, as the tunnels had been blocked by the ground sliding down the slope.

Q'ualel could see well in the dark, but he lit a log, because according to tradition, it should have never been dark in the temples of the gods of light. In the flickering shine he noticed the last of the key elements of the cave - the statue of Tonatiuh in a cat form, and more precisely what was left of it. Fragments. Failure. End. The gilded, dirty surface sent no reflections. The topaz eye seemed dead; the other was lost somewhere. Something like this shouldn't happen even to a snowman. The most important god of Q'ualel was dead. Maybe that's why Tonatiuh had brought him to the cave to show him the worst kind of decadence? To make fun of him in front of him himself? The Onkalot looked sadly at the statue and actually saw the ruin of himself in it. This is what he had become. A zombie. Despair. Twilight. A trace of a warrior. A coward. He had fallen to pieces over the centuries. And he would have probably fall to dust soon.

Aggro stood up and roared loudly, the echo responded the jaguar's call in the corridors.

"Enough," he growled. He couldn't remember the last time he had felt such rage.

He understood why the deity had brought him here. It gave him the strength hidden in the decaying statue, which was the exteriorization of the divine spirit.

If Q'ualel was reborn, Tonatiuh would be, too. "No more passivity," he decided. "No more being an incapable farmer - it's time for a warrior."

He didn't remember much about the monotonous underground crossing in which he finally reached the cave complex, where a stolen silver transporter was waiting for departure.

Q'ualel flew through the wide crater of the extinct volcano, quickly reaching outer space. He chose the direction of the dangerous Capricorn Universe. He knew he was risking everything, but he was aware that only in the criminal sector would he get up-to-date information that would help him find his friend.

***

Anne was awakened by a bone-penetrating chill that was as effective against lethargy as a bucket of icy water, sadistic slapping and shaking by arms together. If she was lethargic at all. She opened her aching eyes and realized with fear that she could see very faintly and indistinctly.

However, she immediately breathed a sigh of relief.

It was just a helmet with a broken visor. Getting it off her head turned out to be quite a challenge, though, because as soon as she started to move, she discovered that she had no feeling in her body.

She got scared again, this time seriously, imagining that she had sustained such great damage in the fall that her limbs would have to be amputated. What if she had broken her spine in the total woods?!

Wait, what fall?

Oh, yeah. The battle, bringing down Beliar, the pursuit of the Kiritian space ace, deactivation of the White's AI, falling in the cyst from on high - the memory returned with the striking force of a mine mole's hydraulic arms. And with the memory back, also fear, uncertainty and questions arose that Sandstorm would surely not get an answer to right now.

Had the battle been won?

Had Beliar survived?

Were the rebels already looking for her?

Had the White survived?

And where the hell was that stupid Kiritian she had shot down in the orbit of a planet ...

Exactly, orbit of what planet?

How long had she been here?

And is there ... oxygen?!?!

I guess there was, since she hadn't kicked off yet with her helmet damaged. Therefore, since there was air that allowed a person to breathe freely, it meant that she was stuck on some planet, either subjected to cyclical or one-time terraforming, the effects of which regulated themselves.

The rebel regained feeling in her hands a few minutes later. She could finally bend her fingers, twist her wrists, even move her entire arm. First, she took off her gloves, then that damned helmet, having grasped it with her hands. Her throat and the chambers of her nose hurt, even her teeth, as cool air rushed brutally into her system through her open mouth; the girl felt dizzy.

She looked around at the surroundings. She was lying in a rock-hardened sandy wasteland where a gentle wind rolled the particles. From the heavy, gloomy sky, looking like an expressive work of a painter who loves grays, was falling snow. A few meters away were the cyst flaps.

Sandstorm ran her tongue over her chapped lips, they tasted of clotted blood. She must have had a little of it on her face, for when she changed her expression, she felt resistance against her skin, as if a layer of dried mud had been left on her face. The bundles of hair stuck together were also dirty with blood, they seemed to be as hard as a bunch of straight, raw pasta.

Sore, she stood up with great difficulty after another minutes, grunting and wincing, complaining of nausea and burning eyes. She brushed dust and snow off herself. She pushed up the sleeves and legs of her suit to see if there was anything broken that would burn with fiery pain as she found a warmer refuge. She saw a few bruises, but no spot swollen like a balloon, bulging with blood. She straightened up and once more looked around helplessly. The lack of damage to her health would not save her if she didn't warm up soon. And it was so terribly cold around ...

Shaking like jelly, chattering her teeth and cuddling her clenched arms, she staggered toward something jutting above the ground - the only thing that stood out in that uniform yellow-gray-white woods.

That sticking out thing was the White ... or rather, what was left of the poor fighter, that is, part of the fuselage behind the flaperons. Flooded, warped chunks of metal and components littered the area of hundreds of meters. The worst thing was that the cabin, the only source of communication, ceased to exist.

Broken down, Anna rested her forearm on the jet of the fighter, and on it, her forehead, and sighed with resignation.

"You served me bravely," she murmured. "Thank you. Especially for the fact that many times you comforted me more than any other person."

She searched the vicinity of the crash meticulously, hoping to find something to wrap herself in. The cyst fired from the cockpit also had taken too much damage to be slammed and used like an incubator: the system didn't work beyond doubt. Using all the strength she could summon, Anna tried to tilt the composite flap to make something like an igloo, but the nearly quarter-ton colossus could be barely swung. At least the effort made her warmer. A little.

She moved forward, where the White's fairing antenna on the ground pointed. Every direction seemed good in this bleak land with no end. Weakened Sandstorm fell to the hard ground several times, with each subsequent rise she did it less willingly. She wanted to sleep; it was so cold ... Too cold to think about anything. All she knew was that she just had to go.

She stumbled again and fell, but this time not because of weakness, but because of a frozen stem sticking out of the ground. Nearby, there was an ice-bound forest similar to Carboniferous terrestrial backwoods. Squat, segmented trunks that looked like giant pineapples. Tendrils. Climbers. Twisted stems. Forked leaves. Rickety saplings. Having walked a short distance, she picked up a stick and tapped the nearest stalk, wanting to examine the strange film, like thin ice, covering all the plants. Maybe it wasn't ice? She wondered why the deciduous forest had been surprised by winter.

Did plants of this type prepare for the changes of the seasons by shedding their leaves with the onset of cold weather? Or maybe she was looking at extremophilic flora, the biology of which she completely didn't understand? Or she had wandered for several kilometers through an area affected by nuclear winter ... It was said that some terraforming morons still used this terrible, primitive, completely ruining weapon. First, they destroyed to build something from scratch. That would explain the barren terrain around. Sandstorm threw the stick. It didn't matter. Why would have she worried about some trees when she herself could froze solid if she didn't think something up quickly?

Taking careful steps on the creaking ground, she plunged into the forest. She carefully observed the clearances between the trunks and the possible threat from the side of dense crowns. She made sure not to fall into a hole or some other trap: the litter, which was cracking under her shoes, didn't look very stable.

Anna found an ice-free pool. She threw garbage raised from the ground into the water, wanting to check how it would behave in an inconspicuous-looking liquid. Finally, having taken off the glove - and clenched her teeth from the cold - she took a risk and, carefully as if it had been fire, stuck her finger into the basin. Nothing happened, the water just seemed to be water. But salty, which turned out when she touched her tongue with her finger. That's probably why the liquid didn't freeze. The girl dipped the hem of her sleeve in the pond, washed the blood off her face and rubbed her hair stuck together and chapped lips.

She found no hiding place in the forest that could protect her from the cold, so she turned back and began walking along the edge of the forest. She realized the peregrination might have not made sense if it was the same everywhere, but she had to go. That was all that mattered: to move her cold legs and not stand still.

Maybe the situation wasn't tragic.

The silhouette of a building loomed on the horizon. It didn't turn out to be an exhausted man's illusion or a pareidolia as Anna stepped closer. The enormity of the building, the stone structure and the mystical aura that seemed to emanate from the depths of the portico guarding the wide, twisted staircase, resembled the Onkalotian ruins of Ajb'atenaja from the H14. But it surely wasn't the Chulimal, unless somehow the dying Kiritian had miraculously carried them both light years away. The girl smiled at this totally crazy thought. The Immortals were - she hated to admit it - amazing in many ways, but they certainly didn't have the portation technology.

She took a small military knife out of her upper, having - horror of horrors - no firearm at her disposal (she was unable to retrieve anything from the White) and, holding the blade as if to stab from her hip, she began to climb the massive stairs. The front elevation turned out to be a lonely, thick wall, about twenty meters high. After crossing the portico, Anna entered what could be considered a giant garden. Instead of plants, flaunted their hideosity destroyed fountains, old monuments on pedestals which depicted something unknown, cracked and twisted columns, stelae, walls and a dilapidated road built of stone slabs covered with lichens, leading to the building itself. Everything was made in the Onkalotian style, reminiscent of the technolytic architecture of ancient human cultures, more specifically the Aztecs and Mayans, which Sandstorm had learned about as a teenager.

The snow stopped sifting. The clouds thinned to reveal stars blooming in the firmament. Anna went up the next stairs, short and narrow this time, lit a flame with the Kiritian little generator that she had once received as a gift from Beliar (she always carried an item stolen from Ajb'atenaja like a talisman, she herself didn't know why).

Inconspicuous from the outside, the building turned out to be a huge, multi-level complex full of chambers. Anna concluded that she might have entered a temple of significant worship that had been used hundreds of years earlier, given its splendor, magnitude and degree of destruction. The earlier guesses about the builders seemed to be true as she sightsaw the site: scenes from everyday life carved in reliefs, a bit indistinct due to lichens, dust and time, testified that the peculiar sanctuary had been built by Onkalots. But what had the humanoid jaguars been doing on a planet so distant from their native Chulimal?

With the little generator in her hand, she walked around the complex for a good hour, checking if it was safe. On the first floor, she discovered an interesting species of bioluminescent colony plants, perhaps fungi, looking like crumbled and scattered sponge. Hairy creatures emitted their own light: red, yellow, greenish and blue, depending on the species. In places where the most colonies accumulated, i.e. in gaps, cracks and on damp walls, Anna could turn off the lights without fear of hitting something in the dark. Another peculiarity turned out to be ... mice and rats! She squealed and jumped back, having accidentally stepped on one sitting in a rosette of lichens. The frightened animal, with a squeak as well, rushed, disappearing into the darkness. For a while, one could hear the roar of stones being moved. Sandstorm realized she had been holding her breath for a long time. It is possible that the complex was visited by people, because wherever they appeared, it soon became infested with filth such as rodents and cockroaches. Fortunately, she was unable to spot the latter, but she found other creatures: something like flattened lizards that didn't respond to the light from a generator or the proximity of humans, but lingered lazily, stuck to vertical surfaces with their paws, at best casually changing position when the girl touched them gently with the tip of the knife.

There were also glowing fungi on the second floor (Anna skipped the tour of the dark underground). Guided by their light, she reached a large room, partially without a ceiling, which, in the form of wooden joists and stone remnants, littered the entire floor. In the light of the stars and the relaxing aura of the fungus colonies, she found the entrance to an alcove, obscured by skipping cobwebs. There were broken vases and pots in the corner of the claustrophobic place, and on the opposite side was an ornate stone slab. The exhausted girl used it as a place to sleep, having lined the hard surface with a large amount of picked up lichens.

Curled up like an embryo, she didn't sleep a wink all night long. Every now and then she was awakened by piercing cold and muffled sounds coming from further parts of the complex. She was also kept awake by short dreams, the content of which quickly faded from her head, but she knew that they must have been nightmares.

In the morning she woke up stiff, sore, cold, thirsty and hungry. She got a workout by doing gymnastic exercises and running up the stairs between the floors. She warmed up and the contracted muscles stopped aching, but when she finished exercising, she felt more thirsty.

She quenched her thirst in the pond found the previous day (she would get sick at most, she could take a chance), which she reached easily, following the edge of the forest. The day turned out to be warmer than the previous one. The rock-hard sand had partially thawed, but the leaden sky returned, and a strong wind picked up, as if the ruthless weather had wanted to compensate with blasts for that day's lack of snow.

At one point, Anna's nose picked up the familiar smells that came with the eastern wind: of smoke, burning, metal, coolant and battery fluids. At first she associated them with the White, but quickly realized that they couldn't have come from the fighter, for, if she remembered correctly, it had crashed in the north. She walked towards the distant mounds, sticking the collected poles into the ground at intervals, so that, standing next to one, she could see the previous one, in case she had to plunge into solid terrain.

After sticking the fourteenth, the rest flew out of her hands when behind the hill, she discovered the source of the mysterious smells.

There was, in a collision recess, a Kiritian combat transporter, so mutilated that it was barely recognizable. It was practically a collection of loose parts, damaged in a plane crash, from extreme atmospheric temperatures and space combat. There was no pilot in the remnants of the cabin, not even his remains. All Anna found was an overturned strobilus helmet filled with sand as well as some blood on the rim of the canopy.

She wandered a little on all fours, examining the junk, analyzing the situation. It was impossible for the aviator to survive. Had the body been taken by the Kiritians who had visited the planet at night? Or maybe it burned down completely in the crash, along with the bones? After all, she hadn't seen a rescue cyst.

Holding her loose hair, which, in a violent blast, attacked the left side of her face, Sandstorm stood up and looked around. In the distance, she saw only barchans and hills, but she found them worth investigating. Maybe she would find valuable elements from the transporter that could be used.

Having reached the desert island a few minutes later, the startled second lieutenant almost fell, feeling a sudden softness in her knees. It wasn't a fustian at all ... but the pilot buried downwind. He was lying on his side, with one hand pressed against his chest, the other extended, and his legs curled up.

Anna brushed the sand off the poor man's face - and fell to the ground in amazement. Her eyebrow rose and her mouth parted in a silent scream. She was motionless for a time, making only wind-broken breaths as if the planet's atmosphere had gone haywire.

"It can't be true ... It's impossible ..."

Forkis was lying a meter from her.

Exactly the same as she had seen in Ajb'atenaja twenty years earlier. Despite her very young age at the time, he had scored himself in detail in her memory. There could be no mistake. Unless she was staring at the clone.

She rested her hands on the sand as if she intended to humble herself before the First Galactic Dignitary, but the momentary state of numbness was due to the shock she experienced. After sitting down on folded legs, she hid her face in her hands and stayed like that for a long time. She tried to think logically. Was her whole life guided by a destiny that finally brought her to Forkis? Or it was a coincidence, pure and unbelievable, like winning a huge sum in the lottery? Or in the sand was lying one of a frigging shams the Kiritians had mass produced in biomedical laboratories to spread propaganda that Forkis was the only one, immortal and invincible?

The man lying motionless turned out to be real - he wasn't an android, as the girl noticed when she examined his neck and face with her fingers. The androids didn't bleed like humans, but had a white or black substitute for the life-giving fluid that circulated in the synthetic insides, and on the Kiritian's forehead and unarmored parts of his hands there were wounds clotted with blood. It is possible that Anna indeed had Xajb'a Kej in front of her, taking into account his sensational aerial feats and brutal combat techniques. The infamous Emperor of the Immortals was capable of such things. Unless it was another propaganda and cult of the leader, because who would have distinguished them in the same ships and naval craft? However, it all didn't matter anymore. There was the corpse in front of her. Sandstorm's multi-year plans went to hell.

After the first shock was over, she set about disarming the Kiritian. Coarse war weapons interfered with examining and determining when the death had occured. She stripped off piece of his armor and outfit, revealing an abs and part of his muscular chest.

She fell on the sand for the second time, this time after touching the area of the lying's heart.

Forkis was alive.

He had crashed to the ground, lain in the cold for a day, without drinking, food or medical help, but he was still, the collapsed star, alive! He was deadly cold, the pulse was barely palpable, but his heart was beating slowly, faintly, like during a cryogenic sleep. To be sure, Anna brought her fingers to the

Kiritian's nose, which she hadn't done before, certain, like of the sunrise on the Nephrida in the morning, that she had a dead man in front of her. A strong wind had just picked up, creating a dust-cloud and small eddies around her, so she sensed nothing.

But he was alive.

So, she had to kill him now.

She had devoted her entire life to one goal - to kill the bastard who had destroyed two galaxies, as well as her childhood. To send him to hell again. Now, by a twist of fate, it had become so easy.

She knelt down and pulled the knife out. She held the blade so that she could cut a deep smile in the neck of the hated enemy. It was enough to bring the blade a few centimeters closer and run it in an arc from left to right. Slowly ... yes, preferably slowly, to feast the mind and eyes. Barely one arm movement. It was that simple.

Having taken a deep breath, Sandstorm put the knife to the throat of Forkis, as helpless as a baby, who had no idea what was going on around him.

She stared at him for too long. Her hand seemed to be petrified. It was not fair to kick a man when he was down.

She didn't implement the plan, for she had a different idea. She spat on the sand.

"When the rebels come for me," she said to him, "and I assure you that they will be looking for their second lieutenant, you will come with us on a little trip to the Lion Universe. There you will stand before the tribunal." She leaned and whispered in the usurper's ear, "It would be wiser to execute you in some grubby room in a basement. I will personally make sure no Kiritians find out about it. I will initiate only a small group of people into the plan, so that nothing leaks to the outside of the planet. Let them look for you to the end of time."

The man's cold mouth didn't move, no muscle of his face twitched.

Anna started to giggle at the grotesqueness of the situation.

"And you see, I turned out to be better." Having gotten up, she stashed the knife into the upper and poked the Kiritian in the stomach with it. "And now I'll take care of you. You will only die when I let you."

There was no way she was dragging Forkis, which weighed more than 150 kilos in armament, by hands across the wilderness to the sanctuary. Nay, she didn't manage to drag him even a few meters. Struggling with the ever stronger wind and the sand ruthlessly attacking her face, she returned to the remains of the transporter and began to rake the scattered debris. After a short search, she concluded that the best improvised trawls would be the punctured horizontal tail fin. She took a flexible metal cable from under the console, pulled it through the holes and used it as a rope.

Groaning and gritting her teeth, she rolled the Kiritian onto her primitive invention. There was still a problem with shifting around. So, she equipped the bottom of the trawls with machine fuselage frames, which she stuck with some non-caustic liniment, thus obtaining unpatented, original skids. After this shift, the transportation of the unconscious went faster and easier, but after reaching the sanctuary located a few kilometers from the crash site, Sandstorm fell on the stairs completely exhausted. Staring at the yellow stain of the star behind the thick cloud shroud, she didn't have the strength to move her hand for a long time. Her shoulders and spine ached terribly, not to mention a knot in her starved stomach.

"And what the hell is this whole trouble for, if are you going to die here anyway?" She muttered to still unconscious Forkis, who was lying beside on his back on the fin. Despite her exhaustion, she found the strength to roar in annoyance. She got up. "Well, since I already dragged you here."

Though she had barely twenty steps to climb, she struggled to drag the man up the landing at the top of them. Twice she had to move him to the right place because the armored body was sliding down the metal ramp. In the temple, she didn't know where to put her prize, and she didn't find the prospect of struggling with this colossus and dragging him to the second floor a good idea. The rebel's thoughts and gaze turned to the unfortunate entrance to the underworld. She stood for a moment, with the Kiritian fire lit in her hand, considering whether it would be a good alternative. In the end, she chose to confront this area yawning cold, gloom and mustiness.

Spiral, cracked stairs led down, separating at the end into two parts limited by a pillar. After going along the left branch, the girl was greeted by the dark gorge of the corridor. In the light of the artificial fire, she could see the dangling sheets of quivering cobwebs.

She walked unsteadily, confined in a small cocoon of light. Pebbles crunched loudly under her shoes. She thought it would be a good idea to light the logs that were stuck in the metal yokes on either side of the corridor and looked, though fragile and old, still serviceable. Before Anna realized this intention, she saw the stone polyhedra of tombs resting on catafalques, fortunately covered with massive slabs. But she also saw exposed graves, the covers of which rested against a dusty mosaic of the floor. Empty. A lot of white cap mushrooms grew around, looking and smelling like mushrooms exported to Nephrida. The ceiling and walls were covered with bioluminescent moss, giving less light than the higher-story plants, but enough to avoid bruising oneself in the dark.

Having no better dwelling for the enemy, an hour later Anna threw him into one of the tombs. A primitive lifting mechanism she used still worked. Once it had had to be used to raise a casket and lower it into the grave. She tied the man's hands with a trawl cable. She searched the two leather bags attached to the sides of his belt. Inside, all she found was an energy pill that pilots used to satisfy their hunger during long space voyages. One was enough for a week in Terrenic units of time. Anna swallowed it immediately.

"Here you are, drink it." She poured down Forkis' throat the water he had brought in a clay cauldron from a garden pond she had discovered as she had rested on the stairs. The rest, she greedily finished herself. "And that would be it. Now we will politely wait for the rebels. For sure they have already identified the White's wreck from space."

"Unless the Kiritians did it faster," she thought. "Then it won't be fun, especially when they discover this place, and it's only a matter of time." Anna glanced at Forkis and felt uncomfortable. Resting in the tomb, pale and bloodied, he reminded her of an enormous, muscular vampire, anyway an evil being of unimaginable power. She didn't believe such nonsense, but the mystical, gloomy aura of the environment could distort the perception of reality and damage logic.

Sandstorm left the basement as quickly as possible and went to wash in the reservoir in the garden. It was getting dark as she returned to her 'bedroom'. Even though she had picked up more sponge-like lichen and balls of wool, she was also shaking like an earthworm in the snow that night. She often woke up because of the cold, and then in her thoughts and aloud she vulgarly complained about her fate.

Once she awoke, drenched in a cold sweat, and sat up abruptly, with the knife in hand. She dreamed that Forkis, with eyes red as an android's diodes, rose from the tomb and was standing over her bed. Of course, she didn't notice anyone.

Chapter VI
With a psychopath under one roof

His people in ancient times had learned to use magic, as was said in the tribe, although in fact wise ancestors had used the ordinary forces of nature to achieve certain goals. But there had been also those who had believed that the power had been given to them by gods. The ancient Nimja members had allegedly harnessed forces so powerful that they had been able to direct the elements, influence the weather, and even resurrect the dead or control dangerous space objects in such a way that they had pushed them off a collision course with the planet. The golden mouse, a living artifact, had been created probably in the heyday of the Great Family, or perhaps it had been shaped by nature itself, as a being with aberrations? Millennia later, when magical practices had almost completely disappeared from the world, being replaced by a pernicious, lethal technology perfectly mastered by the peoples of Earth, no one could say it exactly. However, endowed with immortality, the golden mouse had survived entire ages, living in alienation according to its own rules, revealing itself to the chosen ones (maybe random people - new generations couldn't define it, because Nimja's knowledge was almost completely lost) extremely rarely. The living artifact possessed the miraculous quality of influencing reality as the owner wished, but its resources seemed limited. It could be used several times.

He found the artifact in a time of dire need, when he wanted a vendetta on demons from outer space that fell like thunderbolts from the sky and completely destroyed the civilization of his people and the population of the planet. He believed that it couldn't be a coincidence that the mouse had turned up for him, one of the few survivors, but a deliberate artifact had chosen him on purpose. He asked the mouse for a new body so that he could blend in with the crowd of enemies, and that was immediately given to him. He also craved for supreme power, one that was beyond the imagination of mortals.

If he had the mind and knowledge of Nimja, he would have known that the transformation was based on extremely advanced technology, and the device gave rise to an artificial, though biological process of accelerated transmutation, drastic to the organism, but still survivable. After all, he didn't die, and he retained some of the characteristics of his natural species. Power, in turn, he won himself, because people wanted to follow him. At least that's what he thought. He had no idea the item's gift was crowd control.

Paired with his mind, the artifact still had power supply, but he refused to use it again.

Afterwards, he killed the golden mouse free from disease and old age, but vulnerable to damage like any living, material being, so that no one accidentally used it in the future and knock him off his pedestal. Such a fall from above would have been extremely painful.

***

Forkis opened his eyes, which in the darkness instantly took on a reddish glow of infravision. This remnant of his heritage was taken by both enemies and achijes for bionic modification of the eyeballs. And that was good. The Kiritian was pleased that everyone thought so. He saw moss patches growing on the ceiling, emitting its own light. Raising his sore head, he was slightly surprised to see a brown dwarf rat standing on his chest, which must have wondered if the nipple of this enormous creature could be eaten. Forkis smiled only with the corner of his mouth. The rat that thought it had found the corpse went still. It tensed the tiny muscles and watched closely the man's face with its black eyes, sometimes wiggling its whiskers.

"Damn it ... Great, you put me in the grave." The man recognized the four stone walls bounding him. He knew where he was. During the transport, he had regained consciousness twice: in the wasteland, where he had seen the back of the enemy pilot pulling him, and at the entrance to Ch'amiya b'aq, an ancient temple known as the Bone Scepter, the front of which he had seen much earlier, on a previous visit to the planet. That's why he wasn't surprised to see the stone ceiling instead of the gloomy sky. But what kind of idea was it to put him in the tomb? Were there few better places in the temple for keeping the wounded? He smiled mischievously. The rebel's idea was amusing indeed. "So, we're on the planet Aj."

He easily got rid of the cable partly melted by the explosion that bound his hands. It only took a few more tugs of the wrists to loosen the loop and free the numb hands.

Meanwhile, the stupid rat, instead of getting out of the Kiritian's sight as quickly as possible, continued to stand on his chest and stared as the giant recovered.

It was too late when it decided to escape. Forkis caught him with a quick move of his arm. He squeezed it so that only the tail and head protruded from it.

"How hungry I got," he said to the beast in a pleasant timbre of voice. He sat up, grunting and wincing in pain. He ignored it and tensed, reaching out with his free hand to straighten his bones.

The already well-disturbed rat began to jerk and squeal more and more. The little heart was rattling intensely in its tiny chest like a radiation meter at the site of an explosion. The usurper could have sworn he felt the vibrations through the biometal of the glove.

"And what are you afraid of, little?" He asked in a calm, hypnotic voice, wrapping the rodent's tail around the finger of his other hand. Licking his lips for a long time and staring at the creature with hungry eyes, he stroked its back tenderly. He ran his tongue over its head, leaving thick saliva on its fur. "Look at it differently. If it weren't for me, you would have died under some rock, eaten by bacteria and worms, and you would become part of the most powerful man in the universe."

The Kiritian smiled awkwardly at the sound of these words. The most powerful man in the universe lay in the basement of the forgotten temple, knocked out of orbit by the anonymous rebel turd. He sighed, amused. Well, it was a change. And with the girl, if she was still alive, he would deal later.

"Shhh, calm down." He blew at the rat's mouth, then turned to it gravely, "It will take a moment. It will hurt, at least in a few minutes. But you should like the beginning."

He slipped his paw into his mouth and tasted it delicately with his tongue for a moment. He murmured with satisfaction.

The rodent went crazy, started thrashing and screeching like crazy, fully aware of what was about to happen.

However, it had no chance.

"Have a nice journey, baby."

Forkis put it in his mouth wide open. He played with it for a moment, moving it with his tongue and the muscles of his mouth to moisten it as much as possible. He parted his teeth again and again, creating an illusory gap, and when the animal tried to get out, he locked it and scooped again with his tongue towards the esophagus. Hunger is hunger, but he also had to have some fun. Especially in such circumstances. The confused rodent didn't even think that it could achieve at least it and cut the oral cavity of the attacker.

Finally, Forkis tilted his head back a little and loudly swallowed the rodent alive. He ran his finger along the bulge on his throat as the contents wandered downward. He felt the terrified creature barely tremble, being squeezed by the muscles of his esophagus. The moment of peristalsis of living creatures gave him the greatest pleasure. He felt movements for a time, once the rat was in his stomach, weaker with each subsequent long breath of the Kiritian. But it still lasted quite a long time, many minutes. He patted his belly. He loved this feeling; it had no right to ever get boring. A feeling of unbridled domination as he took the lives of little creatures in a truly barbaric way. After all, he was a killer with a right to everything, so why shouldn't he have enjoyed what was considered even the most macabre pleasures? Why shouldn't he have enjoyed life in his favorite ways? Nobody could stand against him; the gods couldn't punish him because they didn't exist. He had believed in them much earlier, but everything had changed. There was no heaven or hell, no punishment for sins, and no final judgment. There was only responsibility for your own actions. Praise for bastards and contempt for the honest.

He belched. He ran his tongue over his lips. He picked a piece of fur from between his teeth. He could hear and feel stronger gurgling in his stomach.

As he still felt weak, he lay down again on the stone slab. He began to twirl a metal capsule with his fingers - a talisman hung on a chain. He checked to see if he had any equipment with him. As he expected, the pouches at the belt had been emptied, but only he could open both compartments in the cuisses (unless he changed settings). So, the X17A4 - a self-renewing luminous ammo gun that was the basic equipment of every Kiritian - was still stuck in its place, and in the other compartment Forkis found a container with an ampoule and an included microsyringe. The universal medicine was a treasure in the field, because it could both hyperstimulate the immune system in the event of an infection, limit bleeding in case of large wounds that were not arterial damage, as well as neutralize all poisons in the body known to the Immortals' medicine.

Forkis got out of the sarcophagus like an awakened vampire a few Terrenic quarters of an hour later, when he felt his strength returning. He looked at the feral fungi that grew beautifully in the nether regions, once cultivated here by temple acolytes. He knew that the energy obtained from the lousy rat wouldn't last long. And the only energy pill he had had with him had been stolen by the rebel bastard. He didn't care too much; a mocking smile twisted his pale face. He would make his next meal out of delicate human flesh.

***

The next wakening wasn't caused by a nightmare or the low temperature of the temple at night, but by voices coming from somewhere deep within it. Anna heard them even when the sleepy haze had completely dissolved and the mind was fully attuned to tangible reality. So the sounds couldn't be delusions.

Having put on her shoes, and the knife in the upper, she left the alcove. She made her way to the room with the damaged ceiling, where she stopped in the beam of dim starlight.

She listened.

Nothing. Silence.

She descended the stairs to the lower landing and heard the voices again, clearly this time. Human ones! Moving lights flickered in the distance, as if glints were being released across the level.

The girl's heart rate increased, she herself felt great joy and relief. A huge smile appeared on her relaxed face. She moved faster. It seemed the rebels hadn't left her!

Moving in the darkness thanks to the bioluminescence of the fungi, for igniting the Kiritian fire could prove to be risky - she wasn't 100% sure she heard her friends - Anna moved towards the source of voices and the lights roaming the walls, trying to make as little noise as possible. "On the other hand," she thought, "if they were Kiritians, they would trace me with a nucloindector as a living being with a human temperature and certain types of proteins." Nevertheless, you can never be too careful. She made sure she had easy access to the knife.

She took a careful step over a creature that looked like a cross between a snake and a stingray, which, pushing off with folds of skin on the side of its body, crawled over the bricks. Anna followed it with her eyes until it moved a safe distance away. She reached tilted columns and a cornice, in front of which there was a chasm of several meters deep. From there, she had a good view of the first floor, while remaining hidden.

Yes! They were rebels! Tom Lewandowski and eight more men from the 98th Regiment! They were looking for her!

The girl's heart leapt up to her throat, and a cold chill ran through her body as an armored hand grabbed her face unexpectedly, and the other arm, strong like of a factory robot, wrapped itself around her waist and jerked her back violently. Her back was pressed against metal and her hand rested on something warm and hard. She recognized armored breastplate and abs, shaped like in a professional bodybuilder. The face pressed to the side of her own.

"If you start thrashing, I'll break your neck," she heard a soft, threatening whisper at her ear, but making the hair on the nape of her neck bristle. The torturer moved Anna silently into the shadow of the column.

It was Forkis.

Who should have died three times in a day, yet crouched behind her, painfully pressing her against himself and holding by the throat.

The girl was overwhelmed by panic, and a wave of heat poured over her as she realized who the person behind her back was. She felt exactly the same as twenty years earlier in front of his chamber, this fear of a completely defenseless person paralyzing every cell in her body. She started kicking, jerking her head left and right, thrashing like an insect in a spider's web. An insect that had no chance of freeing itself, being wrapped in sticky silver threads.

She stopped when the mighty hand nearly crushed her larynx. "Will it be calm?"

Sandstorm nodded eagerly. She could breathe again. Sand sprinkled into the abyss, and half of an old brick collapsed after it. The light beams of flashlights integrated with the weapon simultaneously turned upwards, towards the columns.

Forkis cursed almost silently, so that only Anna could hear him. He leaned back and, still pressing her against himself, began to feel something with his extended hand. Soon the hissing stingray snake Anna had seen earlier flew down.

The lights pointed to the alleged perpetrator of the upstairs commotion.

"What is this oddity?" Tom touched the animal with the tip of the barrel. He shuddered as it rose halfway, spread a dermal neck frill, and bared several rows of tapered teeth.

"Leave this filth, master." Tom's closest companion grabbed his elbow and pulled him sideways. "It can be poisonous. Wait, I'll bump it off."

The rebel fired a beam of combat plasma, aimed at the body, but burned a hole in the floor, for the frightened animal managed to disappear into the gap between the rock blocks.

"Nice shot." Tom patted his friend playfully a few times on the shoulder.

"Have you seen how fast that reptile is?"

"No, no one has seen it except you. It's good that you gave a comment," added a woman from the team.

"Enough, let's check also that corridor," said the commander.

Anna thrashed desperately in one powerful spurt she could afford. At all costs, she wanted to free her face from Forkis' grip and inform her companions, screaming about her presence just a few meters above.

"Stop it, damn it. You'll spoil everything. And I need you alive for a while," she heard again that reassuring, alluring, but this time threatening voice. Warm breath caressed her earlobe so that she flinched.

She was indeed starting to calm down. She stopped struggling, only over her desperately pounding heart, Forkis had no control. She was breathing deeply and steadily, staring helplessly from the shadow of the column at the companions below.

When, in helpless anger, she wanted to clench her hand crushed between the two bodies, she felt the abdominal muscles of the executioner tighten. He moved as he sucked air into his massive chest. Forkis, despite the pale complexion typical of most Immortals that Anna associated with death, was very warm. Deep down, she was glad to be able to warm herself for a moment after the ghastly chilly nights, pressed against that massive body, and having her cheek regularly brushed by his warm breath. That's why she froze, not minding Forkis' strong arms, still holding her tightly to him. She was scared to death, but her primal survival instinct told her to take advantage of the momentary convenience.

Meanwhile, the rebels went to search an adjoining chamber. They consulted, obeyed new orders, and then left the temple forgotten by the universe. If Lieutenant Sandstorm had been here, they would have found her much earlier.

"Why didn't they track us?" Anna asked, in her voice trembling with emotion a few minutes after the Kiritian finally withdrew his hand from her mouth. He brought his wrist to her eyes. She immediately recognized the bionic inhibitor built into the multifunction device of the brace, which made its host invisible to all military scanners - and with it masked other large living organisms within a radius of several meters.

The Kiritian stepped in front of the rebel and set her free. Tired and broken, she fell to the ground. The man walked over to the edge and rested his arm against the column.

"Your people just flew away forever." He turned to Anna. He still spoke in a nice, calming voice. "They didn't find the body, but assumed you were dead."

"At least someone's looking for me," she said tartly, though she was afraid of him. However, she didn't want to demonstrate again that she was afraid of him. "They say you've ruled for centuries. I suppose your disappearance pleases the achijes. They are probably sick of you, because how long one person can rule? They will find someone else to replace you. You are not irreplaceable, Xajb'a Kej."

Forkis raised his chin. He seemed to pierce the girl with his eyes more effectively than the most sensitive neuromogram, unmistakably depicting the emotional state of a man. He smiled indulgently, amused by her lame attempt at repressing her emotions.

"Bullshit. People like you know nothing about altruism. Your mentality is on the level of a man who is always afraid for their fate, who leaves their loved ones to save their own ass."

"A superman has spoken," the rebel whispered in a voice filled with hate.

"And if you care about succession, Necron will certainly do well in my position. He's a trusted lictor and a great friend. What you are trying to suggest to me is disrespecting other people. Treating your neighbor as an object. But don't taint, kindly, with this behavioral rebel slime, my people, whose degree of morality you completely don't comprehend."

He walked over to Anna. She stood up slowly, sliding her back along the column as if along a rail, as if she had had a dangerous animal in front of her and been afraid to make a sudden movement. She wondered what the monster might have wanted with her. Forkis, a head taller than her, leaned over her, resting his arms apart on the stone so that she was between them. He was smiling again in that macabre, specific way, as if he had relished her fear or laughed silently at the rebel's helplessness and absurd thoughts, knowing them perfectly well.

"That's exactly what your thinking is like," he said. "You don't care about your companions; you choose the lesser evil. You can sacrifice five to save fifty. You give up your search because of presumptions, not knowing the fate of a wanted person. And what's next? Do you think the rebels will come back here? Those poor-spirited terrorists?"

"The achijes left you too. I haven't seen anyone looking for you ..." She fell silent, seeing the finger extended in the warning.

"Kiritians never ignore their people. Never! And none. We are able to look for the missing for hundreds of years, to turn the universe inside out, just to find them. Unless we're 100% sure they're dead."

"What do you want from me?" Anna looked down at her feet, deliberately, so that the cascade of hair obscured her face. She remembered the knife in the upper. If only she could sense the right moment, having convinced Forkis with her behavior that she was harmless, maybe she could correct her mistake. She didn't consider in the script that the bastard would free himself.

The usurper pushed off the column and stood straight.

"For now, I want you to live, Anna Sandstorm. I need you."

Surprised, she blinked. She looked up.

"How do you know my name?"

"I can read your mind." Forkis smiled amusedly. He licked his upper lip lasciviously. Anna shivered.

"Yeah right. You read the name tag ..." She noticed that her chest ID had been lost somewhere. And the mystery solved: Forkis had found it, and now he made a childish fun of her. "Of course. It's impossible to read minds, no human can do it. Research has been conducted on this."

Forkis' widening smile silenced Anna more effectively than an admiral rebuke.

"We've met before," he said. "Yes, I'm talking about exactly what you are thinking about now. Even if I hadn't probed your mind, I would have recognized you by those green eyes looking in such a specific way. I remember them. Human eyes are like fingerprints, all are unique, and in addition they are a mirror image of the soul. Do you want proof that I'm a telepath?" He spread his arms. "Go ahead, try me. Think about anything and I'll tell you what it is."

The rebel, although at first, she didn't intend to take part in his idiotic test, involuntarily thought about the last night spent with Beliar, not very exciting and successful by the way. For the past few months, their relationship had been going downhill.

Forkis folded his arms over his chest and raised an eyebrow.

"Sex with Lieutenant Beliar," he laid on the line. Shocked, Anna crimsoned with embarrassment on her face.

"I still don't believe you. What I thought of is too trivial. All people do it, after all."

"Oh, and all the men in the universe are named Beliar. So, we keep trying. Think of something completely senseless."

She made the effort this time and thought of something totally idiotic: a shod beetle in a green dress with black triangles, dancing on top of a yellow diamond. The Kiritian chuckled, but also this time he read her thoughts aloud flawlessly, making her stunned and anxious.

Forkis outthrusted the X17A4 pistol from a concealed recess in his cuisses. He took it and began examine it ostentatiously, thereby making an all-too-obvious allusion to the rebel. The hope that she would make something with her little funny knife melted away quickly and efficiently. Like the expectation that she would get out of this sick situation alive. She wished she'd tried harder to find the gun while the man had been unconscious and vulnerable. Now water under the bridge, but maybe not all had been lost yet. Forkis was only human and he had to sleep. Anna immediately called herself an idiot in her mind; she wanted to shoot herself. He had just presented his possibilities to her, saying silently that she had no chance with him. And she didn't know the limits of his abilities.

She glanced at him and felt trapped. Forkis 'heard' it all, to which he responded with an amused smirk when their eyes met. He slipped the gun into the compartment, spat into the chasm and began to walk away, leaving broken Anna still leaning against the pillar. The girl was trying hard not to think about anything.

She waited a few moments until the usurper's heavy footsteps died down - and rushed through the complex without thinking too much about what she was doing. Tripping over unevenness and hitting a wall once, she ran through two chambers. She reached the stairs, ran down to the first floor and crossed a large room filled with obsidian idols, heading towards the exit. It was still a starry night outside, giving the meager pink daybreak a chance to seize at most a scrap of the eastern horizon.

Anna sprinted out of the building, calling loudly Tom. She ran across the garden, searching for the flames of nozzles in the sky. She stopped, abruptly, only when she reached a lonely wall separating the sanctuary area from the wasteland of this sad planet.

She wasn't alone.

Her muscles tightened; her heart tried to tear her chest another time. A hand slowly reached for the knife. On the cracked earth, thirty paces away, stood three enormous cats with thick reddish fur, similar to the extinct Earthly smilodons. With their necks bent, they appraised with their orange eyes the lonely human.

Keeping her eyes on the predators, Sandstorm, frightened, stiffly took a few steps back, going up the stone stairs by the seat of her pants. She didn't know completely how to deal with the beasts she came across for the first time. The smilodons also started moving, stopped at the same time as she did. The cat on the right opened its mouth, presenting a pair of yellow tusks, the upper ones were as long as a child's hand. It growled. Huge muscles rippled under the thick fur as it started walking again. Apparently, it wanted to attack, having not felt any threat from this strange, fragile creature - but it let it go. It pricked up its ears and sniffed.

Anna quickly realized what had happened. And she couldn't believe it.

"It was a really stupid idea to run away." Forkis appeared next to her as if having grown out of the ground. He grabbed her arm and looked at the smilodons with his eyes cold as ice and sharp as a military knife. The girl was terrified by this look, though not intended for her. The animals stood still for a moment, looking sharply the Kiritian in the eye, twitched, then turned and just walked away. "Aj is dead as far as civilization is concerned. You will find here only ruins, wastelands and some dangerous fauna and flora. But the cold will kill you sooner. Temperatures drop to minus fifty degrees Celsius."

"Aj? This is the name of this planet? I don't know it."

Forkis, striding, moved towards the sanctuary, dragging Anna with him without finesse.

"It is in the No Man's Zone outside the Scorpion Universe, which is why you've never heard of it. Everyone is afraid of us and therefore rarely venture into this part of the Milky Way."

Anna broke free from his paws as they reached the entrance of the temple. They stopped.

"Who the hell are you?!" She adjusted the stretched sleeve of the flight suit. "Why did these cats leave as if you had dominated them?"

"You've just answered the second question yourself: I dominated them. Little sight war, moreover, they were females. The smilodons of Aj form matriarchal clans."

"You dominated the three big maggots? You think I'm stupid?! For God's sake, each of them weighed at least three hundred kilos!"

"It's good to know, by the way, that you are a believer."

"That's just what I said. I'm an agnostic. Even though we live in a time of planetary conquest, believers and non-believers are still on an equal footing when it comes to this age-old dispute."

"Cool. And I don't need any gods or religions to achieve my goals. Now go inside." The Kiritian pushed the girl towards the entrance. "Unless you want to be the prey of those cats. And know that they will now be wandering around the area every night and closely watching the sanctuary, having sensed your soft, delicate body."

The last words echoed somewhere in his mind. He looked at the enemy walking in front of him and felt a hunger similar to that of the animals brushed off. But unlike them, Forkis was able to refrain from murder for a long time. Long enough to fully win over the victim and attack only when he had fully gotten their trust. He wondered himself where this cunctative thinking had come from.

***

The sun didn't appear that day, from dawn almost until dusk it was eclipsed by a large moon slowly circling Aj. The second and smaller satellite was visible only in the evening. It was blowing so hard outside that the wind almost caused a sandstorm.

Forkis had made a home for himself in the sarcophagus that Anna had placed him in, and he had to admit he this bizarre idea even amused him. He brought a lot of wood from the forest to the temple and piled it next to flammable tinder, which could smolder for hours and also were abundant in the area, then lit a fire in the key racks of all Ch'amiya B'aq. He stuck new logs into the yokes. The sanctuary immediately became more alive, especially the nether regions with vaults, revealing many details and architectural ornaments invisible with poor bioluminescence. It got much warmer. But not for Anna, who spent most of the day sitting, curled up on her lichen bed, and staring into the flames of the little generator standing on the alcove cornice. She had a runny nose from night drafts, sneezed every now and then, and her throat ached. She watched with a slight envy as Forkis was sporting outside and around the complex, only pants and shoes.

Taking advantage of the large amount of unengaged time, she thought about many things. For example, why the rebels had given up their search so quickly, and what were Forkis' plans for her. Certainly, they were specific and not very pleasant, because he would have rather not kept the enemy for company. He stated openly and laconically that he would kill her, and given the fact that the Kiritians didn't lie, it was rather so obvious that it didn't require deliberation. Anna hoped to get out of the sanctuary somehow. She planned to steal Forkis' pistol, which he always carried with him. However, first she must have recovered from the disease that she had gotten, which in the civilized world would have been dealt with in a few minutes with the help of numerous medications to choose from. Unfortunately, she was in the place forgotten by the devil himself, where a man addicted to technology occupied the level of a weak, fragile and completely helpless being.

In such circumstances, she learned who she really was and what it really meant in the face of the power of nature. Cut off from civilization, the creators of space propulsion could die of toothache. Their naked bodies froze without warm sheets. Meanwhile, in such conditions, stupid cockroaches, hideous rats and primitive mushrooms did well. Animals that were worse (was that true?) could survive. Exposed to low temperatures, the plants always exploded with lush greenery in the spring. And who was there at a lower stage of evolution? Man zero, nature one. Anna breathed a sigh of relief, tilted her head back, and closed her eyes. In fever, blues and excess free time, a person thinks about a similar nonsense, instead of, for example, devising an escape plan.

Forkis appeared in her alcove the next day, went inside without asking. He sat unceremoniously on the corner of the jittery girl's bed. He handed her an antique amphora from which the aroma of hot mushroom soup seasoned with herbs was rising. Anna took it hesitantly. The man took off the glove and touched her forehead and ears, then stared at the artificial flame burning beside her.

"Kiritian fire gives light but doesn't heat," he said. "I remember that generator. You swiped it from us, in front of Ajb'atenaja," he added, smiling gently.

"Take it back if you want," the girl replied uncertainly. She held the amphora as if there had been a scorpion inside.

"Keep it." He made an amused face. "Treat it as a gift."

"What do you want from me?" Sandstorm said in a scathing tone.

Forkis touched her hand and pushed it lightly, moving the amphora under Anna's nose. She was surprised that despite the chill air that lingered in the complex, his fingers were very warm.

"I want you to drink it."

"Why would you be interested in me?" She still talked in the cynical tone. "We are enemies after all. You said you wanted to kill me. Is this the moment?"

"It wouldn't be convenient for me if you died now. Don't sulk like a baby, just drink." He ran his tongue over his lip. "Unless you prefer rats."

"I'm not gonna get poisoned with this?"

Forkis rested his elbows on his parted thighs and let his arms hang freely. A mocking smile flashed across his regular face, as if carved in alabaster. "Believe me, if I wanted to kill you, I could do it in a thousand funnier and more innovative ways. Only cowards poison food. Warriors and men of honor call for a fair fight on the beaten ground.

"Sometimes you are a fast talker like a dinosaur."

"This is how it is when you live a long time."

Looking into his brown eyes, Anna touched her lips to the edge of the vessel and tilted it. The taste of the soup turned out to be adequate to its appearance and smell: it tasted simply delicious. Pleasant warmth began to spread through her body, and the throat pain decreased upon contact with the thick, hot liquid.

"Who would have expected that the usurper can cook?" She handed him the empty amphora. "It's really delicious."

Forkis smiled again. He knew from her thoughts that the girl preferred a meat-free diet, so he spared her the details and didn't mention that he had seasoned the soup with rat fat.

"Do you want a real fire in the alcove? I can bring a stand or a log." He nodded towards the wall. "Look, there's a torch hoop over there."

"Could you explain to me why you're not cold? Are you always so warm?"

"As you can see, I'm a little bigger than you and I have greater weight. Also, I'm not a vegetarian. But you already know it perfectly well." He gave her a mocking smile.

"You act like a troglodyte sometimes; I don't understand you at all. You are a strange man."

"Maybe." The Immortal changed the subject, he didn't intend to pursue the question of his past. "I have good news: frost lets go. The local warming season is beginning. It is admittedly a few degrees above zero, but we can't count on more. So the nights will be milder from now on. Aj is smaller than Nephrid, which you probably felt through the gravity when you took your first steps on the planet, because now you are probably used to it. It's circulating faster, the seasons also are changing rapidly."

"You seem to know this planet perfectly."

The Kiritian made an indefinite arm movement, reminiscent of a market trader's gesture, presenting goods. "Some time ago I spent a local year here. Then I learned a lot about it." He raised an eyebrow. "Go ahead, ask anything you want, Second Lieutenant. And the answer to the question that has long been troubling your mind, but you've been afraid to ask, is yes, we knew from the beginning that you were going to attack us. However, when an aphid attacks a hornet, you don't have to worry too much about it."

Anna bridled, sat cross-legged.

"Would you please stop probing my thoughts?" She said reproachfully. Forkis laughed good-naturedly. "However, in your megalomAnnie, you made the most common mistake: you disregarded your opponent. And now you are on some forgotten planet, cut off from information. Anyway, how could you have known about the planned attack? Because you can't read minds within several astronomical units."

"Your rebel army is full of traitors, tempted by the prospect of power and immortality," he said hard like a judge conveying a sentence to a murderer. "By the way, you shouldn't call yourself an army, but rather fighters or a paramilitary community."

Surprised, Sandstorm was speechless for a moment. She bored into Forkis in disbelief.

"What were you expecting? That in such a huge group of people there will be only patriots? What kind of world did you live in, naive girl?"

Anna closed her eyes and rested her head against the wall.

"Who could do something like that?" She asked sharply, lifting her eyelids. "Tell me. Give me the names! Do I know them?"

The usurper's hard, firm gaze was more eloquent than any words that he could have said, "I know who did it, but I won't tell you it." Anna sighed in resignation. She wouldn't get anything out of him on this point, at least not in this conversation.

"I'm so sorry that this is happening in your society," said the Kiritian. "Hypocrisy and lies are common there. We, on the other hand, have nothing to hide from ourselves and the entire Zodiac Universum. Nevertheless, there are various myths and misinformation about us, because people find it difficult to accept the inconvenient, sometimes shocking truth and prefer to invent conspiracy theories. We are unchanging. And above all, we love and respect each other like blood brothers. The ties forged between us are similar to those that existed among the Onkalots. I was inspired by them, creating the nation of the Immortals. This is the reason behind our successes: full trust, no exaltation in behavior, no hypocrisy and spontaneity, which, unfortunately, other nations aren't famous for. The opposition in particular. There is something else, but you don't need to know about it." He got up.

These words hurt Anne, but she knew Forkis was not sharp-tongued, just calmly giving the facts to the best of his knowledge and point of view.

"You know a lot about Onkalots," she pointed out.

"If you lived for hundreds of years, you would also be a walking encyclopedia of knowledge."

She rubbed her forearm in embarrassment.

"Don't go into my thoughts anymore, please. I feel very awkward."

"Are you ashamed of them? Or maybe you are ... afraid of something?" The satisfied smile on Forkis' face widened.

Unpleasant heat spread over her body.

"I just don't want you to mess with my privacy," she said evasively.

"Alright. I'm not gonna surveil you anymore. But know that you have a hard time giving up on something that brings you so much fun," he still made fun of her. "By the way: I cleaned and turned on the underground thermal baths, if you wanted to use the hot water. The pipes work great. I've already performed my ablution."

"Xajb'a Kej?"

The Kiritian, who was about to leave, stopped and looked around. He rarely heard his middle name.

"Is there something you can't do?" Sandstorm asked honestly, without a sneer this time.

"Surely there are such things."

"I'm not a hypocrite or a naïve. Take into account the level of our experiences and the colossal age difference."

Forkis wondered for a moment what she was trying to convey to him.

"Oh yeah, you are referring to what I said earlier. You yourself don't know what you are like and what you want."

"So, what do you see in front of you?"

"I see a lost, jaded little girl, who is not sure which way to go. Worse, she is not sure a chosen path will be the right one."

The usurper left the alcove.

Anna sat motionless for a long time, with her legs curled up and wrapped in her arms, staring at the creeping artificial flames. She felt as if she had been struck by lightning, but at the same time an enormous weight fell from her heart. As unmistakable as ever, Forkis said aloud exactly what was in her spirit. I only wonder if he guessed flawlessly after several days of observation, or he had read everything in her mind before.

"Little lost girl." She snorted.

"Great."

Chapter VII
A Fight in 'Stanislav Skalski'

Anna took advantage of Forkis' offer and went to visit the underground thermal baths, and when she felt a strong stream of warm water running down her naked body in spurts, she decided to spend the entire evening in the archaic bathhouse. She really liked the place. The square room was the size of a living room, perhaps for a dozen people. It was entered through a stone sliding door operated with a gear. The ceiling was supported by rectangular columns decorated with cabbalistic symbols. The chamber was illuminated by portable stands with fire buzzing in bowls as well as oil lamps hanging from joists on tarnished chains, into which Forkis had poured powdered tinder, on which he had put then melted rat fat. In the center was a drainage grate, and above, ancient builders had attached a stone pipe stylized as a jaguar's head. Water came out of an open maw. The stream pressure was regulated with a feedthrough lever.

It was the third time since Sandstorm had arrived at the Bone Scepter - as Forkis called the temple - that Sandstorm didn't grind her teeth. She had fond memories of the bath, like of the hot soup before ... and the body heat of her own enemy. It was enough to cut Anna off the appliances that kept her warm for practically her whole life to make her see what she really meant without technology. Forkis was right to say that a man without their toys was a pathetic, fragile creature, which she thought of as she put a poorly insulating anti-g suit over her dried body. It was a little puzzling because the Kiritian insulted his own kind as if he hadn't belonged to it. Perhaps power and immortality had so scrambled his brains that he found himself a superman. Nevertheless, after all, he was right on practically every point they had raised, which irritated Anna immensely. It made her feel much inferior.

***

Recent traumatic events were not conducive to falling asleep, but Anna as a rebel had it in her head that she should have always found time to rest and recover. She couldn't count on a hard, many hours' sleeps, especially since she was afraid of Forkis more than lying alone on the stone in the terrifying temple. At least she would try to take a nap, then she would be able to stay awake and jump to her feet, if needed. Though she wouldn't do much if the enemy wanted to murder her in her sleep.

She put out the generator. She lay down and was lying for a long time, staring at the shadows lingering under the ceiling, listening to the distant crackling of flames, ghastly gusts of wind in the cracks, and disturbing tapper, as if someone had been climbing stairs and stopping frequently. Twice she couldn't stand it nervously, got up from the couch, but found nothing near the alcove.

Eventually, she was able to calm her mind and lie down longer with her eyes closed.

Anna's breath grew shallow before she heard something mushy drip from above onto the floor. "This," she thought, "is just another mischief of the brain calming down, which loves to mix reality and fiction just before sleep." However, the goo on her hand after another drop was too real, and it made her skin sting. Could such a realistic tapping of something hard on a stone also be made by her dozing off mind? Moreover, there was also a bad smell.

She opened her eyes - and was paralyzed with fear.

In the faint glow of the fire in the corridor she saw the most disgusting creature in her life. Like a terrible deep-sea fish, the being was as long as an adult, and looked and smelled like decaying corpse. The gray-brown, mottled skin clung tightly to its limbs, of which four skeletal ones were spaced apart like in an amphibian, and dozens of smaller ones with hooks moved disgustingly between them. Long teeth protruded in all directions from the wheezing maw. The eyes were hidden under the membrane deep inside the eye sockets. A multitude of white bubbles danced beneath the skin, reminiscent of a larval swarm that may have been responsible for the host's emaciation, unless it was due to hunger during the winter. Anna felt sick. The creature attached to the ceiling hissed and stared at her, and she was afraid to move.

She remembered Beliar's stories about monsters from her childhood (she had even met Forkis in Ajb'atenaja). From then on, bloodthirsty beasts, all too real, had become her phobia. As a girl, she had seen them for years in a room, lurking behind a balcony railing, in dark corners, in a closet, classically under the bed. She could see teeth, glowing eyes, bones and blood. Human blood. Hominal bones. She didn't admit to anyone that she had wet the sheets many times, which she had poured over with aromatic drinks in the morning, pretending to be a wimp.

However, the phobia hadn't gone away with the lost childhood. It got her again in the place even perfect to attack: cold, dark, terrifying, filled with predation, where the strongest one won. It took the form of the beast from the land of death.

Still unable to make any movement, let alone reach for the knife, she screamed, hoping to scare the creature away.

It was a mistake.

Anna got roused from stupor only when the creature jumped on her from the ceiling and clung to her body with tick-like limbs in a death grip. It wasn't heavy, but it could shatter bones well. Weakness overwhelmed her. Driven by instinct, she jumped up from the bed, took a run-up and hit her belly against the wall, but before she reached the cool stone, the monster managed to move onto her back. Its muzzle ruffled her hair, dozens of claw blades sunk in the suit, trying to get at the muscles.

Sandstorm threw herself to the ground, flexing her body and waving her limbs, but also this time she failed to crush the creature, and only broke a few vases. She reached for the knife and waved it hysterically, unable to break free from the yoke of phobia and real danger.

The fast-moving creature changed its position again. Its claws ripped the suit's fabric across her chest. Anna imagined the moving appendages of the quasi-paws digging into her body like parasites from tropical rivers. It gave her a boost. She stabbed the animal a couple of times with the knife, but she might have as well tried to hurt a wall.

The creature intended to reciprocate by sticking its teeth into the opponent, but before its neck rushed with deadly precision, something lifted it high.

Forkis slammed it against the pillar with tremendous force; the crunch of the skeletal armor mingled with the splashing of body fluids. The Kiritian almost immediately grabbed the screeching creature by the tail and flipped it again. A dry crack could mean its broken spine. The pistol shots slightly damaged the carapace, but strengthened the fury of the predator, which, surprisingly, was fine.

The Kiritian quickly holstered the useless weapon and picked up the writhing creature, which hurt him a little, but the man ignored it. He grabbed the skull with his left hand and the ribs with the other and started pushing them in opposite directions. Harder and harder, he gritted his teeth. The tail armed with spikes, flying in all directions, hit his legs several times, protected by armor plates.

Forkis screamed as the head was torn from the body. A stinky, jelly-like goo spouted from his neck. The torso, instead of falling like a dead head, escaped from the alcove like decapitated poultry, leaving a trail of gore behind itself.

Anna felt nauseous, saw darkness before her eyes. She had to lean against the wall. She stared with disgust at the still skull; she was breathing loud and fast. Sweat dripped from her face plastered with hair.

"It's syncars. It's dead." Forkis, standing in the doorway, was holding the knife she had dropped. "There is no danger anymore." He approached the girl and looked down at her. "You hear me? The threat is over, take it easy. That body is about to fall somewhere."

Anna didn't react, continued to look into the eye sockets of the skull. She couldn't stop the trembling of her lips. Only after a moment did she slowly turn her head to the Immortal.

"More," she croaked.

"What, more?"

"There may be more of them."

"There won't be more. Syncarses are cold-loving loners. Epicenes. Each adult specimen produces its own eggs as soon as the weather warms up, therefore it needs a lot of energy.

"This one was going to feed, and you were so lucky that I wanted to come here and save your ass. The syncars could pierce you like a steel virgin and suck all your blood."

"Save yourself the details."

Forkis threw the knife on the bed with a flourish. He turned and left, having taken the head dripping with blood.

Sandstorm felt uneasy when the murmur of footsteps faded away, as she was alone again. She was ashamed and angry that because of her Forkis had to intervene for the second time. But it was not her fault, in the end, that she hadn't known the dangers of the planet, and that the Kiritian hadn't deigned to educate her.

With the attitude that she was an adult and that she should have taken a grip, she went to sleep some time later by the generator's fire burning. Despite Forkis' assurances of safety, she scanned all nooks and crAnnas of the alcove, most often fixing her eyes on the entrance.

Slowly, she started to get tired as she thought she had witnessed the monster kill the monster.

When she heard a murmur, she sprang from her bed and ran out of the alcove as if fired.

***

An hour later, shortly after dusk, as Sandstorm strolled nervously through the fire-lit temple, the chill began to tease her again. The hot water from the thermal baths warmed the chilled body only for a short time, and to the alcove, where was the equivalent of a bed, she certainly wouldn't come back.

Forkis approached her, having noticed that, sitting on the stairs between the floors, she embraced herself tightly.

"Nephrida is a warm planet," he said as he sat down next to her. "If you lived on Aj, you would get used to the temperatures here over time. Man is able to get used to many things."

"I didn't thank you for that," the woman muttered. "Then thank you."

"It wouldn't be convenient for me if you died now."

Anna immediately changed the subject, not wanting to develop the thread:

"You probably never get cold." She moved her gaze from her shoes to the interlocutor. Forkis, who had been looking at the fire so far, also looked in her direction. "As if you were wearing invisible fur."

There was a hint of a smile on his lips.

"In fact, it is as you say: I rarely feel cold, even in the frost."

"You have a good metabolism. Not like mine, chilly ass."

The Kiritian cheered up more, Anna also lifted the corners of her mouth.

"Unfortunately, you have to endure without quilts and heating for some time."

"And more specifically?"

"We'll see."

They sat next to each other for long moments, not speaking, each lost in their own thoughts. Finally, Forkis glanced at Anna, who was picking her nails. He watched her for a moment and, amused, crooked his lips into a wry smile.

"If you say I have a good metabolism ... maybe I could share it with you?" He said. "For you, rebels, is it so hard to tell the truth?"

She looked at him as if he had been an admiral exposing himself to the division.

"Are you proposing kiritianization?" she said the words with difficulty.

"Don't be silly." Xajb'a Kej hung his hands freely, resting on his parted knees, and laced his fingers together. He fixed his eyes on the lizard climbing the wall, but his thoughts wandered in a different direction. "Though ... you would be a pretty good Kiritian, and trust me, there aren't many people who are fit to join the nation. Can't you say outright that you're afraid to sleep alone?" He looked firmly at Sandstorm.

"What do you mean?" She retorted arrogantly.

" Don't play the fool," he said jokingly.

"You read my mind again."

"I didn't have to. It was enough to look at you." He shrugged. "You can sleep with me. Don't gouge your eyes out like that, or they'll fall out. This is not an allusion or offer. I swear I won't do anything to you tonight, I won't hurt you." Forkis stood up and extended his open hand towards her. "Trust me."

The confused woman looked into his hazel eyes for a long moment, but didn't see even a hint of the cool flash of a bluffing killer in them. She saw practically nothing there, except for the utter calm.

"Sorry, but this suggestion is terribly ridiculous. What's in it for you?"

"Don't treat me like an opportunist. I do it selflessly. Well, maybe a bit out of pity. I can't look at you walking around like that and chattering your teeth. So?"

Strange matter. However, Anna didn't have much of a choice: either the hated Kiritian, who was warm and knew the dangers of the planet, or the cold and loneliness in the dangerous temple. She was a little afraid to refuse, because what guarantee did, she has that Forkis wouldn't use force then? With such a disparity in power, size and age between them, he could do whatever he liked in Ch'amiya B'aq. However, since he asked politely and didn't force her to do anything, maybe it wasn't a sick joke, but he simply wanted to help?

Sandstorm hesitantly accepted the outstretched hand, slowly placing her own on it. Forkis responded to the decision with a nod.

"Reasonable choice."

"Are we going to my alcove?" Anna asked and immediately realized how ambiguous the words had sounded.

"Or my sarcophagus." Forkis gave her a disarming smile. "Your dwelling is terribly tight."

They chose the nether regions.

At the sight of the stone mausoleum, lit by fire, fungi and glowing insects flying around that she had never seen before in the temple, Sandstorm shook her head in nervous amusement.

"It's so stupid."

Forkis had lined the bottom of the vast sarcophagus with fluff, rosette-shaped mycelium scraps, the same as Anna had used in her 'bedroom'. He lay down first, on his side, Sandstorm lumbered along right after him. She positioned herself with her back to him and he put his arm around her and pressed her to him. He rested his chin on her head. He was wearing partial armor, Anna just took off her boots, wanting to stay in her flight suit.

A pleasant wave of heat quickly spread over her body and settled in the relaxed limbs. The fear of the temple and the monsters inhabiting it disappeared as if on the spot. However embarrassing and ambiguous the idea of Forkis was, it turned out to be sensational - the girl finally didn't freeze. Moreover, she felt safe. Safe, in the arms of the greatest killer of all time. The thought made her smile indefinitely as she stared at the ancient wall of the sarcophagus. She felt relaxed like never in her life, even blissful. No, it was not a crush, absolutely! but a feeling of blissful peace, a certain form of spirituality, as if Xajb'a Kej had transferred some of his amazing energy to her. He was a very mysterious man.

"What are these glowing insects?" She asked in a whisper. Forkis, who was slowly falling asleep, opened his eyes.

"Fireflies. I located their nests and moved some of them closer to the sarcophagus. You will find such insects in many Onkalotian temples. Humanoid jaguars let them into the corridors, to make them not only give light, but also add a specific atmosphere to the surroundings. They bred there and nested permanently."

"Aren't they insects from Earth?"

"The other way round. They come from Aj. And it was from here that they were distributed to many terrestrial worlds where life developed. Their genetics were changed to suit different conditions. The ancient Onkalots, known as Nimja, or the Great

Family, contributed to this. They mastered an interplanetary portation method that has unfortunately been forgotten with the passage of time, just as people of electronic technology can't comprehend how ancient nations could build mountainous pyramids out of stone blocks, some of which weighed tens of tons. Almost all of Nimja's knowledge was lost with their departure to the stars.

Anna rose on her elbows and turned her head.

"Are you telling me that the Onkalots visited Earth in the distant past?"

"Nimja members, not Onkalots. According to mythology, humanoid jaguars are their children, a fragile, low and weak version of the original. According to some legends, they are not related. It was from the Great Family that the earthly myths about the gods from stars originated. Mesoamerican culture mostly came from outer space, and Nimja members themselves were considered children of the Jaguar God. Thousands of years ago, the cultures of humans and Onkalots were synthesized precisely because of the influence and cosmic journeys of Nimja members. That is why humanoid jaguars speak in Quiché, although it is different from Earth's one, because it has changed over time. The two planet populations had never seen each other until 2480, when the colonists discovered Chulimal, and on it, the Onkalots."

"Amazing ... It's unbelievable. But as a Kiritian you couldn't make it up." She shook her head. "It is a bit disturbing that with the expansion of the cosmos, knowledge began to move towards old myths. And bring them to life. What had been ridiculed began to become a fact. We still know so little about the universe. What happened to all those Nimja members?"

"They're gone. No Onkalot knows their fate. And how are you feeling? Are you still cold?"

"Absolutely not."

She turned to face him, as the hand she was lying on went numb. Forkis pulled her closer to him and rested his chin on the top of Anna's head again. She felt the strong, soothing beats of his heart under her hand. Unknowingly, a blissful smile surfaced on her lips.

Anna couldn't enjoy the pleasant moments of security and warmth, as she fell asleep quickly.

***

She woke up because of a nightmare in which Forkis grew feline fangs. With the animal madness in his eyes, he threw himself at her in the same way he had attacked the unfortunate woman from the ruins of Ajb'atenaja. The dream scene was the same as in the Bone Scepter's crypt, except that the real Forkis was still asleep beside her, apparently deeply, for he didn't react to her flinch. And he didn't have long teeth sticking out of his mouth. He still pressed Sandstorm against him, sharing his warmth with her.

Awakened Anna's attention was caught by a glowworm sitting on the edge of the sarcophagus. To her immense astonishment, the insect spoke in Kiritian:

"You think he does it because he likes you?" The hissing voice sounded more like of a slimy snake than a two-centimeter creature. "Do you think that the danger zone in which you were, and in which death endangered you, remained a traumatic past? You are wrong, human being. He will kill you. Because you are only ... food to him."

Anna moved Forkis' hands gently so that she could get out of his embrace and, making sure that she didn't wake him, moved closer to the firefly.

"No, it's a paranoia. I still must be sleeping." She touched her fingers to her temples and began massaging them. The nightmare didn't disappear when she pinched her cheek, feeling like an utter madman. She glanced at Forkis, then looked at the glowing insect again. "He's done too much for me to kill me now."

"That's what it's all about. He inspired your trust, wanted to let you know that you were no longer in danger from him. He just wanted you not to run away from him again, because the chase is a waste of energy, and you can see the conditions around you. And you, stupid, let yourself tangle up so easily in his intricately woven net. Soon he will kill you and eat you like many women before. Some Kiritians have reportedly seen him swallow the smaller ones whole alive, because his jaws and muscles of his digestive system can move apart against human anatomy. Only for it he has kept you alive for so long. He cares to keep you in the best condition possible. You've probably heard that the best slaughter meat comes from happy animals. Forkis is not what he looks like. You'll end up in his stomach, you'll see."

She thought it was insanity. She must have entered the next nightmare from the current one, because how would some worm from the forgotten planet have known what the achijes or Forkis' dignitaries had seen? Even if the dream seemed suggestive, she might have fallen into some twisted recursion where she dreamed that she was dreaming and pinching herself to wake up. Maybe the fungi growing around were to blame, after all, she had no idea what filth their mycelia emitted.

Nevertheless, anxious, she began to lose her grip. What if this was all true? Were the nightmares not a warning, a signal that not everything was going well? She wasn't sure of her own judgments, yet so obvious and rational a few hours earlier. She glanced sharply towards the usurper to see if he was watching her with a sneering smirk.

"So, what am I supposed to do?" She asked the insect, continuing her way into the madness.

"RUN AWAYYYY!" The glowworm replied in a long, hissing, vibrating voice that seemed to drill into brain tissue.

Anna woke up a second time, this time really, pale and scared. She put her hand to her forehead and began to slide it towards her chin, brushing the delicate skin of her face with her nails. As at the beginning of the talking firefly nightmare, Forkis was fast asleep, holding her in his arms. The girl had to move again because she was lying with her back to him.

Even though it was only a badly messed up nightmare, it made the rebel think. Indeed, when it comes to Forkis, recently she had acted like she drank mescal, and her caution was pent. The usurper might have cared to hold her effortlessly with him until her murder, when the Bone Scepter ran out of fungi and rodents. Could he actually murder and eat her? He could do it ... She saw him eat human flesh herself. So, it made sense, though it seemed even unreal. How long would the person weighing well over a hundred kilos, with a high energy metabolism, endure, eating junk food? How long would it be for the Kiritians to find their Emperor? And if they arrived any minute, what would happen to Anna then? Why would they have cared about the mediocre second lieutenant from the hostile camp? She tasted a nauseating, sweet blood on her lips as she bit them too hard. Whatever she did, she would be on a hiding to nothing. She suspected that Forkis, having cannibalistic impulses, might have bad plans for her, but everything began to wane as she watched him and the incomprehensible bonds were forged between them, the authenticity of which the girl didn't want to undermine for her own peace of mind. She preferred to think Forkis was her temporary ally in distress on this goddamn edge of the universe - not a lurking killer.

It made the most sense to run away, no matter where. It wasn't likely to end well, but there was some lousy chance of rescue. Anna just had to walk away from here immediately, as far as possible from him, his charm, net and slightly crimson eyes in the dark. She didn't want to see him anymore. She didn't want to judge him anymore. Finally, she didn't want to discover the truth about him, afraid to see in the Kiritian the exact opposite of what she had tried to hate him for. All these years she had dreamed of getting to Forkis and slaughtering him like a pig, but now, disheartened, she wanted to run away from him to the other end of the Milky Way. What a paradoxical inversion of ideas. Or maybe it would be easier to kill Forkis, which she had been striving for since pissing in bed at night for fear of him when she was a brat?

Sandstorm carefully turned to the sleeper. When she saw that perfectly formed face, the face of an infinitely cruel, powerful, but also preventive and prudent person, more doubts arose. Forkis' lethal, magnetic charm didn't fade away even when he was asleep. "Connor's ass ..." She had to close her eyes and grit her teeth in mounting anger as she reached out into the compartment with the X17A4 pistol. The mechanism clicked softly as the niche cover shifted. The weapon came out, convenient for a person grabbing it by the handle. The worried girl looked at the still motionless face. Confident that the enemy was still asleep, she steadily took the gun.

To break free from the sleeper's embrace - which didn't come easily to her, not least because the Kiritian held her tightly - and then to get out of the sarcophagus soundlessly, took the rebel several minutes.

She scooped up her shoes on the floor.

At last, she was free in terms of body, but not entirely of spirit. She stopped a few steps from Forkis and couldn't take her eyes off him for a long time, which she didn't like a bit. Not to mention the attempted murder, which ended in a total catastrophe: the extended hand with the pistol dropped by itself. The angry girl would have most gladly hit the wall out of helplessness, if it had been possible to do so without making any noise. The plan, intricately woven over the years, shattered like a knocked down mirror, because she was overwhelmed with powerlessness. She should have congratulated herself on her spirit.

Feeling like a traitor to the opposition, she flashed towards the exit of the crypt among fireflies flying everywhere. The fires of a few torches were starting to go out, but the rest burned briskly, illuminating the way perfectly. Anna put on her shoes on the first floor and immediately moved briskly to the exit, with Forkis' gun in her right hand. She almost sprinted through the garden, hoping that the exercise would weaken the feeling of shame and guilt. She barely noticed that a pale, sunless dawn had come.

She crossed the portico in the wall separating the sanctuary complex from the wasteland and headed towards the forest. A few minutes later, she fell among the luscious green plants and trees, from which the ice-like film protecting against the cold had completely disappeared. Anna immediately thought that it was Forkis who had enriched her with this knowledge of Aj. During the few days she had spent with him, she had learned many useful things, from historical and scientific curiosities to hard-to-accept political facts. She shook her head. Frigging, smart, longtime son of a bitch.

She paced among the trunks with no specific plans. She stuffed the gun into her pocket. If she was lucky, she might appear on the scanners of rebel fighters searching the planet. She would have even preferred to be kidnapped by corsairs from Capricorn or to die of hunger and exhaustion somewhere in the Aj desert, as long as she could be as far away from Xajb'a Kej as possible. Her former purpose, her former obsession.

If she had watched her surroundings more closely, she wouldn't have missed the detail that for a certain distance she had been following the footprints of a huge blue lion imprinted in the soggy earth, one of the modificants created by biologists for enthusiasts of hunting. Therefore, she was surprised when the beast attacked unexpectedly, emerging from a tuft of brush.

Weighing over three hundred kilos, the brown-yellow, spotted animal, whose appearance can most accurately be described as a cross between a wolf and an otter, smashed Anna with its paw so hard that she found herself in the air. She landed painfully on a slope, breaking branches. Panicked, she walked a bit on all fours, protected by a canopy of bushes. She went out into a small clearing surrounded by a swamp and tree ferns.

The predator, growling, covered the same distance with a few heavy but agile leaps.

Ignoring the painful bruises, Anna rose to her feet from the collapse. She yanked the knife from the upper, spat out the mud.

She started screaming and brandishing the blade, trying to pretend to be dangerous, although her heart pounding strongly, she felt almost in her throat.

Her demeanor stopped the beast for a few moments, but it quickly found the glistening object harmless, and moved to attack, grinning its slimy teeth. Its lopsided gait resembled that of a monitor lizard.

Aware that she was about to be trampled by two meters of rushing teeth, claws, and muscles, Sandstorm turned and started rushing towards the nearest tree. She hoped to hide between the tall, exposed roots that made up the cage.

The animal turned out to be faster. It grabbed her shoulder with its great jaws and, jerking its head sharply to the side, sent her a few meters into the air.

Anna ran out of breath, pain exploded in her lungs as she hit something hard. The released knife was lost somewhere, but there was also Forkis' X17A4.

Lying down, she pulled the gun out of her pocket and fired at the charging beast. I mean, almost fired. She pressed a second, third and fourth time.

Click, click, click.

Nothing.

"Seriously?!" She understood immediately what was happening: the weapon was programmed for the specific user. Unlike her, Forkis wasn't a fool, and he had protected himself against her in advance, even though Anna hadn't seemed to pose a threat.

She got up and, screaming in anger, threw the gun at the predator's head. The object bounced harmlessly off an outgrowth above the eye and disappeared under the sheet of a nearby pool.

The animal approached Anna looking helplessly at it. It opened its toothed maw, getting ready to bite off the head protected only by the stick being waved.

However, instead of biting into the victim, it lost its balance and fell into a swamp. The pissed off beast grunted gutturally, with its paws thrashing in the stinky liquid.

"Are you out of mind, Second Lieutenant?!" Forkis, who had appeared in the clearing like from behind the Nimja's porter gate, roared at Sandstorm in a sharp baritone. "If you wanted to die, it was enough to turn to me! On tree! Get on that tree over there!" He pointed to the branch consumed by salt as the startled rebel didn't react the first time, staring at the Kiritian. "Tylakosmils can't climb!"

The girl obeyed, cautiously began to back away.

"Thanks a lot for the bang-stick, by the way," Forkis said dryly, a term that still existed among Capricorn criminals.

"You're welcome."

Meanwhile, the predator rose, brushed off the water and mud. It began to snarl wildly and plow the ground with its paw at the sight of another bipedal weirdo who dared to step into its area - but didn't attack. It broke a thick branch with its jaws, showing its strength.

Without taking his eyes off the tylakosmil's golden eyes, Forkis leaned forward slowly and grasped the handle of the knife Anna had dropped. The Kiritian assumed a menacing expression, not a single muscle trembled on the face reminiscent of a war mask. He straddled and leaned slightly to stand more firmly on the ground. He directed the blade towards the snarling beast that was watching him closely. Moving his head almost imperceptibly, he glanced out of the corner of his eye at the rebel. At least in that matter, he was relieved, because she was a few meters above the ground.

The tylakosmil, roaring, decided to move forward first. It stopped abruptly, however, and tensed as the Kiritian roared, too, louder, making a strong, driving away swing of the knife. All the time the man didn't took his eyes off the animal's eyes.

"Can't you dominate it with your sight like those cats?!" Anna shouted, sitting on the tree limb.

The beast was getting more and more irritated. It jumped up, rose on its hind legs, then hit the ground with its front legs. It backed away, then continued its show, wagging its tail wildly. It was just an animal, but it saw something no human had ever been able to do - that it had the dangerous predator in front of itself. In addition, the male it was trying to scare away. If he didn't go out of its territory, then it would attack.

"On it, cheap tricks like this don't work," Forkis replied. "Tylakosmils despise everything that moves and doesn't belong to their species."

The man and animal tried to circle each other. Forkis reached down and picked up a pole, with his other hand still gripping the knife.

Then the tylakosmil charged.

The Kiritian stopped it, slamming the wood mightily against its drooling jaw. Splinters flew around. He tried to stab it with the knife, but missed, because the predator jumped back and immediately moved forward at the man, with its mouth wide open.

Forkis, howling wildly, threw his arm forward and drove the blade almost to the cross guard near the beast's heart.

Tylakosmil whined. It tilted its head back and grasped the handle with its teeth, and after a few clumsy attempts, it yanked the tool, dirty with greenish gore, out of its body.

"No kidding." Forkis barely had time to comment as he had to prepare for the counterattack again. The opponent stood on its hind legs, obtaining a height of almost three meters.

The tylakosmil didn't overturn Forkis. It fell to the ground, digging its claws into the marshy ground, for the man managed to turn and change position. The creature charged again. It snapped and grabbed Forkis by the metal bracer. In retaliation, the Kiritian began to hit the beast with the remains of the pole. He raised his armored leg and kicked at the great chest, on the groin side. The tylakosmil withdrew its jaws, but almost immediately attacked again and grasped the end of the rod.

For a moment the combatants dragged the wood, each one their way, until it split in half, sending both to the ground.

Forkis got up only to be back on the ground, having received a blow in the chest with the three hundred kilo live bullet. The knife was out of reach because it fell between the stones next to the animal's rump.

Having recovered the vertical with a jump, the Immortal fought hand-to-hand, taking advantage of his speed and body armored with bio metal, when the tylakosmil was far superior to him in strength. He kicked, held, choked, rolled, punched, blocked. He lay down on the ground, trapping the beast in a strong grip of his arms and legs, all the time trying to stay out of reach of its big teeth.

Horrified, Anna watched this brutal, atavistic duel from above. She wasn't even able to move from the impression.

Forkis, who had managed to retrieve the knife and dealt a few severe blows with it, was bleeding from several wounds in unarmored places, including ones under the ribs, made by the claws. However, he had more greenish gore on him. Despite the wounds, the relentless mountain of meat didn't seem to weaken, much less to resign from killing Forkis.

The girl could no longer look passively at the unfolding episode. She was beginning to fear for the life of the Kiritian who would surely lose if the fight was prolonged. She saw him fade. In this situation, primal strength would win with human intelligence and cunning, it was only a matter of time. Anna just realized, when she was unlucky enough to see another beast from Aj in action, that she needed Forkis. When the tylakosmil killed him, her fate would also be doomed. She had acted foolishly and impulsively leaving the walls of Ch'amiya B'aq. If she lived long enough, she would never let the situation happen, in which she made serious decisions in the heat of passion.

But in combat, calm, cold analysis had no right to exist.

The rebel squatted on the branch, then jumped several meters into the pool.

"Keep it a few more moments!" She called to Forkis as she surfaced for a moment to take a breath. She dived in the cool water again, not waiting for a reply, much less wanting to hear the Kiritian's furious protests.

She didn't find the X17A4 until the third dive.

"Forkis!" She dragged herself ashore, tossed him the waterproof weapon. The wound caused by the tylakosmil's claw began to sting her strongly after contact with salt water.

The Kiritian pushed the animal away with his shoe for seconds, but it was enough for him to jump in, extend his arm, and grab the spinning pistol in flight.

Sandstorm gritted her teeth from pain, lumbered to the trunk, and fell to the protruding roots.

Forkis raised the gun. He stood there like an executioner, shooting a predator leaping towards him: stiffly, straight, with an outstretched arm, keeping the expression of a ruthless murderer on his face with a tight mouth line.

The short monochrome red rays etched into the enormous body many times. A few more shots aimed at the head were fired to be sure, though the tylakosmil had already been lying motionless.

Xajb'a Kej also fell to the ground. He leaned against a boulder, tilted his head back, freely hung his arms. He let the X17A4 and the knife slide out of his relaxed hands. He was breathing loud and fast from exhaustion. He wiped the greenish gore off his forehead, which had spattered in a thin stream at his face as projectiles of light had plowed through his opponent's brain. He lay so still for the next minutes, staring at the clouds wandering high above the treetops, revealing the sometimes orange-pink sky and a large full moon.

Getting up, he saw Anna sitting next to him. She had her hands clasped on her feet and was staring at them.

"I'm ... sorry," she whispered. She scowled at Forkis.

He said nothing, kept his face indifferent.

He walked over to the slain animal and prodded it several times with his leg.

"Will you lend me your knife for a while?" He raised the blade covered with gore, turned his head to the rebel. The girl nodded briefly. It didn't escape his notice that she grimaced at the same time. He walked over to her and crouched down besides, then fixed his eyes on the torn suit. "Show me." He grabbed her hand and, having moved the scraps of cloth aside, examined her arm. "It scratched you pretty bad. There may be an infection or other local filth in your blood that you don't have antibodies to."

"I can't catch anything from Aj. After all, I don't come from here and my body is not compatible with this ecosystem. Diseases plague organisms only from the same planet, on which both have evolved," she reminded him, although she knew that as an Emperor who had lived for hundreds of years, he was certainly comprehensively educated.

"Have you seen the fauna here? Does it remind you of something?"

"Late Cenozoic on Earth."

"Exactly. Many animals were brought here from Earth at that time. Little has changed. And with them came the earthly filth."

"How ..."

"Nimja and its travels. It is a very old nation."

"Forkis, these are only Onkalotian myths!" Anna groaned in pain.

"Don't move so violently. There are otomabo leaves growing nearby that can help you. I will also have to smear myself with their flesh. But first, let me sanitize your wound."

The girl tensed her muscles, pulled her hand towards her.

"It was washed with salt water as I dived in the pool."

"And do you know how many pathological halophiles live in this spring?" Forkis made a sly face. "You probably know this notion, you were interested in the nature of the planets as a teenager."

"Have you been rummaging through my head again?"

"Since I gave my word that I wouldn't do it, I will not. However, I allowed myself to use previously acquired information. Now take your hand out of the suit." With a gesture, Forkis ordered the girl to sit down on the boulder, he positioned himself next to her, grabbed her forearm and brought it closer to his mouth.

"What are you doing?" Frightened, Sandstorm jerked her hand so strongly that it hurt again. Forkis, however, held it tight. He looked firmly at his patient.

"Saliva is the best disinfectant with our poor medical supply. Tylakosmils have venom glands near their claws, you never know with which punch the poison will flow. So, the wound needs to be purged while it is still bleeding. The longer you wait, the more filth can get into your bloodstream. So let me help you. You have nothing to fear, I won't eat you."

"But you, in turn, can infect me with some grunge." The man looked at her with pity.

"I'm a Kiritian. We have the best medicine at the Zodiac Universum, and I guarantee you that each of us is completely healthy."

Anna snarled something indistinctly, relaxed her tense muscles and let the Kiritian act. She watched, speechless and disgusted, as he sucked the blood from the scratches and spat it on the ground every now and then. She became concerned only when he pressed most of her hand, which she had rubbed against the stones, into his mouth; his eyes flashed dangerously. She felt his warm, moist, soft tongue move between her fingers. It pleased her for some reason, she suppressed a sigh. She noticed in Forkis' embarrassed glance that he realized he had been overdoing it. He took her hand out of his mouth, slimy but clean. Anna didn't comment on the incident in compensation for the fact that her action with the tylakosmil, the Kiritian also had paved over.

"Done," he said, looking to the side. "In Ch'amiya B'aq we will also seal it with otomabo mush."

"And what about you?" Having brushed the saliva off her hand, Anna pointed to the bleeding claw wounds on his chest. "Should I suck you too?"

The usurper looked at her with amusement, crooked his lips in a weak smile.

"Don't worry about me." Forkis wiped blood off Anna's mouth, stuffed the X17A4 into the compartment, and the knife cleaned against leaves, he slipped behind his belt. He grasped the tail of the tylakosmil, lifted slightly part of the animal, and, standing firm on the ground, started to slowly drag the carcass towards the sanctuary.

"Come on, a great feast awaits us tonight," he said gently to the rebel, seeing her standing under the tree, ashamed and embarrassed. "You helped kill the beast, so you'll have to try a piece, too," he added with a disarming smile, instantly infecting Sandstorm with it, though her smile was not as intense as his, and of other kind - sad.

Not wanting to feel useless, she helped as much as she could with the transport of the tylakosmil.

***

'Stanislav Skalski' was a small inn. It was located on a multi-level service station, drifting in a safe area of the Capricorn Universe, close to the border with the Fish Universe. Order was maintained there by professional police units established by the authorities of the neighboring sector, specially trained to operate in the borderlands. And it was the awareness that the contractual border, barely half a million kilometers away, was besieged by uniformed services, that made the more respectable customers of 'Stanislav Skalski' feel relatively safe here. The police itself also often visited the place famous for its good drinks. In addition, the owner, Mr. Skalski (the object was named after his ancestor from ten centuries earlier, whose aviation merits in the Ancient War went down in history), had recently bought androids, which kept order. So, fights were rare. However, they could always erupt, especially when the room was occupied by guests from feuding social groups.

Aggroteh chose 'Stanislav Skalski' precisely because of the variety of guests, wanting to obtain in the restaurant the necessary information. As an Onkalot, he took a little risk showing himself in public. Though he had taken care of his clothes, a mishap was always possible. He was still listed as a runaway slave in the Zodiac Universum record, though his former owner had long since passed away from this universe. The status, however, couldn't be revoked, the ownership of the livestock had to expire, but it was to happen in a year, that is, in 2957. So far, the humanoid jaguar hadn't been ratted out yet, the few people familiar with Q'ualel's past were on his side. It was from them that he had purchased, at one of the H14 commercial orbital stations, a complete test pilot's uniform with a helmet of a one-way mirror type, behind whose cover the cat's face could be hidden. Into the holster he stuffed an ion ejector used by real mercenaries who made a living by patrolling the orbits of the planets or the globes themselves. On the other side, Q'ualel placed a sheath with an obsidian dagger that he had always carried. Only the problem of the tail remained - an Onkalotian showcase forming a bulge. He untied it by cutting a hole in his uniform, and the extended tail, he tied around his waist, and threw over himself a long poncho with a deep hood. Onlookers would take him for some extravagant person who wanted to stay hidden.

Having landed the previously repainted transporter on the almost full landing field in front of the premises, he pulled the hood over his mouth, which he also tied with a scarf. He left the machine and moved toward the entrance. He would have most willingly gone inside wearing the helmet, which so far had protected his identity, but he would have attracted general attention, because he would have probably been the only client to have it. The weapon, he had to give to the storage room, he was additionally scanned for its presence when crossing the security gate. He managed to enter the room with the metal-free obsidian dagger smuggled underneath the cloth.

The restaurant was styled as an eighteenth-century inn, which is why it was built mainly of wood, wood-like materials and stone. It even had a fireplace against the wall, where a huge fireplace was buzzing, fueled with real firewood, which gave the room a specific smell, reminiscent of ancient times. This caused that many galactic pilgrims and tourists tired of the present, willingly returned here. The furnishings, counter, stairs, and the entire floor with rooms also had the appearance and color of various types of wood. That board evening the inn was bursting at the seams, filled with a dangerous mix of people of all professions and sub-cultures, but there were also a few empty tables set far from the bright fireplace; on each there was burning a candle.

Aggroteh ordered a meat dish and a pint of *pulque*, an agave drink, then took a seat at one of the empty tables. He pulled the hood tighter over his head, for his eyes turned bright red in the twilight, adjusting to an infra-vision seeing. That is why he often glanced at the candle flame interpreted by the eye receptors as daylight. He began pecking at his meal with his fork, wasting time as he listened to the conversations mingling in the lively place.

Having spotted several young men with badges of the 78th Rebel Squadron, the man smiled. If someone had looked at him better, they would have noticed the reflexes of fire on the fangs deep in the hood. Aggro couldn't be luckier. As he was unable to study them using psychometry, which required touch and long concentration, he watched the pilots armed with decanters and mugs. They chatted merrily, joked, nudged each other in funnier episodes of polemics, burst out laughing collectively, but weren't drunk. They seemed to be nice and tolerant people with whom even an Onkalot could get along. The young rebels weren't usually indoctrinated, and they didn't have the stupid things stuffed into their heads that humanoid jaguars were animals fit only for simple work for people. He took a long sip of *pulque*, decided to take a risk and talk.

He was already preparing to get up when into the room broke a noisy group of drugged privateers, who had somehow circumvented the ban on admission to drunk people. They had fancy hairstyles in flashy colors. On their foreheads were protruding multi-vision goggles. Beat-up clothes, mostly in shades of gray and brown, jingled with chains and bracelets sending reflections around the room. Clumpy, heavy boots tapped uneven rhythms on the dance floor. As they made their way to the counter, the corsairs made silly faces at customers, mocked couples kissing, occasionally made gestures as if they had wanted to hit someone and laughed at the sudden reaction.

At the sight of the rowdy group, the bald, leptosomic bartender made an embarrassed face, but then relaxed as the corsairs took care of the drinks ordered, having sat down at the two joined benches.

They were still making noise, shocking their surroundings with obscene behavior, but that was not yet a reason to ask them to leave the place, which was open to everyone with their pockets full, even Kiritians. Of course, all those who knew how to behave.

Aggroteh temporarily resigned from the conversation. He sat in his seat for a few minutes to eat a blowsy meal in peace and empty his mug, only then got up and headed towards the rebels, sure that the pirates, absorbed in their affairs and drinks, had lost interest in their surroundings.

He was wrong.

"Hey dude, and you, who are you? Master Yoda?" One of the corsairs leaned out in his chair and, with a sweeping movement of his hand, slipped the hood off the head of the humanoid jaguar passing by along with the scarf. Staring incredulously at what the material hid, he hit with his stiff hand his friends engrossed in discussion. "Oh, snap, people, look! Kitten!"

"Do you feel worse, Margo?" Muttered one of the nudged, with a green mohawk. Then he was speechless when he saw the humanoid jaguar in the poncho and tester's uniform.

More and more clients began to look at the standing in the center representative of the species that had practically no longer been seen. None of the guests in 'Stanislav Skalski' had heard of Aggroteh from H14, a friend of good-hearted John Schindler. Those less universal thought that humanoid jaguars figured among myths and legends.

Some people held their breath. There was a silence, as if the station covers had been turned off, and a vacuum swept over it. Somewhere a dropped glass broke. Someone cursed violently.

The corsair with the green mohawk sprang up abruptly, knocking over his chair. He pointed to Aggroteh.

"Onkalot!" He roared, putting an end to the neurotic atmosphere.

The bartender, sighing deeply and shaking his head, touched an alarm plate under the counter. He knew this anarchist gang very well, whose on average every fourth visit to 'Stanislav Skalski' ended in a sharp brawl. Had it not been for the fact that the cosmic pirates brought a lot of income to the premises - even if it was dirty uinals - by ordering more expensive liquors, taking rooms sometimes for a few evenings, and the best prostitutes, they would have been banned long ago. So, the profit outweighed the losses. Today's visit, however, fell short of the statistical norm, because the gang of racists, which had been kicked out by the androids during its previous visit for initiating riots, had just attacked the Onkalot.

Nimble Aggroteh quickly dodged the charging thug who tried to hit him with a ring-laden fist. He threw at him the poncho he stripped off. He also released his tail for better balance.

Clients jumped off their chairs and moved to the walls, making space for the fighting in the center of the room. The rebels Aggroteh had intended to talk to earlier sat in amazement and stared at the prelude to the show.

Margo threw a chair at the humanoid jaguar. The latter made a quick dodge, and the projectile swept the contents of the table behind him. The angry man, screaming, rushed like a bull towards Aggroteh. The green mohawk charged from the other side.

The humanoid jaguar jumped back, grabbed their clothes and pulled them, taking advantage of the men's impetus, then sent both with their heads smashed together to the ground. He didn't take a full breath, and the third thug was already running at him with some multifunctional weapon that he had managed to sneak through the gate.

Aggro made an annoyed face, his ears clung to his skull. Using the speed and dexterity he had acquired at Chiq'aq as a warrior priest, he performed a backflip, letting the man run harmlessly by, then kicked him in the butt. The corsair having lost his balance, slammed his face against the edge of the table, then fell heavily to the ground, groaning and holding his bleeding nose.

The green mohawk attacked next, tearing a leg out of a broken chair and began swinging it. The Onkalot efficiently avoided all blows at different heights and angles, and when the man charged more passionately, he began to run away, jumping on tables on four limbs or throwing dishes and objects under his feet. Finally, he whipped the wooden club from the man's hands, and they started fist fighting.

Aggroteh was hit in the nose so strongly that his head snapped back. In retaliation, having thrown his gloves on the nearest table, he left five bleeding claw wounds on his adversary's face.

"Kill that fucking cat!" wounded, he shouted to his companions.

The man with the broken nose, cursing violently, began to rise from the floor. He kicked brutally and mindlessly some man passing by and cursed him. The person hammered in the kneecap turned out to be an as big as Forkis, bald, beefy from steroids neo skinhead in black leather clothes. She growled and looked at the corsair with hatred.

The bartender had his hands on the counter, ready to crouch and cover himself at any moment. He carved in his mind that if his inn wasn't smashed to matchwood that evening, he would blow off political correctness and somehow change the rules so that members of conflicting social groups weren't together at the same time.

The space pirate, wounded in the nose, flew a few meters and fell on a wooden table, shattering it into two parts. The companions of the victim, who was bleeding more profusely from the nose and now from the cut on his forehead, transferred all the anger from the Onkalot to the neo skinhead - who hadn't come here alone.

The brawl in the air erupted as quickly as it spread across the room. The presence of the Onkalot was merely an igniting spark for the drunk representatives of various subcultures. That evening at 'Stanislav Skalski' could be classified as exceptional, as it rarely happened that members of several culturally, morally and behaviorally different groups gathered in one place and time. People who wanted to keep their set of teeth full went outside. Those who tried to calm the drunk or sober but furious company asked themselves to become living projectiles or moving shields for flying objects.

"Come on, let's help him." Tom Lewandowski, who felt a sympathy for the humanoid jaguar who was fighting and cracking scathing jokes, encouraged his companions with a gesture of his hand. They nodded, shrugged and charged at the two privateers who wanted to attack with broken bottles Aggroteh, defending himself with the stone knife.

The rebels grabbed the pirates not seeing them from behind, kicked the bottles off their hands and pushed them towards the already shattered tables.

"Thanks for your help, but now you'll also get hit," Q'ualel said to Tom, who stood behind him, waiting like an anthropomorph to receive more blows. "I'd like to talk to you."

"No problem. You wanna talk now?" The rebel replied in a casual tone. Q'ualel embraced some corsair attacking him. Seeing Tom's meaningful expression, he turned the man towards him so that he could punch him on the tattooed face. The intruder slumped to the floor.

"I would prefer at a drink," Aggroteh smiled, "but you can see for yourself that the circumstances are not favorable."

"You fight great."

"Thanks."

"What's your name?"

"Call me Aggro."

"I'm Tom."

They both fell flat as a bench flew towards them.

"Holy shit, what a rumble. I've never seen one like this here," Tom said as they crawled to the fireplace, with objects flying over them.

Aggro roared like a jaguar as someone brutally tugged his tail, causing him to lose his balance. He was shifted a bit before he outthrusted his claws and caught them on the point of contact of the flooring strips. Mumbling threats, the thug picked him up by his uniform, then pinned him to the bench with his back to it. A cutlery knife blade flashed in his hand. Q'ualel quickly bit the exposed hand, having shifted his head to the side before the knife reached his throat. The opponent cried out in pain, grabbed his hand, having dropped the tool. The humanoid jaguar struck the man with his forehead, lunged at him, and they both flew onto the opposite table. Aggro stood with his hind leg on the man's chest and, growling, brought the obsidian blade to his heart.

"You want furballs in your old age, huh?" He grunted. "Did you have a concrete teddy bear in your childhood?"

He had to jump away quickly, because from the left side was charging thug, red-faced from alcohol, screaming. Aggro sighed nervously as he grabbed his clothes. The man staggered and almost fell.

"Good idea. I propose to take an even greater run, and the wall will be found for sure," having said that, he sent the juicer ahead with a thrust and kick in the buttocks. But before he hit the wall with impetus, he was stunned with a flying bottle and lay unconscious on a bench. The glass shards hit Aggroteh as well but didn't harm him through the uniform and fur.

The group of androids awaited by the increasingly irritated bartender burst into the room. They also were scolded before they managed to deal with the company and throw all the participants of the brawl in front of the premises.

Tom and Q'ualel made no resistance as a taurine android more carried them than led out of the room, then slung them easily through the front doorway.

"It's time to ventilate the exoskeleton, gentlemen," he said flatly, and turned back for another batch of adventurers.

The humanoid jaguar and man looked at each other's cuts and scrapes as they lay on the birclone driveway - made of organism-friendly synthetic plastics, apart from the admixture of clay. They laughed, but then grew serious.

"I hear you have a business with me," said Tom. "What could an Onkalot want from a human?"

"I'm looking for someone." Aggroteh glanced at the entrance to the bar, from which more wild guests were flying out. "Someone who took part in your last battle with the Kiritians." The surprised rebel looked at him more closely.

"Who exactly?"

"Sorry, but I can't tell you. I just want you to give me the exact location of the battle. Could you do that much for me?"

"I can. It's no secret anyway. Are you here with someone?"

"No, I have my own ship."

"Then I'll send you the bearings."

Half an hour later, after analyzing the data received from Tom, Q'ualel was studying a human-drawn holographic map of the space sector where the Eos Endymion skirmish took place. He compared it with a map of the Ancient Onkalots, and he put together all the information he had obtained about missing - possibly killed, as many believed - Forkis since leaving the Schindler family. He made an instant analysis of the facts. He frowned, looking at a specific planet on the map.

"Then Aj," he murmured. He knew the commander of the Immortals too well, so he couldn't have been wrong on that point.

Chapter VIII
Lost Hope

"It was so stupid ..." Anna sighed on the verge of audibility. She didn't want Forkis, who was sitting nearby, to pick up nuances in her behavior that showed that she was still shaky after the recent episode. However, when she glanced through the cascade of hair at the bloody Kiritian, she noticed that he was grinning under his breath, skillfully dressing the slices of obtained meat with the knife. He's been smiling a lot lately. Much to her annoyance, all the smirks seemed indulgent, as if he had seen Anna as a spoiled child.

"I acted like a bitter and twisted bobbysoxer," she said to the flames that buzzed merrily in a fire in a stone circle in the center of the room with the damaged ceiling. Glowing dust rose towards the stars. Anna contemplated the past, remembering all the times she had spent with the Kiritian when she had made a fool of herself.

Forkis stopped removing fur, tendons and fat from a huge slice of meat to watch his next culinary creation.

"I don't deny it. But I have no grudge against you. On the contrary. If it hadn't been for your escape and meeting this beast, it would have been you who would have lost their life," there was a sharp tone in the usurper's voice, his hazel eyes flashed unpleasantly. "It's not easy to catch something big here. Syncars are poisonous, and smilodons, I don't touch."

Anna felt uneasy. She looked at the man with a searching gaze.

"I don't understand."

"You understand perfectly. You are not stupid, although feisty. Often you do something first and then you think. You know for what, only and exclusively, I have kept you from the beginning."

The rebel swallowed.

"Could you ... could you really ..."

"Eat you," he finished. As every Kiritian, he didn't hold back from anything. Telling the truth, even shocking one, came naturally to him. "I could. I love human flesh." He gave her a cruel smile, ghastly even because of the tylakosmil's gore with which even his face was dirty. In addition, he ostentatiously licked his lips so that Anna flinched and looked away. "They say that the way to a man's heart is through his stomach."

"You're crazy. Sick. It's cannibalism! It must be healed."

"Isn't it abnormal to die in the name of rules devised by agitators stoned on fanciful ideals?" Forkis snorted. "Mere law of survival, dear Anna. The oldest and most powerful of all living creatures, which will always prevail in unfavorable conditions, even when they instill in you pseudo-legal, artificial civilization norms from the first days of your life. It's genes, Anna. Code of the universe, not of man."

"You're talking like some drunk sectarian again. And you are insolent due to that directness."

"So, you would prefer a lie that makes you happy?"

"I didn't say that." The girl touched the shoulder dressing made of a fibrous stems' lint, under which the skin was being warmed by a specific consisting of saliva, a cobweb and fragmented otomabo, carefully prepared by Forkis.

The Kiritian pointed with the blade at the sticks with pieces of meat beaded on them, which hissed by the fire.

"Get yourself one, they're already roasted." Without cleaning the knife of blood, he reached to his stick with it, speared it, blew on it several times, put it in his mouth, chewed and swallowed. "Be my guest. It tastes good."

"You know I'm a vegetarian."

"We've had a deal." He wiped blood off his face with a hairy moss.

"You made it up. I didn't approve anything. It can hurt me anyway."

Forkis looked at Sandstorm with pity, smiled meanly.

"And rat soup, you ate like a horse. And you even praised it. Whoops ... I wasn't supposed to tell you this."

"What ...? Don't tell me you added a rat to the mushroom soup?!" Anna jumped up from her seat, she felt immediately nauseous. She leaned down and rested her hands on the empty pedestal.

"Rat, no, but I made an essence of it. Stop making a scene."

"How could you?!"

The Kiritian burst out laughing. He laughed louder, the stronger the grimace of indignation on the rebel's face became.

"And you died? So, meat doesn't hurt you."

"You carelessly ignored my choice, completely disregarding what I might feel afterwards! Who gave you the right to decide anything for me?!"

"Oh, what a pugnacious she-wolf. Well ... The answer, as always, is as simple as for all your twisted questions," Forkis grew serious, or at least tried to look like that. "I'm stronger, much bigger, more intelligent, I have experienced and seen more. And so on and so forth. So, I am the law. Besides, you didn't forbid me to use spices as I wanted."

"Are you making fun of me?"

He swallowed another large shashlik, whole this time. Anna was surprised that a human could do it at all. She remembered that sick dream with the firefly again.

"Eat. You won't endure for a long time, eating mushrooms." Sandstorm grabbed the end of the stick, brought it closer to herself, but grimaced.

"I can't."

"It was customary among Onkalotian hunters that each of them had to eat some of the prey they had hunted together. It forged tribal bonds. Failure to do this ritual is offending the rest of the warriors. And you don't want to make me angry, do you?" He winked at the girl. He went back to his interrupted work on supplies.

"Why do you allude to humanoid jaguars so often? You like them, yeah? This is why you have the Onkalotian middle name."

"I just admire them. They are, or rather were, the most organized society I have dealt with, in which every member was important. Virtually everyone was altruistic, thought first about others, then about themselves." Forkis put the next batch he had prepared on a pile. He started on another one. "By the way, I'm surprised by the vegetarianism of the killer."

"I'm not a killer, don't call me that."

"You are, and so am I. We are cut from the same cloth, Anna. Except you are going in a little white wobbly cart while I am going in a black, big and stable one that will never fall off the tracks. Unlike yours. You can change the colors naturally; I've used them to illustrate the opposite."

"My cart is as stable as yours," she said thoughtlessly, feeling offended.

"Which you showed at the syncars, and then escaping from the sanctuary." He glanced at her from under his eyebrow. "If it hadn't been for me, the cart would have derailed and quickly fell into the abyss."

Unfortunately, he was right. Anna chose to pave over this matter. She didn't want to argue and be perceived by Forkis even worse. For some reason, she wanted him to think of her as a useful person.

"I try to avoid meat," she said. "I feel sorry for the animals. I have some inhibitions. Blockades unrelated to upbringing or provisions, the breach of which means that I will later agonize over guilt. Something like you called it, the code of the universe. I have no influence on it."

The Kiritian finished his work. Instantly, he reached for something behind his back. Anna felt anxiety tugging at her lower abdomen as she saw the tail of a struggling mouse in his hand. Having known the usurper well enough, she understood immediately what was happening.

"I prefer not to hold back." Forkis lifted the mouse and opened his mouth wide.

"No!" Anna rushed towards him, took the rodent from his hand, then returned to her pedestal. "No ..." she repeated softly.

To her indignation, the usurper started to laugh, clapped his hands.

"You fell for it. I wish you could see your reflection. Your face was insane!"

The rebel narrowed her eyes menacingly.

"Do you enjoy it? You guys are like big boys. All of you!"

"Anna Sandstrom, think! Why would I eat scraps when we have countless kilos of better-quality food?" The dark humor quickly left the Kiritian who sighed broodily. "Anyway, I prefer to skip mice."

Letting the curious rodent walk over her hands and tickle them with constantly moving whiskers, Anna looked more closely at the interlocutor.

"Why? It's something like those smilodons?"

Instead of answering, he unfastened the notorious capsule chain from around his neck. He handed it to her.

"Open it."

The rebel put the mouse on the stones, which immediately vanished into the meanders of the temple. She opened the metal capsule, twisted the knobs in opposite directions, and almost dropped its contents.

"It's a bone." She looked questioningly at Forkis.

"That's right. This is the thigh bone of a mouse that contributed to my success."

She looked at him as if he had lost his mind.

"How did the mouse contribute to your success?" Fortunately, the question sounded serious.

"Sorry, it's a private matter," Forkis said even more seriously. The girl watched the reflections of the flames dance across his impassive face. "I can't say that to you or Necron, my most trusted lictor, or any other friend."

"Can I at least know the reason? It's not fair that you start something, interest the recipient, and then dummy up."

"Everyone has their own secrets that they keep. And, believe me, my secret would be a shock to the entire Zodiac Universum." Forkis looked at her with a gaze she had never seen in him before. She couldn't tell what it actually meant. "Also, for you."

"As you wish. I respect other people's secrets. So, let's end, assuming that it is your amulet." Sandstorm handed the chain back to the Kiritian. She smiled. "People say different things about this item."

"For example?"

"That inside is the essence of your power. And when it is destroyed, you will fall off your pedestal."

"This cannot even be called a conspiracy theory."

They both laughed for a while. Anna tossed the logs into the fire.

"Anyway, it's no wonder." Forkis took the chilled coal and crushed it to dust. "Where knowledge ends, there are fear, uncertainty and ... ambitious explanations." He smiled as he saw the girl nibbling on the shashlik, maybe not very eagerly and wincing, but still. "And you see, it's not a blockage."

She shrugged.

"By the way," he added. "I think I know what your problem is."

Uncertainly chewing on the crispy skin, Sandstorm glanced at her interlocutor with a passing interest. She perked up as she heard the next words:

"You are simply afraid of your own feelings, that is, of a certain category of them. You think it's something wrong and try to suppress them with anger and aggression."

"Let's drop the subject," she whispered so softly, lowering her gaze that the flames popping briskly could be considered a shrill cacophony compared with the hissed words.

"Of course. I have my secrets and you have yours." The smile appearing on Forkis' face widened suddenly. "Let's move on to the prizes." Having reached with his arm behind a block of stone against which he was leaning his back, he outthrusted from the shadows a brown, mottled fur stripped from the back of the tylakosmil. He got up, walked over to intrigued Anna, and placed the skin on her hands as she put the stick away. At first, she held it stiff and unsteady, but then she pressed her fingers into the soft fur. "Here you are. Soaked, fleshed, smeared with preservative plant pulp."

Sandstorm got up. Holding the skin by the corners, she unfolded the rest and looked at it with undisguised delight.

"Not bad."

"I don't think you need me again tonight," Forkis said, suppressing a smirk. "If you want, there is also this."

She became speechless when the prepared skull of the predator baring its huge fangs appeared on the usurper's hands. Anna was surprised that he had obtained these things when she had gone only to nap. She wondered where he had learned to dress animals, since food was commonly artificially produced or bought.

Forkis snapped with its rattling mouth in front of her nose, making the girl jump back with a playful squeal.

***

She saw the glowworm again when she was lying, alone and naked, in the sarcophagus on the skin of the tylakosmil. Sitting on the edge, the firefly stared at the rebel with thousands of independent eyes, making up two huge ones.

"You want him, baby. You want to make love with him," the insect croaked brazenly with its comic, thin voice. And then he started laughing nasty.

"Shut up." Anna threw her arm forward, trying to kill the insect with her fist, and that woke her up. The same move, she made in reality. She must have fallen asleep as she had sat in her alcove, enjoying the warmth of her new, large coat.

The specter's words terrified her more than if another syncars had hung over her head.

***

Forkis carried the freshly prepared food to the basement, where he had set up a locker in one of the darkened recesses, then left the complex. Anna, who wandered around the sanctuary, unable to fall asleep, saw him step outside. She thought he must have gone to gather another batch of wood and medicinal plants. She became concerned when she heard strange noises coming from the garden. She decided to carefully examine the source of the noise.

As she came closer to the entrance, clasping the haft of the knife in her hand, murmurs similar to those made by the tylakosmil came to her ears. These were, however, quiet and gentle, though more bass, as if their fully calm owner had been pleased with something. For example, hunted prey.

At first it occurred to the girl that the predator surprised and killed Forkis. Shaken, she immediately trotted down the last stretch of the corridor, forgetting about caution.

She almost jumped out of her shoes when the Kiritian, without making the slightest noise, appeared unexpectedly on the landing of the stairs leading to the garden.

"Forkis ..." Anna put a hand on her chest and breathed a sigh of relief. She gave him an angry look, making a face like 'I almost got a heart attack because of you.'

The Kiritian smiled at it.

"Come on, you'll see something nice. I'm sure you will like it. You can hide it." He pointed at the knife.

Sandstorm followed the usurper uncertainly across the garden. She stopped abruptly and tensed her muscles as she saw a two-meter-tall, tan saber-toothed tiger shuffling its paw across the ground by the pool. She looked at her companion with concern.

"Don't worry," said Forkis. "Look."

He approached the huge animal, raised his hand and boldly began to scratch it behind its ear. The predator, eager for caresses, purred throatily, contentedly closed and opened its yellow eyes with horizontal pupils. Finally, it lay down in the sphinx position, then rolled over onto its back, revealing a white belly, curling up its massive front paws like a dog. Its reddish brindle tail swept the ground steadily. Forkis put a piece of meat into the animal's mouth and, kneeling on his knee, started scratching the cat's fluffy throat.

"Go ahead, try it." With gestures of his hand, he encouraged Anna to come closer.

"You must be crazy."

The girl thought for a long time, finally she was convinced by the trust and attitude of Forkis, who wouldn't have exposed himself unnecessarily. Nor did she have a feeling that he would have lured her here just to sic that hairy beast on her. She crouched down, extended her hand fearfully. She gently touched the thick, warm fur with her fingertips, then began to stroke the animal more boldly, not seeing any disturbing reactions from it. A smile grew on her face like in a carefree child who discovered a place for fantastic games.

"How did you do that?"

"I bribed her a bit." Forkis handed the she-cat a second portion of meat. "It's partly a merit of my ancestors."

"What do you mean?"

"The smilodons of Aj obeyed them. Unlike the tylakosmils. The latter couldn't be tamed in any way, they remained wild."

He amazed her once again. She didn't understand much of it. But seeing that Forkis didn't want to dwell on the subject and responded curtly, focusing more on the animals than his family, she wasn't going to be nosy. She already knew him well enough to know that he cut some matters at a standstill, especially those related to his mysterious past.

"And now ..." The Kiritian spoke aloud some incomprehensible word, probably in Onkalotian language. The female rolled over, took the position of the Sphinx again. Forkis straddled her back. "I would like to prove to Miss skeptic, who tried to see for herself that there were no people in the area, but only a certain completely mismatched pair of survivors." He extended his hand invitingly.

"You mean ... we're going to ride this thing?" Anna pointed to the smilodon, which slapped her own nose with the broad tongue, then purred delightfully, which sounded like she was pouting.

"Exactly."

Forkis grabbed Anna's wrist, not letting her think further, and with a yank, persuaded her to take a seat behind him. Surprised, she shyly embraced his waist; The Kiritian grabbed a bunch of long hair that was densely growing on the cat's shoulders.

On command, the smilodon jumped up from the ground, easily lifting the two adult people. Forkis directed her, pulling her fur and saying strange words, towards the gate in the wall.

Sandstorm, clutching, gradually began to relax as they left the miles behind. She was getting accustomed to the female's steady movements, her powerful muscles undulating under the thick skin of her back, her shaggy tail with a ragged brush slapping Anna's arms and back again and again. A serene smile crept onto her face.

"Hope you know what you're doing."

"Hold on tight, it's gonna shake."

"What do you want to do?" She asked confused.

Forkis didn't answer, hit the sides of the animal with his shoes and screamed. He felt the small hands gripping his waist tighter; the girl inhaled loudly.

The smilodon roared as if in response to a command, then rushed forcefully into the open space. A faint smirk passed over the Kiritian's face as Anna clung to him tightly like a koala baby to its mother. And then she attacked him with an avalanche of pleas and warnings: that he would pay the price, that she was going to puke, that she was about to fall, that she would kill herself, that her ass hurt, that the cat should have slowed down immediately, which Forkis dismissed with more and more intense, spontaneous laughter. He also incited the animal to run faster.

The night they raced with the speed of a young hunter chasing a prey wasn't very warm, but it was cloudless. Two moons hung overhead, sufficiently illuminating the barren countryside. They lost sight of the walls of the sanctuary much earlier, and soon after that, of the forest and both crash sites of the machines. They found themselves in an endless semi-desert swarming with fanciful boulders and rocks.

The animal raced on breathlessly, genetically adapted to long, exhausting chases. Her powerful paws created fountains of sand as they hit the ground hard, and in the more steppe regions they threw out chunks of cracked earth. They were both in good spirits already. A joyful scream sneaked out of Anna's throat; she began to wave her arm without fear of falling. It was the first time she'd ever ridden any animal on the back, and she loved it immensely, especially the wild wind blowing on her face - an unfamiliar feeling when you constantly flew behind a canopy. She liked it even more than lonely sallies with the White or simulated fights with Beliar. She wasn't entirely sure if it was a matter of cutting-edge entertainment or company.

"And? I didn't lie to you, saying that we were alone here." Forkis said to his companion long after the night was fully ripe. The female stamped slowly along the temple wall, carrying them both towards the gate.

"I believed you from the beginning, and besides, telling the truth is your domain. Thanks, Forkis, for this nice trip." Anna tried to shape with her hands her carelessly spiky hair into a civilized hairstyle.

The Kiritian smiled to himself. He directed the she-cat back towards the garden, patted her above the shoulder blade in thanks for the daring journey.

***

The slight warming following the frost period was usually accompanied by strong winds that continued on Aj for most of the year. A dust storm began in the morning and turned out to be so strong that Anna had to stay in the sanctuary. She knew her surroundings well enough now that she could help Forkis with fetching wood and lichen with her eyes around her head. They didn't think about any serious plans. It made more sense to stay in the conspicuous building than to attempt the crossing of Aj, for then they might have missed the search party that the Kiritian believed would surely arrive sooner or later. Besides, scanning a terrain from above had been disturbed on the planet more than once.

The gale didn't subside until the end of the day. It raged also for the next ones, turning the air into an orange ordeal full of matter, but as soon as it weakened, they left the Bone Scepter. Forkis went towards the forest to find wooden elements that could be used to repair the broken thermal baths, while Anna went looking for mushrooms and lichens, the supply of which was depleted. These grew in colonies among the rock massif several kilometers west of Ch'amiya B'aq. According to Forkis, the place was safe, because a plant with a predator-repelling smell had its stand there.

Sandstorm didn't listen much to his disquisition - she thought about their recent relationship, and the rest of her attention, she focused on his slightly crimson eyes. She nodded when he finished, but she couldn't remember why. At first, Forkis was against splitting up, but Anna was stubborn and convinced him that she would be prudent, besides she wanted to walk a little alone. The Kiritian gently bent his promise and learned Sandstorm's thoughts, thanks to which he wasn't afraid that she would make another escape attempt. The girl, moreover, acknowledged this uncomfortable fact that without the Kiritian she wouldn't be able to do well on the planet for too long.

The rock massif consisted mainly of carbodur, a highly ferromagnetic compound that additionally disrupted electronics, and even caused system failure at high concentrations of elements. Anna's shoes took on a rusty color from carbodur filings mixed with sand as she walked with the amphora towards the monuments standing close together. When a stronger wind blew for a moment, she choked - so much of it swirled in the air.

Before she sank into the labyrinth of rocks, she stood for a moment and listened, not wanting to get naively in trouble again, especially since the pool of luck might have already been exhausted for her. However, she didn't catch anything disturbing with all her senses. As she plunged into the meanders, even fifty meters high, curved like the fingers of a hand holding an apple, her anxiety decreased. The worst thing that could happen to her turned out to be a whistle of wind announcing another spurt of matter. In the clearances she saw a growing wall of sand, gravel, and rusty carbodur torn from the rocks. She felt brushes against her hair. She looked up; it started raining. Forkis had explained earlier those rains on Aj weren't toxic to humans. But she had to hurry anyway, because dust storms at this time of the year blew up one after the other.

Searching for a colony of mushrooms on the boulders and walls, she kicked the ribs of a skeleton covered with sand. From the jaws of its massive skull protruded fangs. "It must have been one of the big cats that inhabit the planet," she thought. I wonder why it had died. Did it have anything to do with the plants that Forkis had sensitized her to? But then he would have forbidden her to come here. Maybe they hadn't been here for a long time because she hadn't noticed a single one so far? She walked cautiously on, leaving footprints in the sand sticking to the soles of her boots.

She found no mushrooms, in the amphora had rested only a lousy bundle of green lichen so far, looking like matted hair pulled off a brush. But Anna discovered something interesting. One wall was covered with a fluff fungus, similar in appearance to cauliflower, except that it was purple. A ledge above gave it a cover against the rain, which had stopped pouring down anyway. Sandstorm would have loved to explore it with a stone she was holding, but she chose not to risk it. She set off on further searches, which she would have to finish soon, as the wind was getting more and more vicious.

Apparently, the fungus decided to persecute her, because she stepped in the same species, covered with sand, as soon as she turned behind a monumental boulder. Spore haze flew into the air like fan-treated flour. They flew into the woman's nose before she could cover it with her sleeve, and when she had a fit of sneezing, she opened her mouth for a moment and felt a stinging taste on her tongue.

She stopped dead; the amphora flew from her hands. Anna was getting weaker and weaker from breath to breath, she felt a strong prickling in her temples and lungs. Her pulse sped up rapidly and she was shivering. Suddenly panic overtook her. An incredibly strong urge to run, over which she had no control, led to her crashing with a rock and sliding unconscious at its foot.

***

The music in the cockpit had brightened Corporal Tsar Seymour's search from the moment he had separated from a devemer squadron. This is what Kiritians called small combat or civilian transporters, with the best masking technology at the Zodiac Universum, which were visually stylized as Ordovician cephalopods. The achij, who had been kiritianized eighteen years earlier, was singing every now and then to the words of a vocalist from Calvary, a planet of flourishing crime, but also many interesting talents. He, too, came from this globe circulating in the Capricorn Universe. However, he couldn't say whether he liked the notes of Calvary because they emanated an aura that attracted the listener, or simply aroused nostalgia. It is of little importance anyway. Seymour was a free spirit, so he could always and everywhere kick back, which pissed off his unit more than once. Beautiful women, drugs and strong impressions were all he wanted in his life. He had changed since traumatic family events of his foggy past, and when he had become a Kiritian, the word 'seriousness' had ceased to exist in his vocabulary. Permanent relaxation, however, didn't prevent Tsar from being an exemplary, albeit cruel, achij. From practically every action against the enemy, he took the head of the defeated, which he then prepared. He boasted that he had over a hundred skulls in his apartment on Morascrik, occupying specially designated shelves. He hadn't tanked a single mission since joining the Immortals, though his beginnings had been difficult because of drugs. He had even risked being expulsed from the nation, but it had soon turned out that the man, stimulated by drugs, had worked more effectively than when sober. With time, the comrades-in-arms got used to their peculiar comrade with dark blond, almost red hair, always slicked-back, and medically modified red irises. They even liked him because he was able to relieve tension with his way of being and simple but accurate slogans. Seymour owed his place among the Kiritians to his father, who had had no better idea what to do with his son, who had never graduated from school, had had no job, and could only deal with pushing and brawls like many of the Calvary slum dwellers. He had dragged Tsar before Forkis' face almost by force. It was one of the few moments in the young man's life when he had felt fear, something strange, so different from the blissful satisfaction circulating in his blood. He had been afraid of the emperor, the infection with the super virus, in a sense the loss of his masculinity, and the future life that the army would give him, with the prospect of taking what he had loved. Tsar's physical and mental tests had fared perfectly, and he had been accepted. Thanks to an entraser implanted in the brain for the data transfer period, he had assimilated a great deal of Kiritian knowledge and many new things, but that hadn't changed his person. He had quickly realized that Forkis had given him the most beautiful gift that an ordinary man like him could receive - happiness to the end of time, unless someone put a bullet in his head first. Seymour didn't think about the future, he lived in the moment, forever perpetuated in the body of the twenty-seven-year-old, which, according to him, was the best time. He was afraid that if the super virus had reprogrammed his body at the age of sixty, he wouldn't have been interested in what he idolized now, and his life would have been like eternal boredom. General Velkee Vandringen was so old, and he was still pissed off, serious and puffy like a buffoon. And Seymour didn't shy away from anything that gave him joy, like unprotected sex - the Kiritians paid for their immortality with fertility. Diseases were not a problem for their medicine either. Tsar didn't have great needs. He considered himself happy because everything he needed was at his fingertips. And he didn't desire palaces, fame, or cartloads of uinals.

Waving his hand in front of a human skull attached to the lectern next to the control board and nodding his head, Seymour sang with a vocalist the chorus of one of his favorite songs, written in archaic English:

Don't worry, die happy ...
Don't worry, die happy ...
Don't worry, die happy ...

The devemer, in which he had taken off from an astro-carrier hangar, brought to be used in search for the Emperor, rushed over the desert of the planet Aj. Black as obsidian, the machine was adapted to the fast transportation of a maximum of a few people, but it was also ideal for searching for living targets from above, scanning the area with a thermo-inductor that interpreted temperatures, a bioctovisor allowing to distinguish a dead environment from a living one and also capturing biological traces, as well as a nuclo-inductor focused on searching human proteins. The planet's weather was fickle, but Seymour hoped it wouldn't interfere with the search. He knew little about Aj. He had been taken from the near sector of space, quickly instructed, then ordered to enter the devemer and fly with a squadron of twelve. The rest of Kiritians available in the area of Eos Endymion skirmish was busy exploring other sites.

Unexpectedly a powerful dust storm arose. Its forefront hit the canopy like a battering ram, bombarding it with boulders even the size of a fist.

"Isn't that frigging cute?" The corporal turned off the music. Increased flight altitude.

"Corporal Seymour, how are you? Report," accosted Sergeant Victor Shane on the squadron's private channel, to whom Tsar was assigned.

"Looks like sector seventeen is clear." Tsar crooked his lips in a smile, looking at the gale warring from each side of the devemer, completely obscuring the visibility. Scanners in a radius of tens of kilometers didn't detect life or a corpse. "There are small problems with the weather, but not serious enough to endanger me or the mission."

"Alright, report as soon as you notice anything. And remember, we're looking for the First Galactic Dignitary, so focus, achij, because the task is priority. Especially since an officer should be sitting in your place. We were unlucky to be in the region of the planet. Shane, over and out."

Seymour knew about Aj as much as he had learned at the briefing and couldn't have known that the detail of the presence of carbodur in some areas would cause him to tank his first mission in his life. He flew high above the remains of Forkis' ship, then of the White, detecting nothing. Carbodur was flying literally everywhere.

"I can't see anything in this crap," he gasped. "As if someone threw feces at the fan, right?" He asked the jawless skull staring at the corporal with the blackness of eye sockets. "What do you think, should we turn around and do the same lap in a while?"

Tsar glanced to the right. Finally, he noticed something - the outlines of a techno lithic building, even several, connected to each other. However, he quickly lost interest in them, trusting devemer's silent scanners. The whole area seemed deserted.

"What this time?" The transporter hit turbulence so strong that the pilot was thrown. After a while the machine began to lose height, and Seymour a good mood.

***

Using trawls pulled together by Anna, Forkis transported several boughs to the gates of the sanctuary, struggling against the wind that started to blow stronger on the last stretch of the road. Leaving ballast outside the doorway, he entered the building, spitting sand and shaking it out of his armor and clothes.

"Anna?!" He exclaimed loudly. The girl should have come back before him. He waited a moment and thundered again, but to no avail. He didn't care too much about the echo and the whistle of the wind that might have drown out his scream.

Searching the complex hastily took him two quarters of an hour. He was surprised that the absence of the rebel, which after getting food, he kept alive for pure entertainment - because for what else? worried him so much.

"Anna Sandstorm! You will regret it if you hear me and make fun of me!"

Angry, he went outside. For a moment he considered waiting in the sanctuary until the storm was over, because if Anna found herself a safe hiding place among the rocks, she would be safe, but a bad feeling told him to go west.

Fighting the gale, he left the garden and walked through the hole in the wall towards the rock massif. He called the rebel, though he knew the words were carried away by the wind; he tried to spot some traces in the sand. He did it soon, when he was already surrounded by rocks. Just because he knew what to look for, he found shoe prints on the damp ground.

The hurricane eased, but the sand mixed with carbodur still hovered within hundreds of meters. Forkis found the colony of tissue-free, toxic plants growing on the rock that Anna had looked at earlier, mistaking them for mushrooms. Considerable humidity neutralized the poison spread by the thallus, so the Kiritian wasn't afraid that the dispersed spores would harm him.

Soon he found the rebel covered with sand at the foot of the high rock.

"Anna?"

He knelt down and started to examine her. She looked terrifying. She was lying on her side, almost purple, with her mouth open, drooling, barely breathing. She twitched, her eyes open, with iris-sized pupils stared in terror at the void. She didn't react. Forkis knew this state of the organism very well - the last, pre-death phase of blood poisoning. Soon the strong toxin would start to dissolve the organs. The girl had the last minutes to live.

"You idiot, I warned you not to cross the eastern tunnel!" He hissed. He had been only slightly worried about the rebel earlier, but now he was terrified. He remembered he had an unused medical ampoule with him. He opened a cuisse compartment and found the gun, the other one was empty. The man slammed his fist against the rock with a roar. After all, he had left the container in the sanctuary!

The chances of saving the girl were small, the poison had been in the body for too long. However, the Kiritian took up a race against time and started running towards the building.

He stopped abruptly, as if a snare hidden in the sand had slammed on his feet. He took a noise at first to be the wind that blew through the rocky maze, but as it began to rise, Forkis had no doubts. Such sounds were made by flying machines without masking, whose pilots didn't care if they were noticed. Or even they wanted it.

A thin whistle suppressed by a thick casing.

A tiny, powerful engine.

Devemer.

He guessed well, judging by hearing. He soon saw the barely visible silhouette of the devemer high above, flying at the speed as if the crew had been searching for something. Or someone.

The Kiritians had come.

To take their emperor.

"Hey, I'm here!" In a sudden impulse, he began to wave his arms naively, although the cloud of sand and dust combined with the narrow clearance of rocks overhead effectively limited the pilot's visibility. Forkis wasn't sure the combat transporter's scanners would pick up anything, since carbodur was swarming everywhere and the air turned orange. He knew that he had to leave the massif as soon as possible and get out into the open space, maybe then he would achieve something. To his delight, the devemer began to descend. With this angle of inclination and speed, the pilot should have landed a few kilometers from Ch'amiya B'aq.

He was about to start running when the thought of Anna pinned him as effectively as the discovery of the transporter earlier. The girl would die if she didn't receive help immediately. Even if Forkis managed to reach the machine - if it did settle down - and take the first aid kit from there, he would waste too much time. Especially since he didn't know the cause of the landing: disruptions by carbodur or noticing the wanted man. However, in the case of the second option, the devemer would have landed vertically, and not descend gently for kilometers like an ancient plane. By running to the sanctuary for the ampoule, Forkis would still have had a chance to save Sandstorm, at least half, because it was not known if the drug would have worked on this poison.

Seconds passed, and the Kiritian stood torn in two. Why would have he actually saved the rebel girl? If she died, fate would settle the matter for him, and Sandstorm wouldn't have to suffer long, left alone on this forgotten planet while he returned to Morascrik. After all, he had planned to leave her here. Besides, wouldn't have he killed and eat her, if the food in the temple had run out? So, what drove him? Why was he wondering and wasting time at all? Compassion? Mercy? Maybe something else?

"Make up your mind, you big idiot!" He screamed at himself in his mind.

The devemer or Anna? Salvation or stupidity?

Damn it."

Forkis looked sadly at the empty sky, bounded by the clearing, and ran towards the sanctuary.

***

Seymour managed to control the flight and at the last moment turn on the reverse thrust, so the devemer didn't nose into the sand, but scrubbed with his underbelly for several dozen meters, losing speed. On-board diagnostics indicated that all systems were operational and that the energy levels were high, "so the cause of the disturbance must have been an extremely strange dust storm," the pilot interpreted. According to the scanners, the area was clear, at least in terms of the presence of living organisms, because the visibility behind the canopy was tragic, as if the devemer had lain at the bottom of a dirty, silted lake.

"It's completely empty. It's nothing here for us," the corporal said to the skull. "We have to get out of here."

The auto pilot didn't work, so Seymour had to switch to manual control. The anti-gravity drive, best for moving over the planet's surface, also couldn't be turned on. So, the corporal used the most primitive one, which was used to take off on the earth-orbit section, which, paradoxically, in such unfavorable conditions turned out to be the least unreliable.

After a short fight with the machine, Tsar managed to change the angle of the nozzles and rushed diagonally into the sky, leaving a swirl of sand beneath him.

***

The contents of the ampoule injected into the system saved Anna's life, although for the first moments after the injection,

Forkis was sure that the girl would give up the ghost. When her pulse and breathing stopped, he immediately gave her artificial respiration and restored her vital functions, but not consciousness. He carried her to the alcove and buried in the bedding.

The girl fell into a coma, he stayed with her for the next days.

One night, sensing a herd of smilodons following him nearby, the Kiritian went to investigate the area where the devemer might have landed. There was no trace of the sandstorm, over the wasteland, blue in the glow of the night, loomed the sky full of stars, without the slightest cloud. One moon was diminishing, the other was a narrow crescent on the way to become full. Even the wind didn't trouble, as if it had lost all strength from its recent attacks and needed rest now.

Forkis searched all night for the landing site, scoured vast swaths of land and found absolutely nothing. Even if the machine rested somewhere on the ground, the shifting dunes had long since covered the tracks. So that would be it when it comes to rescue. Achijes would search for him until they found him alive or dead, but they may have not returned to the same place if they thought they had combed it thoroughly. "I wonder if they took into account that the failure of the mission was caused by carbodur," Forkis considered. He had forbidden the exploration of this planet, so the Kiritians didn't need to have perfect knowledge about it.

"And all because of Anna Sandstorm. No," he corrected himself quickly, walking angry across the wilderness to the sanctuary. It was his fault, his decision. Wanting to vent some of his anger, he screamed and kicked a fustian.

Upon his return, he was still so annoyed that he wanted to destroy the reason for his stay on this planet. He took the military knife of still unconscious Anna, with the intention of slitting her throat. He stood over her, with his fingers gripping the haft so tightly that his knuckles were white - and that was it. He studied her tiny face, eyelashes, eyebrows, delicate body. The undefined blockade and the conflicting feelings that gnawed at him became too strong to kill the rebel. He wasn't willing to light the fires.

He went to the heart of the darkened sanctuary, where bioluminescence didn't reach. Only the points of stars visible above the ceiling of the damaged room gave poor lighting. Forkis' red-glowing eyes needed a minimal amount of it to see perfectly at night. He stood still for a long time, wondering about his future. He decided that if Anna recovered from the disease, he wouldn't tell her what had happened and cast in her teeth that he had to save her a third time, because she could have taken on all the blame and broken down. He observed that she bothered. And he didn't want to see her in bad shape anymore. He honestly didn't want to.

Chapter IX
Stockholm syndrome

After a few days, the girl regained consciousness. Forkis looked after her carefully as she lay in the alcove, indifferent to everything. Therefore, when she woke up, she was refreshed and regenerated. The Kiritian told Anna part of the truth: that she had hit her head, and he had brought her to the sanctuary. She thanked him, but for the next hours she retreated into herself and avoided his company. Only in the dark could she be persuaded to talk. However, the conversation was desultory, and there was an awkward silence between them. The girl decided to interrupt it first.

"It's all so ... incomprehensible. Yes, that's probably the perfect word," she said to Forkis as they lay on the temple's almost horizontal mansard late in the evening, looking up at the starry canopy and taking advantage of the warm, fresh air. Against the chill of the roof, they were protected by the tylakosmil's skin.

The Kiritian looked at the interlocutor.

"And specifically?"

Sandstorm shook her head.

"For example, the fact that I don't feel hatred for you anymore, and I should. She shifted her gaze from the stars to the man. "You're still an enemy to me."

Forkis smiled without cheerfulness. He looked at Anna for a long time before he replied:

"Another of your doubts has a very simple explanation. Would you like to know it?"

She propped herself up with her shoulders behind her, so that she was more sitting than lying. She sighed, shook her head, looking at the toes of her shoes.

"I have the impression that many of the things I have been taught are not real. I don't know what I want anymore."

"But I know perfectly well." Forkis also sat down. "You need a solid signpost, made of hard stone or dhurnsteel, not some paper sticks with arrows that will tip over with just any blast. Stones last for millions of years, and of dhurnsteel, we make warship armor."

Anna half snorted; half smiled. She wrapped her arms around her legs and put her chin on her knees. There was another longer silence, which this time was extinguished by Forkis.

"I can show you the right way," he said in a soothing voice, carefully filtering his words, "although it will be for you ... quite a dramatic experience. Shock. Upset. Unless you already know it but are afraid to take the first step on it."

As she hesitantly turned towards him, she noted that Forkis was looking at her meaningfully and affectionately.

"Would you like to?" He said with a slight emphasis.

Sandstorm was afraid. Of something, damn it, she was afraid. The truth? Forkis? His closeness? Her weakness? What the hell?! Yet she nodded. Once. Barely noticeably.

She was frightened, but didn't back away, when Xajb'a Kej moved closer to her and grabbed her chin. For a few moments he looked at her seriously in the eye, before he placed a gentle kiss on the girl's lips, as if he had tasted them. Finally, she brushed the second lieutenant's nose with the tip of his tongue. She noticed that he was struggling with himself - he wanted to do more, but hesitated.

Anna didn't resist, didn't seem surprised by the incident, as the Kiritian thought having looked at her after moving away his hand and face. He didn't give up only on a long gaze.

This time she moved closer to Forkis, put her arm around his neck and kissed him harder than he had her before. She didn't back away, pressed harder and harder, letting in this surprising moment completely act, every woman's secret, strongest desire - to be close to an alpha male. The one that the smilodons respected. She put her other hand on his back, and the Kiritian allowed her to do everything, not gaining momentum himself, so as not to scare the girl. At first, her behavior with the brakes released seemed amusing to him. He gently wrapped his arms around her waist and brought her closer to him. Anna kissed him more and more passionately and aggressively, sighing again and again.

Forkis, within which a flame of desire was suddenly kindled, barely controlled by him, pulled her onto the skin, and he himself was above her. He gave Anna a series of light kisses, even though he wanted to even attack her with them.

Sandstorm slowed down at one point. She looked at Forkis with frightened eyes full of disbelief, as if she had been roused from the hypnosis she had fallen into against her will. She moved an arm's length away from him, sat cross-legged, covered her face with her hands and began to sob even though she was trying hard not to let that happen. It was the second time in her life that she cried so openly. The first had happened quite recently, and it was because of Beliar, the second guy who had made her cry. Those tears, however, had been of a completely different kind - they had flowed from the broken heart of the young woman who had still believed in true, bookish love. The ones here arose from the contradiction of feelings that had just initiated a violent war within her. Anna had always successfully suppressed her sorrows with anger, demonstrating it even ostentatiously in her childhood so that it had never occurred to anyone that actually she had been sensitive. Now, however, anger failed her, it went somewhere, pulled a fast one with her, didn't have her back.

"Fork ... since when ..." she said more in her mind than out loud.

The Kiritian lay on his side, rested on his elbow.

"How do you know there's anything at all? Maybe I just want to show you your true path, because I have known mine for a long time and I'm constantly following it? And maybe it is different than you think?" He smiled, partly ironically, partly with happy satisfaction. "You're all the same. You imagine too much, you still overinterpret something."

Anna began to shake her head and wiped her eyes with her wrist. She wanted to punch the guy, and harder herself - for being stupid.

"It means that you at all ..." And she exploded: "Pig! You're a frigging bastard!" She pushed her hair back from her face with a nervous movement of her hand. Her nose was pricking, heralding another ripple of tears. Fortunately, anger was taking up the baton again. "I'm just a mascot for you! You play with me like with those poor basement rats you swallow alive! You think I didn't see this grunge?"

"You spied on me?" Forkis smiled broadly. Of course, he had to lick his lips. "Very ugly."

"No! I saw it by accident."

"You judge me too hastily, and such judgments are usually wrong. Especially when you wear blinders and have your brain washed with propaganda."

Sandstorm looked at him reproachfully.

"You're raving again. If you don't care about me, why you are doing it all?"

"Did I say that I don't care? You're insinuating something again." He raised an eyebrow. "Besides, there's not much to do here. We have to wait patiently for my people and deal with something in the meantime."

"How you love to tease me," she hissed, but already without emphasis. This time she wouldn't let herself be provoked.

"Alright, then cards on the table," Forkis said more sharply. "Before you forbade me to penetrate your memories and thoughts, I had been able to see a lot in them. Enough to say that you are quite an interesting and complex person. In the beginning, I had planned to kill you, as you know. Then, when circumstances changed, I thought to show you the true source of your eternal torment. A source that you may have partially figured out in the past, but you had no real friend with you to help you interpret your problems. You are like a volcano with a pipe crushed by a thick layer of rock. You don't explode but implode." Forkis sat down. Anna didn't interrupt him, listening with fear and fascination. "Do you know what would happen if volcanoes didn't erupt? The earth's crust would crack due to the build-up of pressure and magma. You, too, must vent the conflicting emotions that have accumulated in you for years, especially hatred, and you must do it in the right way. As befits not only a woman, but above all a flesh-and-blood soldier you name yourself. Otherwise, you will become a human wreck. For you, this vent has taken the wrong form, your lava should burst from the crater in a clean, uninterrupted stream, and not press into the crevices of the mind and accumulate in them as toxic intrusions." He moved closer to Anna, lowered his voice. "Only then will you regain your composure. And you know perfectly well that I am the key to freeing you from this disease. A key that you should use for its intended purpose, and not try to destroy it."

The girl slowly shifted her look from the tylakosmil's skin to the interlocutor, crossing her gaze with his. She couldn't decode him. Was he still having fun? Did he say honestly, or just wanted to vamp and seduce her? And then kill like many women before?

"But I can't," she whispered.

"Explain." The Kiritian stepped back.

"I don't know how to say it."

"Just tell me like a man what gnaws at you."

"You may get pissed off and do something to me."

"This stage is probably behind us." He smiled.

"Alright. So ... You are a war criminal, psychopath and cannibal rolled into one. A ruthless murderer, an oppressor of the planets. Perfect manipulator, you deceive even strong minds. You created a nation of monsters." Anger was being released in her again. "I, in turn, and my comrades-in-arms, fight against people like you. You murdered half the human population for no reason. For the mere pleasure of killing! And you dare encourage me to hang out with you?!"

"And everything is clear." Trying to keep his face straight after hearing such a stream of nonsense, Forkis stood up abruptly. Anna followed him with her eyes. He did get pissed, but not because of the invectives, but because of the young woman's naivety. "Your head is stuffed with ideological, terrorist shit."

"Am I wrong? Maybe you will tell me that you belong to a pacifist group and that you bring peace to people of good will?" Sandstorm said with undisguised amusement.

"Then, I'll be on the square."

"Go ahead."

"At first, I honestly admit, I was oriented to the total extermination of humanity, but then I began to conduct conquests wisely, craftily using the powerful base that was the Kiritians I had created. We attacked selectively," he began to walk in front of Anna, gesturing, "only those who could endanger us sooner or later. You understand: the tactic of destroying the weed when it is in the form of an ovule. We have reduced the underclass, leaving only a harmless group from the Capricorn Universe. We have overthrown governments that have been given dozens of chances to make humanity better and have not taken any of them, only caring for their own fat, self-righteous asses. From the politics of conquest and genocide, I switched to liberal totalitarianism, also known as hybrid, which prevails today. In this system, only those who ask for it die, don't follow the rules from above. Wise rules. We have everything under control. We have imposed restrictions on our globes so that no one can ever gain an advantage over us, but we allow civilians to live their own lives, including having a small army necessary for the internal protection of the colony. We don't need planets that are beyond our control. But wait a minute ..." He theatrically lifted a finger. "Now, maybe let's move on to the rebels for a change. Where did you come from in the universe arena at all? What do you know about the opposition, what synonym do you name yourself with?"

"We were created as a counterbalance to your expansive activity at the Zodiac Universum."

This time Forkis couldn't resist and laughed loudly before speaking again, becoming more serious.

"Bullshit. You come from the New Order Army."

"What?" Anna got up as well. "You're saying we are the descendants of global government representatives from Earth?! What utter nonsense!"

The Kiritian twisted his face in an indulgent smirk, amazed at the interlocutor's ignorance of her own history.

"You got something wrong. The NOA soldiers were an army operating under the command of the Illuminati who took over the Earth after series of wars. Using holographic projection, they simulated an alien attack on Earth that the nations believed in and then showed themselves as those who had driven the enemy away. They created universal surveillance and one global religion. Also, the super army, which carried out the entrusted orders flawlessly. The soldiers didn't even blink their eyes when they were ordered to slaughter children with their fathers and mothers, entire families, to turn cities to dust. But then appeared a new player who beat the old one - us. The NOA didn't want to assimilate with the Kiritians, we had conflicting visions and views. And in our place, no one was indoctrinated and oriented to mindless execution of orders, even suicide attacks. The NOA army had to go underground, because in the open field, facing us, it would have been turned into dust. This is figuratively, of course, because these people scattered across space. They regrouped over time, trying to make a larger cell. It was then that they began to define themselves as rebels, good fighters against evil Immortals, to make it sound heroic and patriotic in the ears of new generations forgetting the past. But the truth is that the weaker felon yielded to the pressure of the stronger one. Yes, Anna Sandstorm. You belong to the criminals too. Perhaps your ancestors were soldiers, but not in the service of the people, but of a government working against nations. The NOA began to take shape in France, many Muslims were enlisted, with roots in the Islamic State. And it was a terrorist organization that wanted to ideologically and forcibly conquer the whole world. You are not even an army these days, although that is what you call yourself. More like terrorists, a paramilitary group that has stolen equipment and technology from others in order to be able to fight with us. I saw what Commander Lacetti was doing near Eos Endymion. He can't fight a battle at all! He dispersed you, he shifted the responsibility of the command onto the pilots! It's a terrorist technique: target and destroy, you are unimportant. Anyway, it was not the first time that Lacetti urged a rebel to sacrifice their life for a cause, and he would probably do it again in the future."

"I didn't think ..."

The usurper didn't allow himself to be cut in on this time and ruthlessly pressed on:

"Did you know about the campaign in the Universe of Aquarius? About burning with the solar head, the surface of the planet Horix where many settlers lived? It was not the Kirtians who burned it, but you rebels, wanting to prove and show to the whole

Zodiac Universum how cruel we are! You put all the blame on us after we destroyed the weapons whose projects you had stolen from CERN on Earth. Because you must have heard the version that we supposedly destroyed Horix. The rebels started killing civilians and adding bills to our account, wanting on the one hand to get money and combat equipment, and on the other to gather as many supporters as possible for their cause, spreading propaganda about us. And the century-old massacre in the Dormo asteroid belt? Who arranged it?" Forkis spread his hands, then lowered them. "The answer is rebels, not Kiritians!"

"Stop it."

"Why? I'm just getting started, baby! Let's go further. 'Massacre of the Innocents', that is, the murder of the population of the planet CD4G5 in 2770. Now it is called the Planet of the Spirits, because it seems to be haunted. It is also the opposition, not the Immortals! The scenario was as usual: you needed weapons and raw materials to fight us, and the natives showed you the middle finger. And finally, Onkalots ..." Forkis assumed an angry face, such that Anna was afraid that she would get owned for the actions of her ancestors. She had no reason to disbelieve him, knowing the rule of Kiritian truthfulness, even though it all sounded absurd. "It was decades before the fall of the NOA, but both your ancestors and colonists destroyed this techno lithic community that was unable to resist humanity." He came so close to her that she could feel his hot breath on her face. "Yes, my lady, you annihilated almost the entire species! You took their lives, homeland, families, everything! And it was in the times when you were still called the New Order Army!"

"For God's sake, what do Onkalots have to do with it?! Why would you care about a mediocre, virtually non-existent species of slave? You admire them so much? I don't understand it."

The girl felt uncomfortable, even fear, noticing in Forkis' narrowed eyes an ominous gleam like in an angry murderer. As if he had been about to lunge at her and tear her apart with his bare hands. She took a step back, tripped over a wrinkle on the skin, and fell on top of it. She had gone too far on some point, but that was all she knew. "Slaves, you say ..." Forkis smiled, widely and menacingly. He leaned over Sandstorm, so close that she could see the details inside his open mouth. The upper tusks, too large for a human, were particularly noticeable. If it hadn't been for his human appearance, she would have sworn that a hungry smilodon was standing over her.

"No," she whispered, certain he wanted to do something to her.

"Then I'll tell you something," Forkis, however, began to speak calmly, as if he had been telling a child a fairy tale. Despite this, his closeness made the girl shiver. How is it possible that she just wanted to kiss him? "You come from the really lovely planet. Very special, because it is extremely rare in the universe. I'm talking of course about the Blue Planet from the solar system, from the Old Zone. No rocky globe, even after thorough, repeated terraforming, will be equal to the Earth, because there is simply no such second natural treasure in the entire cosmos. Rather. In terms of civilization, people started practically in line with Onkalots." He blew a flying pubescence with seeds off her hair which stopped there. "In their cultural development, the humanoid jaguars focused on the natural resources of the planet and the forces governing the cosmos, which they understood quite well and learned to use them widely. It was once said that the heart of the universe beat on Chulimal. On the other hand, the Earthlings chose a technology based on oil, coal and the atom. A few thousand years later, the world of Onkalots remained unchanged, clean and friendly to its inhabitants, and the Earthlings had to salvage themselves, escaping into space from the garbage they had created for themselves. So, a little more respect for those who know how to use wisely what has been given to them. And don't forget that the humanoid jaguars were not once slaves and a relic of the past, but it was you who destroyed them. Your ancestors."

"I'm not responsible for the mistakes of my ancestors."

"Yes, you're not. But what about the children who have become exactly the same as their forefathers? A variety of human minds cannot be changed, even evolution has capitulated. People who destroy everything around them, but themselves first, can only be brainwashed, have their memory reset to zero, and be taught everything anew. Or simply be eliminated."

"Maybe they were supposed to lose this fight?" Anna said in a whisper. "Onkalots, of course."

"Or maybe the inversion occurred?" Forkis replied enigmatically.

"I don't know what you mean. You often talk in riddles." She gave him an eloquent look, hoping he would explain the point to her. Forkis merely smiled friendly and froze in quiet silence. "By the way," she added, "you should make a list of the things that annoy you, and I guarantee that I would swot up on it."

He sat down next to Anna and began to stare at the sky, while she, embarrassed and subdued, couldn't take her eyes off the ground. Again, she came over as a know-nothing in front of him. Forkis' words shocked her. But had she had any influence on what knowledge the rebels had passed on to her? Could she justify herself this way? She had been among them from birth, she had trusted them, they had been an inspiration and a role model for her. She hadn't even dared to think that they might have distorted facts.

"This is Ajtojil, or Guardian Tohila in Onkalotian." The Kiritian pointed to one of the constellations, then moved his finger to the next. "That little collection over there, with the seven bright stars, is the Hidden Gorge, or Ewab'al Sivan. To the west is a piece of Tepew Q'ukumatz, the constellation of the Omnipotent Feather Serpent."

"Isn't that the name of one of the ancient earthly deities? I associate something. By the way, you know Onkalotian quite well."

"Yes, it's about Kukulkan. I already mentioned to you that the Nimja had made interstellar trips. Elements of their culture were taken over by the tribes from Mesoamerica, because they landed there, but also visited other places on Earth. An example is the Onkalot language, which on Earth was called *quiché*. Hence, so many similarities between humanoid jaguars and ancient humans, species that didn't come into contact with each other until the colonization of space."

"The Onkalotian culture must have orbited cruelty since the ancient Earthlings took over from them hecatombs and other genocidal rituals."

Anna quickly regretted such bold words, remembering Forkis' earlier outburst. Fortunately, he remained calm.

"I think you've mistaken Onkalots for Nimjas. What the latter really were like, nobody knows, but they were surely wise. Onkalots are generally a peaceful species, at least when compared to humans.

They exploited the surroundings, but so that they didn't destroy it and let it regenerate. They didn't sacrifice their own members, at least most of the tribes. What you are describing is invented by people who are eternally thirsty for blood. They feared Nimja members, gave them the hearts and gore of sacrifices to soothe their divine anger. They are just like that. It's their genes. Program. They kill even when they aren't hungry, and their lives are not in danger." Forkis leaned on his elbows. "And referring to the earlier point, which is probably bothering you." The girl looked at him searchingly. "I'm not probing you, like I promised, but it's all written over your face. Yes, that's right, I started to care about you. You, on the other hand, have felt the same for me as I feel for you, but ... for twenty years."

Hearing his words spoken so unexpectedly, practically carelessly woven into the tale, Anna felt as if she had been hit with something hard in the head. And strongly.

"That feeling," Forkis continued, "sheer fascination, you once took for a curse. You pretended it wasn't there. You would gladly tear it from your heart without finesse, if there was such possibility. More than anything, you tried to change love for hate. At the very beginning, I terrified you. I was nothing more than a children's nightmare, a demon that is stuck under the bed, hides in the closet of the dark room. Then that feeling matured with you. You finally started wanting me. You were delighted with my body, gaze, strength, even cruelty, success, the aura of power and authority accompanying me. You were afraid of this feeling. You thought it was something wrong, that it was a crime to love a Kiritian, slandering rebel honor, to which you admitted yourself. You thought the only way to be free from this curse would be to kill me." He made an amused face. Sandstorm, however, didn't notice it, for she was sitting still, with her head bowed and hair hanging down, like a scolded girl. Forkis saw to his satisfaction that she was trembling slightly, not least because of the cool wind that came from the north. "The nemesis wouldn't be gone though, oh no. Repressing your emotions is like a plaster for a fracture. It would have been even worse with time. An insatiable desire would have killed you in the end. Spirit, heart and at the end body," he whispered the last words in her ear. "If you need me, I'm at your disposal." He got up and walked away to a ladder he had built himself recently.

Anna remained where she was, deeply shaken, with a fire burning in her soul. And with those goddamn butterflies chugging along in her stomach. Damned Forkis was right as usual.

***

The next day, she decided to spend alone. Taking advantage of the lack of wind, sunny weather and quite warm air, she wandered aimlessly around the garden for hours, and for the next ones she sat on the roof of the sanctuary, sometimes changing position due to numb limbs or aching spine. Conflicting feelings and thoughts were constantly fighting in her mind. She didn't feel like anything. Most of all, she didn't want to see Forkis. She had to understand what she felt for him, think through many things, especially the indoctrination in her society.

The Kiritian called by her on the roof when the next day she was still stuck in her torpor.

"Eat at least a meal," he said louder, from the last rungs of the ladder. The girl sat motionless in the distance. "This time I made a

100% vegetarian dish. Only young shoots gathered in the forest." He placed the amphora with steaming soup next to the exit. He stared at Anna's profile for a moment, then shook his head disapprovingly, waved his hand carelessly, and began to descend. He thought maybe it was a good thing that he had never been in a relationship longer than a few months.

He went to the thermal baths, where he spent a lot of time under a lukewarm stream.

Late in the evening, Forkis was sitting in the basement on the catafalque, staring casually at the tylakosmil's skull in his hands, grinning in the light of the lamps, the bioluminescence of mushrooms and the abdomens of fireflies. He placed the parts of his armor and clothes next to the sarcophagus, remaining only in pants. He smiled at the stupid thoughts and slipped the huge skull over his head like a macabre mask. It almost fitted.

He heard the sound of footsteps, and in a moment, he saw Anna walking towards him. He got up.

The girl was silent, the seriousness got preserved on her face. She was wearing a thin T-shirt and pants, and on her shoulders rested the corners of the tylakosmil's skin held by her hands, similar to a heavy, flowing cloak. Anna smiled with the corners of her mouth when she saw Forkis with the terrible skull on his head. She went to the sarcophagus in which he slept, and carefully spread out the skin removed from her shoulders on the stone bottom.

The Kiritian raised an eyebrow.

Sandstorm stepped back, took the skull off him and placed it gently on the floor. She ran a fingernail over his bare, muscular chest, from the neck to the underbelly. She stopped her hand, grasping the bio metal belt. With the other hand, she grabbed

Forkis' right shoulder, stood on tiptoe, and placed a weak kiss on his lips.

In return, the Kiritian raised his freely hanging arms and pulled the girl towards him, clasping his hands on her tense buttocks. Anna threw her arms around his neck and entwined it tightly. She clung even tighter to Forkis, her kisses became more and more voracious.

The Immortal began to kiss, lick, and bite the Sandstorm on the neck and face. With a swift move of his arm, he deprived her of her T-shirt as she raised her outstretched arms high, then undid her bra and tossed her clothes onto the forehead of the skull lying at their feet. They began to embrace each other more and more stridently, making sensual sounds. They stuck their tongues into each other's mouth and caressed each other passionately. Forkis lowered himself more and more, first catching Anna's nipples with his teeth, then kissing her flat stomach for a long time, he stuck his tongue into the navel. In the use of teeth and tongue, he was a perfectionist. His eyes glowed like animal's. He put a lot of effort so that the passion of love didn't turn into a desire to eat a warm, living victim.

Anna, with a groan, pressed his head against her belly. Inadvertently, she unfastened the chain with the talisman which fell to the ground with a metallic clang. Soon after, the rest of the girl's clothes landed on it.

Forkis didn't realize that he was not carrying the amulet. For the entire universe had reduced itself to one goal, delicate, soft, and brittle, with its backs to him, which he had been wildly coveting for several days. A goal that finally came to him willingly itself, whom he didn't have to take by force, about which he had thought more than once. Finally, he would be able to satisfy the hunger he experienced in such a bizarre form for the first time in his long life.

He took the girl in his arms and laid her carefully in the sarcophagus, facing him, while he himself stood on all fours above her. They smiled sadly and gently to each other. The Kiritian leaned over and showered her prey with kisses, gentle at first, then more and more predatory, sometimes taking his blissful partner's breath away.

Sandstorm folded her arms around his neck. Every now and then she purred sensually as the strong, fleshy, slimy tongue moved from top to bottom and back again. Forkis took her hand to his mouth, as he had done after the fight with the tylakosmil, and began to suck it, the same he did with Anna's feet, which made her very relaxed. She lay motionless on the soft skin like an android with the battery removed, letting Forkis do whatever he wanted with her. Finally, she got into the bio metal belt of his pants, which they pulled off together and threw on the pile of things next to the sarcophagus.

Anna groaned, loud and lustful as he plunged into her like a rocket into the enemy ship's nozzle. It hurt at first: Forkis was much bigger and stronger than any of her previous partners. However, she quickly got used to the nuances of his powerful body and felt the happiest woman in space as he repeated the same movements over the next minutes, with varying intensity, driving her to screams, climaxes and jimjams.

"More. I want to feel you deep inside me," she whispered in his ear more with hotter, intermittent breath than with mere words.

"I'd like to have you inside me, too," he replied unexpectedly and emphatically. "Whole, tight and alive."

She became concerned as he opened his mouth above her head, as if he had been going to throw himself at her throat - and even swallow her alive if it was possible. She was aware of the danger when she came to him, she knew about Forkis' deviations, but she took a chance. She saw in his gaze brushed with infra-vision and marked with affect, a fight between man and something animalistic, alien and primal. Something that had been stuck in him for a long time, and which she completely didn't comprehend. Forkis struggled with his sex-induced paraphilia, and it was hard for him.

"Contain it," she hissed. She put her hand to his cheek. "You will win with it, Xajb'a Kej."

Forkis' real name acted as a keyword which unleashed the parts of the brain responsible for logical thinking, obscured by the tarpaulin of paroxysm. The warm, gentle touch of the dear person somewhat drove away the madness. After a minute, Forkis relaxed, sighed with relief. He won with his sick urge to fill his stomach with human flesh, at least he temporarily suppressed it. It meant salvation for Anna. However, he made a point of running his tongue down her face, brushing her with the warm air from his throat.

"I won't do this to you," he said emphatically, and kissed her forehead. "You're different."

He smiled lustfully and willingly complied with her earlier request, making the girl scream and groan every now and then. He didn't quit his course, even when she jokingly asked him to stop. For he knew that her body and mind wanted something different, wanted more, though Anna herself was beginning to mumble pointlessly, just like Corporal Tsar Seymour on drugs, recently one of the most recognizable achij among the Kiritians.

They made love all night long with breaks only for catching breath and brief rest of their sweaty bodies. Although Forkis was her fifth partner, Anna had never had a dozen orgasms in a matter of hours. She had also never felt so exhausted and so happy at the same time, pumped by the happiness hormones.

In the late afternoon of the following day, they renewed the sexual marathon with even greater fervor. First, they kissed and fondled in thermal baths under the streams of lukewarm water, then they moved to the third story, to a room with a view of the stars, where they made love in the open air. Forkis won the personal fight and made no more attempts to eat his partner; the obsession of Anna who from childhood had wanted to kill the First Galactic Dignitary was forgotten.

On the third evening they made love on the roof of the sanctuary, taking advantage of the fast-coming warmer days, drawing an audience of smilodons that stared up from the garden, often tilting their heads in astonishment.

"Forkis ... I have never been better in my life," Anna said for the umpteenth time. She had no more strength for further amours.

The man smiled jauntily, kissing her head tenderly.

"That's how it is done among Kiritians."

"I can't believe it."

"What?"

"Many things. But I'm especially bothered by the fact that I have turned from a rebel officer to a traitor ..."

"The question of treason depends on the point of view. The important thing is that you are, and finally stopped destroying yourself."

They lay naked on the unfolded skin, staring at the twinkling stars. The girl, muttering contentedly, laid her head comfortably on Forkis' broad chest, while he put his arm around her and began rolling her dark auburn hair with his fingers.

"Admit, which one am I in your life?" She asked.

"I don't know." Forkis sounded embarrassed. "After four hundredth I stopped counting." They laughed. "Almost all of the previous ones were lame vermin which thought it would achieve their own goals through the bed of the First Galactic Dignitary. Without scruples, honor, lofty prospects. Mere crap and that's it. Inane bitches for a few nights of entertainment. I checked each one's mind in turn for a hint of something of value, but all I found was slime, abyss and devils. I was convinced that people like them shouldn't be shown respect.

"And that's why you started killing them," she said uncertainly.

"Too."

"Many people have had problems with their partners, they were disappointed with them, but this is not a reason to punish them with death. You don't shoot a mosquito with a fighter."

"That's not the main cause of my paraphilia," he replied seriously.

"Will you reveal it to me?"

"I'm sorry, I can't." Forkis unexpectedly sat up, grabbed the girl's face with his hands as she rose with him. "Anna, fly with me to K'otz'ib'aja, our capital on the planet Morascrik. I will give you immortality. We will have all eternity to ourselves," he said in a lively voice, "as long as there is life, unless something kills us first."

"So, we're not going to be immortal." Anna smiled.

"A Kiritian cannot die of old age. Thanks to advanced medicine, the best in the Zodiac Universum, they easily throw off any disease, about which I already boasted to you. However, it is possible to damage their body just like of any living thing. Nevertheless, we will continue to expand throughout the universe. Burn, beat, murder, rape and plunder, slaughter wives, old men and children." If it had been just a joke, Anna would have responded to it with a pitying look, but she laughed a few times, realizing Forkis was sneering at the rumors about the Immortals. "But at night ..." He smiled lasciviously. "I promise that every night I will bring your body and mind to a higher state of consciousness, foretaste of which you already got to know. And rest assured, I can do much more."

Anna ran her fingers over Forkis' shapely chin.

"If it takes place without trying to eat me, maybe I'll reconsider your offer. Does it hurt?" She asked a few moments later, which Forkis spent caressing her cooling body.

"What, eating?"

She collapsed into giggles.

"Kiritianization. How is this done at all? This is a black hole in the knowledge of oderses. Is it secret?"

"No, but we don't put people right. It's interesting to see them spin theories about us, and we're not expansive. What had been once known, was forgotten by successive generations. Regarding the transformation. At the beginning, a potential candidate stands in front of me, and I penetrate their thoughts and assess whether they sincerely want to join our ranks and become a brotherly blood Immortal, or they do it as a spy, for revenge, conspiracy or dozens of other unwelcome reasons. It takes me the blink of an eye, it's like a flash. I personally choose each would-be Kiritian, as you probably already know. Technically, there can be dozens of people in the room for selection, amongst which I walk. Anna Sandstorm, however, already got this test over and I'm happy to say that she passed it successfully. Psychologically, you qualify to be a Kiritian. And believe me, one person in hundreds is fit. Such that won't go haywire with time, weighed down by the yoke of immortality, who is contrary to the biological and psychological program of man."

The rebel twisted her lips in a weak smile.

"Are you sure that I'm not a spy? That I will not betray? That in the future I will not change and bring down your nation? History knows many such cases."

"At the moment I'm sure of my judgment. And once you see for yourself what kiritianization and the nation can offer you, you will definitely not want to act against it. Coming back to the point. The candidate after the selection," continued Forkis, "goes somewhat on an internship. For weeks, months, even years, they belong to the nation, but are an oders. They become a full-fledged Immortal only when infected. Kiritianization is a process that is dangerous for the body, especially a young one, due to the developing immune system or a cytokine storm. The challenger must therefore be of the appropriate age or, when they are already an adult, choose their calendar age in which they want to be preserved forever. Admittedly, the disease - because immortality is nothing more than a disease - can be treated with serum, but now it's not about that. Our candidate is taken to a medical office, where specialists inject into their blood a super virus created by our best scientist, Dr. Maksimus Figam, on my recommendation. And it all really started with some kind of immortal jellyfish, specifically the idea itself," the Kiritian interlarded with a smile. A super virus, which we have never named, and whose colloquial term we have kept, changes the program of the body's cells, much like an ordinary virus. Except this one is different, made from the genetic materials of the most dangerous pathogens at the Zodiac Universum. The super virus infects all cells in the body, without exception, it undergoes reprograming, but it is not an infection in the negative sense of the word. Immortality is a side effect.

The disease causes the body to recover to the state it was in at the time of infection, on average, every five years. So, for example, if someone was forty years old at the time of infection, at forty-five their cells begin trans differentiation and regain the structure and properties they had five years earlier. The body is mortal in principle, but constantly renews itself, which prevents it from achieving massive cellular apoptosis. That is death from old age, calling a spade a spade. The initiated super virus itself is an individual pathogen, one cannot be infected with it in any way, because it gets attuned to the host's genome at the moment of first contact with the body. The pathogen before injection is called the inert form of the super virus. It's just a clump of proteins kept cool. You asked if turning into a Kiritian hurts. It depends on the organism itself. The rule is - this is not the norm, of course, but a statistical average - that the stronger the body, the more drastic the transformation is, because more perfect immune system will defend itself more fiercely. This is the storm I mentioned. In turn, still undeveloped system will be exposed to attack like a naked man being machine-gunned. That is why we don't kiritianize children and adolescents. So, one person will fall asleep after being injected with the super virus, which means that their transformation will be gentle, the other won't feel anything at all, and the third will start to writhe on the ground in painful convulsions and beg for a quick death."

"And how do your candidates want to be kiritianized? At what age?"

"The range varies, but mostly between twenty-three and sixty years."

"And the military ranks? How do you deal with brevetting?"

"So far, everything works fine. We don't give them away too quickly and for anything. Remember also that there is some mortality in our place, then there are vacancies. So, what is your decision, Anna Sandstorm? Do you accept my offer?"

"Give me some time, I need to think about it. This is not a choice that you approve with a click." Anna closed her eyes and lay down on his chest. She muttered contentedly.

"Alright." The Emperor began stroking her head. "You've got time until my lictors find me."

"Anyway, what's the difference between your lictors and dignitaries?"

"Now none, the words are synonyms. Lictors used to be close to me as security, over time they became the auxiliary elite who helped me rule. They act like subcontractors. This is how the Council of Dignitaries was created, the number of which changed over the years. I am the highest, as the First Galactic Dignitary, then there is the Second Galactic Dignitary, but also the lictor, or Necron, who sometimes replaces me. The Zodiac Universum covers the sectors of two galaxies, but the former title has been preserved and is still in use. Below Necron is the Council, the most important dignitaries. Then in the hierarchy there are other lictors. Below them are achijes, among which there are military ranks, civil or hybrid statuses, such as batab. As for achijes, it is a bit difficult for Oderses to understand it, but we also refer to each other using this notion regardless of the status. So, all Kiritians are achijes."

"Then your dignitaries have been looking for you for quite a long time."

"Maybe something stopped them. But they will come. I'm 100% sure about that."

"If I join you, I'll betray my people," Anna whispered after the time needed to take a deep breath, stroking Forkis' belly with her fingers. "What am I actually doing?" She smiled sadly. "You vamped me completely, you took my mind away."

"That's true, your feelings for me have a considerable influence here. You are very young, and in emotional matters you are still controlled by hormones. But the truth is, you've been wandering like a child in a fog all your life. You felt subconsciously that something was wrong with it, that you didn't do what you should have. Making a choice coming straight from your heart when nothing limits you, when you get to know the other side of the conflict, is no betrayal, but common sense. A decision that requires a lot of courage. Often you also have to go through tears, suffer a lot, spend years reflecting in order to finally find your place in the universe. However, there are many unfortunate people who are born and then die without finding their calling, or who are afraid to reach out to their designated enclave, and because of it suffer all the time that has been given to them. It is a real misfortune to waste the most precious gift - life."

Anna stood up and glanced at the interlocutor's face.

"You think my transformation will be painful? I'm Terran twenty-four, so I'm at the bottom of the limit, at the line of risk."

"I don't know it. So, I can't guarantee anything. It may be that way. You have a strong body, for fights in the air and space, they don't take just a runt from the street, not to mention the mental and physical health of the pilot, which must be perfect. What's going on?" Forkis smiled as the girl started giggling.

"We've done it many times, and without protection. If I get up the duff, you'll have to take me with you." Sandstorm rested her chin on her cupped hands. "Because you won't leave me here then, will you?"

"All Kiritians happen to be sterile."

"Seriously?"

"It's a price for immortality, a rent for nature. Something for something. You can't have everything. I ordered this myself during the recruitment of the first Kiritians. We are immortal, so what is the point of reproducing when our genetic material is indestructible? Of course, excluding situations where we die of random causes or in combat. Admittedly, our reproductive cells can be restored to their species efficiency, it is enough to make an injection, and, in an hour, we are again full-fledged women or men, but offspring among Kiritians is rare. The permission to have a child is given to the couple by me personally or the Council of Dignitaries takes care of it."

"You'll never cease to amaze me, Forkis."

"And since we can do it without any restrictions ..." The Kiritian gently pinned Anna to the roof, and he himself was above her. "How about one more time, my little girl?"

Sandstorm laughed, infecting her partner with it.

***

When Sergeant Victor Shane, accompanied by Corporal Tsar Seymour, got onto the captain's bridge of a space shuttle floating in cosmos, he found the Second Galactic Dignitary in front of the No Man's Zone map. Gloomy, tired Kiret 'Necron' Biffter reviewed bit by bit, invoking the holographic projection with the motions of his hand. He was a pale, tall, well-built achij, usually with a melancholy look of his hazel eyes. He wore a silver Christian cross around his neck.

"We're reporting as ordered, sir." Viktor and Tsar saluted.

"At ease." Necron turned slowly towards them. Meanwhile, Tsar, under Shane's threatening gaze, managed to stuff a protruding bag of drugs into his pocket. "And, Sergeant?"

"As I said in my initial report, sir," said Victor. "No squadron pilot noticed anything. We didn't find a living human, nor any remains or traces of them. And we scoured the planet Aj thoroughly."

Kiret started to rub his chin, thinking. He turned to the map and rested his arms on the tabletop.

"It's weird. The Emperor was last seen battling with a rebel XRS series fighter. No one from the opposition joined the duel, probably thinking that their officer militated against a low-rank Kiritian. In addition, Forkis forbade me to interfere even though I insisted. And we could have shot the XRS bastard and in a jiffy it would have been over." He began drumming his fingers on his lip. "An XRS fighter with its armament wouldn't be able to destroy a Kiritian combat personnel carrier. In the worst case, savage it a little, but only if there was a poor pilot at the controls. But if Forkis had died by some impossible means, we would have traced the remains of the wreckage long ago. So, he must have landed somewhere. Or he was attracted by the gravity of a large object if he lost control of the machine. Come and see." As Tsar and Viktor approached, Necron enlarged one of the No Man's Zone star systems on the map. "The first planet is out of question because the average annual surface temperature there is five hundred degrees Celsius. The second has no biospheric atmosphere, like the third one. Besides, their surfaces have already been searched. The fourth is Aj, which is fit for human life. Then we have un-terraformed dwarfs and gas giants." He looked at the Kiritians. "So, it must be Aj, because the rebels didn't kidnap him. Are you sure that no detail has escaped your attention?"

Seymour spoke before Shane opened his mouth and assured the deputy emperor that the hastily assembled achij squadron had made no mistakes:

"I saw a building underneath me," he said in his usual laid-back, non-statutory tone, as if he had been talking about an incident at a bar. "Probably uninhabited ruins, the devil knows whose. I did a scan through the ceiling and walls from the devemer, also checked the area."

"And what about this building?" Kiret, as always during the conversation with this specific achij, felt amused. Beside him, Shane pretended to be interested in the puronax cover of the bridge. Kiritians, of all ranks, talked friendly at times during their service, but Seymour never distinguished between serious discussions and trivial ones. Or he didn't care about good manners.

"Oh, nothing, Mr. Lictor. A dust storm arose, strong enough that I had to land for the devemer to gain strength."

Kiret ran a hand over his shaved head before enlarging a fragment of Aj's surface to a high resolution.

"Was it this building?" He pointed to an object in ruins, erected at the foot of the mountain.

Seymour shook his head.

"It's not it, it's too fu... I mean damaged. That building was complete. This, this one, sir!" He waved a finger towards the element as Kiret moved the map. "Buildings, around it a dry grocery store and a wall. Beside rocks."

"Ch'amiya B'aq, a sanctuary," Necron read the name next to the description.

Viktor was bothered by something. He waited patiently for Tsar to finish talking to Biffter.

"Wait a minute," he said. "Are you saying, Corporal, that the dust storm caused the devemer to malfunction?"

"Yeah. But that's normal, isn't it?"

Usually cheerful Shane was carried away. Now he, too, forgot at whom he found himself.

"Normal probably for rebels, but not for us. Fuck, Tsar! You reported a break in the weather, not an Aj-specific hyper storm of the sand!" Victor hissed so as not to yell and be heard on the whole bridge. "You must have fallen into a strong inhibition field or, as usual, you got drunk! Before the take-off from the Astro-carrier, the devemers were checked and they were operational! I would like to remind you that we are looking for the emperor himself!"

"It seems, dear achijes, that here lies the rub." Kiret twirled his finger over the specification of the object. "Carbodur. The storm must have sprayed it everywhere. Good thinking, Shane." He encompassed Seymour with a judging look. "And you see, Corporal, someone here didn't get acquainted too well with the information about the target?"

Seymour shrugged, smiled stupidly.

"Sorry, sir. I'm only a human. I didn't think the usual naming would be a problem."

"You're rather a silly donkey, Tsar," Shane muttered agitated. "You probably have a brain as ballast, so that the wind doesn't toss your head like a dry leaf!"

"Enough, Sergeant. We will discuss later the question of the achij Seymour." Necron deactivated the map. "Since you're already here. Shane, whichever task your supervisor gave you, I exempt you from it. Take the corporal, arrange transportation. Gather some of your men. We're flying to Aj. Just in case, we will land outside the zone of activity of carbodur, about four hundred kilometers from the structure, and start scouring Sector 17 again overland towards it. Get to work."

"Yes, sir."

Shane left the captain's bridge by exiting through the sliding door. Kiret glanced curiously at the motionless corporal staring at the backs of the officers working at the control panels.

"Come on, Seymour," he said sharply, frowning. "You got the orders."

The corporal followed Victor on his way out. Though he didn't show it earnestly, he was concerned that it was the first time he had screwed up, being with the Kiritians. He stuck his hand in his pocket and felt the soothing bulge of the bag. He smiled immediately. He had to console himself somehow.

***

Maksimus Figam, a self-taught person well versed in physics, technology and biology, who hadn't graduated from any university, entered the lecture hall and displayed in front of the audience holographic projections he had prepared. The University of Szczecin, located in Poland, a strong right-wing country that was the leader of the Visegrad Group, was bursting at the seams on July 20, 2511. The free conference on medicine and human health was attended not only by world-renowned scientists, but also amateurs wishing to enrich their knowledge with scientific innovations.

He also came there. After accelerated transmutation with the usage of alien technology, he was in human form; changed from one species to another. He appeared as an ordinary street citizen who wanted to spend some time listening to scientific debate. He sat down in the back row and watched the presentations for hours, one by one. He was slowly getting bored, casually scribbling in a holonote symbols well-known among his people. A conference participant sitting next to him, seeing these figures drawn with great precision, mistook him for an anthropology linguist.

Maksimus Figam immediately aroused his interest. It was like a flash, the recognition of a perfect, sought-after element. Boredom passed immediately, as soon as he saw the pretender scientist of extraordinary knowledge, who, however, behaved modestly and culturally. Figam spoke with youthful verve, proudly presenting his many years of research work on the use of viruses to immortalize the cells of the human body. Unfortunately, the halfway point of the presentation scarcely passed, and he already was attacked by old, wise, bald academic heads that trashed Figam. They laughed at his 'pseudoscientific' theories, because the turd-amateur absolutely couldn't be right. Just couldn't, and that's it. A bucket of hatred was poured over him. As Figam was the last to speak that day, people began to leave the room, shaking their heads with pity, sending ironic smirks at the slightly saddened scientist, raising their eyebrows eloquently. So Figam was almost alone with his subdued enthusiasm and gathered presentation material.

Among the few who chose to stay and listen to the complete lecture was him. He began to clap when Maks reached the final, then approached the young man and greeted him warmly, giving him a false identity.

Due to reasons which he didn't understand, Maksimus was charmed by the stranger who looked like a soldier at the age of forty. Therefore, when, after numerous praises and expertly spoken words about medical knowledge in the field of immortality, he received an offer from him to work for the army, and in his own home laboratory, Maks felt like in seventh heaven.

Since then, Figam worked for him, covertly, in secret from the world, on reprogramming and synthesizing viruses that, as a new product, would have been able to infect all cells of the human body. Break the code of the gods, give man the most desirable trait in history. The stranger gave Maks a lot of clues that were trivial knowledge among Nimja members, but for people the knowledge from another planet seemed even divine.

Six years passed and the super virus was ready. It acted lightning fast, surpassing even Martian Ebola in the speed of infection. Meanwhile, he got another man into his plans: the 34-year-old defector of the New Order Army, Kiret Biffter, later nicknamed 'Necron', with whom he befriended (he wondered how this had happened because he despised all mankind. Only the most trusted Necron and Figam were exceptions to this rule).

As the day of the coup, he set September 11, 2517. He entered the global government deliberations in London unhindered - and murdered alone with a combat plasma launcher, about a hundred people. About a hundred cruel, hypocritical obstructionists who controlled the population of the Earth, and their fortunes amounted to the wealth of three-quarters of the rest of the population. The building of the parliament, decorated with splendor, was monitored and guarded by dozens of robots and automatic cannons; the edifice floated in the sea of police and army. And yet he managed to break through, not even cut himself in the course of this terrorist attack. He was completely successful. Nobody knew how. No one could explain why no weapons had been fired at him. Even confirmed skeptics started talking about aliens, witchcraft, and evil spirits.

In the first point, they were right - the artifact of the extraterrestrial civilization had worked, inhibiting machines and enslaving minds.

As the sun was setting, he stepped outside the white parliament building, stood at the top of the long, wide stairs, and raised his weapon in triumph. Ordinary people from the street cheered that someone had finally taken the courage and done it for them. The army and the police appeared, but no one was able to fire a bullet at the unusual terrorist, as if he had been protected by an unidentified force field, additionally affecting human will.

Kiret and Figam were next to him as agreed.

"The time has come of the conquest of space and the unlimited power of the Kiritians, a new nation!" He shouted to the crowd. "Join me and I will give you immortality and indescribable riches. Here is the proof that I'm not lying!"

And he fired the plasma gun at Kiret, killing him on the spot. The inert body fell with a thud on a heated stone. Streams of blood ran down the white marble steps as if down the stairs of ancient El Castillo, on the day of human sacrifice.

The crowd fell silent. There was consternation. The neurotic atmosphere seemed to weigh tons and fell on stunned people's heads, get into their throats as no words were spoken. The babies were silent. Not even the dog barked.

He, in turn, summoned a random person from the crowd, who with fear climbed to the top of the stairs. He ordered them, closely watched by the speechless people, to check whether the former NOA soldier with the gunshot wound to the head was indeed dead. After the terrified man confirmed his death, he instructed Figam to inject the late Biffter with the super virus that stimulated the work of a group of genes that only functioned after death.

A few minutes later the electorate saw the miracle.

Writhing at first in convulsions like a grub being pricked with a needle, the body came to life. The man, nicknamed Necron thanks to that event, stood up and raised his hands above his bloodied head like a winner. To the astonished people closest to the stairs, it seemed that the gunshot wound was starting to close.

Then he stuck a needle into his neck and injected into his system three hundred milliliters of straw-colored liquid.

He suffered terribly as his immune system was losing with the super virus reproducing at a bewildering speed, attacking the entire body with modified DNA and RNA. However, he stood upright and proud, like a courageous patriot in front of a firing squad. He wanted to yell, scream, curl up with pain on the landing, but he didn't even allow himself twitching of his eyelid.

He survived, changed in front of the crowd. His skin turned a bit pale as a side effect of the super virus, although in the next infected, complexion didn't always change. For everyone was different.

"Join me and you will become like me, equal to the gods!" The message was infantile, but effective because it struck a chord with the minds of ordinary citizens.

The earlier spell of bewilderment and consternation broke. People started screaming and clapping. From the landing of the high stairs, they resembled a great, wild, bratty mass. Having broken the police groups and troops like a mighty storm an old pier, they started to run in droves up the stairs to glorify the new hero of their time, the savior, the killer of the tyrants of global government and existential monotony, deprived of prospects for a bright future. They gladly went to his side, and he chose only the smartest, richest, strongest and healthiest among them. And with a psyche that could last forever. He told the rest to go home and enjoy the life they had. Then he needed an elite, for ordinary achijes there would be time.

The army, forming at a surprisingly fast pace, he called Kiritians. He made Necron his deputy and lictor, and Figam - a chief scientist.

He promised the moon and was the first man in history to keep his promises, even handsomely. Therefore, forty years later, he had over two million achijes on his side, ready to lay down their immortal lives for him in the numerous skirmishes he had to fight to gain absolute power in the Milky Way and Andromeda. Achijes became a militarized nation, the colonies became the Zodiac Universum.

***

Forkis lifted his eyelids and smiled more inwardly than on his face. Since Anna had been with him, he'd had dreams about the past quite often. It was nice to recreate past, delightful events, he would have loved to relive them a thousand times more.

The sky speckled with stars was still dark, one of the moons was shining, but soon the first signs of dawn would appear in the east. The warm breeze gently brushed the Kiritian's back like the fingers of his new mistress. Wrapped in leather and with her back to him, the girl was fast asleep. Her breathing was steady and calm, the subtle smile of an angel was still lingering on her face. Of an angel who finally stopped complaining about the cold even though she wasn't wearing clothes. Forkis pressed Anna closer to him.

Having heard in the nighttime wilderness, a specific low hum of an anti-gravity engine making sounds at low frequencies, he immediately understood what that might have meant. He untangled himself from the skin, wrapped the sleeping rebel with it, and took her, muttering something, in his arms. He carried Anna to the warmer alcove. He himself went to meet the stranger who had found the sanctuary, and in it the emperor.

Chapter X
Return home

"Anna, get up."

Having groaned, the girl rolled from her side to the back, rubbed her sleepy face with her hands. She dreamed about something unpleasant that was unceremoniously interrupted by the shake of her shoulder. The oneiric visions almost completely disappeared.

"They all just wanted to score me ... but you honestly ... love me ..." she muttered, barely understandably.

Forkis raised his eyebrows. He shook her once more as she slipped her hand under her cheek and began to fall asleep.

"What's going on?" She asked, opening her eye. She opened the second one in a flash and rose on the bed of the alcove, having noticed the black silhouette leaning over her against the background of the torches in the corridor.

"A transportation has come for me," Forkis said cheerfully.

"What transportation? I mean, Kiritians? They are here?"

"No, just Firley, my little AI personal transporter that, along with the orbs, scoured the zone after separating from the Immortals. The achijes already know that I'm in Ch'amiya B'aq. They wanted to come here immediately, but I told them through Firley to give me some time and that I would go to them myself."

"Are they far?"

"About three hundred kilometers from here."

Forkis sat down next to Sandstorm, ran a hand through his hair, plastering it down. "So, what did you decide? Are you flying with me or staying here? If you choose to stay, I will understand. You won't die here. I'll tell the rebels to take you away. Unless you want me to drop you off in the Lion Universe."

"It won't be necessary. I've thought everything through carefully. You were right. For twenty years I suffered because of you until you showed me the reason. You are the only one who showed me a path that I don't want to deviate from, since I have already stood at its beginning. So, I offer you love, and devotion to the nation."

The Kiritian gave her a serious look.

"But you know what it means. If you want to be with me, you will have to become one of us."

"I want this," she said firmly. "I'm gonna be a kiritian." He smiled grimly. He brushed her hair back from her forehead, then, holding the former lieutenant by the chin, placed a subtle kiss on her lips. Anna hugged him and returned the gesture tighter.

"Get dressed, then, and let's go," he said after they pulled away from each other. "Meanwhile, I'm going to scatter the rest of our supplies for the animals."

***

Hanging above the ground, Firley resembled a diving bird of prey, but four meters long. The brown and black hull was covered by armor stylized to resemble organic tissues, which was the hallmark of Kiritians' bionic machines, who drew inspiration from nature to the liking of the First Galactic Dignitary. From the chassis was coming a slight blast produced by the fans of the magnetic anti-gravity motor.

It was just beginning to dawn when they both reached the landing of the stairs in front of the sanctuary. The machine waiting in the garden immediately turned its narrow fairing in their direction and flew up.

"Here is my Firley. Good to see you again, kid." The Kiritian tapped the hull, then spread the tylakosmil's skin over the seat, which Sandstorm wanted to take as a sentimental memento. He straddled the machine. "Anna?" He extended an open hand towards her, inviting her to his world.

She looked into his mysterious eyes that gleamed red in the dim morning light. She didn't hesitate, she wanted to stay with this strange, terrible, but also extraordinary man, even if it meant the complete opposite of her life so far. Everything drew her to Forkis, even his faults. On the other hand, she felt sad, she was afraid of something new, when she realized that she was unlikely to come back to the past. Even if she wanted to, she would be rejected by the rebels, if not killed. She wasn't going to joke with the Splinter anymore. She wouldn't go with that slut Julie - whom she might have forgiven everything - for a hen session. She wouldn't take part in the next breakneck flight sparring with Beliar. It was possible that she would not meet him again, possibly as her enemy. If he had survived the skirmish near Eos Endymion.

She let the wind toss her long-uncombed hair before she shook Forkis' hand and settled down in the back.

The machine made a series of low-pitched sounds, turned towards a breach in a wall, and sped forward, accelerating to a quarter of Mach in a few moments. Anna looked back at descending Ch'amiya B'aq. She saw the four-legged inhabitants of Aj, who threw themselves on the provisions taken out of the building.

They set off into the waning night. They raced through the hard-surfaced wasteland, creating two walls of dust that turned to sand waves as they reached giant desert barchans. They crossed a huge crater filled with silvery dust that had been made by a comet thousands of years earlier. They passed among herds of scaled, winged animals similar to mythical griffins, scaring them away. Firley chose a way along old lava fields, taken over by pioneering vegetation, then weaved through the rocks until they were back on a deep steppe.

A small space shuttle appeared in the field of view, illuminated by green and blue lamps directing the light upwards. It stood on cracked ground at the foot of a great monolithic rock.

"Relax, everything will be fine!" Forkis tried to outshout the wind, feeling that the girl gripped his waist tighter at the sight of the Kiritian ship.

The machine resembling a cyborg cuttlefish was gaining in size; Firley was losing speed slowly. Finally, it fell softly to the ground, having deactivated the anti-gravity engine.

Five achijes in armor of the nation's distinctive colors: black and inky with indigo elements wandered at the outthrust, crude hatch of the hangar. They warmed up when they saw Forkis, who screamed and waved at them.

"Wait a minute," he said to Sandstorm. Stepping off Firley, he nudged her shoulder consolingly and winked at her.

Joyful, the achijes went in droves towards the commander, and he went to meet them.

The frightened girl in the rebel uniform felt warm in her spirit, a sad smile appeared on her wind-chilled face when she watched the men greet warmly, as if Forkis had been a team's favored soccer player after a significant goal. Immediately in her mind appeared the comparison of the Kiritians with the rebels, who also tried to waive the unyielding military rigor in favor of a fellowship as such, but it wasn't going too promisingly. Now she understood that the cause of the discrepancy could have been the different past of the nation and the opposition: Onkalotian norms, adherence to ideals, truthfulness and cooperation versus terrorism, hypocrisy and the progenitor controlled by the global government. This didn't mean, of course, that things were bad among the rebels, but they were having a hard time creating something better.

Her heart pounded as she realized that all the achijes were looking at her.

"Please come here," Forkis repeated. The other Kiritians were silent, their gazes were curious and expectant.

Sandstorm moved her leg over the seat, shook off travel dust, and walked slowly toward the group carefully eyeing her up.

"Dear gentlemen, I present to you Anna Sandstorm," Xajb'a Kej put his hand on the shoulder of the confused girl, "former second lieutenant of the 78th Squadron of the 99th Rebel Fighter Regiment. She wants to be with us. I've checked on her and seen nothing disturbing."

Forkis then provided the Kiritian identities, out of which Anna remembered Biffter, Seymour and Shane.

"How pretty." Kiret smiled slightly, grabbed her hand. "Call me Necron. Since you are recommended by the First Dignitary, we welcome you to our humble abode." He kissed the back of her hand with satisfaction. Anna felt her face flush.

The achijes laughed.

"Humble." Sandstorm eyed the high-tech space shuttle.

"Come on, you'll see something. I guess you will be pleased." Forkis led her to the cargo bay and opened the bulkhead.

Anna covered her mouth with her hands, sighing slightly.

"The White." She looked at Forkis with questioning eyes. "From where ...?"

"I ordered the achijes to collect scrap. We will repair your fighter and it will be like new. We gave up on mine, it was too destroyed."

"Thanks." Sandstorm cheered up, but she also gloomed. The rebels must have seen the XRS-14 near the sanctuary, but they left the wreckage there and probably closed their search, presuming the second lieutenant dead.

Forkis flew into the hangar on Firley. After him went the achijes with Anna.

A red rotor flashed, and the massive airlock closed with a thud. The achijes went to an orlop in the center of the shuttle; the pilots from the bridge started anti-g engines.

They took off.

Sandstorm peered through the meter-thick oval porthole at the declining landscape until it vanished behind the morning's thick cloud cover. She thought about the life she had ended and the new one she had chosen for herself, which was evident on her sad face. Necron, sitting opposite, would have gladly accosted her, but he stayed his hand, aware that the girl had had to go through a lot and needed a bit of privacy to sort everything out in her head. Moreover, Forkis had already taken care of her.

Anna turned away from the armored cover, having felt a soothing touch: the emperor wrapped his arm around her, drew her closer, and kissed the top of her head. The gentle expression on his face was better than the unspoken words of consolation.

She talked little during her journey to the planet Morascrik where was the Kirtian capital of K'otz'ib'aja. She occasionally sent casual smiles to her neighbors, each of whom seemed sympathetic, especially Tsar, whose texts amused her to tears, and irritated Shane. She gave polite answers when asked about something. In spite of good company, she would have most willingly sat in the corner and gaze into the boundless cosmos, wandering with her thoughts elsewhere. She was constantly tormented by one: whether she had acted wisely, going blindly after the guy who had stunned her mind, though had helped to chase away the nightmares of the past. Or maybe she had done the right thing and chosen the right side? Was it treason to join the hegemonic nation, but using reason in its expansion, thanks to which it had managed to eliminate the chaos in which mankind had been for millennia? Were domination and violence an indispensable domain of order? Were the Kiritians bad or maybe needed by the Zodiac Universum? Had they attained absolute power by chance, or it had had to happen, since they had been led by the right person? What was so special about Forkis that she followed him like a sheep a shepherd, just as the people who had decided to become Kiritians? There was something missing in it, some significant factor.

She was relieved to hear that the skirmish near Eos Endymion had ended in a draw: the aggressor had withdrawn from the battlefield, and the Kiritians had gotten to looking for the emperor. She wondered anxiously about Beliar's fate. The couple of years' relationship hadn't been lost like a stone thrown into an abyss - she was still worried about him.

***

Surrounded by bioluminescent mushrooms, Aggroteh crouched over the tylakosmil's skull, keeping his paw spread out on the occipital bone. He was in such a position for several minutes, fully focused, with his eyes closed, immersed in contemplation of the past events, to which the abandoned skull had been a passive witness. The bone looked freshly prepared. The presence of the remains of a crashed Kiritian combat carrier near the sanctuary clearly indicated that the pilot, who had somehow survived the crash, had had to visit the Ch'amiya B'aq ruins. However, with the completely destroyed wreck there was a problem during psychometry.

Non-chronological, broken images began to appear in his head, mainly the last scenes from the life of the owner of the huge skull. Q'ualel's nostrils widened as he watched Forkis drag his prey to the sanctuary. He growled, feeling the hunter's primal call as the Kiritian ripped with his teeth the intestines out of the knife-torn belly. This was happening when Anna went to fetch wood to light the fire. Aggro grimaced. The quite natural thing among Onkalots looked strange in the performance of the man devoid of tusks and claws. In turn, when he later saw Xajb'a Kej making love passionately with the rebel, his cat ears went up high, as did his eyebrows.

"Well, well." He sighed disapprovingly, taking the paw off the skull. He opened his hazel eyes, which immediately turned red at the scant amount of light. "That's all Forkis."

He was astonished to see under the skull the abandoned chain that must have belonged to Xajb'a Kej. He recognized the characteristic cigar-shaped amulet capsule, engraved with Onkalotian symbols - perhaps the only such thing in the universe, custom-made. At first, he thought that the rebels from Eos Endymion had returned to the sanctuary and enslaved Forkis, who had lost the chain in the course of the struggle, because he had never parted with the bone of the living artifact. Then he pondered whether Anna had killed the Kiritian, for example while he had been asleep, but immediately dismissed that absurd thought. Forkis was a monster, but not a fool. He found some of Forkis' jet-black hair ripped out on the catafalque. However, it too didn't provide an answer as to what had been happening since the romance with the rebel from underground.

"Thank you Tonatiuh for all the pointers." Stuffed the hair into the empty spaces of the capsule, making the bone immobile.

He gripped the coiled chain with his cupped paws as if holding a butterfly. He closed his eyes again, calmed down, and began recalling the next batch of images to his mind. These, in turn, proved to be more interesting, provided a lot of useful information, as Forkis had worn the chain long before staging the

London coup, his first bloody success, implied by the power of the Nimja artifact, incomprehensible to Q'ualel.

He spent many hours underground trying to find the most valuable information, but when he finally opened his eyes, he immediately closed them again, completely exhausted. Using your mind on this scale, even having the practiced skill and researching simple everyday objects, consumed a lot of energy. It took her as much as a quick several kilometers run to repeat the events of several centuries.

The humanoid jaguar didn't remember when he had dozed off, curled up on a lichen carpet. After waking up, he regained his depleted strength. He tucked the chain capsule into a pouch attached to his belt, nibbled on some edible mushrooms, and headed across the complex towards the garden, where he had left his transporter. He already had a plan. Brave, almost daring.

Before taking off, he checked the scraps of the tylakosmil's skin. It was something new - Forkis with his paraphilia didn't kill the girl, but took her to Firley, and they both headed for the Kiritian shuttle.

Chapter XI
Machinations

Aggro hadn't yet had the opportunity to fly to the area of the Lion Universe where Cargoo orbited, though it was illuminated by the same K'ajolom star as Chulimal. It was there that the rebels, participants of the skirmish near Eos Endymion, set up makeshift barracks. After collecting another batch of information in addition to those obtained during the psychometry, the Onkalot decided to meet with them. He needed rebels to help him implement his plan.

The planet visually resembled Mars in the Old Zone, from where humankind had spilled into the Zodiac Universum. Viewed from space, it was brownish-red due to the enormous amount of encrusted iron oxides. Numerous old craters testified to the intense bombardment of the surface by space bodies in the past. It was only nine percent larger in circumference than the Earth, yet it had four tiny moons. A day lasted twenty-seven Terran hours. Cargoo hadn't changed much since its discovery in the twenty-fifth century and regarding it as a moderately habitable terrestrial planet. Apart from setting up atmosphere synthesizers on the surface, and then planting several species of agriculturally unattractive plants, mainly shrubs, it hadn't lost anything of its original appearance. In the end, it hadn't been inhabited, except for a dozen or so operating mine infrastructures with hydro stations nearby, which had drawn deep-lying underground water. Dilapidated surface, practically flat areas left after weathered rocks, and resulting from it raving winds, blizzards and hard, barren soil, didn't make the globe a prime candidate for farmers or lovers of premises under palm trees. Therefore, the rebels had used it - like the Immortals Eos Endymion - for military exercises or temporary stops, as now. Sometimes someone stopped on it when their machine broke down, but no one lived here permanently.

Once in the biosphere, Aggroteh observed the vast skins of fungi and primitive plants growing on rocks that produced little oxygen as an alternative to the synthesizers. His silver biplane was quickly surrounded by three fighters belonging to the 2nd Squadron of the 98th Rebel Fighter Regiment, which escorted him to the headquarters of the opposition. At dusk, the machines landed on a lamp-lit pad near the camp, which consisted of a swarm of tents. There were a lot of fires there. In the Kiritian-free sector there was no threat that the enemy would see the lights from space.

After leaving their machines, the three rebels approached the biplane. Having gotten out of the transporter, Aggro stood on the landing pad, stripped off his headwear and threw it into the open cabin. He smiled culturally at the surprised faces - the pilots expected to find a human.

"Hey, what the hell?" One of them began politely, a recruit, according to Q'ualel, because he had no bars on his suit. "Onkalot-fugitive?"

"Wait a minute, man," the older man moderated him, holding his hand, which had managed to tighten on the butt of the pistol. Giving the co-pilot a meaningful look, he turned to the humanoid jaguar, "Welcome to Cargoo. I'm Lieutenant Cirix."

"Q'ualel from Chulimal, from Chiq'aq city and tribe, also known as Aggroteh."

"Now I understand why you didn't give your full identity when we were in the air, but only asked for permission to land. We thought you were a civilian and got a failure, so I spared you our lovely military procedure. But I understand that with your transporter," Cirix glanced at the silver biplane, "everything is fine."

"Of course. I came to meet you. Specifically, it is about the 78th Rebel Squadron of the 99th Rebel Fighter Regiment, whose lieutenant is a certain Beliar Drunkenstein, because it is he who I would like to see."

Cirix frowned slightly.

"Can you give the purpose of the visit and tell why you are looking for that particular person? Are you acting on behalf of someone else?"

"Sorry, but I'd rather settle it with the command that participated in the skirmish with the Kiritians near Eos Endymion. Can you take me to it? Examine and search me, I have nothing to hide. I guarantee that I don't endanger you in any way."

Cirix smiled slightly. He was clearly impressed by the attitude of the mysterious humanoid jaguar who had come here alone. He dismissed the pilot reaching for the gun, ordering him for his behavior to go on foot and inform the command of the civilian's arrival, while from the other subordinate, he took a multifunction scanner, which he moved along the Onkalot's body. He sensed nothing disturbing. He took the weapon from the newcomer in accordance with the procedure, including the dagger.

Before the messenger returned with the information from the command that it had agreed to receive the Onkalot, a small group of curious people had gathered at the landing field.

"Aggro?" One of the young men stepped closer. "Of course, it's you!" He extended his hands and pressed the confused humanoid jaguar to him for a moment, like a brother he hadn't seen in a long time. "What are you doing here?"

"Tom Lewandowski?" Q'ualel also recognized the rebel who had participated in the brawl at 'Stanislav Skalski'. He smiled heartily. "Hello, hello! In lake`ch a la ken."

"Do you know each other, cadet?" Cirix asked.

"Sure! Aggro is fine, you don't need to fear him, sir. If you don't mind, I'll take him to Commander Lacetti. I can vouch for him."

The second lieutenant stared briefly at Q'ualel.

"Alright, Tom. So, take care of the matter. We're going back on patrol." He motioned to the pilots and moved towards his fighter. He drove the audience away with his hands like a housewife a flock of poultry. "And you, what are you staring at? Go away!"

"What the hell are you doing here?" Tom repeated his earlier question as he and Q'ualel entered a gigantic encampment set on a rocky plateau. Everyone they passed stared at them with more than a passing interest. A few people got up, but the cadet soothed them with a careless wave of his hand.

"I'd like to talk to your commander."

"I know that, but what for? Unless it's too confidential for such a fool like Tom Lewandowski." The man smiled playfully.

Aggro returned the smile, but almost imperceptibly and briefly.

"I can tell you a little," he said, "it's no secret. I want to find a scientist who once dealt with Forkis. Maybe he can help me defeat the usurper."

Lewandowski stopped abruptly as if he had hit an invisible wall.

"What the hell are you talking about?! You don't know anything?! Forkis is dead!"

Everyone nearby turned their eyes to the unusual duo. Even those who hadn't paid attention to it before, busy with their own affairs.

"A little quieter," Aggro hissed, glancing discreetly to the side. They moved on.

"What's with that Forkis?" Lewandowski asked in a whisper. "After all, he died in the skirmish. Everyone sounds off about it, the whole Zodiac Universum!"

"Oho, sure." The Onkalot made a mocking face. "Protected by forces beyond your comprehension, the highly intelligent usurper died in the skirmish with, with all due respect, rebels who can't even hold a candle to Kiritians. Have you seen his body?"

"I haven't. But apparently, he did..."

"Forkis is alive, like you and me," the humanoid jaguar interrupted him. "I have evidence for that. He has crashed and been on the planet Aj for a while, but the Kiritians have already found him, safe and sound, and taken to Morascrik."

Tom stopped again, glanced at his companion with skepticism, even suspiciously. The Onkalot also stopped.

"How do you know that?"

"I'm a psychometrician." Aggro explained quickly, seeing the embarrassed expression blossoming on the person's face. "I can recreate in my mind past events about a specific person after touching an object that belongs to that person or with which they have come in contact. It is as if there was a cellula for monitoring mounted on this item, but sometimes with a very damaged and incomplete record. If you don't believe it, I can prove it to you."

"I didn't say I didn't believe it. I have heard that Onkalots have psionic abilities, which has been scientifically proven, but ..." Tom sighed in resignation, raised his hands a little, then dropped them on his thighs, "everything is getting more and more messed up."

"I understand your consternation, but I have no reason to invent such incredible stories. On Aj, in a former Onkalotian temple called Ch'amiya B'aq, I have found some of Forkis' belongings and in this way learned that he survived. Psychometry told me a lot."

Though he didn't have to do this in front of the low-ranking soldier, he showed Tom Forkis' capsule.

"Oh shit ... It seems genuine, as in the reports." The cadet was examining it with his fingers. "Where did you get this?"

"Forkis lost it in Ch'amiya B'aq." Aggro put the item in the pouch.

"Okay, let's assume the emperor is alive. And you want to destroy him? Seriously? Alone?! What do you have to do with him? Why do you care about - I presume - not your case? After all, Kiritians like Onkalots. Explain this to me."

Aggroteh looked at the stars. He managed to see three of the planet's moons in different phases.

"I can't. Sorry."

"Well, don't be angry, but ... the Onkalot, whose species hates people, first asks me in front of the bar about the Eos Endymion battle, and then shows up in the rebel camp, looks for Lieutenant Drunkenstein, wants to meet with the command and even makes plans to overthrow the usurper's corpse. You see for yourself what it sounds like."

"I don't hate people, I can forgive," Aggro said gently. "Yes, I know what that sounds like. But if you knew the whole story, dating back hundreds of years, with all the details, you'd be confused. It is a very tenebrous and difficult story that I will have to convey to the command in such a way that they don't put me in a psychiatric hospital."

Tom raised his open hands.

"Alright, man, as you wish. I won't get into it, but I'm being consumed by ordinary human curiosity. Can you give me at least the identity of that scientist you mentioned? Or it is also top secret?"

"Doctor Maximus Figam. Does that tell you something?"

"I've heard that he worked for the Kiritians. Then they either kicked him out or he left them himself. That's all I know."

Aggro looked around the seemingly endless barracks. There was a relaxed atmosphere at the fires. People laughed, drank, sang obscene songs, played music, and every now and then loud shouts of joy erupted.

"Are you going somewhere?"

Tom shook his head.

"For now, we are stuck here, and we don't know what to do next. This has been going on since the withdrawal from Eos

Endymion. The staff doesn't send any orders, so after licking the wounds, we slowly started to get bored. However, at any time of the day or night, there may be guidelines for mobilization and departure, which would be the best move to serve our cause, since Forkis is considered dead. Momentary perturbations of the opponent without the commander will make it unstable. Personally, I think it would be good to carry out concussion, guerrilla attacks on them."

The Onkalot shook his head with a sigh.

"It won't fly. You will just piss off Forkis and he will just wipe you out. He will consider you a threat."

"How can you be sure?"

"Let's say I know him well and can predict his moves."

Tom didn't like the direction the conversation was taking. He looked suspiciously at the humanoid jaguar.

"The enemy doesn't know where we are staying," he emphasized. "Where our bases are."

"Sure it knows. It just doesn't bother."

"It doesn't make sense. If it was true, they would have attacked us after the action with Forkis. Do you know anything about the case?"

"When you see ant tunnels under a flagstone in your garden, you are unlikely to step on them, even if they sometimes get into your apartment. That's how Forkis thinks: he eliminates only the real threat, but once he gets down to it, he doesn't leave a stone upon another."

"Over there is Commander Lacetti's tent." Lewandowski, sure that he wouldn't learn anything more, pointed to a canvas giant on a small hill, in which could be arranged an intimate banquet. "You can get in. The commander is probably sitting there alone with reports. Oh, one thing," he said in a whisper, slightly embarrassed, "On Nephrida, several Onkalots serve the rebels. I have nothing against you, on the contrary - I really like and admire your kind. I'm an open-minded person out of principle, but senior officers are more skeptical about the matter. If you know what I mean."

"I know. I have already gotten used to the fact that many people give me grudging glances and wonder why I'm free."

"Of course, don't take my words personally. I just want to sensitize you to what to expect."

"Thank you very much for showing me the way and for this advice." The cadet raised his fist, and they gave each other a bro-fist. "If you want, we can talk also later."

"Sure, I'd love to." As the humanoid jaguar went away, Tom murmured, "I would pour water into the tunnels of those ants."

***

The cavernous tent, lit by solar crystals, wasn't empty, as Tom had assured. In the separate, largest part, besides Commander Lacetti, there were three more people. The silver-gray uniform of the lowest rank was decorated with the lieutenant's polished bars. The men sat at a metal table. The Onkalot noticed that it was a social gathering, because the tabletop was covered with drink bottles, some of them still full, and old stuff had been placed carelessly on a dresser next to folding bunks. Under the ceiling there was a cloud of irritating nostrils cigar smoke.

"Hello." Lacetti was a man with blue eyes, a narrow face, a dark complexion, and generally the archetype of a city slicker." He got up and shook the stranger's hand. "Commander Aveo Lacetti."

The Onkalot returned the handshake, introducing himself.

"Here's a chair. Would you like something to drink?" The commander suggested when the humanoid jaguar sat down, closely watched by the rest. Out of the corner of his eye, Q'ualel saw a lie detector not well hidden behind the dresser. "Maybe a cigar?"

"No, thanks."

Aveo began to introduce the rebels seated at the table one by one; each called out made a formal nod of the head:

"Captain Ivan Andreyev. Further the freelancer and temporary captain Arcadius Croft, who received the most deserved rank for his services near Eos Endymion, including coordinated actions that contributed to our safe retreat. I hope he will change his nature of a lone wolf and want to stay with us for longer. The blonde man with the trimmed sides is Lieutenant Beliar Drunkenstein. All the gentlemen of the 99th Rebel Fighter Regiment that took part in the skirmish."

Q'ualel stopped his gaze at the blond for a longer time, then shifted it to the commander.

"So, what brings you to us, Aggroteh?" Aveo sat back comfortably in the chair. Ivan reached for a bottle of vodka, which the man took for a beer at first, filled half a glass and raised it to his mouth. Beliar was leaning on the tabletop with his hands clasped into the basket and watched the newcomer closely.

"First, I would like to inform you gentlemen," Aggro began officially, "that Xajb'a Kej, the First Galactic Dignitary, survived the last skirmish near Eos Endymion. Quite recently, he was found by the Kiritians and transported to the planet Morascrik."

Beliar made an amused face; Ivan stared at the humanoid jaguar with an oblique gaze and tapped his glass ostentatiously on the table; Arcadius waved his hands and muttered something under his breath, throwing a grimace on his face that unquestionably expressed doubt.

Aveo smiled doubtfully.

"Nonsense. Commander Kiritian was killed, brought down by our second lieutenant Anna Sandstorm, who also, unfortunately, fell in this skirmish."

Aggroteh almost summoned onto his trap a bitter, mocking smirk.

"You were looking for the body on the planet Aj where, according to your calculations, Forkis might have crashed. But when you didn't find him, you stopped the mission and presumed him dead. But he survived," the Onkalot looked at Beliar, "as did Second Lieutenant Anna Sandstorm, who was taken with the Kiritian to K'otz'ib'aja."

"What?!" To the Onkalot's well-concealed satisfaction, Beliar sprang from his chair, knocking it over. "This is nonsense! Anna ... is gone."

"It can't be," said Ivan with a distinctly earthly Russian accent. Running his thumb over his long mustache, he looked at the confused Croft.

"Sit down, Lieutenant," said the commander. Drunkenstein picked up the chair and plumped himself down on it. "Can you give us some compelling evidence, Aggroteh?"

He showed the capsule to Tom as before, holding the chain for a moment. This, however, didn't convince them.

"Dummy," Ivan announced. "You don't even let us to peek inside."

"I can't do that, and I won't explain why. My words are also my proof, gentlemen, and you probably know that Onkalots as well as Kiritians who model themselves after them, don't descend to lying. I'm a psychometrician. I 'read' the past, sometimes the present, from items related to the person I want to learn about. Just like humans are born with some talent, such as beautiful singing, we, too, have psionic abilities specific to our kind. They reveal themselves in the early youth," the humanoid jaguar explained it just in case. He didn't know if the Onkalots of the Nephrida had revealed their secrets to them. "I have done my own research. I've investigated the site of Forkis' crash on the planet Aj. I've arrived at the Ch'amiya B'aq temple, known in your language as the Bone Scepter. It turned out that the usurper had been there for some time until he was tracked down and found by Firley, his personal transporter, that drove him to the Kiritian shuttle. Before this happened, Ch'amiya B'aq had been combed by the rebels. However, they had been deceived by Forkis and simply left, confident that the sanctuary had been abandoned. As you can guess, I know all this from the items with which came into contact the usurper as well as Anna Sandstorm while staying with the Kiritian in the sanctuary.

"Great, it's getting better. Getting better!" Croft unconsciously tightened his hand on the edge of the table.

Beliar paled. He began to speak with emphasis:

"Anna was in the same place as Forkis!? What happened to her? What did that bastard do to her?!"

"Beliar ... sit down," said the commander as Drunkenstein started up again like a scalded cat.

"I think the girl is fine. I have no idea what has happened since Firley took off." Aggroteh didn't want to mention the rebel's affair with the Kiritian. He would need Beliar to carry out his plan and would have preferred not to take with him the bundle of nerves seeking revenge.

"I guess I'll have to talk again to the people I sent to penetrate the planet." Ivan made a lower. He ran a hand over a tuft of hair on his almost bald, tattooed head. "Killing, even kidnapping Forkis, would confuse the enemy, which we could take advantage of." He encompassed Aggroteh with a stern look. "As long as our exotic guest tells the truth."

"We'll interview our subordinates again later, Captain." Lacetti turned politely to the humanoid jaguar, "Forgive me for asking you to, but I'd like to conduct a little test. I will give you an item and you will tell me a bit about its owner. It's not that I don't believe you, because I don't see the point in you covering such a long distance of the Milky Way just to tell us a drollery, but I'd like to see your phenomenon with my own eyes."

The Onkalot shrugged.

"No problem. I'm asking for the item."

"Captain, the watch." The commander extended his hand towards the Russian. Andreyev grasped his wrist.

"Why me?"

"What's the difference, who? Come on."

Ivan reluctantly undid the mechanical watch, modeled on pre-colonial devices, and handed it to the commander, who passed it to the Onkalot.

"Give me a moment, gentlemen. And I'm asking for silence." Aggroteh focused on the watch in his paws, completely ignoring the surroundings. After a few moments, images of Ivan's life began to appear in his mind. The Onkalot's face changed according to the events he saw: he was amazed, amused, shocked, ashamed.

When he finally opened his eyes, he saw the concentrated men staring at him expectantly. Only the owner of the watch, supporting his head, admired the nearest frame of the tent with keen interest.

"And?" The commander encouraged the Onkalot, seeing that he hesitated.

"Do I have to say it? I respect male honor."

"You don't need anything!" The Russian said sharply.

"You have to," Lacetti said simultaneously. He didn't know what Ivan meant, and he absolutely wanted to check on the newcomer.

Before he could report, Aggro looked apologetically at Ivan, who was still staring at the extremely interesting detail of the prop, but probably would have liked to admire the rocks far beyond the tent.

"So ... Captain Andreyev likes to pour sugar into vodka."

"Sugar into vodka?" The Splinter gave the man a questioning look. "This is sacrilege!"

Andreyev, in turn, threw him a murderous one.

"Can you say something else, Onkalot?" Lacetti asked, folding his hands over his chest. What only the captain and I know. It would be plausible for me. Could you?"

"Okay. Oh, let it be this. Although I don't know if the event was told to anyone. There is a rebel base on the planet Mezzo. Captain

Ivan Andreyev came down on a private from the barracks one day - but why he went personally to the soldier of such a low rank, I don't know - then left his room and went to use the toilet in the same building.

"Let a black hole eat you all!" Andreyev grimaced and waved his arms. The commander grinned, knowing the story.

"The private," continued the humanoid jaguar, "was in conflict with his colleagues from the floor. The drunken rebels were mistaken because they confused the captain who was leaving the room with the private, turned off the light, threw a large cotton bag over him in the cubicle and had a blanket party. Then they laid ..."

"Enough!" Ivan stood up as abruptly as Beliar had before. He moved the chair with a strong shove, then walked to the designated area next door, having slid the canvas cover open with a sweeping motion of his arm. "Ugly bastards ..."

The other men at the table sat with comic expressions, except for Lacetti who started laughing.

"He's nervous by nature," Croft whispered amused, turning to the humanoid jaguar.

"The cat has told the truth," Muttered Ivan as he reappeared. "Except for the honorable commander, no one on Cargoo knows about it. Apart from the fact that I was immobilized and smeared with tar, my clothes and even this darn sack were also taken. I had to go back through the building with a soap dish at the loins and blood on my face. Everyone laughed. I was new to the base from the assignment, and I had been promoted young, so they mistook me for another youngster who had gotten into somebody's black books. The blanket party cornballs tossed the uniform into the bag and didn't even look at the ribbons. It was only in the gatehouse that I was given some clothes. Fortunately, I was later assigned to lead the company of these jokers." Ivan grinned in a triumphant smile.

Soon Andreyev, Lacetti and Croft were giggling. The Onkalot smiled out of courtesy. Beliar didn't react at all, he had been distrait from the moment he had heard about Anna. Ivan went to the table, took the watch and put it on. He sat down in his seat again and poured himself another portion of esophagus-burning vodka, which he gulped down.

"Very useful ability," the commander said to the humanoid jaguar once he regained his seriousness and wiped the tear from his eye. "But let's get to the point. What exactly do you expect from us?"

"I have a plan to kill Forkis, but I'm going to urgently need Lieutenant Drunkenstein's help." Aggro glanced at Beliar. "You have to believe me that the usurper is alive."

"All right, let's assume he didn't die in the skirmish. But how does one Onkalot intend to solve the dilemma that the rebel regiments have wrestled with for centuries? And to no avail."

"At the outset, I would like to get the bearings of Dr. Maximus Figam, a scientist who once collaborated with the Kiritians. I haven't been able to find out where he is now, and I know," Aggro looked around at those present, "that you can give me this information, because you have it."

The commander glanced at Captain Croft. The latter nodded affirmatively.

"Maximus Figam," began Arek, "has created some kind of super virus, which supposedly gives the Kiritians infected with it immortality. We managed to establish it recently and by accident.

This pathogen is heavily guarded by usurpers, and in its neutral form it has never escaped from their laboratories. From myself I will add that it is surprising that no Kiritian has blurted it out. It is contrary to human nature."

"Captain," Lacetti urged.

"On Forkis' order, Figam created a pathogen for the arising army of the Immortals. He, too, was infected, against his will, because Forkis wanted the doctor always with him. He was taken on Morascrik to the capital Kotzaba ..."

"K'otz'ib'aja," helped Aggroteh.

"Yeah, thanks." Arek smiled slightly. "Sorry, but your Onkalotian names are bizarre and difficult. The scientist, however, created a serum for the super virus, which he injected himself a dozen or so Terran years ago, and he again became an ordinary, aging and sick guy. He wanted to leave the Kiritians because life among them was just starting to tire him. Forkis, with whom they somehow got along, relieved him of all duties and let him go his way. However, he selectively reset his memory so that he forgot all the projects he had ever created for the Immortals. So Figam left the Kiritians, apparently became a recluse, and laid up in a hermitage on a sparsely populated planet in the Libra Universe. Currently, he provides his services there, but only to people whom he has taken to, regardless of their cultural, racial or political affiliation. He accepted me and Beliar when we visited him recently, asking for the creation of a new weapon for the rebel army. We've got a tamari cannon from Figam, he also told a bit about his history."

"You say they erased some of his memory," Aggro said. "But he still works scientifically?"

"Of course. He just remembers nothing - and doesn't want to remember, for his own safety - of what he did in the Morascrik laboratories. Fortunately, no one presses him or descends on him, because unofficially the doctor is still under the auspices of the Kiritians. After all, he was friends with Forkis, although they quarreled more than once. If you want to know my opinion, he'll probably come back to the Immortals. They'll need him, you'll see," Croft added the comment according to his nature.

"Since they were friends, I wonder why he withdrawn from the life he led?" Ivan asked his cigar, which he was lighting.

The Splinter shrugged.

"Maybe he wanted to rest from everything. Hardly anyone has the predisposition to be an Immortal, and they probably go crazy after a long time. Give up fertility, watch loved ones grow old and die, struggle with boredom after centuries of life ..." He shook his head. "That's probably why there are only eight million Kiritians."

"But they make up for in quality, you have to give it to those bastards," said Andreyev.

"I know from unofficial information that many of them quit their profession after years because they would have had a mental breakdown. The average person loves mundane matters, they would finally go mad without any changes in their life."

"Do you know if Figam currently deals with cloning or biotechnology?" Aggro asked.

Everyone looked at him more sharply.

"I don't know, but I suppose he does," said Croft. "The Kiritians have even developed necro medicine related to the work on the super virus, though I have no idea what it is about. Maybe it concerns genes that activate only after the cessation of vital functions. Dr. Figam is a multi-talented scientist who achieved almost everything on his own."

"Why did you ask about cloning?" Said the commander.

"This is part of my plan to overthrow Forkis. The humanoid jaguar looked into his narrowed blue eyes. "Everything will depend on the extent to which Figam has mastered the ability to obtain genetic material from organisms already dead. This whole necro medicine, if he still remembers something of it, could prove useful."

"Another virus?" The Russian raised an eyebrow.

"I'm very sorry, gentlemen, but I cannot give you any details."

"Dear Aggroteh," the commander rested his clasped hands on his belly and leaned back slightly in his chair. "Since you are already trying to establish cooperation with us, you have to introduce us to your plan. Carefully, thoroughly and sufficiently. From now on, the case will no longer be yours, but ours. I need to know what I'm going to get my soldiers into, if your idea proves to be meaningful."

The Onkalot scratched his nose.

"I will only need the white ship and Lieutenant Drunkenstein to accompany me to the Kiritian capital."

"The white ship?" Beliar blinked. "And what am I here for?"

"Tell us everything you know first," Lacetti demanded. "I need to have a ringside seat and assess if we can help you at all. I will also have to consult with the headquarters of other regiments." He fell to the legs of the chair, looked at the anthropomorph with the opinionated gaze of the senior officer. "By the way, I'm interested in the Onkalot's relationship with the Kiritian. Could you elaborate on this interesting thread? Because you still haven't explained what you have to do with Forkis."

"I'm his friend, at least I was a long time ago. Forkis grew up among the Chiq'aq people, just like me." Aggro chose his words carefully so as not to say too much.

The atmosphere in the tent was heavy and neurotic. It felt as tangible as the thick puffs of smoke coming out of Ivan's mouth and nose.

"Are you making fun of us now?!" The Russian muttered.

"Seriously?" The Splinter chuckled. "Bugger me!"

"That would explain a lot," Beliar announced to his fists resting on the table. He scowled at the company and rolled a gloomy gaze across their faces. He took a sip of vodka. "Forkis may have been an orphan. He grew up among the Onkalots, he felt like one of them, and when they were attacked by the colonists, he swore revenge against the entire human race in retaliation for his exterminated pupils. He dehumanized the Kiritians to exclude them from the liquidation list."

"Well, well, interesting theory," Croft said appreciatively. Aggroteh didn't challenge the lieutenant's deduction, though it amazed him. He prayed silently that he wouldn't be asked about other details of Forkis' past. He would have had to hedge; he would have lost the rebels' trust and his whole plan would have gone up in flames. And he couldn't have realized it himself."

"We already know from whom he took over the custom of cannibalism." Ivan snorted in disgust.

"Onkalots aren't cannibals!" Aggro retorted quite sharply. "Only those of the people of Jun Kame were them, but it has nothing to do with Forkis, who has become such by himself," he didn't develop the thread again.

"So, I understand that you know Forkis quite well as his ex-friend?" The commander asked. "Disclose the details of the whole story. Say what you know, you can help us immensely with this. Focus especially on the usurper's weaknesses."

Aggroteh asked for a glass of water, drank, and after a short thought, began to recount everything he had learned through his ability - from the London coup, when Forkis had begun taking power on Earth, and then in space. He enriched the rebels' knowledge of the Kiritian with many facts. He told - albeit reluctantly - his own story as well. He omitted only the thread of Nimja's artifacts that influenced reality. People unrelated to the Onkalotian culture wouldn't have understood that it was one of them that had contributed indirectly to Forkis' success.

And most of all, he didn't explain who Forkis really was, allowing the audience to take Beliar's theory as fact.

"That's why it's important to me to get to Maksimus Figam," he announced an hour later. The rebels listened eagerly without interrupting. They gained respect for the guest. "I have an Onkalotian biological weapon - so to speak - the nature of which you unfortunately cannot comprehend. That's why I skipped a lecture on it. However, I need the help of a scientist to activate this weapon."

"And what do you need Lieutenant Drunkenstein for, Onkalot?" Ivan asked.

"I don't know how I'll be received in K'otz'ibaja, even as an old friend of Forkis." Aggroteh looked at Beliar. "On the other hand,

Mr. Drunkenstein would have reason enough to go to Morascrik: to demand the girl's delivery."

All pairs of eyes turned to the lieutenant, who zoned out for a moment. He was tapping the fingers of his left hand unconsciously on the tabletop, staring at it with glassy eyes. His facial muscles were tense, his furrowed eyebrows almost contacted. He clenched his fist just like his teeth.

"I agree." He rose from his chair and rested his hands on the edge of the table, rolling his eyes over the audience. "I'll do anything to get Anna back. I owe her that. I will fly with you," he turned to the Onkalot. "You can count on me."

"You will also go with Aggroth to Dr. Figam, because you know the route," said the commander. "You will settle the matter regarding that biological weapon and return to Cargoo immediately. If Central Command from Mezzo won't mind - and they shouldn't, if I present them reasonably logically, without, forgive me Aggro, nonsense about the paranormal - I'll prepare a white ship for you as well. Does it have to be a specific unit? And why exactly does it have to be white?"

"Ideally, it would be a civilian ship with weak, regulation armament," Aggro replied. "The Kiritians will take us better then and appreciate our courage. White is a symbol of peace, non-aggression and negotiation, among humans as well as humanoid jaguars. Since Xajb'a Kej's power is based on the Onkalotian code - he is a fundamentalist rigorously adhering to the doctrines and principles of centuries old - the Kiritians will not touch a messenger in such a unit. He or she will have no problems landing, as well as taking off."

Lacetti smiled sadly.

"Well, well. We've had an enemy on our backs for centuries, and we know so little about them. We had no idea about the representatives' white ships."

"How were we supposed to know it anyway?" Splinter said. "Kiritians are not effusive. We learn practically everything about them by accident."

"It's just an extra precaution," the humanoid jaguar pointed out. "The Kiritians have never, in their history, killed any hostile envoy."

"Yeah ..." Andreyev said, nodding. "Even though they are frigging bastards, they can follow the rules. You have to give them that."

"They should also listen to everyone," added the humanoid jaguar. "Forkis always receives representatives in person. He trusts the Council of Dignitaries, but prefers to settle such matters on his own." He said after a moment of silence, he got serious, "But what I'm going to do, may end badly. That's why I sensitize you at once to the fact that the mission may end in our catastrophe."

"I'm not afraid of death," only Beliar muttered.

He and the commander exchanged enigmatic glances. There was some kind of agreement between them.

"So settled," said Lacetti. "We'll end here, gentlemen." He stood up, gave Aggroteh his hand as he too rose from his chair. "Thank you for choosing to cooperate with us. And congratulations on your incredible courage. May this plan succeed."

"The pleasure is mine," replied the humanoid jaguar casually. "I also thank you for your trust and offered help."

"You will go with Lieutenant Drunkenstein at dawn to Dr. Figam, you don't need permission from the headquarters, mine is enough. But the second flight depends on its decision, so I will have an interplanetary conversation with Mezzo shortly. However, the organization may take weeks to complete if the plan is approved. Right away someone will take you to the guest tent."

Ivan extinguished his half-burned cigar in an ashtray.

"And I'd love to talk to that bunch of morons that I commissioned a search mission on Aj to."

Chapter XII
Operation 'Trojan Horse'

Walking under the starry carpet to a tent set on a side, pointed by some corporal, Aggroteh noticed a dropped holonot. He picked it up and examined. Though he didn't intend to refer to his abilities, chaotic, broken images from the object owner's past began to appear in his mind. The lost item turned out to be the property of Lieutenant Drunkenstein. A few days earlier, it had been lying next to a lonely fire where Beliar had kissed, then made love, with some rebel. Disgusted, the Onkalot immediately interrupted the relay channel, hid the holonot in the pouch. He shook his head disapprovingly. He remembered Beliar's behavior at the Commander's meeting apparently caused by the shock after finding out that Anna Sandstorm was in the hands of the Kiritians. The menacing gleam in his eyes and the nervous gestures seemed real. The Onkalot had no doubt that the lieutenant wanted to beat the usurper, but he doubted that the girl was the cause of his dislike. It was more about male pride and the feeling of your property being taken away. "Anyway, that's not my problem," he thought. All he cared about was the young Drunkenstein turning out to be useful in the mission, the details of which Aggro constantly refined.

Sometime later, Tom Lewandowski came to Q'ualel's tent and persuaded him to join him, and his companions interested in Onkalots. Soon, the four of them were sitting among the rocks, by the joyfully buzzing fire, talking about situations in the barracks and everyday life, drinking beer.

"Tell me something else about your people, preferably about its habits," asked the girl one of the men, who joined the company. Aggro told eagerly, being listened to as willingly as at the meeting with the commander. In the meantime, another people were joining the group. It started to get merrier; the beer was already flowing in liters.

Looking for the holonot, thoughtful Beliar was walking by when the topic of challenges among humanoid jaguars was raised. He stuffed his hands in his pockets and stopped on the sidelines behind a thorny bush to listen out of curiosity. He didn't want to approach low-ranking rebels.

"Did you have any habits regarding women?" Asked the same girl as before.

"Oh, a lot," said the humanoid jaguar. "For example, if males fought for the favor of a female, the challenging person threw a stone red as blood to the ground in front of a competitor, because usually such fights were the bloodiest, as were those for the position of chief. If anyone healthy refused the duel, he was treated by the tribe as a coward, and this meant the greatest disgrace for a warrior. Therefore, resignations were rare."

Aggroteh heard the sound of pebbles falling, and as he turned, he saw Beliar standing by the bush. He got up and went to the lieutenant.

"You had to drop it." He outthrusted the holonot towards him.

The man looked at the Onkalot with a fleeting indifference, then stared blankly at his lost item. Aggroteh didn't miss the slight embarrassment on his face in the form of the quivering eyelid and corner of his lip, as well as the gaze that escaped to the right, as if Beliar hadn't wanted to meet his eyes.

"Thanks." He took the holonot and put it in his pants pocket. He managed a forced smile. "So, see you tomorrow. Have a nice night, Aggro."

He turned and marched towards the officers' section of the barracks, leaving the slightly surprised humanoid jaguar on the rock.

***

"Can we talk for a moment?" Beliar didn't go to rest. He accosted Aggroteh on his way back to his tent.

"Of course."

"I know you didn't tell the whole truth in front of the commander. I saw your hesitation when you talked about Forkis before the London coup and avoided the subject of Anna. Lacetti noticed it as well, but didn't dwell on the subject, as he knew you wouldn't say what you chose to keep to yourself anyway." The lieutenant shifted the weight to the other leg. "I, however, would prefer to find out the truth. In case you didn't notice it, I'm too on this mission."

"Why don't we go inside?" The Onkalot nodded towards the tent.

"No need, no one else is here."

"What exactly do you want to know?"

Beliar's eyes narrowed.

"Did Anna fly with the Kiritians voluntarily, or they took her captive. Tell me the truth." He gripped Aggroteh's arm forcefully as he saw him staring at the distant point. "I will extract this information from you, even if I have to try until morning. Otherwise, I will not go anywhere."

"Your commander has already given the order. Do you want to challenge his words?" The Onkalot looked at the interlocutor with reddish eyes full of gentleness and something else. "But what?" The lieutenant wondered. "Compassion? Mockery? Disgust?"

"Just tell me what happened. I know you haven't summarized even half of what you found out. Understand: Anna is my girlfriend ... Okay, we had a bit of a fight because I screwed up, but I still love her. Therefore, I would like to know everything, no matter what the truth may be. Tell me!"

The Onkalot jerked his arm out.

"Sorry, I'd rather not."

"So, it's bad, right? She was captured?"

"Not exactly."

"Come on, spit it out, damn it!" The lieutenant growled. "Otherwise, I won't leave you alone."

Aggro looked at him coldly.

"Anna is not the Kiritians' hostage."

Beliar understood immediately. He rubbed his face with his hand. He walked away a bit and leaned against the boulder. He didn't speak for a moment, staring indifferently at the lights of the encampment.

"I knew it. I sensed it." He turned abruptly to the Onkalot. "She has a crush on him, doesn't she?"

"I don't know if you can call it that. I don't really understand this relationship, you can't thoroughly outline such things with psychometry."

"It doesn't make sense! You must have been wrong." Beliar walked over to the humanoid jaguar. "After all, she hated Forkis as if he had murdered her entire family by himself! Where the hell is logic here?!"

"It is said that the line between love and hate can be very thin."

"Thanks for telling me." The lieutenant spoke calmer.

"Just don't do stupid things. Once we start working together, it would be better for both of us, as well as for all the rebels, if the plan went according to the guidelines."

"I won't. Those who make mistakes don't become officers." Beliar gave him a confident smile that even emanated affectation. Massaging his neck, he turned and went away into the night. "Good night, Aggro."

Q'ualel stood in front of the tent entrance for a moment, wondering what the gleam in his eyes he was given on parting could have meant. So often seen in madmen or terrorists who no longer cared about their future, which could lead to a tragedy.

***

The Utza'm Achij hall from the capital K'otz'ib'aja, originally a complex of several interconnected caves, was so huge that when a lot of fire was lit in its center (it was customary that modern lighting was not used here), the darkness lingered by the walls and ceiling. In the development of the space, was chosen naturalism: it was filled with stalagmites, stalactites and columns of monumental dimensions, as well as fountains, ponds, balustrades, balconies, terraces, swimming pools and other recreational attractions - and everything was created in the living eruptive rock, using ingenious mining and construction techniques. Most of the Morascrik surface was seismically active. The immortals have learned to use the enormous amounts of energy stored in the earth's crust. Their civilization was innovative and state-of-the-art, at the same time a lot of flashes and references to the Onkalotian culture could be noticed, the creators of which turned out to be masters when it comes to bending nature to their own needs, harmless to the planet itself. Therefore, on the Kiritian mother planet, there were many places similar to Utza'm Achij, whose name Forkis borrowed from the Onkalotian language, and which meant War Corners. War conferences were held in the cave hall, but over time it also became a place of recreation and entertainment, where thousands of people could be present at once.

Anna liked this enigmatic and atmospheric place at once. Being in the hall soothed the senses, calmed the mind, regenerated strength, especially when she had the opportunity to walk here alone, like a young acolyte waiting for mental contact with her professed god. She liked to contemplate for hours the vault, facets and cornices, multi-colored Kiritian fires, as well as flames creeping on stands stylized as mythical beasts and animals, feel the warmth emanating from the bowels of the earth on her skin, inhaling the scents of incense. She chose for strolls the time when there were few achijes in Utza'm Achij. Forkis often joined Anna, as soon as he finished his duties.

Although she had been in the Kiritians' capital for many weeks, still as an oders without the super virus, she was given access to all facilities (In general, any achij was free to move around K'otz'ib'aja, except in places where they might have disrupted someone's work. Thanks to Forkis' Kiritian truthfulness and telepathy, there was no monitoring or other form of surveillance anywhere, which worked). In addition, Forkis, with his own plans in mind, inducted Anna into the Council of Dignitaries, also known as the Council of Five. The organ performed advisory, sometimes judicial functions, when the opposing parties were unable to reach an agreement individually, or relieved Forkis in matters that it assigned to him. Sandstorm's voice as a specialist in rebels' matters and an objective person in Kiritian domestic politics was significant among the council members, other lictors, and generals. Though she still didn't belong to the nation, she was liked and trusted thanks to the recommendation of Forkis. At least in public.

Utza'm Achij that evening was filled with Kiritians having fun on no special occasion. The Emperor tried to organize such meetings every month so that people could relax and get crazy with the participation of sex, music, stimulants and liquors brought from different universes. The aggressive fun was in full swing, but Forkis, busy with plans to develop the moon U1 and destroy parts of the asteroid belt, joined Anna and the lictors a few hours later. They had the highest terrace at their disposal, which overlooked a large part of the hall. Forkis found the girl briskly talking to Necron.

"As always, you show up when the best is over." Smiling, she pointed to the amused crowd. "The party is slowly ending."

"Ending? Yes?" Forkis scooped her up in his arms, seemingly protesting, walked over to a leather-lined chair and sat on it, clanking his weapons.

As the androids began to carry more drinks across the terrace, an officer approached the Emperor kissing Sandstorm and whispered something in his ear. Utza'm Achij's thick walls interfered with communication signals, especially during the plasma ejection of Betelgeuse, the red supergiant that provided Morascrik with energy, so information had to be passed on verbally more than once.

Forkis sighed nervously.

"Great. They won't give a man even five minutes of privacy." He got up and turned to the officer, "I'll come right now. Take these two to the throne room." He kissed Anna as achijes moved away. "Forgive me, baby. Wait for me politely."

She shrugged her shoulders.

"Needs must when the devil drives."

"Come on, Kiret." As Forkis passed by, he nudged Necron in the shoulder. He also summoned another lyctor occupied with his bottle.

The men, accompanied by two androids, descended the stone steps to the level of the hall and disappeared into a side corridor.

***

A white merchant ship, encircled by a Kiritian squadron of mini ships, was flying through the planetary system towards

Morascrik under the envoys reception procedure. Why exactly in the vicinity of such units, where one could destroy twenty ships - no rebel knew for sure. It was supposed that the Kiritians were either demonstrating their strength or sending ships due to the military nature of the nation. Maybe both.

Though nothing bad had happened so far, Beliar had been sitting as if on a hedgehog from the moment Aggroteh handed over their personal details to the squadron's achij. His anxiety was bigger the closer they got to the planet. He sincerely admired his comrade sitting in the co-pilot's seat, for his stoic calm, he even envied him a little. The Onkalot must have had great control of his nerves, or he did know Forkis well enough to believe that he didn't endanger them as deputies. Drunkenstein would have definitely preferred the latter option.

Though light-years away, enormous Betelgeuse hung over them like a harbinger of death. They entered the Morascrik's upper atmosphere, which from space appeared as a black-brown geoid interwoven with red lava veins. They quickly broke through the dark clouds and found themselves above the rocky, rough surface. The planet had been fully terraformed in the past, and yet it still looked Precambrian and dangerous.

The machines began to slow down as they neared the capital.

"It's time." Aggro activated the autopilot, disconnected all safeguards and apparatus. He pulled a plunger with a needle from a compartment next to the control panel and walked over to Beliar.

The officer flinched, instinctively rubbed the suit's fabric on his shoulder.

"Is it really necessary?"

"Forkis can read minds from about a hundred meters away. If he probes your mind, what he will do first, we can forget about the success of the mission. Even about life. This undetectable inhibitor from Figam will shield your brain tissue, then no sensory expert will get to the information. This works more or less like a Faraday cage blocking an electrostatic field. I repeat what the doctor told me."

"You didn't inject yourself with that filth."

"I'm an Onkalot, I can block myself from Forkis, I already explained it to you. We used to spend time together often. It can be learned, but it takes a lot of time and the presence of a telepath nearby."

"And more puzzles. I don't know anything anyway. You didn't share your arch brilliant plan with me."

"It's for safety. It's enough for Forkis to find out prematurely that we visited Figam and we will be screwed. I asked the doctor to remain discreet. I'll tell everything myself in good time when Forkis has no way back and can't stop me. Don't whine but give me your hand or inject yourself."

Beliar got rid of the breastplate. In his nerves, he pulled off the entire suit, remaining in a military camouflage outfit.

"It will work in a minute or so," Aggro informed as he injected the contents of the little vessel into the man's system. He also got rid of the uncomfortable anti-g suit, staying in the loincloth, tooth necklace, and belt with the obsidian knife. On the other side, he attached a cage covered with cloth (at least it looked like a miniature birdcage), the contents of which Beliar had not been able to determine throughout the journey, and the fellow passenger, silent as a statue, hadn't wanted to talk about the strange object. "Act ordinary."

The officer chuckled.

"Two sheep are going to a party with a pack of hungry wolves, and you are asking me to behave as if I go to a pastry shop for cookies?"

"At least don't bite your nails." The corners of the Onkalot's black lips rose slightly. "And don't take your weapon."

"I know, damn it! We've been through this a million times."

They fell silent and held their breaths as in front of the canopy, they saw the first sky-high - literally - K'otz'ibaja towers. In fact, they were reminiscent of mammalian intestines, collectors of enormous caliber reaching above the clouds, drawing from space every kind of energy available in the sector, then feeding it to city's processing tanks to make it inexhaustible source of power for the city next to geo-energy. The sight was both fascinating and creepy due to the huge size and complexity of the devices. The city's mostly pyramidal buildings, sometimes hundreds of meters high, were mostly made of dark rock blocks of volcanic origin, with stunning precision and attention to detail. Numerous constrictions and openings allowed free electronic communication. Both Beliar and Aggroteh, who had seen similar buildings in ancient Onkalotian cities, couldn't take their eyes and thoughts off them. The Kiritians mastered a technique of stone processing incomprehensible to the Oderses, which they did as easily as if they had been using soft, flexible metal alloys for building materials. That is why K'otz'ib'aja was associated at first glance with the ancient cities of Mesoamerica, except that the forgotten techno lytic techniques were not only rediscovered here, but also improved. They made it possible to create literally everything from stone, from a well-presented government building to ergonomic barracks. The capital was definitely a dark metropolis, as its inhabitants liked: although it was close to noon, dense, dark clouds lingered there, occasionally letting the bloody beams of Betelgeuse through. Manufactured artificially, they blended in with the microclimate, and the overall effect was enhanced by high cones of a distant forest of extinct volcanoes. Indefinite, usually bulky, maggot-like units hovered over the metropolis; technical orbs flew in all directions.

"It's weird that all this won't fall on their heads." Beliar glanced curiously from left to right as they glided slowly through the capital. "The ground is said to be shaking here often."

"Kiritians only build metropolises in the middle of great tectonic plates," Aggroteh replied, also watching the view eagerly through the canopy. "These are aseismic areas, also they choose places far from active volcanoes. For them, nature doesn't provide for any surprises. They have everything under control."

"It's obvious," Beliar admitted reluctantly. He had envied Kiritians literally everything for a long time. "But you did your homework."

They landed on a vast, multi-level pad in front of Utza'm Achij cave, connected by a tunnel to the government building. Several armored achijes approached the ship's fairing. The squad leader signaled the passengers to leave.

Beliar looked questioningly at his neighbor. Aggro, keeping his face serious, nodded at him, then used the control panel to slide back the canopy.

Drunkenstein took a deep breath as he descended the extended ladder.

"Amazingly clean air," he said to his companion. "It's like I'm in the mountains, in some forest. I admit that I've expected smoke and sulfur."

"Welcome to K'otz'ib'aja," the Kiritian officially spoke to them. "I'm the batab Gareth, this is the title of the commanders of the city guard here. For some time you will be under my auspices, so I'm asking you to follow all instructions."

He made them stand facing each other and raise their arms high, then instructed the two achijes to run their multifunction scanners along their bodies.

"And what is that?" Asked the man checking Aggroteh, pointing to the small cage covered with the cloth, strapped to his belt.

"For good luck." The Onkalot grinned in an innocent smile. The Achij whispered something to the other controller. The latter, slightly confused, shrugged, then spoke to Gareth. Irritated, the batab took the device and made a detailed scans of the cage and its contents himself, then waved his hand dismissively.

"Onkalots and their superstitions. But he's clean. You can put your paws down."

The achij, who was examining Beliar, held a holographic mini monitor at the height of his chest for a long time. He looked significantly at his supervisor.

"Have you had lung cancer?" Gareth Beliar asked. Aggro looked first at the rebel, then at the Kiritian. The uneasiness that appeared in the blink of an eye on the lieutenant's face didn't escape his attention, quickly replaced with a dispassionate mask. The batab noticed the same thing because he was frowning for a moment.

"Yes," Drunkenstein replied matter-of-factly.

"This is rare, especially in our time." Gareth looked into his eyes but could read nothing but his insistently demonstrated indifference. He simply assumed that the rebel was afraid and was acting reckless. He ordered the visitors to be checked again for weapons and suspicious objects. "Follow me, please. The First Galactic Dignitary is waiting for you." He pointed to an open double-leaf gate leading to the Utza'm Achij cave.

Gareth led, followed by Aggro and Beliar bordered with achijes, who were ready to overwhelm them with energizers if they did something wrong. The newcomers watched the Kiritians wandering around. They couldn't get rid of the feeling of being overwhelmed as they stared at the majestic, detailed, and artfully crafted structures that challenged the sky. Beliar felt like a cottage peasant who was given the opportunity to see a city and palace.

Having passed the gate several meters high, they entered a vaulted, chamfered corridor drilled in the living rock with machines commonly known as moles. It was illuminated by artificial fire and solar crystals. Delving into the complex where aliens could easily become disoriented, they passed Kiritians interested in them, especially in the Onkalot.

Aggro noticed that the closer they were to Forkis, the more concerned Beliar was. He was breathing hard, he was looking nervously to the sides, he wiped a bead of sweat from his temple with his finger. He was acting like someone afraid of caves. Or a convict who is fully aware that he is going to be executed.

"Is everything alright?" He asked in a whisper, walking closer to Beliar. He flinched, looked at him with more than the legitimate concern of a person surrounded by enemies.

"Alright?" The humanoid jaguar repeated, carefully looking the man in the eyes. They entered a corridor with a stone colonnade leading to the meeting room.

"Yeah ..." Beliar fixed his eyes on Gareth's back. "But you'd better tell me everything. We'll meet face to face with the Kiritian emperor in a few minutes, and I don't even know what you want to do."

"You'll find out soon." The Onkalot placed his paw on the dangling cage at his hip.

"Here is the audience hall." The batab pointed to the gate at the top of the short, wide staircase, decorated with engraved animals and Kiritian letters reminiscent of ancient signs. On the left and right sides of the entrance guarded by two achijes, artificial flames burned, sending vivid reflections down the gray-brown metal.

"So, here we go," commented Drunkenstein as the clearance appeared.

The humanoid jaguar didn't speak, just inhaled deeply.

***

As the group entered the warm, monumental room, Forkis sat nonchalantly on a diorite throne. As if by the very posture he had wanted to humiliate the guests.

"Q'ualel! By the gods who don't exist ..." He stood up, not hiding his surprise to see Aggro strutting proudly on the synthetic carpet.

He had been warned that a rebel with an Onkalot had wanted to see him, so he and his dignitaries had had their minds set on additional entertainment on Orgy Day, but he had never expected such a thing in his life. Not Aggroteh! Having contained his emotions, he bowed his head slightly in greeting, which had nothing to do with the ruler-subordinate relationship but was an Onkalotian tribal greeting. Anyway, Aggro was several dozen years older than him. The achijes in the throne room, ignorant of the custom were surprised why the First Galactic Dignitary was behaving this way towards the arriving anthropomorph.

"Xajb'a Kej," the humanoid jaguar returned the greeting. After this deliberate test, Forkis got rid of all the doubts. He felt uneasy. Aggro knew everything. That's why he had come here. It was up to him now to find the emperor out. And Kiritian truthfulness, the eighth rule of the decalogue, might have proved fatal in this case. However, Forkis was able to control the fear he felt so rarely.

"I've thought you've been long dead." His eyes showed sadness, but also joy. "I'm glad I was wrong."

"I was in captivity for a time, but then lived as a free Onkalot on a human farm," the words sounded like an accusation.

"And specifically?"

"On Chulimal."

Beliar frowned. He was no less confused than the rest of the people. He didn't understand the bond forged between the two, who began to communicate without words. From the side, it looked as if Forkis had been gesturing silently to Aggroteh not to say something. He rolled his gaze across the guards and the five dignitaries seated at their posts beside the throne. There was only one member of the Council of Dignitaries among them, the highest of the highest lictors: General Velkee Vandringen, though more often referred to as a Warfighter, with his disfigured face, whitish eye and menacing gaze. Anyway, they couldn't expect the rest of the welcome flower, since Beliar wasn't someone important to the Kiritians. The general was probably also here for entertainment. The guards stood motionless by black rock columns that edged a carpet. Drunkenstein realized that they would have reacted 100% effectively if he had decided to commit any foolishness.

Forkis dismissed Gareth and his men with the wave of his hand.

"Come closer," he ordered the newcomers. He himself also began to climb the gentle steps separating the landing from the floor. When he stopped in front of the guests, he smiled slyly as he eyed Beliar from head to toe. The rebel felt a sudden weakness in body and mind; his back was damp with sweat. "Who can I see? Beliar Drunkenstein, lieutenant of the 78th Rebel Squadron."

"Beliar?!" From the side of the entrance to the hall came a woman's voice. Forkis, Drunkenstein, and Aggro turned simultaneously to see Sandstorm bumping into Gareth, who was just coming out into the corridor. "You're alive!"

"Anna?" The rebel's eyes seemed to grow in an instant. He took a step back, shook his head in disbelief. "So, it's true," he added in a whisper.

"You weren't supposed to come here," Forkis said reproachfully as the girl walked briskly towards them.

Anna stopped a few steps from the surprised officer. The joy swelling on her face turned into a grimace of uncertainty. For moments that seemed decades, they looked into each other's eyes.

"What are you doing here?" She asked.

"I came for you." Drunkenstein raised his arms outstretched invitingly. To his surprise, Anna didn't move even an inch. She was standing stiffly like the guards at the columns. Beliar's smile crawled off his face, replaced by anger. "What is it about?"

"You thought your arrival would do the trick? You will smile nicely, and everything will be back to normal? That you're just gonna stretch out your hands like a little boy and I'll fall into them? Beliar ... I don't belong to your world anymore. I came here voluntarily."

"Well, well, Judas has returned to his last supper chamber and still wants to wreak havoc," Forkis said sarcastically, then laughed ruffly.

Necron left the platform. He walked over to Sandstorm, discreetly grasped her arm, and pulled her aside.

"What are you talking about?" She asked Forkis, alternately looking uncertainly at him and the lieutenant who gave the man a glare. Beliar shook his head barely noticeably, as if he had had some sort of deal with the Emperor too, and he didn't want it to come out into the light of day.

"About the fact that your former partner perfidiously stand you all up." Forkis began to walk around agitated Beliar. Having stood behind his back, he placed a hand on his left shoulder and shook him slightly. "Didn't he, Lieutenant? He sold you down the river." He looked at Anna. "He didn't share this happy news? Oh, damned rebel. Well, maybe I'll do it, since it's time to reveal innermost secrets. Well, Lieutenant Beliar Drunkenstein wanted to be one of us. He desired immortality and glory at all costs, he was even ready to give his soul to the enemy. Therefore, he unscrupulously warned the Kiritians against the rebels flying towards the Scorpio Universe." He put his other hand on the lieutenant's right shoulder and smiled wickedly at him for a moment. "The betrayal of your colleagues is, however, the greatest evil an intelligent being can commit. So, the lieutenant got pissed when I sent him away to the disliked mom. The information turned out to be redundant, the rebels are not able to threaten us anyway, even if we had no idea about their plans. Nevertheless, we didn't ignore the warning and dispersed in time into battle lines. The act of treason, however, will remain the act of treason, shitting into one's own nest, whatever it is like."

Forkis' face, as he moved away from the man, was marked with a scowl, like in a mafia boss from Capricorn. "And treason of the highest level should be punished ... by death."

"Beliar, what's that supposed to mean?" Anna shook her head, making sure her voice broke. She wanted to go over to Drunkenstein and look him closely in the face, read the nuances in it, but Necron kept holding her arm. "Tell me it's not true."

The rebel in response looked at her hard and apologetically, his hands were alternately opening and clenching.

"I can't believe it ... You were such a cheerful, brave and helpful man. And a friend. What happened? Why?"

"Descendants of the NOA. What were you expecting?" General Velkee said dismissively, sitting at the desk with his arms folded on his chest. He certainly didn't understand Forkis' decision, why he wanted Anna to join the Council, but he supposed it had to do with the information and better control of the opposition. Nevertheless, the hypocritical girl was fun and harmless.

"Many of you simply have betrayal and desertion in your genes."

Necron moved uneasily and gave the general an indifferent glance, certain that the words were addressed not only to the rebels. He himself had been once in the NOA but had escaped and risen to the position of the Second Galactic Dignitary. He sensed

Velkee was angry about it, because he wanted more powers than he had in the Council.

"Times have changed, Anna," said Beliar. "I also had to change to adapt to new conditions and survive. Although I no longer care about the latter." He looked hopefully at the Onkalot, but he too gave him a grudging, judgmental look. The rebel clenched his jaws. So, he was alone. "We'll never win against the Kiritians. So, it is wise to join the stronger. Isn't it?"

"What? Adapt? By turning into a traitor? What are you raving about?!" Sandstorm spat.

"The innocent has spoken."

"I have never revealed any of our plans to our enemy." She continued speaking, but Beliar began to ignore her words. Anyway, like water off a duck's back, completely not bothering him. Anna was only an irrelevant addition to this meeting. He stared defiantly at the usurper, who had stopped circling annoyingly, amused by the situation as much as Velkee. The other dignitaries simply waited for the course of events, watching and not interfering with the conversation.

"Xajb'a Kej." Fearing his upset companion might have done something inappropriate, Aggro quickly took the initiative. He stepped forward. "I came here to ask you for one thing: abdicate. I know who you are, you probably figured it out. The madness you have woven all these centuries is enough. This is not a place for you or me. Quit, please. It's not too late."

A few dignitaries chuckled. Laughter could also be heard from the guards.

"It's getting more and more interesting," Velkee muttered.

"Another artist." Forkis put his hands on the hips. He still carefully hid his anxiety under the cover of irony. "The circus from which the clowns escaped came to us? Are you crazy, Q'ualel?!" He raised his voice defiantly, pointed to the humanoid jaguar with his finger. "You come suddenly, practically from beyond the grave, you enter my territory and order me to reject my life, which has required so many sacrifices? Is that the only reason you came here? To order me around?" He ended the question with an amused smile.

"Think about it," hissed Aggroteh. "Consider who you really are. You've already done your revenge. Millions have died on your orders ..."

"Yes," the usurper interrupted him, "a long time ago. And then I created something phenomenal that I must not give up now as the person responsible for it. I didn't plan it, but I don't regret it. I'm even proud of it."

The humanoid jaguar smiled defiantly.

"Maybe you can change your mind now."

He grasped the material covering the cage with his claws and yanked it off.

The guards raised their weapons, ready to pierce the Onkalot. However, they didn't notice the threat, but they were confused.

The golden mouse kept in the dark, exposed to the brightness of the solar crystals and artificial fire, perked up and began to squeal.

Necron blinked in surprise. Velkee leaned forward with interest. The other lictors, Anna and Beliar, also stared at the cage like a halfwit, not understanding anything.

Forkis, on the other hand, stepped back as vigorously as before a knife heading toward his chest. Emotions prevailed over him.

"Where did you get this?! I killed it!" He screamed, pointing at the cage with a trembling finger. "It was dead!"

"Maksimus Figam is familiar not only with viruses and making technological masterpieces," the Onkalot replied calmly, keeping his smirk full of satisfaction, "but he also turned out to be a great geneticist and expert on necro medicine. Imagine he extracted genetic material from your talisman's bone marrow and raised me a mouse in less than two weeks. A living animal artifact with identical properties to the destroyed one. He succeeded, although he didn't know what he was doing, because he messed with the knowledge of the gods." He narrowed his eyelids. "You know what it means."

Forkis instinctively touched his chest below the neck. True, he had lost the capsule somewhere in the Ch'amiya B'aq temple, most likely while making love to Anna in the crypt. That damned Q'ualel must have gone to the sanctuary and found the talisman. He growled like an animal.

"So, what's it going to be?" Continued the humanoid jaguar. "Are you flying with me, or I should show a curiosity to your achijes?"

"You're not gonna do this ... my friend. Don't get involved in matters that you don't understand and don't concern you."

"Is that so?" Aggro asked, more confident. "I'm doing this only for the benefit of all of us. I really don't want to hurt anyone."

"You're alive, that's great, I'm happy about it, but you can now go back to your forest and mud." Forkis smiled with relief as he remembered something. "You can't spoil my work, and you know why? Because the powering of the artifact will suffice only for one more command!"

The usurper jumped up like a hunting panther and in a split second found himself at the cage.

"Let everything that your holder says not come true!" He shouted to the golden mouse.

Aggro laughed softly, and the laughter echoing off the ceiling and walls became the only sound heard in the vast room. People stood as stiff as after eye contact with Medusa, surprised by the usurper's incomprehensible reaction, as if he had lost his mind. Apart from the two discussing the matter, no one understood anything of this.

"I anticipated that you would like to block the artifact." The humanoid jaguar shrugged. "But you misunderstood the way it works. The golden mouse seems to have infinite power, but a given person can use it three times; this is how this device was designed, synchronizing itself with the mind. Another user, on the other hand, can leapfrog the will of the former, imposing their own, canceling their intentions. That is why I made the request earlier, asking the golden mouse not to obey your last command, which you didn't feel like using hundreds of years ago. So, I can use it three times, I already did it once. You no longer have power over it. Now it's my turn." He pointed to Forkis with his claw. "I wish you to show your true face to everyone."

Nervous, Forkis could only watch helplessly as his body was undergoing an accelerated regressive transmutation. As his pale skin got covered by orange-yellow-white fur, black spots bloomed on it, the face lengthened, and the fangs of a big cat appeared in the mouth being shaped, as hazel eyes turned green, a tail getting long pressed against the lower part of the armor, as claws grew out of his hands becoming thick.

The shocked guards simultaneously looked at one of them.

"What the fuck have you done, you half-assed idiot?!" It was the enraged voice of Corporal Rasmus Darkoris, who forgot completely where and with whom he was. He looked at Tsar Seymour, also mounting guard during the meeting.

"Get off me. It's not me!" Tsar waved his hands.

"You sprayed some shit in the air!"

"If it was a drug, you would see visions everywhere, not just have a kick regarding one object."

Shocked, Anna fell to her knees with a thud, when Kiret, holding her, suddenly lost his strength. She got motionless, with her mouth open in a silent scream and her hands pressed against it. Necron's eyes widened, and he stayed that way, as did Beliar. The stunned lictors and the disciplined, full of rigor achijes, who had made sure many times that the audiences were held smoothly, reacted in a similar way. A gun fell from someone's hand and hit the part of the floor without a rug with a metallic rumble. Velkee got up and put his hand on the compartment with the X17A4.

Forkis snarled. He eyed Aggroteh with a hateful glance, while Aggroteh looked sadly at his old friend and pupil, whom he was unlikely to regain.

"Wh ... what the fuck is this?!" The lengthening stupor was first interrupted by Beliar. Pointing a finger at Forkis, he looked at Necron with his eyes demanding an explanation from him as he was closest. The still stunned Second Galactic Dignitary didn't realize that he was being asked the question.

Meanwhile, the emperor threw off part of his armament that pinched him, released the cat's tail. The transmutation was complete, and in front of the meeting participants, stood now the second humanoid jaguar, taller, heavier and more muscular than Aggroteh.

"Xajb'a Kej, known in our language as the Deer Dance Square, and in your place as Forkis, is an Onkalot," Aggro began to explain. He moved from one person to another. "The truth is that for hundreds of years mankind has been controlled by the humanoid jaguar who has claimed to be a human being. This is," he detached the cage from his belt and lifted it upwards, "a golden mouse. A powerful, living artifact created by Nimja, an extremely advanced technology that sometimes manifested itself and gave the owner the ability to influence reality usually three times." He lowered the cage. "Craving a vendetta against the people who had attacked Chulimal in the past, Xajb'a Kej was lucky to meet the golden mouse and used it twice, thanks to which he achieved almost divine power. Since he had obtained everything, he wanted, and had no idea for his last request, he killed the mouse, not wanting it to get into someone else's paws. He turned softly to Forkis, "Sorry, but I had to do this. The game is over, brother. Now you have no choice but to quit it all and fly away while you still can. Let's admit that revenge has been completed, and with a vengeance."

"You don't understand, Q'ualel," Forkis said gently, having swallowed his anger. He spoke loud and clear for everyone to hear, though he was looking at Aggroteh. "You are right about the beginning of the crusade. I had only one goal: to exterminate the entire human race. However, this changed, as I already mentioned. Being at the head of the enormous army in which any achij was ready to die for me, even sacrificing immortality, although I hadn't cared for any of them at first and intended to get rid of these people at the right moment, I had come to the point where I had to abandon my insane attempts and to be responsible for the empire I had created. I couldn't back out anymore. For I had introduced a new order among Oderses constantly militating against each other. I had created the nation that had persisted despite acting contrary to human nature." He glanced at Necron. "I had also loved the Kiritians. They had become like brothers and friends to me. I could also give my life for them. Most of the Onkalots were the species of creators, they didn't destroy what they had built with great difficulty. And I, too, couldn't act otherwise."

"Wow." Tsar Seymour, who had often had many different visions, was the first to get roused from shock. Anyway, it lasted for a short time in him, and by definition suited more to surprise. "This is better than the best kick I've had."

"I hope Dr. Figam can explain that to us somehow," Darkoris said. "Because otherwise I will go crazy."

"But why were you lying to us all the time?" Necron asked Forkis in his voice trembling with emotion, having finally gotten it back.

"Would you have trusted me? At most, you'd have thought I'm a madman who can successfully block lie detectors. I would have lost power. Only the Nimja artifact was able to reverse the process of transmutation that I had succumbed to and thanks to which I changed from one species to another, but I destroyed it. I didn't even think Dr. Figam would be able to recreate it. However, it wasn't important to me to return to my earlier form. The human body is better." Forkis hung his head. Those watching him from the side could have sworn that he abased himself before his lictor -

for he knelt on his knee in front of him. "Kiret Necron Biffter ... do with me what you want. I'm ready for anything."

Necron helped Anna, still unable to come to herself, pulled her aside and crouched down next to his lord and commander. Biffter's serious face softened from a warm smile. He put his hand on the usurper's shoulder.

"Nothing has changed, Forkis. You are still our emperor to me. An achij like all of us." He hugged mannishly the surprised humanoid jaguar.

"Necron." Forkis returned the friendly hug. "Remember that these are just your words."

Kiret moved away.

"I suspected there was something wrong with you for a long time," he said softly. "I have lived by your side for hundreds of years and have observed a lot, but rarely did I want to pursue the topic. You know it yourself. Although you tried to hide it, it was an open secret that you sometimes eat people alive. Or you were extremely drawn to Chulimal. But I wouldn't have expected something like this in my life."

"We also support the words of Kiret Biffter." It was the hard voice of General Warfighter. The guards and lictors who approached Necron and Forkis were of the same opinion. They got up from the carpet. "By deed you proved, sir, how valuable you are."

"By their fruits ye shall know them," quoted Biffter.

"As you can see, sir, you have no enemies here," Tsar said cheerfully, spreading his arms. "A look doesn't matter. A genre neither. Actions count, as was said."

"Probably for the first time in his life, he has said something wise." Darkoris relaxed the atmosphere even more.

"It's not what I've expected, gentlemen." Forkis had to make sure his voice didn't break. He approached Anna who smiled weakly. It encouraged him, but he didn't smile back.

"All your deviations and inhuman deeds now make sense," she whispered. "Though I still can't comprehend what just happened."

"And it will probably affect ..." Sandstorm hesitated for a moment, staring at the alien but well-known being. However, she found the courage and hugged the soft, warm cat's fur, throwing her arms around the usurper's neck.

"Of course, it won't affect our relationship. Your achij Tsar Seymour summed up the topic perfectly."

"Anna." The Onkalot repaid with a much stronger hug. He discreetly wiped the wetness off his eyes, now green as they had been before the first transmutation. He hadn't been so moved in ages. On closer inspection, he had never got so moved in life, immediately accepted by the creatures he had once despised.

Aloof, Beliar had no reason to be happy. He was seething with rage as he watched the two hug.

"Forkis!" He shouted, drawing the attention of the rest.

He acted instantly.

He pulled something out of his pocket and threw it at them. Thinking it was an explosive, Forkis pushed Anna hard, and she landed in Necron's arms.

On the carpet, at the Emperor's feet, lay a red topaz the size of a plum.

Forkis, like Aggro, immediately understood the intention of Beliar, standing in a truculent position.

"The challenge accepted ... Lieutenant," growled Xajb'a Kej, stressing the last word. Among Onkalots, hierarchical fights between males significantly different from each other in the social ladder were rare. Challenges were sometimes accepted by the mighty with the mind and strength of a ruler, if they were justified. In turn, challenges regarding a female were never rejected because they had nothing to do with authority. "I see you've done your homework with Aggroth."

"Lieutenant Commander," corrected Beliar, smiling and making Anna stunned again that day. "You have rightly noticed that I have prepared myself for the audience. We went through it with the officers and decided that after my promotion you will be more willing to talk to me. However, the meeting happened anyway, but it's better to have an ace up your sleeve. By the way, I didn't get the promotion for free, but I deserved those two levels higher."

"Will this merry-go-round of laughter and absurdity never end?" Tsar commented. Everyone ignored him, though most thought the same.

"All that's left for me to do is congratulate you, Lieutenant Commander," Forkis said with a slight irony. "You don't lack bravado, but imagination, you do. You don't seem to realize what you want to get yourself into." He ostentatiously outthrusted and retracted his long, strong claws.

"Could the fight take place in a few hours?" The officer asked, pretending that Forkis' hint was unimpressive.

"Let it be so. I propose to fight in public, in the arena of gladiators next to Utza'm Achij.

"So, everything is settled." The Lieutenant Commander crooked his lips in a cynical smile, inadequate to the uncertainty and fear he felt. He realized that the fight couldn't end in anything other than drastic changes. In a way, it would be a duel between the Kiritians and the rebels, fought by the ancient rules. Who loses, would also bring down his own companions. Forkis was a formidable opponent, and after the transformation he seemed invincible. However, Beliar also had countless fights to his credit, often with a stronger opponent. If not by force, he would try to do something with a stratagem. In addition, he had a plan that only a few people knew about, including Aveo Lacetti. The commander wouldn't have sent him on a mission to K'otz'ib'aj if he had had any doubt that Drunkenstein would fail. That's why he couldn't screw up.

Anna freed herself from Necron's embrace. She stood in front of Forkis, gave Beliar a questioning look.

"Beliar, what is it?" She pointed to the topaz lying on the ground, which no one deigned to pick up. So, she bent down and did it herself. She looked at the usurper. "What is this?"

"A stone, as you can see," he replied. He turned to Necron, "Take Miss Sandstorm to the chamber and make sure that she doesn't leave it for some time."

"Come on, Anna." Kiret grabbed her arm and started to lead her firmly towards the exit. Sandstorm was unable to interpret the reluctant, even hateful look Beliar gave her when they accidentally looked into each other's eyes. After his double betrayal, she wanted nothing to do with him, nevertheless it hurt her when he looked at her that way. It was as if had been going to alienate her. But why.

"Maybe you can explain to me what's going on here?" She asked Necron, steadfastly leading her forward.

He shrugged.

"I wish I knew it, honey," he sighed. "This is the craziest day in my hundreds of years of life."

Chapter XIII
Duel

Within an hour, all Morascrik knew about Forkis' origin. The unheard-of news rushed at superluminal speed into space, rapidly infecting consecutive colonized planets, causing shock and disbelief to all the inhabitants. However, no Kiritians hated Forkis after discovering his true identity. For them, he was a symbol of perfect power, stability and order, the giver of glory and immortality, the personification of power, the bearer of hope. Regardless of the character. Only a handful became disaffected with Xajb'a Kej but accepted him, while another group needed time to understand the situation.

An arena stylized as an ancient Roman one was built in the times of the nascent capital, K'otz'ib'aja. At first, bloody life-and-death duels with the participation of prisoners and criminals took place here, then animals brought from the Zodiac Universum colony were added to it. Busy conquering the Odersian planets, Forkis rarely visited K'otz'ibaja, so he was unaware of the colosseum massacres. When the cosmos became stable under the rule of his steel hand, enemies were crushed to dust or effaced, and the planets conquered, he could afford to rest in the capital. He then banned barbaric intraspecific fighting, so fitting for the cruel human nature, in favor of duels to first blood or a minor bodily injury that could be quickly healed in a medical center using machines, bio nanites or molecular glue. These were the times when the young military nation was stuck at the stage of germination - it had in itself more human than a perfect being, modeled on the statistical Onkalot, for which the usurper wanted to create the Immortals. The idea, it was said, came from Kiret, who persuaded Forkis to soften the nature of the fighting. Others argued that the First Galactic Dignitary himself feared these duels. For he saw in them a reflection of the nature of a wild animal, the exteriorization of his own indomitable ego, which he wanted to suppress as the centuries passed. Deaths after reformed fights still happened in the arena of the coliseum, but they were rare.

One of them was supposed to take place in the evening. Only one combatant was to survive.

The Emperor hoped for an intimate duel that would take place in the presence of a few guards, lictors and Aggroteh, so he was extremely surprised when he saw at the end of a passage for gladiators, on stone bleachers, jostling crowds.

"Where's Necron?" He asked the Warfighter.

"He should be here soon."

Forkis made sure that a knee-length loincloth material - the only garment he was wearing - didn't restrict his movements. The group passed under the raised grate, and he entered the sand arena, over seventy meters in diameter. Cages with logs attached at regular intervals were burning on the circular wall. An additional source of light was in the center of the colonnade and had the form of a giant torch burning in a syenite bowl, supported by four squatting winged creatures.

The usurper looked around at the gathered crowd, moving and undulating like ants, into whose mound, someone stuck a smoking stick. He shifted his gaze to the blood-red sky, cut by black bands of clouds heralding the coming night, then to the steep peaks of volcanoes that had become extinct thousands of years earlier. He stood slightly astride, wagged his tail, raised his arm and roared mightily, lingeringly and loudly, showing his fangs. To his almost atavistic satisfaction, the crowd boomed wildly in response, undulated even more. The achijes wanted great entertainment like in the old days, that's why they came here, and he would provide it for them. He didn't have to limit himself anymore.

From the other entrance, yawning blackness mucky by the dull glow of cressets, emerged, naked from the waist up, Lieutenant Commander Beliar Drunkenstein. He was accompanied by five achijes. He moved a seemingly indifferent gaze across the crowd, and finally fixed his eyes on Xajb'a Kej smiling and purring like a cat, moving the tip of his tail. He became even more concerned to see him in all his glory, well over a hundred kilos of fur, perfectly shaped muscles, sharp claws and fangs, waiting to crush him with his aggression and power. Beliar had at his disposal the athletic body, nearly one meter and ninety centimeters tall and weighing eighty kilos, so he had to rely on speed and cleverness in the upcoming fight. Everything seemed so unreal to him.

"Crush that kid," Warfighter said to Forkis, going back into the hallway. He had a call to a riot control center on one of the planets and was unable to watch the duel.

The escort who had led the fighters to the arena went back to the walls of the breacher. Although no command was given, the onlookers fell silent. The grates under which the opponents had passed dropped heavily to the sand.

Beliar looked around at the crowd once more, trying to estimate the size of the audience: there must have been at least a few hundred achijes. He thought it was better than he had expected, because his only target was to be Forkis. The grates dropped, both behind his back and in his mind. The bridge was burnt down. There was no turning back.

The opponents faced each other, between the colonnade and the entrance to the arena from which Beliar had come. Had it not been for the sizzle of the fire, one could have said that the world was completely silent, held its breath, as if it had wanted to see the fight without missing the smallest detail.

The Lieutenant Commander noticed that Forkis was holding something in his hand that, when thrown carelessly, found itself in the sand between them. It was a small military knife.

"I would like to fight a fair fight," said the Onkalot. "I hit clear; you will be able to use this tool."

Beliar snorted in response, made a mocking, arrogant face, and scowled at Forkis.

"Are you making fun of me? Are you trying to baste me?"

"I want to fight fairly, as equals," the Kiritian replied honestly.

"You don't even know me, and you don't know what I'm capable of."

"You will have the opportunity to prove your skills in a moment." Forkis glanced at the lictors to see if Necron had already arrived. He looked at Aggroteh with that funny chest at his hip. Q'ualel nodded to him, folded his arms over his chest. "So, he'll be unarmed?" He turned to Beliar. He was stubbornly silent, eyeing him with an ice-cold gaze. "As you want."

Xajb'a Kej rushed to attack.

He fell on four limbs and ran like a hunting jaguar towards surprised Beliar.

"Oh shit ..." Rebel quickly got self-assured, shouted, and started running as well. He flashed past the lying knife, ignoring it.

The distance between the opponents was melting down drastically quickly.

Aggroteh held his breath. It would have seemed that everyone in the breachers did the same as the silence became overwhelming.

Forkis jumped, hit Beliar as if he had been ramming him with Firley. He knocked him off his feet, and they fell to the sand together. The fans screamed. Some rose from the benches when the lieutenant commander thumped his back on the ground so painfully that he groaned and clenched his teeth, crushed by the Onkalot's weight.

First blood was shed. Human.

The fight began.

***

"Don't make a scene but let me out!" Anna Sandstorm hit her fists again on the door of her private chamber. "Necron, damn it. You can't keep me here. Deactivate that goddamn lock!"

"I'm doing it only for your own good, sweetheart," replied Kiret from the corridor. He glanced at the control panel, which he had recoded as soon as the girl had entered the room. Now only an outsider could open the door. "I got the order."

"Just let me go there."

"Better not, really brutal things are happening there."

"Forkis will kill him. I gotta stop them, is it getting to you?" Banging on the door again.

Necron leaned against the wall next to the panel, stared at the ceiling, and took a deep breath.

"You can't do anything."

"You have no right to imprison me, I'm on the Council!"

"With all due respect, but this is a case between men. You will only disturb them. Don't think that the fight is for you, well, maybe a little bit. Beliar wants his honor back after Forkis took him down a peg. Poor rebel fool. In addition, a traitor."

Hearing these words, Anna stopped pressing against the door and fell to the floor. She was still angry with Beliar. And she still felt the pain of his betrayal from months earlier, fainter but still lingering in her heart with a heavy sediment. Maybe she should have let him die? After all, it was his decision to fly there and engage in this idiotic fight ... No. Then she wouldn't forgive herself for it, she would torment herself with Drunkenstein's death, if she could help him. She would save not Lieutenant Commander Beliar Drunkenstein, but the man who had gone astray and chosen the wrong path. The kind, helpful boy with leadership qualities who had saved her from the Kiritians in Ajb'atenaja twenty years earlier. The Kiritians she had recently joined ... It wasn't until she felt the pain that she realized she was biting her lip to the blood. She wiped off the reddish saliva with the back of her hand.

"If you don't open it, I'll go out the window," Anna said to the door.

"You are about thirty meters from the ground," replied Necron from the other side. "So, good luck. I have to go to the arena. I'll come back to you later. And don't delude yourself that someone will come and open it for you."

"Then I'll go onto the roof."

Unaffected, Necron didn't take even a few steps when he heard the bang of the window being cracked nervously.

"She's crazy."

He turned and released the lock, quickly running his armored fingers over the bright green panel.

"Anna?" He jumped immediately to the open window and leaned out.

The door to the chamber got slammed behind him, and the Kiritian turned around. He reached it, but it was already locked. He heard hurriedly taken steps in the hall, which quickly died away.

"Kiret, you're the idiot of the year." He banged his fist on one of the pillars supporting the canopy of the bed. He pulled a PDA out of his pocket, a better version of a rebel holonot, and found the right contact. "Gareth, will you help? I'm stuck ..."

***

Beliar, in which adrenaline boiled at the sight of the humanoid jaguar leaping at him, managed to curl his leg before he fell to the sand. Lying, he pressed with his shin sharply and threw Forkis off himself. It cost him several claw wounds on his forearms. He ignored them, rolled over his right shoulder, and quickly stood up; Forkis also regained a vertical position.

The humanoid jaguar attacked immediately, surprisingly lightning fast for his size; the man couldn't even take a full breath. Forkis swung his paw, wanting to leave five bleeding marks on his opponent's chest.

Beliar threw his arms and jumped back, causing the man to plow air. However, the second, outspread paw, was already gliding towards him. The rebel fell to the sand, rolled over, and rose a bit further, barely avoiding the crushing blow to the head by the Onkalot's hind limb.

Forkis pressed without respite, striking too fast for Beliar to be able to make any counterattack. He constantly forced him to dodge defensively, thus taking his revenge on the pride of the man who thought he could defeat him with his bare hands.

"You will die, you fool," he hissed in the face of grounded Beliar, trying to clench his jaws on his throat. The lieutenant commander prevented him from doing so, pressing his arm hard against his throat.

Beliar grabbed a handful of sand with his free hand and threw it in the Onkalot's eyes. He took advantage of his momentary disorientation and kicked him off himself. Then he leapt onto his back and tightened his arms around his neck, pulling him toward himself.

Forkis, who regained his normal vision after many blinks, tripped his opponent with his hind leg. They both fell to the ground.

The rebel put his hands to his ears and rose with a leap, throwing his legs out in front of himself. He did a backflip when the Onkalot, already standing, tried to grab him. Another feint of Beliar failed, Forkis, bouncing off the ground, grabbed his shoulder and tried to ground him again. Trying not to lose balance, the rebel pressed from the other side, so that both of them were now struggling like wrestlers.

However, Forkis was stronger. The boots of Drunkenstein clenching his jaw with the effort began to ride across the sand, yet their owner didn't let go of his opponent, painfully digging his claws in the back. He did the only thing he could practically do in such a sticky situation: he swung his head and hit the Kiritian with his forehead in the face.

The Onkalot growled, took a step back, grabbed his busted nose. He didn't lose even a hint of vigilance, however, and reacted immediately as thrashing Beliar was about to send him on his back with a jump kick. Forkis grabbed the opponent's shoe and pushed it, causing the man to do with himself exactly what he intended to do with the opponent.

The rebel got up and took a defensive position, putting his foot backwards for better balance, tilting his body and preparing his outstretched arms for any eventuality. He expected everything ... but not a tail slap in the face. He was hit in the eyes, which he automatically closed. It hurt like a blow with a belt wrapped in a wet rag. He lifted his eyelids just as Forkis' right hook flew towards his nose.

Drunkenstein blocked that quick blow by bending down and grasping his fist with his hand. He helped himself with his other hand, performed a quick pirouette and found himself behind Forkis, painfully twisting his paw.

The Onkalot roared. If Beliar had been wearing a shirt, he could have grabbed it and throw away the increasingly annoying rebel. Instead, swallowing a wrenching pain in his elbow, he swung his twisted arm as much as he could. He succeeded. Beliar fell on the sand a few steps away.

Forkis leapt into the air, intending to hit the man with all four paws and crush as many bones as possible. Beliar rolled at the last moment; the Onkalot hit the ground.

The lieutenant commander kept rolling until he reached his target - a sand-strewn knife. He understood that without it he would have been lost. He scarcely got up from the ground, and he had to block with his blade the impact of the claws put together, so strong that sparks flew. He supposed one of his metacarpal bones had fractured, because his wrist had hurt a lot, and a nervous current had momentarily paralyzed his entire arm.

"You're dead," Forkis said sharply in his face. He kept pressing his claws against the knife. "You should have estimated your chances first, and then throw stones."

"I've thought through everything. Have you not been taught, Emperor, that no enemy should be ignored? It is you who will die this evening. We'll both die!"

The humanoid jaguar's eyes flashed wildly. He opened his mouth wide and, having struck a lightning blow, sunk his teeth deeply into Beliar's left shoulder.

The rebel screamed, torn by a wave of throbbing pain. The hand with the knife dropped, but the latter didn't slide out of the palm. Streams of blood began to flow from between the fangs of Forkis, whose jaws tightened more and more.

He jerked his head back, once, twice. Beliar had the impression that his eyes escaping deep into his skull were about to explode and merge with his brain; more and more foamed saliva appeared on the lips.

On the third pull, Forkis tore a large chunk of muscle from his body, splashing blood around him. He looked into the eyes of the terrified man, bared red teeth in a cruel smile. Making sure that Beliar was watching him closely, he swallowed ostentatiously what he held in his teeth and licked his lips. "B Rh-," he said.

***

Corporal Zira Aytar, on duty at the arena, tried to block Anna's way when she ran into the corridor for gladiators. Sandstorm didn't let herself be turned back, she had used her privileges and threats effectively.

She burst out into the arena like a storm, catching the attention of most of the lictors in the box, following the duel. Barely catching her breath, she covered her mouth with her hands, seeing Forkis' bloody face and scraps of what was left of Drunkenstein's shoulder.

She intended to go to the combatants and separate them, not caring that she would have made a laughingstock of the Kiritian elite, but Aggroteh turned her back to the wall.

"He's going to kill Beliar," she hissed in his face. "This madness must end!"

The Onkalot blocked her way with his shoulder.

"You can't do anything. Anyway, you shouldn't be here. Where is Necron?"

"Screw Necron. Forkis, stop it!" Anna shouted towards the center of the arena. The Kiritian turned his head to the unexpected source of noise. And that cost him a knife blow.

***

Stress-driven Beliar grabbed the knife handle with his right hand and, yelling, plunged the blade deep into Forkis' side, just below the ribs. He felt the blade dig into the tense muscles.

Anna was no longer able to scream, she just groaned. Aggro hissed as if it had been he who received the blow. He looked away.

The screaming crowd fell silent in cryogenic silence.

The medical team wanted to run into the arena, but Forkis forbade them with a scream to do so under the death penalty. He would have rather died than taint his honor.

The Lieutenant Commander, panting heavily, raised the corners of his mouth high in a maddened smile. He let go of the handle of the knife stuck deep in the opponent's body and grasped with his good hand the heavily bleeding shoulder.

Staring at the man with eyes open wide with astonishment, Forkis took a few wobbly steps. He looked at his side, covered in Beliar's blood, as well as in his own. He grasped the knife handle and, grimacing, yanked it out of the wound with a movement devoid of finesse, then threw it away. The blood stemmed by the metal immediately spurted in a thin stream. The Kiritian almost fell as his pressure dropped; the world suddenly spun madly; the sounds faded. However, he managed to stay on his paws, overwhelmed his weakness. Despite the throb twisting intestines, he pulled himself together and lunged at the opponent with the simplest possible attack - a charge.

This move left Drunkenstein in undisguised astonishment: after such a knife blow, inevitably fatal, Forkis should have fallen to the sand and writhed in agony.

Moaning with throbbing pain radiating from his shoulder across his whole body, Beliar crouched down and reached for the knife lying nearby. He swung his healthy arm wide fractions of a second before colliding with the Onkalot. He left him a streak that stretched from his lower rib to his muzzle. Forkis stopped abruptly. The long wound started to bleed at once, the well-sharpened knife wasn't restrained even by the thick fur.

The rebel dealt one more blow to weakening Forkis - right between the ribs. In counterattack, he got a stab with five dagger claws in the same place.

Beliar knew he had received the killing blow. The claws dug into the windpipe, heart and lungs, but he began to laugh ironically, at first softly, but immediately with his full chest. Then he gurgled and spluttered like a man possessed, less and less, for the rapidly weakening body was no longer capable of such an effort. Thick blood appeared between the crooked lips.

The stunned onlookers were stuck in the breachers as rigid as catatonics. They were sure like about the stars after sunset that Forkis would smash this pathetic little man to pieces, which he delayed only to raise the tension.

The usurper yanked his claws out, having twisted them a little in the opponent's chest. However, he didn't touch the knife stuck in his body, as he would have bled out of the damaged aorta right away.

The world ... no, the whole universe fell silent. Even Anna was silent, whimpering like a dying animal in a trap a few moments before.

And Lieutenant Commander Beliar Drunkenstein continued to laugh, gasping for air as desperately as a fish washed ashore.

"You are fools, everyone! To a man!" He spread his arms and turned to the breachers, presenting the onlookers his bloody chin, shoulder, and five red holes in his chest. "It was I, and only I, who won today, and Dr. Maksimus Figam helped me achieve this goal!" He spat blood.

Still standing on his paws, but barely, Forkis tried to probe the mind of this startling man, to see if he was trying to convey something specific, or he was completely mad and raving like a man with nothing left to lose. The inhibitor injected into Beliar's system was still working: Forkis might have as well been reading thoughts from the wall of the arena.

After the rebel's words, something began to get to Q'ualel, but nothing concrete to take appropriate action. He associated how, after arriving at Figam's home on planet B9, Drunkenstein had gone with the scientist for private talks. Once, they had both disappeared for 24 hours in his underground laboratory. At the time, he had thought that the people had simply wanted to sit in their own company, exchanging information not intended for his ears. Aggro remembered that intriguing gleam in Beliar's eyes as he had spoken to him at the rebel camp on Cargoo. I think it was then that he had begun to devise a specific plan. Single. It's more likely, though, that Lacetti had given the lieutenant orders, taking advantage of the fact that Aggro had flown to them as the perfect ticket to enter Morascrik. The Onkalot had hidden from Beliar the reconstructed Nimja artifact (he had also asked Figam to recreate it in secret, so that next to the inhibitor for Drunkenstein, he would have double protection against Forkis' telepathy, in case the inhibitor failed), the latter repaid with something similar. But what? What secret could it be?

Beliar fell to his knees, with his arms still spread wide, and looked up at the darkening sky. There was a sense of triumph on his fading face.

Anna tried to free herself from Aggroteh's arms, but he held her tight and didn't intend to let go. All she could do was swallow her own tears and say curses.

Forkis finally broke through Beliar's mental shield. The inhibitor began to malfunction in the damaged body, flooded with hormones.

He was shocked to find out what was thinking about the rebel, whose chest began to glow unexpectedly, as if a miniature sun had been forming between his ribs.

"Oh shit," he managed to cough up, amazed at the ingenuity of the man kneeling in front of him.

He felt no fear (as did Beliar having ancestors among terrorists, who knew perfectly well that he would die in K'otz'ib'aja at the moment of agreement with Figam, so he had a lot of time to come to terms with his death), only surprise when the payload placed in the rebel's right lung exploded with force and the brightness of a little star, engulfing the arena and breachers.

***

Minutes after regaining consciousness, Anna finally decided to open her eye. Above her, she noticed a dense canopy of tall tropical plants. I guess. She wasn't dreaming anymore. And the dream about the wilderness in which she watched the great, majestic cat was indeed beautiful. When she opened the other eye, she noticed a faint beam of sun piercing through the juicy green barrier, as if to greet the recuperating girl with warmth and joy.

Wait, what tropical forest?

She sat up abruptly, rested her hands in the back. She could feel the softness of the spongy ground beneath them. She was indeed in a tropical forest, more precisely in a tiny clearing where leaves, branches, vines, and flowers intertwined overhead, almost obscuring the sky. There were boulders to the right, rubble beyond, and at the edge of the field of vision - a stone pyramid absorbed by the jungle.

On a collapsed stele sat the Onkalot with the cage strapped to his belt. He held in his paws and stroked a small animal. It looked like a mouse, but with golden fur.

"Aggro?"

He looked at Anna as she rose. She felt dizzy, everything turned blue for a moment from tiny dots flying everywhere as she approached the rubble.

"Carefully, the journey has exhausted you a bit," Aggro said as Anna hovered over him.

"Journey?" Sandstorm blinked. And she flooded the humanoid jaguar with a stream of questions, suddenly animated and terrified as she remembered the recent drastic events, "What about Beliar? Where is Forkis? What happened? Where are we?"

"You'd better sit down." Q'ualel pointed to a boulder opposite. He glanced at a paradise bird with a long tail chirping in leaves. How extreme it was compared to Anna, who looked like a colorless bundle of despair. Aggro, however, didn't intend to color his account. "When you were unconscious, I sorted out all the facts. It turned out that Beliar had injected into his chest an explosive custom-made by Maksimus Figam. On planet B9, where we flew together, I heard scraps of conversation about digging a tunnel on Cargoo to create a mine, in a very hard rock, resistant to moles - it was claimed that a charge was needed that could be squeezed into a deep crevice the diameter of a pin. Beliar must have bought the scientist with this story; Figam is smart and intelligent, but good-natured and trusts people too much. I swear I had no idea Beliar smuggled the microbomb in the body onto Morascrik. Now I understand why he was constantly so ... wired. I thought he was afraid of meeting Forkis and had trouble hiding his emotions. It is difficult to say whether the terrorist act was his idea, or he acted as a kamikaze on commission of the rebel staff, but I'm betting on the first option. The Kiritians didn't have the pattern of this prototype microscopic payload, probably secured with some kind of cover, so they didn't detect it when they checked us after landing in K'otz'ibaja. When Forkis injured his body during the fight, the microbomb probably activated."

The girl started shaking her head.

"So Forkis ..." She sobbed quietly.

"I don't know. I'm sorry." Aggroteh turned back to petting the golden mouse. Satisfied, it squinted and began to fall asleep, still twirling its long whiskers.

"Nimja artifacts are amazing items. I didn't even realize that it could be such a powerful technology, whose essence of action we may never understand. I demanded evacuation, using the artifact for the third and final time. I did it in desperation, but I didn't think the method would work. The artifacts are related to Onkalots as descendants of Nimja, so theoretically the mouse should have transported me and Forkis to a safe place, but instead carried you.

It seems Tonatiuh has some specific plans for you. I prayed to him, maybe that's why we survived."

The girl rubbed her red nose and eyes with her hand. The story, though sprinkled with Onkalotian mythology, made an impression on her.

"Is he some god of yours?"

The Onkalot nodded.

"He protects people with brave hearts and faith in their abilities. You asked about the location: we are in a Chulimal jungle."

"Where?"

"On H14."

Anna sighed and tilted her head back for a moment.

"Which is where it all began. It's hard to believe ... It feels less real than a dream." She glanced at the ruins. "Isn't it Ajb'atenaja?"

"That's correct."

"Why did you transfer us here?"

"It wasn't me, but the artifact. Maybe the god. I just wanted us to be in a safe place."

"And what will happen now? The planet is abandoned, how will we get out of it? I need to find out what's going on with Forkis!" Anna jumped up from the boulder. Aggro stood up, waking the golden mouse in his paw.

"It is not abandoned, but sparsely populated. Only the rebels have abandoned it. I have a friend on Chulimal whose family I lived with for a while. The Schindlers will help us, but they are a few days away on foot."

"So, let's go to them," Sandstorm said firmly. She almost fell over.

"We'll go in a few hours when you have a good rest and eat something." Q'ualel walked over to the bushes, crouched down, and set the mouse on a huge tree root. "Come on." He waved his paw in the direction of the forest. The bird he had been watching earlier flapped its wings and flew away. "You are free. And too dangerous for anyone else to use you. Better not show yourself to anyone else."

The mouse stood on its hind legs, looked at the Onkalot with convex eyes, swayed its whiskers, then dropped to its paws, turned and disappeared into the thicket of underbrush.

EPILOGUE: Anna

The trip to John Schindler's farm took us more days than Aggroteh had estimated. And all because of the aggressive gang of lycans who flew into the Chulimal jungle to catch exotic species of birds. We had to choose a longer route and run through the forest, because the wolf-people decided to hunt for entertainment also for our strange duo. Eventually, we managed to hide in an underground chamber of some forgotten ruins, where we waited until they gave up on crowding us and flew away into space, probably having caught enough birds for sale.

The Schindlers were overjoyed to see Aggroteh. Only Eredal sulked. She was jealous of me in spite of the assurances of the humanoid jaguar that I was someone else's faithful partner.

Aggro insisted that we stay on Chulimal for a while, for the sake of safety, until things calmed down. I was not persuaded and demanded an immediate take-off. Due to the days spent in the jungle, we didn't know the current situation of the Zodiac Universum. Apolitical John could say little about fighting or politics, at most talk about inflation in the trading stations. In turn, about the terrorist attack on the Kiritians' capital, he knew nothing. We didn't learn more until reaching the orbital station, where he took us on a transporter. Unofficial information circulated in space that Forkis had died in a bomb attack orchestrated by the rebels. The official information, given by the truthful Kiritians ... was unfortunately the same.

Then I felt as if I had lost my grip and begun to drift off into dark, deep space. As if some intracorporeal larva from the wildest planet had eaten all my insides, leaving an empty shell, a human wreckage. Like a syncars from the planet Aj. I locked myself in a room over the inn rented for a day and silently, but for a long time cried.

Exactly, I cried.

It had happened too often to me recently. I guess I had stopped being that tough girl who in the past had reacted to all sorrows and failures with kicks and anger.

John Schindler was doing great on the farm. Despite the greater activity of lycans and other thugs on H14, no one invaded his family and destroyed their crops, and selling the fruits of labor at vacant orbital stations went excellently for him. Therefore, he could afford a long-term charter of a small civilian unit for Aggroteh, with basic, statutory armament, which was equipped with a simpler version of Kiritian Alcubierre propulsion.

We reached the Kiritians' capital without any problems. We were greeted at the landing field by Necron himself. The Second Galactic Dignitary, or rather, the temporary governor of K'otz'ib'aja (it seemed that he would become the new emperor under the succession) confirmed the news of Forkis' death. Beliar Drunkenstein, lictors watching the fight, part of the city guard and many Kiritians from the breachers also died in the explosion. Overall, a third of the arena was blown up. There wasn't even anything to collect.

It is difficult to describe the emotions that accompanied me after digesting the distressing news, finally heard from the reliable source. Terms for similar things have never been and won't be invented. You just have to experience it for yourself - I don't wish it to anyone, of course - to understand the feeling of overwhelming love and then overwhelming emptiness, suffering and loss when it turns out that the closest person is gone forever. It made me realize how much I love Forkis. Listening to Necron's words, my face paled, my legs buckled under me. He and Aggro had to support me so that I didn't fall on the landing pad as if hit by a sniper missile. Except a sniper's victim won't suffer anymore.

Necron said that I had saved his life when he escorted me to the chambers. I caught his words with one ear and let out through the other. Then I fell into apathy. My glassy eyes stared at the terrifying great wheel of Betelgeuse hanging between the black cones of dead volcanoes.

I spent the next few days in my quarters, mostly lying on my back on the bed, staring at the fabric of the canopy, rolling my tousled, unkempt hair. It was announced that I was indisposed. Excluding robots, I didn't want to see anyone and take medication. My body had already gotten messed up since I had arrived at K'otz'ibaja, which made me stop having my period. Maybe this was what happened when an adult moved to another planet, different from the previous one? I don't know. But I didn't talk to anyone about it, believing that the changes were normal and that everything would stabilize over time. The Kiritians were not in the habit of harming their own citizens. I just had to go through it myself. Aggro and Necron, despite the visit ban, came to me anyway. They declaimed wisdom, probably invented thousands of years ago by ancient monks and philosophers and brought food that I unwillingly stuffed into myself.

On the fifth day, I looked out the window at rising Betelgeuse, and a change took place in me. I left the room, found Necron, and demanded that he inject me with the super virus I had feared so much, seeing my own death in it in a way. Biffter was surprised by this sudden change, but quickly accepted my choice. He had an irritatingly serious expression. He took me to a medical center and had a geneticist named Alejandro Cortez, a nice boy with scared rabbit eyes, examine my mental and physical condition. After both were satisfactory, I lay down on a couch and was immobilized. Andro gave me an injection in the arm with a small plunger.

I hadn't thought completely about the transformation. In my indifferent mind, it was comparable to eating a meal or going to a restroom - something so common that you don't pay the slightest attention to it. The injection chased away the remnants of lethargy. It was only then that I started panicking, glancing nervously from side to side like a hunted animal, so that Necron had to calm me down with his hands and words, and finally attached me with extra straps. The medics couldn't give me any sedative, because the contact of the active ingredient with the super virus could have resulted in a biochemical catastrophe. A patient's blood should be as pure as an angel's heart, as Corporal Tsar Seymour once sang to himself.

Andro did his job, Necron ordered him to leave the office. In my case, the super virus acted as an anesthetic, in the positive sense of the word. An office lamp reminiscent of the glistening belly of a ray seemed to fade away. Everything became clearer, the picture dreamily blurry. A tunnel with a light at the end appeared. And a smile on my face.

I was plunging as if into a narcotic sleep.

I was dying painlessly.

I felt Forkis' kiss on my lips. I answered, moving my mouth as I held out my longing arms towards him. There were tears in my eyes. Maybe I dreamed about it. Or maybe I was kissing Necron who - how could a woman not notice it? - had had a crush on me since our first meeting on Aj. He had never told me this, and hadn't signaled it otherwise than with rarely sent, affectionate looks when no one could see it. During the reign of Forkis, adultery had no right to exist. It was the sixth commandment. In cases of infatuation, platonic love remained.

But it's possible my brain was generating some nonsense and Necron wasn't even with me. Hypoxia, psychological shock, instant infection, cell reprogramming, happiness hormones and those things.

But I didn't die.

I underwent the transformation very gently, as if I had been in a coma for several days. However, I woke up as a different Anna Sandstorm. I was reborn, although I remained physically the same as before. In my case, there were no phenotypic changes.

I changed a gown to a light Kiritian armor. I felt stronger and safer in it, like a grain in a lignified shell. As if I had been sitting in the White again.

Necron made me the captain of one of the Kiritian company stationed in the capital, because the previous commander had been killed in an attack in the arena. Incidentally, I barely felt sorry for Drunkenstein. But I immeasurably pitied the wonderful boy from two decades ago, with a radiant smile and a warm, sincere heart, as flawless as a tabula rasa. The boy in whom such a terrible change had taken place. At a meeting of the Dignitaries' Council in K'otz'ib'aja, I supported General Warfighter's idea of retaliation against the rebels. It ceased to matter how many people were behind the attack and who specifically had organized it. Kiret, still as viceroy, opposed it, was afraid to disturb the balance of the Zodiac Universum, and so did the member Vitani Kinsey, but Velkee, me, Roger Larsen, and Richard Durand were in the majority. The general even crushed Biffter with arguments; it was obvious that the two with different views and characters didn't like each other. We didn't argue for long, eventually the Council of Five decided to take the bombers under occupation. As emperor and absolute ruler, but not deaf to the advice of experts in various fields, Kiret could have accepted or rejected this decision, but he hadn't yet had such power.

Guided not by revenge, but many weeks of thoughts, I supported the idea of a total war. I was fed up with the hypocrisy and mess that prevailed outside the Scorpio Universe. I found out, to my own amazement, after getting to know the Kiritian people from the inside, that only through the dictatorship of intelligent organs could order and peace be established. I know, it makes no sense. It's like putting out a fire with fire. However, the Immortals had shown many times that this method works. They were the best suited to wielding power, although many oderses disapproved of the ways in which they operated.

Organizing anything among the Kiritians took place lightning-fast, so we quickly built an armada by bringing in Astro-aircraft carriers, cruisers, bombers, destroyers, combat transporters, support ships, and many other machines from various stations in the Scorpion Universe, including some Morascrik units. The Zodiac Universum hadn't seen such a fleet in nearly two hundred years, when the Immortals had shifted from territorial expansion to a policy of stability, having subjugated all the planets they had cared about.

Aggroteh followed the launch of part of the armada from K'otz'ib'aja. He wasn't satisfied with what we were going to do. Soon someone was to take him to H14. I watched his silhouette diminish from a flagship war shuttle that looked like an armored fortress the color of blood in Betelgeuse rays. However, even the flagship couldn't compete with the kilometer-long Astro-aircraft carriers (colloquially called citadels), the Kiritian patent in the form of a pole with strung station rings, used to transport units through the Zodiac Universum. Thanks to this, it was possible to save a lot of space when jumping with the Alcubierre drive (the mass was concentrated in one place, not dispersed as air formations), which translated into energy consumption.

As the armada flew through the Scorpio Universe, more units as well as Astro-aircraft carriers that filled up with ships and naval craft joined in, ready at any moment to spill out and attack the enemy like bees from a prodded hive. Random Odersian pilots escaped from our route as quickly as possible; courses of scheduled flights were changed.

Once the full fleet was assembled, it was time to switch to subspace drives.

We couldn't get to the Lion Universe, our destination, with only one jump because of the great size of the citadels. Even Figam hadn't solved the problem of the horrendous energy consumption in the case of the transfer of units exceeding a certain mass in the subspace tunnel. That is why we moved by leaps and bounds. On average, we emerged every few astronomical units, and after regenerating the energy necessary to open the gate and subsequent mass transfer, we made another jump.

In the Capricorn Universe, the criminal sector, no one got in our way. A couple of carelessly formed bandit regiments even joined the armada, moving in the back like hyenas after lions, counting on a loot they would surely find when the predators hunted and sated their hunger. And the Kiritians didn't care about the harmless thugs.

The Libra Universum was empty. Only near the border with the Lion did a couple of rebel suicides resist but were swept away by the powerful citadel cannons and long-range missiles - not even the smallest devemer set off to engage in the skirmish.

Something started happening again as we emerged from the subspace tunnel on the outskirts of the Lion Universe. The rebels had had time to prepare (let's say) for our arrival. We were attacked first with messages: questions, warnings, even threats, and finally attempts at negotiation, because we didn't even say a word, leaving them in fear and uncertainty. We just flew, all the ships and naval craft kept the same speed.

The citadels were arranged on a solid plan, the transported units poured out into the interior. There were force field-generating warheads on the Astro-aircraft carriers that were activated. It was supposed to consume energy missiles or to disperse them. Kiritian missile ships, located near the citadels, protected the warheads from enemy ballistic missiles.

The rebel cannons drifting in space, used to destroy both enemy units and rocks that threaten the planets, attacked the first.

Since it was an energy weapon, it didn't do any harm to the Kiritians protected by the field.

We were disrupting enemy communication with inhibitors. No one from the opposition had any doubts that we came here with bad intentions.

After the cannons - quickly destroyed - we were attacked by Cargoo regiments constituting the first line of resistance. Two other planets joined the rebel spearhead. In their ignorance, they shot at our shield with energy weapons, intending to weaken it, but the absorbed energy only replenished the losses resulting from maintaining the field. Kiritian fighters and drilling craft - after approaching, could use drills larded with blades on their nose to pierce armor and shred the enemy machine's innards - spilled out in a counterattack as the enemy attempted to smash the citadel warheads. However, we turned them off ourselves when we reached the Lion's center and scattered in it like the genetic material of a virus across an infected cell. Hence this citadel trick was called the capsid tactic: protect, fly in, release.

In the space battle that spread to the inhabited part of the universe, I didn't take part. I asked General Warfighter to let me go on a mission to Nephrida. He didn't want to allow me it, seeing that I was getting emotional about it, but after Kiret's intervention, I got permission.

More than a dozen fighter regiments as well as several destroyers and cruisers were sent to the planet. The former reached the surface of Nephrida, the others assisted from the stratosphere, conducting supporting fire.

We left the civilians alone but destroyed with air-to-ground missiles power plants, airports, factories, air defense cannons, military bases and arsenals. Also mechanized, intelligent ground units, which, due to their inferior technology, resisted poorly. In the future, we planned to raise a different type of buildings here, made of distinct materials, so we could afford to destroy key objects, instead of taking them over and then incur huge modification costs - it was cheaper to get rid of them.

The planet fell in three days.

Krystian Sandstorm hated me. He quit the service, not wanting to fight against his daughter, and returned to the unoccupied native Calcaris in the Libra Universe.

The bases that resisted were wiped off the face of the earth. Those who laid down their arms - and there were quite a few of them - didn't lose a single human, robot, or android. Unfortunately, my former base wasn't one of the latter, but it didn't get completely destroyed. It defended itself until I landed and left the White in the same place from which millions of years ago, I had flown to the Scorpio Universe to defeat a small Kiritian unit ...

Taking off the helmet and showing the face was more effective than the weapon paralyzing dozens of defenders, because so many were in the base when it was captured. Rebels, former comrades-in-arms, but also crooks, criminals and heirs of the NOA, stared at me, bewildered and amazed. Perhaps Forkis himself in the form of an Onkalot wouldn't have aroused such a sensation if he had now stood in front of them on the landing field.

'It's over, lay down your arms and no one will be hurt,' that's all I managed to cough up of my speech prepared during the flight, barely controlling my voice. The rest of the words escaped, perhaps a deep sadness trapped them in my larynx, signs of which began to bloom on my face. I looked away and headed for the White. General Warfighter was right - I shouldn't have come here. But I didn't want to chicken and engage in some tasks taking place far away from Nephrida, but to face what I had brought about.

Maybe it would be better for everyone if Forkis had devoured me then in Ch'amiya B'aq.

The rebels obeyed, broken and resigned, giving up without a word. Since the burning base was in a strategically key place on the planet and was one of the most extensive (it had even well-developed interplanetary communication), the Kiritians allowed the losers to extinguish fires and save undamaged equipment.

Among one of the watched groups, I noticed Arcadius Croft. He was close enough that I could see the seriousness and compassion on his face. Compassion meant for me. We looked at each other for a while before I continued my journey to the machine. Yes, a journey. The longest twenty-five meters in my whole life.

'Don't harm a hair of this rebel's head,' I said to Sergeant Victor Shane, accosted on the way.

"I will take care of it, Captain, don't worry," he replied cheerfully as always. So, I didn't have to fear for the Splinter's life. A Kiritian never breaks their word.

Orders were given, the situation at the base became stable; I wasn't needed so I could take care of myself. I cut off communication after warning Necron that I needed privacy.

The sun was almost set, being replaced by stars, two visible moons, and the glow of a citadel stationed in orbit. I flew to the town of Ramondoor. The Kiritians paced the conquered streets, followed by civilians' eyes expressing a bit of everything. The sky was often crossed by machines from Morascrik. Surrounded by a few low-ranking achijes, Corporal Tsar Seymour was dealing in some dingy alley, at least in his case no political or ideological walls had the right to exist.

At the parade of winners, I saw Julie Croft and Marlena. The fairy turned her head and, though I was standing far on the sidelines, glanced at me, having apparently sensed someone's gaze on her. Perhaps in fact nature had given her a substitute for psionic abilities like Onkalots.

Just like Forkis.

Wrapped in a green cloak, with her black hair flowing in the wind, the woman approached me. She stopped and eyed me gravely, as had done the Splinter before. I endured her gaze for a moment, but then began to stare at the last rays of the sun. We stood there, not talking, like two pillars of salt.

'You were right, but I changed the face of the Zodiac Universum,' I finally said as if stoned to Marlena. She put her hand on my shoulder, I couldn't read anything from her expressionless face.

Another bland, therefore terrifying mask.

I sighed deeply, shook my head. With my helmet in my left hand, I walked down the alley of the little houses quarter, leaving Marlena on a hill, accompanying me with her gaze.

I dropped my headdress on the ground somewhere on the border of the polis with wasteland. I set off aimlessly into the night, not caring about the lighting. I just kept walking on the sun-cracked ground covered with sand, anew getting used to the gravity of Nephrida that I had once known so well. Once I climbed, another time I ran down the rocks, like the last idiot perfectly exposed to the line of fire of pissed off rebels. I didn't care about it.

I wandered so for hours until I reached the foot of the mountains. I sank to the ground, thirsty and exhausted. The warm wind was blowing from all directions, throwing grains of sand in my face and keeping me awake.

The old order was changed. The friends turned out to be crooks.

The enemies turned out to be friends.

Forkis was dead.

Sleep didn't come.

And I felt like philosophizing.

I crouched down and grabbed a handful of sand, letting it slide between my fingers spread apart.

I didn't react in any way when someone landed nearby. I recognized the devemer by the sounds of the dying engine. I didn't turn my head at the sound of the increasing murmur of the steps taken, even when the stranger stopped behind me.

He moved and sat on a boulder for me to see him. It was Necron. He played with the helmet he found for some time.

"I think it's yours." He leaned over and handed me the item. Then we were both silent, I am staring at my helmet, and Kiret resting his elbows on the spread legs, at something distant.

'You came here alone, unprotected?' I glanced at him. Necron looked at me seemingly scolding.

"And the captain is supposed to be better?" He smiled slightly.

I wasn't in the mood for jokes, so my expression remained depressed.

"I flew to Nephrida to see how the achijes had dealt with the mess. I saw you in the town, you were going somewhere. I figured you wanted to be alone for a while, but why here?" He looked around at the rocks. "In the perfect spot for an ambush."

I shrugged.

"You are a Councilor now, Anna. Not a rebel in the middle of the military hierarchy. Except in Morascrik, where each of us is safe among their own compatriots and can walk wherever they want, you should pay more attention to safety. I didn't come here alone. Behind that hill," he waved his hand, "achijes in the fighters are waiting. I tracked you down with a bioctovisor, fortunately you are completely alone in the area. It's even nice here in its own way." He looked at the moons. He took a deep breath. "At least it's calm. A monastery or a temple could be set up here, where people would regain their inner balance. It's a perfect place for my taste." I looked at him askance. Kiret had never been good at drolleries, as long as it was supposed to be a kind of humor. He picked up a little rock of celadon color from the ground and began to twist it with his fingers. "You loved him very much. I miss him terribly too. We were the oldest Kiritians. I thought we would survive for many more centuries. But maybe not all is lost."

I looked at him with undisguised interest. He got up from the boulder and approached me. He crouched down, took something out of the armor compartment and placed the object on my open hand.

It was Forkis' talisman in which he had carried the golden mouse bone.

"Aggroteh told me to give you it," said Necron. "Look inside."

He took out the X17A4 and turned on a flashlight with a bright white beam. Running my fingers over the concave Onkalotian inscriptions, I turned the knobs in opposite directions and glanced at the contents of the capsule.

Black hair.

I immediately guessed who they belonged to. Nice memento. But so, what that it was Forkis' hair? What was so happy about it that Necron's widening smile didn't want to crawl off his face?

"If we visited Doctor Maksimus Figam and persuade him to help us," he looked me in the eye, "maybe something would come of it. This is the only genetic material left of Forkis. His Onkalotian remains were burnt to dust in the explosion."

'Cloning? Necro medicine?' I sighed. 'Kiret, recovering the body won't bring Forkis back. You should rather think about your power, for you will soon be proclaimed emperor."

"Body reconstruction is only the initial stage. We will have - sorry for this term - a shell. Before I left, I spoke to Aggro and he accidentally mentioned a thing, but then he didn't want to talk about it anymore. We argued about view matters and his religion. He went back to the H14."

Necron embraced me comfortingly, pressed me against him, and rested his chin on my head. Forkis had liked to do that too.

"What's your point?" I asked. Hope and fear are a terrible mix, and I began to feel this amalgam of extremes.

Kiret smiled soberly and soundly.

"That there is a chance to bring him back to life. We just need to find a Nimja member alive, or at least its lost knowledge."

And all hope, unfounded anyway, went haywire.

"Didn't you crash somewhere in that devemer and hit your head?"

End of Volume I

From the author

The book was written between 1997 and 2020, so it's a mixture of styles. A lot of things had to be changed and deleted. It was edited by employees of three publishing houses, also beta-readers added a bit. Initially, the novel was about something completely different and was entitled "First Fire". Its printout circulated here and there, for private use. The plot evolved over the years, took its final form in around 2013, and in this version, it was released for the first time two years later. After regaining the rights to the text, other minor fictional and linguistic changes took place in it (okay, not so minor, because the characters from volume three and two found themselves in part one, Forkis contracted vorarephilia, and Anna - I hope - ceased to be a hysteric and Mary Sue pissing off all readers). However, this is a longer story that I plan to present in a Zodiac Universum free guide someday, in which I will put up also notes about heroes, machines, inventions, technology, planets, and so on.

I count on your opinions and reviews on the Internet :) I would love to know what the good side of the text is, and what is the weak one. Which characters you liked, and which you would launch into space. 'See you' in the second volume!

www.ingramcontent.com/pod-product-compliance
Lightning Source LLC
Chambersburg PA
CBHW020837020726
47497CB00005B/1132